PURCHASED FOR PREGNANCY

DARK MAFIA ROMANCE

GREEK MAFIA ROMANCE BROTHERHOOD
BOOK 2

JAMILA JASPER

WWW.JAMILAJASPERROMANCE.COM

ISBN: 979-8-3302-8369-9

Thank you to my Patreon subscribers for your support with this book. I could not have done it without you. www.patreon.com/jamilajasper

✽ Created with Vellum

GREEK MAFIA ROMANCE BROTHERHOOD

Purchased For Submission

Purchased For Pregnancy

Purchased For Seduction

DESCRIPTION

Every woman Loukas loves ends up dead.
He's given up on love...

Then he meets Tisha -- the last woman on Earth he should ever want.
His daughter's best friend from college.

She's perfect... with light brown skin.
She's Innocent. Alluring.
Loukas wants to be her first. He desperately wants to claim her.

But if he has his way with Tisha, he'll ruin everything.
His daughter's life. His family. His career.
Worst of all, he'll ruin Tisha.

Book #2 — a steamy BWWM mafia romance novel. Check your undies at the door for this high-heat black woman white man bad boy romance story. If you enjoy muscular alphas, dark mafia

romance and steamy romance with African American women, dive into this smokin' sequel...

Thank you to my patrons for your ongoing support. This new edition is only made possible because of your support.

*Here's to manifesting your **happily ever after...***

Click here to subscribe:
www.patreon.com/jamilajasper

READER OPINIONS

"I didn't think that this book would be better than the first book, boy was I wrong! The drama, the suspense and the sex! OMGosh, it's all in here. Loukas, Tisha, Carlotta, sheesh. I couldn't wait to find out this would end. So good! On to book 3!!"

TN MAMA BEAR

"I choose my rating because reading about mafia life is crazy good. Especially the Greek mafia with all the killing and betrayal and love."

KINDLE CUSTOMER

"I eagerly awaited this second book in the Greek Mafia Romance Brotherhood Series. Although this book was quite dark, I expected it after reading the first book. This love story of Loukas and his daughter's best friend, Tisha, was a ROLLERCOASTER RIDE for SURE! OMG! Ms Jamila Jasper and the voices in her head, are at it again! The Pagonis' are one crazy family! I enjoyed how Ms Jasper decided to take a different route in revealing how Loukas and Tisha's relationship developed; from present day to past and back around again. It kept me on my toes and wanting to read MORE!"

THEA W

CONTENT AWARENESS

BWWM Dark Mafia Romance

This is an adults only read for fans of diverse romance, dark romance and high-heat relationships between black women and white men.

When I say dark, I mean DARK so expect mention of the following topics: big age gaps (all over 18 years old), pregnancy, abuse, violence, drug use and other unsavory subjects.

As this is a fictional story, Jamila Jasper does not condone any of these actions. <u>Don't try any of this at home.</u>

ONE
A FIRST GLIMPSE AT MY FORBIDDEN LUST

"Papa!" Carlotta shrieks from the boat deck, "Papa! It's Stavros!"

I don't want to go above deck because if I go above deck, I'll have to face her. Not Carlotta, but her friend Tisha. *It's been ages and I don't want to see her now. I can't see her now.*

Tisha will be above deck and since she's returned with my daughter, I've been avoiding both of them.

Tisha has full lips, and she's slighter of frame with smaller breasts and a much bigger butt. *I shouldn't even think these thoughts.*

She's lying on my pool deck *right now* and Carlotta lent her one of the tiny pink thong bikinis I told her to throw away. My daughter never listens to me, which is why Tisha is here in the first place. I remember forbidding her to bring that girl around.

I poke my head up the stairs.

"Stavros?" I ask my daughter. "Where is Stavros? What are you talking about?"

Carlotta calls out to me loudly, "He's on the phone."

I run up the stairs and avoid looking at the girl lying to my left, covered in tanning oil. What the hell does she need tanning oil for?

The girl is one of the darkest I've ever seen. I'd like to look at her again, despite the guilt I feel. My body responds like a beast to hers. She's young. Beautiful. Very curvy.

She's my daughter's age, which is just the first reason even glancing at Tisha is wrong. I'm a killer. That's another good reason to stay away from her. There are about a hundred more that run through my mind as I walk past her and snatch the phone from my daughter.

I left it upstairs for a reason. I don't want to talk to my brother, so this had better be a fucking emergency.

"What do you want, Stavros?" I snarl at him, hoping to scare him away from needing me. That doesn't work.

It's about Helen. She isn't tired of the drama she's caused, forcing Stavros to save her life with the final remnants of his sanity.

Why can't the people in this fucking family keep it in their pants? I can. I had to learn my lesson the hard way, but at least I learned it.

If Helen hadn't been so loose with her morals, her idiot ex-boyfriend wouldn't have had it in his head to raid our family villa.

Stavros just got there to clean up their mess, but apparently that wasn't enough.

"Nikola shot Helen," Stavros says. "We need you here. Now."

"Fuck. Are you sure?" I grumble. "It's *Helen.*"

"I know," Stavros says. "But that's no excuse. We need you. Hurry, Loukas. I don't have time to deal with you."

Someone shot Helen. I don't mean to be cold, but she's plunged herself into danger continuously since she was a teenager. We're lucky this hasn't happened earlier. Still, Stavros needs me. So I'll go.

I hang up and toss the phone to Carlotta.

"What is it, Papa?" She says, peering over the railing, letting her hair fall in brown ringlets to her waist. *It'll be impossible to keep her out of trouble, won't it?*

"We need to go," I tell her, cutting our little boat ride short by steering us sharply toward starboard. "I'm taking us back to the villa."

I don't want to tell her about Helen yes.

"Papa, I'm working on my tan with Tisha, can't this wait?"

"No, it can't."

"This is so not fair," Carlotta says with an irritated pout. "Tisha, come over and tell him this isn't fair."

Tisha ignores her because she's fast asleep on the boat deck, lying on her stomach with her underwear scrunched between her butt cheeks. I look away from her quickly. This argument is between me and Carlotta anyway.

"Your brother's in trouble. Someone shot your aunt," I say calmly.

Carlotta rolls her eyes instead of having a normal, human response. "Cassia? She has Sandros, Gal and Stavros to protect her. I don't see why they need you."

"She's already been shot," I remind her. "And it's Helen. Now go wake Tisha."

"I'm not waking Tisha. You do it."

I run my hands over my jawline. Why are we always fighting?

"Don't make me repeat myself, Carlotta. We're fifteen minutes away and I need you dressed by the time we get to the marina."

"I *hate* you," she hisses. "You promised us a boat ride and tanning time and now you're making up some stupid excuse."

"I don't care if you hate me," I reply. "Get your clothes on."

"I hate you!" She shrieks. "Aren't you listening to me? I hate you. You always ruin everything. Isn't it enough that you killed my mother? Do you have to ruin the rest of my life?"

Her voice gets higher and I try not to let Carlotta's words get to me. *She's using her mother's death to make me angry. I never killed her mother and it doesn't matter what she thinks because I know the truth.*

Tisha's nervous American accent rises above my daughter's clatter. I hate fighting with Carlotta. She looks too much like me — blue eyes and hair the color of coffee beans.

"Carlotta? Is everything okay?"

She rolls over and I can't tell if it's a blessing or a curse that I can no longer see her ass in that thong bikini. The view from the front feels less lewd somehow. Her thighs cover her crotch, but her smooth stomach draws my attention with a piercing through her navel. She's so young, like Carlotta. I don't like young women, I remind myself. I'm forty-one years old and much too old for a girl my daughter's age. I'm much too old to go after a girl like this and have her end up dead.

Carlotta glowers at me as she answers her friend.

"I'm fine. My dad's just a total *loser.*"

Carlotta storms off downstairs and I storm off to the railing. *Fuck.* I am such a shitty parent. Ana would have known what to do with the children. I met her when Carlotta was fifteen and she wanted to be a mother. My kids didn't scare her. Then she got pregnant. After she gave birth to Zoe, she died. Murder, like all the others. I sent Zoe away to live with her aunt after what happened with Matilda. She's safer away from me.

I corrupted the other children already, but Zoe doesn't have to turn out just another fucked up Pagonis. Carlotta will never forgive me for sending her sister away.

I feel a small hand on my shoulder and jerk back, thinking it's Carlotta returning to slap me in the face. It won't be the first time Carlotta's slapped me.

If YiaYia ever found out...

I tell myself that I won't let my grandmother hurt my children the way she fucked up Stavros or Galanos. Or me. As the eldest boy, I was her favorite for a while. But YiaYia prefers Galanos. He's more cruel like her.

I was always the idiot older brother. The daredevil. Ha. The older I get, the more that changes. There isn't an ounce of that reckless idiot left in forty-year-old Loukas.

The hand on my shoulder is Tisha's and I turn around with such a fierce look on my face that she jumps back.

"Sorry, Mister Pagonis," she says with a soft voice.

She's wearing a beautiful dress that hugs every curve on her body. I don't think she's wearing a bra because I can see her dark brown nipples poking out of the dress. I hate myself for noticing.

I clear my throat, stifling anything near an inappropriate thought. She bites her lower lip, genuine concern that she's bothering me written all over her face. Hm.

She has a beautiful American accent with a voice that's more breath than force.

"It's fine. You startled me. Are you enjoying the view?" I say, trying to sound calm and put together.

"Oh, this is awesome. I love the ocean. Greece is so beautiful. It's way better than Brooklyn."

"Is that where you're from?"

I don't know much about her or her past or why her parents allow her to wander the streets of Greece in tiny skirts and crop tops. Do her parents care that she has her navel pierced?

"Uh huh," Tisha answers, leaning on the railing and rocking back and forth just enough to let the wind pick up her hair. It flows in gorgeous waves around her head. She grins with genuine pleasure. She likes it here.

"Hm."

I don't know what to say to her next. She's breathtaking and it's all I can think about. She draws my attention away from the Greek coastline just with her smile. I can't stand it.

I've never been skilled at talking to beautiful women, and Tisha isn't just a beautiful woman. She's young. A ruby pendant hangs around her neck, drawing my eye to her ample breasts.

And she's wearing a bathing suit that no Greek man in his right mind would have ever let his daughter run out in — at least when I was a young man. I haven't been a young man for a long time.

"I heard you and Carlotta fighting. I wanted to see if you were okay."

"You're more worried about me than your friend?"

I instantly regret the question. It's too forward. The question itself is nearly flirtatious. She leans against the railing next to me, her breasts nearly falling out of that tiny bikini top. I will myself not to stare at this young woman's breasts, even if temptation menaces me.

"Don't tell Carlotta I said this but... she's rude to you sometimes. She doesn't appreciate all this stuff. I'd kill for a boat."

My heart swells with pride. Every parent wants that acknowledgement from their kids. Every bullshit job I do for my father, every gun I've ever sold, I've done it so my children can have a better life. Carlotta doesn't see it that way. Unlike Tisha, she sees more than the boats, the villas and the cars. She sees the darker side of our Thessaloniki wealth.

"No need to kill. Just work hard and one day, you may afford one."

The statement is the boldest lie I've told all week. But I have to set a good example for the girl.

Papa gave me the boat when I killed three men at seventeen, long before Tisha was ever born.

Her smile is fucking beautiful and her breasts... She squeezes them up against the railing, trying to lean over and catch the sea breeze in her curls but inadvertently making my cock rise to attention.

Hey, asshole, there's a beautiful woman standing next to you and you haven't gotten any in months!

I can't do hookers. I need emotions for sex. I have needs, but... I'd prefer one woman.

Yiayia claims I have the Pagonis curse — excessive virility, she calls it. YiaYia will believe anything as long as it makes the Pagonis name look or sound good. She thinks we're Gods.

I realize I'm awkwardly silent and worse... I'm staring.

I wet my lips and realize something far worse than my erect cock or my intense gaze. *I fucking want her.* Tisha notices. She stands up straight and adjusts her top so those marvelous plump breasts escape my view.

"I'm going to check on Carlotta, Mister Pagonis," Tisha mumbles awkwardly.

Fuck. The first chance I had to get close to her and I blow it by being staring Tisha. It's blatant. I can't help myself. I watch her disappear below deck. She's already seen me staring. It can't hurt to look at her ass. It's plump. Deliciously round. Even in that dress, it bulges out with soft-looking cheeks.

The slightest glance in Tisha's direction *aches.*

My sister's hurt and I'm thinking about a woman. Maybe YiaYia's right about men. We're too easy to manipulate. And I know Tisha's name. I just can't bear to say it because of what happened. What was all my fault...

TWO
THE LUST CHAPTER

Loukas
39 years old
Tisha
17 years old

I haven't been this drunk in ages. Matilda and I fought. Again. She doesn't understand how dangerous my family is. One wrong move is all it takes. What she doesn't understand is that what I'm doing isn't controlling. I'm trying to protect her. She's *new*. She doesn't understand my family and what it means to love me.

I groan and polish off a bottle of vodka. I wish Stavros were here. He'd cheer me up. Take me to a strip club. That's what I need. Hot strippers who now think I'm an old man. When I was their age, I could get every girl in the club. Fuck. I am old. Almost 40. Why don't

I feel forty? Isn't my sex drive supposed to disappear with age? That would make life easier.

Carlotta strides into the kitchen with her friend from university. She folds her arms, a sign I'm going to get a telling off.

"Papa, you are drunk! It's embarrassing me in front of my friend. Tisha's parents don't strut around drunk all the time!"

She grabs the bottle and throws it out.

"There was perfectly good vodka in there," I slur, making a mental note of where I keep my backup bottle in case Carlotta catches me drinking again.

"You don't need vodka! You need to pull yourself together."

Carlotta drags my collar up and shakes me. Ugh. *Don't get sick all over her.*

"I'm sorry," I groan.

Fuck. Is there a Pagonis who doesn't have a drinking problem? I can't pull myself together, anyway. Matilda doesn't see what's coming, but I do. I've lost three women this way. Three. They get too close to me, they say they love me and then they die. I won't allow that to happen to Matilda. Why do I fall in love so quickly?

Carlotta yells some more and then struts away. Her friend Tisha stumbles into the room afterward, and I take a faint smell of something strange on Tisha's clothing.

"Marijuana? Were you and Carlotta smoking marijuana?"

I lose control of myself and forget she's a stranger visiting my daughter from school. I grab onto her shirt and wrap it around my hand so she can't move.

"You smell like marijuana."

She trembles as I sniff her clothing, starting at the base of her hoodie and up to her neck. She whimpers and I let go. What the fuck am I doing? Smelling a seventeen-year-old on the off chance she's smoking?

She runs. Fuck. She'll probably tell Carlotta I'm a pervert and she'd be right.

But if they were smoking marijuana, I'll tan Carlotta's hide. I won't have my daughter turning into a common Thessaloniki whore. Before I can slink away in shame, Antonio struts into the room, singing "My Neck, My Back". I thought that song died with low-rise jeans and thongs sticking out the back. Fuck, my back hurts. Too old for clubbing teenagers and getting drunk on a Wednesday.

"Papa!"

He sounds surprised to see me and I act like I don't notice him wiping off his eyeliner quickly before I can see. I know my son and I've known what he was hiding before he even knew he had to hide it to survive out there in the world. He's not a pussy. That much I made sure of. If anyone doesn't like his mesh tank tops and high-heeled boots, they'll find themselves on the receiving end of Pagonis violence.

"Where were you?"

"Out."

"Smoking weed?"

"Yes."

"Meet any nice girls?"

"Nah. They all had boyfriends who looked like they could kick my ass."

That's part of the game, pretending I don't know because he hasn't told me yet. I don't know if that makes me a good father or a shitty one, but it's better than my father would have treated any of us. I miss my youngest. After her mother died, I sent her away to a boarding school in the town where her aunt lives.

When I can be sure she'll be safe from this, I'll send for her. But that doesn't make it hurt any less. I slink up to bed and fall asleep. When Carlotta brings friends, I prefer them at one of my private residences, not the villa where the entire family hangs around. I don't want Galanos near any female over the age of ten. He's Yiayia's favorite, and that's as good enough a reason as any not to trust him.

I hear a thud downstairs in the middle of the night. My first thought is that Carlotta was sneaking out and I load a single bullet into my pistol — in case it wasn't my daughter. I would kill any man before letting an intruder near my sleeping teenagers.

If Cass hadn't killed Ofek, I would have done it. None of my siblings believe me, but they're different. They're not patient.

I don't mind waiting to get what I want... I'll wait as long as long as I have to.

I tiptoe downstairs, concealing the gun and pull it on the person standing in the kitchen who definitely isn't Carlotta. The poor girl lets out a loud shriek and drops the carton of milk. Fuck. I lower my gun as milk spills around her feet, soaking her completely.

"Mister Pagonis! I... Don't shoot!"

"Sorry. I thought you were an intruder."

Her eyes widen. The milk puddle grows.

"You would have *killed* an intruder?" She asks.

She doesn't look like she believes me, but there's no point in lying.

"If my family were in danger. Yes," I respond. "I would kill someone."

Her eyes flash to mine. Her lashes are ridiculously long as they frame her wide brown eyes. She has *very* beautiful eyes, and they're the largest features on her face.

"Shit," she says, her gaze never leaving my face. "Intense."

"Watch your language, young lady," I say, trying to sound like a parent. I sound a little more gruff than I mean to.

"Sorry."

Shame courses through me as she says that word because of the reaction it provokes. I round the kitchen island and reach on top of the refrigerator for blue kitchen towels, the cover of Santorini roofs. I hand one to Tisha.

"We can clean this up faster if we work together," I say more gently.

"Uh huh," she says, still staring.

She's not paying attention to what I'm saying. I notice her youthful gaze on me and my shame increases. She's staring at my bare chest. I don't think twice about walking around the house shirt-less. Greece can be painfully hot and my upstairs bedroom can be worse. I clear my throat and crouch to the ground, sponging up milk. Tisha crouches and helps me.

"I'm so sorry. You don't have to help. I should clean this up."

"Nonsense. It's my job to help."

It takes six towels to clean everything.

"Your clothes are still wet."

She glances down at her chest, which causes me to glance down instinctively. Shit. I shouldn't have looked down because whatever thin dress Tisha borrowed from Carlotta doesn't cover her chest well. Soaked with milk, I can see her body through the dress and my cheeks darken.

I want her. But I have to suppress every bit of emotion. She's seventeen and I'm... *too old for her.* This is beyond wrong.

"I can change in my room," She says.

She stammers over the words uncomfortably and I realize I've been foolish. My gaze maybe lingered a little too long, or I stared too blatantly at her breasts. Maybe it's my dick. She's had an effect on my dick too. *I'm too hard to think.*

"Yes. I know," I mutter awkwardly. "You'd better do that. No point catching a cold or something..."

I sound like a fool. I move to conceal myself. *Please, don't notice.*

My cock stands at complete attention in my trousers. I've never been this hard before and even moving my thighs to adjust my hard-ness barely works.

"I'd better be going," I say as I leave the room, certain she noticed my erection.

THREE
FALLON AND STAVROS...

By the time we get home, the panic is for nothing. Helen has the man on the ground and Stavros has his boot on the man's face. Fallon peers over the balcony and yells at him.

"Stavros! Get off him!" Fallon screams.

Poor girl. Her attempts to make my brother a better person appear to be working. But instinct kicks in once anyone endangers his family.

"He tried to shoot my sister. He knows what will happen!"

Fallon can't run downstairs as easily as she used to. With a baby on the way, she's getting large. She never thought she'd get pregnant but Pagonis sperm finds a way. She's about to pop by my estimates. Six weeks fly by.

"Loukas! Stop him!"

I hate Fallon knowing I have a heart. This woman has the insane ability to understand us, and without Fallon Iverson, we may have all killed each other. I suppose it's good luck that my brother was a big spender before he agreed to tie the knot.

Fallon pushes me out of the way and drags Stavros away from Helen's boyfriend. Helen steadies the gun in her hand.

"I'll shoot you, Nikola! It's your fault Khalid got me."

Fallon jumps between Stavros, Nikola and Helen

"Don't jump in front of a fucking gun with my child growing inside you," Stavros screams.

Fallon folds her arms and plants herself steady.

"Helen, put the gun down."

"I agree with Fallon."

I offer my words of support, but everyone gives me a disappointed look. Do they know how tiring it is to be the eldest brother to a bunch of untamed hooligans? Not only did I do my round of parenting my siblings, but Papa never seemed to stop having them. I had kids of my own while he impregnated one mistress after another. Only Helen, Stavros, and I share a mother.

Carlotta mercifully sneaks Tisha upstairs and away from the drama. She doesn't need to see this. While they renovate our summer home, I have the girls here. I couldn't take Tisha back to the summer home after what happened there. It would hurt too much.

"See? Shooting him won't solve anything."

Helen can't hold the gun anyway because Nikola fired off a shot that grazed her shoulder. I can see the flesh wound now. She'll survive, but it'll hurt like hell to pull the trigger because of the kickback from the gun.

"Put the gun down, and I'll kill him. That way, Stavros can keep his hands clean and Fallon can carry her unborn child to safety."

Helen lowers the weapon.

"What do you want me to do with him?"

I don't mind that Stavros is the boss now. Papa has spent months at sea with Yiayia until she cools down or pushes him off the yacht and drowns him herself. He's keeping her entertained with sheikhs and other rich old ladies who share my grandmother's sadistic streak. I don't doubt she'll return to Thessaloniki, but I doubt she'll return without exacting revenge on all of us for standing up to her.

Stavros speaks coolly, "Take his passport, identification and give him £500. Drop him off in Italy. If he shows his face in Greece again, we kill him."

Fallon never hides her discomfort with the business of murder, but even she has to make moral compromises to get along with the family. I wonder if she would have chosen differently if Stavros hadn't knocked her up. I'm not clear on the reasons she has for staying, but I don't mind her. Stavros has had worse girlfriends. And they'll be married soon. I never thought I'd see the day...

Helen sits in the kitchen and Fallon returns with a First Aid kit.

"I think you need stitches. We should call a doctor."

Mafia families breed certain instincts in you. Helen and I both shout, "No!"

Yiayia always made us stitch each other up, especially when the family doctor left town.

We can both do good sutures in short order. It comes in handy. Fallon purses her lips in disapproval but slides the First Aid kit to me across the kitchen island. She eagerly sits on a stool, her belly protruding and nearly hitting the counter. She sighs.

"Pregnancy sucks."

"If it were a girl, she would have stolen your looks," Helen says, "Don't worry, it'll be a boy."

"I don't care if it's a girl or a boy. I just... want the kid to be happy."

Helen and I smile at each other. It's absurd that a cynical cretin like Stavros ended up with a woman like this one. But I won't deny Fallon's beauty. I dab alcohol on Helen's wound and she utters several colorful phrases in Russian.

Fallon watches the gruesome scene of do it yourself stitching. But she appears impressed in the end.

"Not bad."

"Yes... one of my many talents," I tell her.

I wink, and Fallon folds her arms.

"You should flirt less, Loukas. I know you're still hurting, but maybe it's time to get back out there. Meet someone."

Helen leans on her good arm and wriggles her caterpillar brows.

"She has a point," Helen adds gleefully. "When is the last time you fucked a woman? Matilda died eight months ago. It hurts, but you have needs. And everyone thinks you would have a much better temper if you had sex."

Fallon covers her mouth to stifle a laugh and fails miserably at her task.

"What the fuck is wrong with my temper?" I snarl at my sister.

Carlotta and Tisha strut into the kitchen. Helen cackles and I whip around to see why.

"You aren't leaving the house wearing that!" I snarl at my daughter.

Heat rises to my cheeks. Fucking hell, she is infuriating. Where the hell does she think she's going dressed like that?

Carlotta folds her arms.

"You're not my boss, dad. Get over yourself. I'm not a little girl anymore. I can dress however I want. And Tisha doesn't have to listen to you. You're not her dad either."

Tisha's eyes meet mine, but I glance away.

"This isn't up for discussion. You aren't running around Thessaloniki with your thighs hanging out. You're begging for rape or worse. Is that what you want?"

Carlotta appears mortified. Mostly because of Tisha. She thinks I'm too crass and old-fashioned for her friend. She isn't wrong.

"I *hate you!*"

Carlotta screams and throws her phone at the sliding door. Her phone shatters on the tiles.

"I wish you died instead of mom!" Carlotta screams.

This is my daughter, clean from all drug abuse. I shudder. I try to be a good father, but I'm woefully incompetent at it. I don't have that way women do... I get all angry and emotional with the children and then I fight with them. They ought to fear me, but Carlotta hardly respects me. Antonio... well, he's too busy hiding his secret escapades to notice me at all.

And Zoe. I miss Zoe. I had to send her away for her safety, but I want her back.

"I'll go talk to her," Fallon says, instantly stepping off the stool and trying to help.

I restrain her gently.

"Don't bother. Go back up to Stavros. Make sure he isn't thinking about taking Nikola out. I'll go out with Gal and handle it."

"Don't kill him."

I lean over and kiss Fallon's cheek, "I won't. Bye, sister."

Fallon acts uncomfortable whenever I call her sister, but she's become a sister to me. I'm glad Stavros has kept her alive. Tisha returns to the kitchen and sighs, wrapping a blanket around her shoulders. At least she had the decency to cover up.

"Uncle Loukas, we should talk," Tisha says with a trembling voice. She doesn't like conflict, but there's nothing for us to talk about. We can't afford to talk anymore. Neither of us can handle talking.

"We have nothing to talk about. Tell Carlotta to change and then I don't care what you two get up to."

She sighs and continues, "I didn't mean about Carlotta."

"We can't talk here," I murmur.

I don't want to talk to her at all. What I've done is bad enough. I tried everything in my power to make sure I didn't see her again, and now she's standing here. And I have to fight the urge to protect her. *What I'm doing isn't protection. It's... abuse.*

She tightens the blanket around her shoulders.

"We have to..."

Her eyes well with tears. I can't help myself. Seeing her cry tugs on my heartstrings. I touch her shoulders and she gasps. Does she want this? Does she want more? I want to pull her against my chest, but I resist the urge. This is my punishment for not resisting the temptation before.

I kiss her forehead. *No. You're letting go again.*

"What's wrong, Tisha?"

What I want involves more than kissing.

"I'm pregnant," she says, her breath catching as she sheds a few more tears. "Don't worry. Carlotta doesn't know."

Her body shakes as she hides her face in her hands. No... This can't be. She can't be pregnant...

How?

FOUR
GROUT ORTHODOX

Loukas
39 years old

Tisha
17 years old

I am not proud of what I do when I leave the room and shut myself in my bedroom. It's not hurting her to think about her. I touch myself and when I finish, I know I'm broken. I'm a dirty bastard for the way I feel.

It doesn't matter if I'd never act on my attraction to her. The lust is just as bad. In the morning, I exercise and plan to get the teenager out of my house. It's five in the morning, too early for her to be up, but early enough I can secure the trades with Ofek.

Again, I step into my kitchen and hear a gasp. Tisha. Again. She's pressed up against the refrigerator, kissing... a *boy*. Not Antonio. My seventeen-year-old brother. Gal.

"What are you doing here?!"

Gal grabs her cheeks and kisses her again, forcing his tongue into her mouth and smacking her bottom. Tisha yelps but doesn't pull away from him. Her body rests against his and I sense her wanting him. *No.* I can't be jealous. Galanos is *her age,* and I'm old enough to be her father. I'm her *best friend's* father.

Gal wipes his lips and kisses Tisha's neck, "Sorry, Lou. I thought you would be cool."

"Get out of my house, Galanos."

Tisha reaches for his hand and Galanos snatches it away.

"I'll pop your cherry some other time, babe."

He winks and saunters out of the room. Whistling. If I didn't know better, I'd say he was whistling to piss me off. Tisha and Gal? He can't be her type. My brother is immature and vain. *And too much younger than me.*

I'm old enough now to know when I'm jealous, but now my envy and rage form a ball of something disgusting within me and I direct all my loathing at the innocent teenager standing in front of me. She's not sure whether it's okay for her to go back to Carlotta. Then it occurs to me that if Tisha snuck out to be with Gal, Carlotta isn't home.

"Where's Carlotta," I snap, my thick Greek brows bunching above my aquiline nose, bent slightly from a bar fight in Tel Aviv.

"I-I don't know."

"You two went out last night?"

She bites her lip and shakes her head guiltily before answering.

"No..."

"Don't lie to me, Tisha."

"Yes. We went out. But I didn't want to! Carlotta wanted to meet

—

She remembered she wasn't supposed to be talking to me about her best friend's love life. Tisha doesn't know my family well. So I have to pretend to be a normal father of a teenager. A man who can be reasonable. She doesn't know that when it comes to protecting my daughter, there's no room for reason.

Every woman I've ever loved has died, and I won't let the same thing happen to Carlotta.

"Tell me. I promise no one will get punished if you tell the truth."

"Carlotta's dating a guy who owns a nightclub. She promises she hasn't slept with him yet. I know your family is really religious. Grout Orthodox and everything."

I stifle a laugh.

"Did you say *grout* Orthodox?"

"Did I get that wrong? I can never understand Carlotta's accent when she says it."

"Greek Orthodox. You're a college student and you've never heard of it?"

"Sorry! I'm not the one who's religious."

"I'm not religious. I just need the name of this nightclub owner. I'll pick Carlotta up and she'll be safe and sound before you know it."

Tisha bites her lower lip and her tawny cheeks gain a tinge of red to them. I've been a dad long enough to know when a teenage girl is lying.

"What is it?"

"She's not at the nightclub."

"Then you know where she is?"

"She went on his boat. She said she was coming back tomorrow."

"And she left you here?!"

"She said Galanos would take care of me. We were coming here to get my clothes."

"Yes. My little brother. Sit down."

Tisha stomps her foot and snaps, "I wasn't doing anything with Galanos!"

"I said *sit*."

She obeys. Which I like. I wonder what other commands she'd

obey, and then I remember she's seventeen. Too tall to be seventeen, I think. And too fucking gorgeous. She'll break some man's heart someday. Tisha folds her hands in her lap and lowers her gaze.

"I'm sorry, Uncle Loukas. I won't kiss boys or disobey your rules. And I'm sorry I let Carlotta out of my sight. Honestly, I think that's the only reason Gal was kissing me. To help her."

"That doesn't sound like my brother. Helpful."

"He owes Carlotta money for —

"For what?"

Tisha groans and massages her temples, thinking otherwise of spilling the beans, "Carlotta's going to *kill* me."

"For *what.*"

My stern "dad voice" intimidates her enough for her to spill — perhaps with more details than necessary.

"She spotted him €200 for an ounce of Platinum Bubba Kush and he lost his wallet so he couldn't pay her back."

"Okay. You're telling me my daughter was *smoking marijuana?*"

Again? Carlotta knows my rules. No more drugs. We're past that point in time. She told me she would stop doing drugs when I stopped drinking but... fuck. She's the kid. I'm the one who it's too late for. She's the one I want to protect. The one I always fail to protect.

I nearly lose control of my cool dad facade. Tisha covers her face with her hands.

"Please don't make me snitch, Uncle Loukas."

"Calm down. Calm down."

I reach over the counter and touch her shoulders. This is fatherly. I mean nothing by it. She wriggles and my hand falls off her shoulder. I don't move away from her.

"Tell me the truth. I won't punish any of you."

Except Carlotta. And my idiot brother, Gal.

"Yes. We had *some* marijuana. But we sold most of it for —

"For what?"

"Carlotta said MDMA was better, but I promise we didn't do it!"

Fuck's sake. My daughter's doing hard drugs and hanging out with older men. And which nightclub owner? Luigi perhaps? We should stop letting fucking Italians live in Thessaloniki.

"I'm sorry, Uncle Loukas."

"Give me the man's name."

"Adrian. I only know his first name."

"Thank you."

She grabs my arm. Tightly. The contact makes me want to press her up against my chest. And kiss her. I forget she isn't a woman. She's my daughter's best friend and my desire to turn this contact into more makes me a sick person.

"Are you going to hurt him?"

"No. I'll have my brother wait for him on the docks that way he can help Carlotta home."

Stavros will have the perfect answer to a man threatening my daughter's honor. It's not like he hasn't killed before. It's not like I don't suspect him of killing the three women I've already lost.

"If my dad heard all this, he'd have whooped me so damn hard."

I raise an eyebrow.

"You sound like that's what you'd prefer."

Fuck. I hate myself the second the words come out of my mouth, but she's too young to get the innuendo. Or maybe she thinks I'm too old and hideous for it to be innuendo at all.

"It's weird having a calm presence around," she says. "That's all."

She barely knows me, so I understand the mistake.

"Carlotta would disagree. We fight endlessly."

"She fights back."

"You don't fight back with your parents? They're lucky. Or maybe you're lucky. Carlotta fights because I'm a shitty dad."

"No way. You let her do whatever she wants."

Except have relationships. Except go to college alone. Not even Carlotta knows I have men following her to make sure nothing happens to her while she's away from Greece. I couldn't bear to lose her.

"I don't let her do whatever I want. I'm strict."

Tisha scoffs.

"No way. She has her own apartment. She has all the money in the world. Everyone's jealous of Carlotta."

"Including you?"

Tisha shrugs. She's opening up to me because she sees me as a father figure. I can't help but feel drawn to her sweet nature. I want to put my hand on her shoulder again, but I'm terrified of what will happen if I make contact.

She's only seventeen.

Tisha finally admits, "Yeah. I'm jealous of Carlotta."

"You have nothing to be jealous of."

My English sounds rough and hurried. Tisha glances at me and tilts her head to the side curiously. She's not experienced with this. She doesn't know what to do with what we both feel. But I'm the adult. So I know what to do. And I know better. I lean forward and kiss her forehead. Slowly.

I pull away and she gasps...

"Uncle Loukas."

"No," I growl, "Loukas."

I grab her cheeks and kiss her on the lips. A rough, urgent kiss. Then I pull away. She sits in shock and shame courses through me. This moment of sanity is all I need. Just one moment to make the correct decision.

I leave the room. Furious with myself. My desire overwhelms me. I can't breathe. I can't be near her again. I don't trust myself.

FIVE
THE ABORTION CHAPTER

"How can you be pregnant?"

My heart pounds as I ask her. The idea of my daughter getting pregnant flashes through my mind and sickens me. It would ruin her.

Tisha replies casually, "The usual way people get pregnant."

I ought to punish her for that smart mouth. I fight my urge to control her behavior. To act like I'm a father figure to her when we both know — I'm far from it.

"What are you going to do about it?"

"I'm going to have an abortion. Obviously. But I need money."

Abortion? How can she say it with such ease, like she's decided? I tell myself that this kid isn't mine and I have no claim to her body. That doesn't work against twenty years of parenting instincts.

"You're in Greece. It's free."

"I'm only here for another two weeks and then I'm going back to America. I already have an appointment at Planned Parenthood, but I need \$800. I can't ask my parents. They'll kill me. Please, Uncle Loukas."

I am useless when she pleads. Her face scrunches up and I'll do anything for her. But then she goes and calls me... uncle. I scowl.

"Don't call me that."

"Will you give me the money?"

It's my fault she's acting like this. I remind myself of the ways I hurt her. How I deserve this. I'm an ATM to her now.

"Yes."

My fists clench and my knuckles turn white. Tisha steps onto her tiptoes and kisses my cheek. I loathe what the simple touch of her lips does to me. Tisha's *pregnant*. I have to sit down with another drink as soon as she leaves the room. After all this experience as a father, I can stay in control most of the time. Carlotta's the only one who can get a rise out of me.

Fuck it. I can't sit here and know she's pregnant, doing nothing. I'll give her the money later and then I'll ask Fallon to monitor the two of them while I sail off to Somalia or some fucking place where I don't have to deal with this.

I storm out of the room toward the pool. Unlike Galanos, I don't spend all my time out in the sun. I need to come up with a plan. I'm a father. I have three children and I can't know about another and allow...

Abortion. It's none of the man's business. I understand. I have finely honed fatherly instincts now. I've made mistakes before, but for my children, I'd make the same mistakes over again if it meant they'd be safe, happy and rich as fuck.

It occurs to me. I don't know the baby is mine. A second thought occurs to me. The baby isn't mine. It *can't* be mine. Because it can't possibly be my child, my first suspect is Galanos. She kissed him. And if she's like most women who kiss Gal, she liked it. I don't know what they see in that vain little shit.

Carlotta comes into the room dressed in sweatpants and a crop top with her navel showing. She dresses like this to piss me off and it works. It's her tiny act of rebellion against me.

"Come for your phone?"

"Shut up, papa."

"I know you're angry with me. Always. And I know it's my fault."

"Good. I *seriously* hate you. I'm surprised Tisha's always asking to visit Greece because you're such a piece of *shit*."

Carlotta snarls every word, baring her teeth and looking like Yiayia. I never allowed my mother much time with her grandchildren in the past, but looking at Carlotta, I wonder if I've allowed them too much. I calm myself with the reminder that Yiayia is far away from her... on a boat with my father.

All I have left when Carlotta gets like this is pleading with her.

I promise her, "I'll get you a new phone. The newest one."

"You can't keep buying my love. But uh... it's €1,500. And I need this new Prada bag."

She takes her iPad out of her tote bag and shows me a teal leather bag on some website with a €5,000 price tag.

"Are you fucking crazy?"

The bag looks nice enough, but I don't understand why women don't simply wear clothing with pockets instead of emptying the bank on hideous sacks.

"Daddy, seriously? This is how we work. We piss each other off and then you buy me things and we forgive each other."

"Is that all it takes to get forgiveness?"

Carlotta throws her arms around me, and I pull her close. She's too beautiful for her own good, like Helen.

"Yes, daddy. I could never be that angry with you."

I worry that she's about as mentally stable as Stavros.

"Fine."

"And daddy, no matter what happens, I love you."

"Hm."

"Aren't you going to say that you love me too?"

She pulls away from me and leans against the counter, reaching for a cigarette. I shouldn't let her smoke, but it's one of the many battles I've lost against my daughter. At least she's still pure. Untouched. And we'll find her a rich Italian husband. An attractive one. And a young one. I don't want any harm to come to her. Papa might not look after his children, but I look after mine.

I touch her hand.

"Look at me, Carlotta."

She looks up at me. Her eyes are fierce, but there's darkness between them. She lost her mother and that pain never left her. I caused that pain and there's nothing I can do to heal it, even if I try everything in my power to keep her safe.

I continued, "I don't need to say I love you all the time because I show it. I would go to the ends of the earth for you."

"Hopefully not the ends of the earth."

"No. I would. I would comb through hell with a toothbrush if something happened to you. You're my eldest daughter. And you will have a good life. You're my universe, princess."

She kisses my forehead and struts off with her cigarette. Her legs are so thin. I hope she's eating enough and staying away from drugs. I can't get her to quit the cigarettes, but I can at least get her to eat some fucking pasta.

I spend the evening drinking with Stavros and Fallon. I'm the only one drinking. Fallon holds her tummy and muses about possible baby names.

"What about Sage? It's my favorite spice," Fallon says.

Stavros eyes my drink enviously and then growls, "We aren't naming our baby after a leaf."

"Why not? I suppose you think we ought to name him AK-47."

"A.K. Would be a nice nickname," Stavros says, perking up and kissing Fallon's shoulder.

She pushes him off, and then he grabs her and kisses her. Babies. *No.* I don't want to talk or listen to anything about fucking babies.

Hearing the conversation pushes me over the edge. With Carlotta safely out of sight and her best friend far enough away not to hear,

"She's fucking pregnant," I snarl under my breath, but loud enough for Fallon and Stavros to catch a few words.

Stavros and Fallon exchange worried glances. Fallon gives him a look as if to say, "I've got this."

Then she puts her hand on my knee.

"Loukas. Are you hearing voices?"

"No! She's fucking pregnant. FUCK!"

I throw my bottle into the fire. It shatters, only deepening Fallon's concern.

"Who? Meghan Markle?" Fallon wails in a mixture of distress and anticipation.

I don't know why Fallon thinks I know why this "Meghan Markle" is. Or why I'd care that she's pregnant.

"I can't tell you… I can't… I fucked up. I fucked up."

"It can't be that bad. Give her money for the abortion and send her on her way," Stavros answers coolly.

Fallon hits him for his clearly unhelpful comment. I am glad we both put our differences behind us in favor of hitting Stavros whenever he says something idiotic.

"I don't want her to have an abortion. We're talking about *Pagonis blood.*"

Stavros groans and accuses me of sounding like YiaYia, which earns him another kick from Fallon.

Fallon tries to comfort me by saying, "Whoever she is, it can't be that bad. You can work together in harmony to co-parent."

I don't know what Fallon learned as a psychiatric nurse, but it sounds like Hindi to me.

"Oh, it's bad," I grumble, "And no psycho-babble can fix it. Don't mind me, I'm going to kill myself now."

I stand up, but I'm too drunk to stand. Thankfully, I'm too drunk to find my gun. The next thing I know, Stavros catches me before I fall and I hear Fallon hissing, "Put him to bed! I think he's stressed about losing Matilda."

Matilda…

All the ways I hurt Matilda. I deserve to die for that alone.

SIX
GEMINI

Loukas
40 years old

Tisha
18 years old

Carlotta's home for my birthday in June. Her flight gets in just in time for her to come to the enormous celebration at the villa. Even Yiayia's in a good mood. Stavros isn't here. He's pissed at me. Again. He's frustrated. Even if I disagree with him publicly, Stavros is right.

Defying our grandmother and father isn't as easy as he thinks. I walk into the party to see Gal sitting on the counter, a joint between his lips and a thin tower of white powder on the table.

"Credit card, Seb."

His friend tosses Galanos the credit card and he cuts the cocaine. Seb is apparently famous in America, so my brother constantly craves his company. I don't like the platinum-haired little shit. And Gal gets too loose-lipped about family business when he wants attention. Which he's addicted to. Seb bends his nose to the kitchen counter and laughs like a jackal once the ice hits his nostrils.

Seb turns red and Galanos laughs. I grab the joint from my brother's mouth and toss it in the sink. Afterward, I take a swig from my flask. I need liquid courage to talk to Gal without wanting to punch him. I was wild at his age, but I didn't run around kissing my niece's friends.

Okay, now that I say it like that. I'm worse. And I'm forty. But fuck, it's my birthday. I take another drink.

"Don't smoke in the house," I snarl at Gal, mostly because I'm drunk and need to snarl at something.

Galanos grins and says, "Happy Birthday, Lou."

"Hm."

A pale girl with short brown hair has her arm around Gal and one hand on his cock. He's ignoring her entirely while she giggles. Embarrassed, I look away. How old is that girl? My brother's only eighteen. Like Tisha.

Gal reaches into his breast pocket for a gold chain. I snatch it from him. I'm eager to get out of here. Horny teenagers scare the shit out of me. Thankfully, Helen taught Carlotta about her period. Helen made me pay her a €4,000 consulting fee, which she promptly wasted on Ferragamo boots. At least she got the job done and I didn't have to suffer.

"Where the fuck did you get this?" I snarl at the gift. Galanos doesn't have any money. I handle the family accounts and I know he doesn't get enough for delightful gifts. Giving Galanos too much money would be like giving Charles Manson a sorority house.

"Families *without* reptilians typically exchange *gifts* for birthdays," Galanos explains. He does a line of cocaine and his pupils dilate, covering the blue.

"Did you steal it?"

"No. It's custom you twit. And it's yours. Solid gold."

Galanos sounds proud. I snort and stuff it in my pocket. There's music coming from the pool deck.

"Carlotta's here," Gal announces as he meticulously divides more cocaine into three distinct lines, "She's brought that girl with her."

"What girl?"

"The black one."

There can only be one black girl. I don't want to believe it's Tisha. Gal kissed her. And probably worse. Shouldn't he know her name? I have to find out if it's her.

"Where are they?"

My eyes dart around the room quickly looking for an escape route when Carlotta stumbles into the kitchen hanging onto a man, drunk and wearing a bikini that leaves her nearly nude. His hands dig into her waist and his cock juts lewdly from his thin bathing suit.

The thin yellow straps almost blend in with Carlotta's deep Greek tan. His hands tighten around her. Her body is far too exposed and she's my daughter. I can't have my daughter walking around this. *I can't fail to keep her safe.*

Rage courses through me.

Then erupts.

"CARLOTTA!"

She squeals and pushes the boy with his arms around her off like she didn't want him touching her. She slaps him.

"Pervert! Daddy, he was *mauling* me."

Everything about our relationship has been horrible lately.

I scream at her, "That's ENOUGH! It's my birthday and you're humiliating me by acting like a whore! Don't you have any respect for this family?"

I'm drunk. Too drunk to parent. I grab Carlotta by the hand. She's screaming and I know people are looking in from the patio. I am too angry to care. She brought Tisha back. After everything, she brought that *girl* into my house. I can't control myself around Tisha, and I can't control myself now. I slap her. And hit her again. I hit Carlotta until she screams.

It's what she'd do as a child. When she'd had enough of me. When she was tired of being the victim of my emotional outbursts. I let go of her. She grabs her face and runs out of the room. Sobbing. I grab hold of the man who had his arms around my daughter. I take my gun out.

"You. Get the fuck over here."

The man listens. Most people make it a point to show they aren't listening. If you're at a Pagonis party, you know exactly who we are. You didn't see shit or hear shit once you cross the threshold of the Pagonis driveway.

"What's your name?"

"Gabriel."

"Last name."

He bites his lower lip and shakes his head. He doesn't want to give his name. But someone doesn't want young Gabriel's bad luck spreading to the entire party.

"Morello!"

I have his last name. I lower my gun and pat the boy on his shoulders.

"Have fun tonight, Gabriel. Enjoy my birthday party."

I walk out of the kitchen, away from everyone. Galanos is already mocking the way Carlotta cried out. My daughter knows better than to run around in her bikini on the property. And on my fucking birthday. She doesn't care about how hard I work to protect her. She doesn't know the details of what happened to her mother.

She can't. Carlotta blames me for her mother dying. She wants to blame me for everything. I never wanted three children. I never wanted *one.* But when I saw Carlotta, I knew I would die for her. I'd die to protect her.

Someone around me kills the women I love. With Carlotta's mother, the murderer did worse. It's the only reason I have to believe Stavros isn't the killer. He'd never had a woman like that. But every man has demons. And they can't always avoid temptation. I still have to keep him close.

Now that Carlotta's nearly a woman, I won't be able to protect her the way I used to. She could go anywhere. She could meet anyone. I could lose her. My angel.

Once I held this baby in my arms, I couldn't be Loukas the party animal or Loukas the womanizer. She became the only reason I was alive. When her mother died, Carlotta was the only reason I didn't kill myself.

Carlotta is my everything.

Tisha stomps out onto the side patio toward me. She's here. The corners of my lips turn up in a smile. She's more beautiful than I remember. And she looks older. She must be eighteen now. Like my daughter, I remind myself shamefully.

"Tisha, Good —

"How dare you!"

She takes her sandal off and flings it at my head. I grew up with too many siblings to let her shoe catch me in the head. But the second one is harder to dodge. I catch it instead.

"Welcome back to Greece."

"Don't do this, Uncle Lou. You *beat* Carlotta in front of everyone. What were you thinking?"

"I disciplined her."

"Disciplined her? You hurt her. I saw the marks. I didn't think you were that type of parent. Sorry to see I was wrong."

"*Young lady*, how I discipline Carlotta is none of your problem. I'm her father and I'm perfectly capable of raising her."

Tisha pouts and pops her hip. I don't scare her.

"Since you 'disciplined her', mind sharing what she did wrong?"

"Carlotta has the tendency to dress and act like a street prostitute. This is not acceptable behavior for a young lady."

"How dare you."

"What is it now?"

She leans in and hisses, "You *kissed* me. Don't play dumb, Uncle Lou."

"Have you told people about this?"

"That's what you're worried about?"

"I wouldn't want to damage your reputation."

We both know that's bullshit. Tisha folds her arms and glares disapprovingly. Is someone my daughter's age supposed to make me feel guilty for being such a fuckup like this?

"You can't lecture Carlotta about boys, when you kissed me. I don't know if you remember, but I wasn't even *eighteen*."

Ouch. I know it's true, but it stings. I hurt her. I *touched* my lips to hers. Looking at her was one thing, but kissing her was another entirely. And she's right. I'm a horrible father. It doesn't matter if I was drunk.

"I'm sorry I kissed you, Tisha. I shouldn't have done it."

She scowls harder and makes a huffy little teenager noise before continuing her lecture.

"All Carlotta wants is for you to care about her."

"Care about her? I do *everything* for Carlotta. I have always done everything for her."

Tisha snaps, "It isn't good enough then. Try something else."

She turns to walk away and I grab her arm. Tisha swings around and her body is close to mine.

"You talk to no one about what happened between us."

She gasps and struggles.

"I am serious, child. What happened between us will never happen again. Nod if you understand."

But she's close enough to me I'm not sure about the words coming out of my mouth. She doesn't resist my grasp. It's like she's beckoning me. Tempting me. Carlotta could walk out of her room any minute. She'd feel betrayed. Her best friend sleeping with her father?

Not like Tisha would sleep with me.

That would be too much for my daughter to bear. She hates me enough already.

She whispers, "Was it because I was young? Is that the only reason?"

"No."

"So you aren't a..."

"No! I... It was a mistake. It was a stupid mistake. If I hurt or traumatized you..."

Her eyes well with tears. And I realize that I have. I've hurt her. And now I want to make it better. But holding her will only make me act on the urges I want to suppress. I imagine her skin is warm. And soft. And supple beneath my fingertips. I imagine how her lips would taste salted with her tears. Imagining her flavor makes me hard.

"You haven't," Tisha says.

But her voices warbles. And I have a teenager, so I know all their tricks.

"That's not true, is it?"

"You're like an uncle to me, Loukas. Not an *actual* uncle. But... I trusted you."

I grip her forearm tightly and she winces.

"Please... let go."

But I don't want to let go. I want her.

SEVEN

GONE CARLOTTA

Knock. Knock. Knock. Knock. Knock. Knock. Knock. Knock. Knock. Knock. Knock. Knock. Knock. Knock. *Jesus.*

I stumble out of bed and throw the door open with an enraged, "What the hell do you want?!"

Tisha's eyes are wet.

"She's gone."

I lower my voice.

"The baby?"

Fear and guilt surge through me. Not a miscarriage...

"No, Uncle Lou. Carlotta."

"Where has she gone? Tell me the bastard's name and I'll pick her up."

Carlotta and I go through this repeatedly. She runs away with some man who believes her when she says her father will never find him. I find the man and give his name to Stavros. The man isn't a problem anymore. But Stavros has given up killing, which means I have to do the dirty work.

Stavros was always a better killer. And I want to set a good example to my children.

Kill only when necessary. Better yet, don't kill at all. I want them to be better than I ever was.

"You don't understand," Tisha continues, "you won't be able to find her this time. She's gone for good."

"She's twenty. I brought her back home at seventeen, I can bring her back at twenty."

Carlotta's a little older than Tisha. Tisha probably turned nineteen recently. And she's pregnant with a baby that probably isn't mine. It's my fault for *sexualizing* her.

"I told her not to go, Loukas. The guy she's with is dangerous. I tried to warn her, but I don't think this man will let her out of his clutches."

"Do you know this man's name?"

All I need is a name and I can get the whispers in Thessaloniki to spread the word that I'm looking for him. If he's smart and wants his family spared, he'll come right into the lion's den.

"I don't know. She spoke in Greek to him, but I don't know more than that."

My desire to hold Tisha in my arms mounts. I've given up that option. The baby she's carrying is only proof that I have no business near her.

"Does Gal know about this?"

The gentleness in my voice surprises me.

"No. He wasn't with us last night."

I eye Tisha suspiciously. If she's still in touch with my youngest brother, I want to know. If he's the father of her child, I'll kill him.

He's not ready to be a father. He'd only fuck the kid up — even worse than I fucked my kids up. Tisha's round russet-brown face shows no hint of deception. Only genuine concern for Carlotta's life.

"I need you to tell me everything you know about her plan."

Tisha gives me the details she can recall. She thought Carlotta was joking because she always talked about running away.

This time, my runaway daughter had it all planned out. Burner phone. Thousands of Euros stashed away. She got her passport from Yiayia by pretending they were going to Milan on a shopping trip. Tisha sobs by the end of it and I put my arm around her. At first she resists, and then her head touches my chest.

"Don't worry. I'll find her."

"These guys were bad news, Uncle Lou... I don't know what they wanted with her, but I don't think she'll be happier there."

"You can stay at the villa while I look for her. Stavros and his fiancée are here. You'll like Fallon because you're both... you know... *similar.*"

"You mean black?"

"Yes. But there isn't anything wrong with that," I add quickly.

"Why would there be something wrong with that?"

My cheeks redden.

"Nothing. I come from a different time, I suppose, when women of your skin color faced harsher judgment."

Tisha rolls her eyes and mutters, "Whatever, Loukas. But I'm not staying here."

"It isn't a discussion, Tisha. You're staying at the villa."

She's pregnant. The last thing I want is to run all over Greece with my daughter's pregnant best friend. That would hurt her reputation, especially if she really ends up living here like she plans with Carlotta. I have to think about her future.

"I'm not staying here unless you give me money for an abortion first. I'm not going back to America without the money," Tisha says.

I clasp my hand over her mouth, and her fierce brown eyes meet mine.

"Are you crazy?" I hiss, "You can't speak so loudly about that here..."

Her muffled screeching gets louder.

"Sorry! But I need to get one. I'm too young to have a kid."

"You mean you have too much partying to do? You're my daughter's best friend, I'm sure you can't wait to get back to drinking, fucking strangers and snorting coke."

"Uncle Lou! You can't talk to me like that."

I want to ask her "why not" but we both know why not. I glance down at her belly and concern replaces my outrage.

"Have you been doing everything right?"

"Who cares? I'm flushing that thing down the toilet like a used napkin."

"That's a horrible way to speak about ending a life," I snarl at her.

Tisha rolls her eyes.

"It's not a life. It's a parasite. And it's going to make me all stretched out and ugly, and everyone will look at me like I'm some stupid stereotype."

"That's not what having a child is about. It's a magical, beautiful thing. This life inside you means something."

I want to touch her stomach, but I know what will happen if I allow myself. I can't even look at her. Her voice gets soft and timid. Teenagers. They say things that are so calloused and cruel that you can forget they're not actually evil.

She whispers, "It means nothing to me."

Then she quickly remembers she's angry with me.

"I *don't do drugs, anyway.* You're thinking about my best friend. My best friend who by the way, is the best reason we have to get rid of this baby. I don't want to get attached."

Is she suggesting the child is mine now? If she's going to have an abortion, perhaps it's best that I don't know...

"You're only a child, Tisha, so perhaps you don't know that you don't get a choice. You're already attached."

"How dare you call me a child? How dare you," she says. Her eyes swim with tears and I force myself not to feel sorry for her. Pregnancy hormones, I tell myself, they make women crazy.

"I won't be discussing this further. I'm leaving to find Carlotta and when I get back, we will discuss... this."

"I don't want to wait."

Young people can be so impatient. She gazes up at me with soft brown eyes. Desire stirs between my legs again. I loathe the control she has over me. She doesn't recognize it. Or perhaps that's what I tell myself. Maybe Tisha has me wrapped around her finger and I'm too foolish to realize that feminine wiles have her advanced beyond her years.

"Uncle Lou... please. I want to fix this."

Her eyes water and I feel weak as I watch her emotions bubble so close to the edge of an explosion. I shouldn't be the one making her cry.

"Tisha. Trust me. I will fix this. But I need to find Carlotta."

"Let me come with you," She begs. It's nearly impossible to resist her, but I can't just think of her this time. My fatherly instincts have always been strong. I forbid this.

"Absolutely not. It's too dangerous. You're pregnant."

"I don't want to be pregnant. I want to find my friend."

"Please. Stay here. For me. Because I asked."

"Okay."

I raise an eyebrow. I have two teenagers. They don't give up that quickly. Maybe I'm used to brattier kids than my daughter's best friend.

"Good," I say with the confidence of a won battle.

"See you later, Uncle Lou."

I pull my phone out. Whoever has Carlotta can't be far. I'll get the boats ready to leave in the morning and have two of our guys pinpoint her exact location.

"Have her readied for me in four hours. I don't want her getting far. Make sure they don't cross the border. Call Papa if you have to."

Tisha scurries down the hallway back into her bedroom. How can she speak so casually about getting rid of a child? There's truth to it. The generations get worse as you go along. We fucked up bad with my daughter's generation.

That much becomes clear the way they have their heads buried in phones. Galanos never stood a chance. Papa's weakest sperm in his youngest hook-up and now we have Gal...

His mother left him on the doorstep of the villa and never looked back. Good riddance. She was younger than Stavros.

I have to remind myself that Tisha isn't different. She's a *child*, just like Galanos. It doesn't matter if a piece of paper says she's eighteen.

I allowed myself to go too far. And even if she's a legal adult. And she was when it happened. That doesn't make it okay.

She's my daughter's best friend. I'm more than twice her age. There's no way what exists between us is *love*. I can't allow myself to think that.

She's young enough to get confused about where we stand, but I'm old enough to know better.

I catch a few moments of sleep before I drive to the docks. Three of our boats hold up my daughter's out in the Aegean Sea. It'll be an overnight journey, but I can get there before things get out of control.

EIGHT
LONG SUMMER

Loukas
40 Years Old

Tisha
18 years old

Summer is too long. I'm in over my head with Tisha. Nothing happened, but she saw my desire for her and she's avoided me ever since. I can't sleep because I can't stop thinking about her. I can't help wishing that she were older or that there's a way to justify this. There isn't.

I'd never recover my relationship with Carlotta if she knew what happened between us. And if Matilda found out... I'm a total dick. A drunk idiot. I'm a fucking monster.

Matilda's right here. I belong with Matilda.

I stumble into bed after another night, avoiding Tisha. Matilda's warm body coils against mine. It isn't Tisha's. But I wish it were. *Fuck*. What is wrong with me... and why can't I get this teenager out of my head?

My cock stiffens. I roll on top of Matilda.

"Wake up and service me, woman," I growl into Matilda's ear.

Matilda likes dominant men. Perhaps more dominant than I am. But I need to make love to her. Hard. I try to get Tisha's face out of my head, but it's impossible. Matilda notices my troubles afterward. Her fingers dance across my chest.

"How much is Carlotta's tuition?" Matilda asks, raking her fingers over my chest hair.

"Oxford. Fucking expensive school. For an international student, £35,000 a year. Worth it for what she's studying. I'm proud of her."

"But Carlotta doesn't do well in school. She isn't grateful for all you're spending."

"You think I spoil her."

"You always have money for your daughter's tuition, but you never have money for what I want. Your friend Sal buys his wife new breasts and a new nose in the same year. She's half his age. How do you think that makes me look?"

"Christ, Matilda. I don't care about new breasts or a new nose. I want to fuck the same woman. Every day."

Except today. When I want to fuck Tisha. My daughter's eighteen-year-old best friend. *Black* best friend.

Matilda complains, "I want to fuck a man who doesn't cheap out on his woman."

"You want new tits, fine. I'll have Henrik transfer the money tomorrow."

"Great. I'll schedule an appointment."

Matilda kisses her way down my chest and thanks me in the way I hope. We have an understanding. And it's as close to love as I thought I'd get after my youngest lost her mother. Carlotta blamed me for that death too.

I should end things with Matilda.

When Matilda finishes, she gets dressed. She's three years younger than me but fitter than most women in their late twenties. Perfect. Narcissistic. Violent. She understands my family and Yiayia likes her. I can't get her to stop butting heads with Carlotta. But my daughter doesn't make it easy.

"Carlotta deserves worse from you. If you spoil her, she'll ruin your reputation. It's embarrassing that my friend's husbands look at her in those skimpy dresses. They talk about her."

"Who looks at her?"

Matilda's too smart to reveal more of her hand.

"She's out of control, Loukas. One day, she'll break your heart."

"She's my daughter. She's supposed to break my heart. That's part of the deal. I don't want to talk about Carlotta. So either fuck me again or shut up."

She shuts up. And doesn't talk to me for two days. By the third day, my tight grip on Carlotta's movements dissipate. I rework the sixth contract with Ofek. I don't know why we bother with contracts. We're all fucking criminals. You fuck with the wrong guy, you end up dead. But Ofek likes to launder his money, so it looks legitimate, and we're willing to help him along. He brings in too much money for us to piss off.

When I get back to the villa in the afternoon, I hear giggles from the living room. Then soft moans. I barge in, expecting Carlotta and one of her paramours, but find something worse. Much worse. Galanos naked. On top of Tisha. Her legs spread even if she's clothed. Galanos' hands slip out from under her dress. He puts two fingers into his mouth as he sees me walk into the room. It drives me insane.

All hell breaks loose. Tisha escapes. I grab my brother and wrap my hand around his neck. I want to kill him. His face turns red. I hear

Tisha yelling. She drags me off him. I punch the wall next to Gal's face and he flees, leaving Tisha to face my wrath.

I turn on Tisha and scream.

"What the hell were you thinking!?"

"He told me you wouldn't be home! I'm sorry! We weren't..."

"You *fucked* my brother?!"

She flinches and runs behind the couch. I chase her and grab her by the forearm. Her dress falls off her shoulder. She isn't wearing a bra. Her breathing hurries as she struggles to wrestle her arm away from mine. She's weaker than me. As old as my daughter.

"Uncle Lou... stop," she whimpers.

My voice trembles but emerges low, icy and terrifying.

"Did you fuck him?"

"N-no..."

She wriggles her shoulder to cover the breast that fell from her dress, but it doesn't work. The cold air teases her nipples to full attention, and she freezes, gazing at my eyes which fixate on the hardened nubs. My thighs bristle as my hardness grows between my legs.

I have to remember she's only eighteen. Too young for me to be reckless with.

"Where's Carlotta?" I murmur, trying to force my volcanic emotions to settle.

"With a girl."

"A friend?"

She nods.

"Good."

I let go of her forearm, but I can't make myself meet her gaze. I'm too guilty. She tiptoes and kisses me on the cheek before walking away. Is it pity? Sympathy? I wonder if I am the seducer or the seduced. I can't bear to look at her as she walks away, but the image of her bared breast with its ochre color, green veins and hard umber nipples remains burned on my brain in riveting and colorful detail.

No fantasizing about her, Loukas. You promised yourself. She's too young, anyway.

I need to handle my brother. Gal lounges by the pool, updating his millions of followers with a rendition of the story that paints me as a crackpot criminal. He pans the camera over to me. I grab the phone and toss it into the pool.

The fucking phone is waterproof — naturally — but that doesn't stop me from wanting to ruin my brother's stupid fucking obsession with bragging about guns and money where anyone can see.

I smack Gal on the back of his head.

"That *girl* doesn't need you knocking her up and ruining her life," I growl at him. *I want to hurt him for touching her.*

Galanos snorts, ignorant about how close he is to having me throw his skinny ass in the pool. He might be muscular, but I'm still older and more experienced at knocking men the fuck out.

"If I knocked Tisha up, I'd push her down the stairs until she got rid of it," Galanos says. "Relax."

"Fuck you," I say to him. "She's Carlotta's best friend and she's a good girl."

"She's a slut."

I slap him again. "Can you stop that?" He says.

"I ought to drown you, you little shit."

I can't go that far, but he fucking tempts me.

"It's called dark humor, brother."

"I don't care what you fucking call it. You go near her again, I'll rip your balls off."

"What the fuck, Loukas. Can you relax? She's just a girl."

"She's *not* just a girl," I snarl at him. "Get anywhere near her and I'll fucking kill you."

"I'm going to screw her," Gal says. "And you can't stop me."

I grab onto a handful of his hair and throw his head forward until he yelps. Blood courses through me as I consider tossing him into the pool or maybe right there on the concrete pool deck I could knock out one of his teeth.

I hit Gal hard in the side until he stops struggling and fucking listens.

"You won't fuck her, finger her, touch her or even think about her," I growl. "Stay away from her or you *will* regret it."

"Fine. But she would have let me fuck her ass. She has that look in her eye, doesn't she?"

I smack him again but don't respond to his comment.

"Don't talk about Tisha like that. Or any woman."

"Says the man who has a new one every week. Stop worrying about who I'm fucking and get laid once in a while. Everyone's sick of you whining."

By a new woman every week, he means that the women I love keep dying. It's easy to see why Galanos is his grandmother's favorite.

"Shut up."

"Have a fucking drink, Lou. You aren't my boss."

He storms off, furiously typing on his stupid cell phone. When did that little shit get a second phone?

I don't follow Galanos because he's right. I need a drink. I consider walking back to Matilda, but I push the door open to Carlotta's room without knocking.

Tisha squeals and draws her towel around her naked body. I stand in the doorway, but I don't apologize. I watch her.

"Uncle Lou!"

"You ought to cover up more," I tell her, "You wouldn't want anyone in this house getting the wrong idea about you."

What the fuck am I saying to her? And why can't I stop looking at her? I'm ashamed, of course. But that doesn't stop me. I just have to look at her. *I must.*

"I-I was changing," she stammers.

When she gets nervous, I stiffen again. I lean against the frame, keeping her locked within my gaze. Eighteen.

"Drop your towel," I command.

"N-no. Uncle Lou... you have a *girlfriend.*"

A girlfriend who doesn't hold a candle to her. A girlfriend who hates my daughter. I'll have to dump her for that alone. Carlotta comes *first*. Every woman I meet knows that about me.

"I want to look," I tell her plainly, "You're a beautiful girl and I want to see how beautiful."

Her towel falls. She's not sure whether to feel proud or embarrassed. Her eyes drop to my crotch. Her back straightens and her perky breasts bounce a little. The hard nipples stick straight out at me. Her hips curve a bit and she's soft around the tummy. No panties on. And waxed. Completely hairless.

Something catches in my throat as I ogle the hairless mound between her legs. I stumble an inch back and humiliation courses through me. I'm so hard I nearly burst. She's gorgeous and unabashed about her looks. And her nipples...

Leave, Loukas. Get out of here before you have her.

"I'm sorry," I whisper, "But I had to look."

NINE
STUCK WITH ONE BED

have the men ready the boats so I can leave *alone* and on time. There's only one bunk below deck, so when I get Carlotta back, we'll have to share the bed on the way back home.

We haven't done that since she was a toddler. I'll probably sleep on the floor. Or not sleep much. I want to look after her. She hasn't been this reckless in ages. She was getting better, I tell myself.

I turn the little boat away from shore and watch the city of Thessaloniki disappear behind me.

A few miles away from the shore, I hear a thud downstairs. Someone's on my boat. An assassin? Or worse...my son Antonio. Didn't I say he could take this vessel out fishing sometimes? But the idiots who got the boat ready should have discovered him.

"Antonio?!"

I race downstairs with my hand on my gun in case it isn't my son and throw the room open. Tisha screams.

"What the hell are you doing here?!"

She yells, "It's too late! We're too far away from shore."

What the fuck is Tisha doing in here? How did she sneak onto this boat?

"I could still throw you overboard. And I ought to!"

"No, Uncle Lou! Don't!" She screams and throws a hair clip at me. Was that meant to be a weapon?

"Why not? I give you one damned instruction and you can't listen to that."

"I'm *pregnant* so you can't throw me overboard."

"Not for long if you had your way. Isn't that what you want? Get it over with? I'll fling you into the sea and end both your lives."

She ignores me, stubbornly folding her arms and stomping her little foot, "Carlotta's in danger, I'm coming to help."

"You can't be here. We have one cot. When I find Carlotta, I'll have to take her back to the villa and there's only one cot for us to share."

"I'll sleep on the floor."

"What the hell will she think when she sees you here? That we've spent a night in the same bed."

"We'll find her soon and we can honestly say we never spent the night together."

"This journey will be at least overnight. We don't have a choice."

We exchange glances. Because we couldn't honestly make the statement, anyway. We could never truthfully say that again.

I say to her plainly, "Don't tell Carlotta. Not yet."

"We're *never* telling Carlotta," she sneers.

I feel foolish, like I'm the irresponsible one. I suppose I am. What was I thinking? With *her*. Stavros used to joke about me having a weakness for the wrong women. Usually that meant addicts, gold diggers or waifs.

Not girls like Tisha — girls who were far too young for me.

"I knew that," I stumble over my words.

"You're giving me the money for the abortion. I don't care about your old school crap. I want my body back."

"You shouldn't have come here," I growl and move toward the door to leave. I don't want to have this conversation with Tisha anymore. Even if I've lost my ground to stand on. She lets me go and when I surface on deck, my loathing intensifies.

Fuck. After everything I went through with Carlotta, I thought we'd found a solution. She brings her friend here and we repair our relationship. We've never been on a shakier footing. I wrongly assume Tisha will spend all her time below deck either pouting or catching up on sleep below deck.

"Why won't you look at me?"

That's what young girls are like at that age. They want to be *looked at* and they don't even know why yet. I know because I have a daughter her age.

"Tisha, I can't look at you and we both know why. You should head below deck. It's not safe out here."

"If it isn't safe, you shouldn't be out here alone."

I ought to be the adult here, but I can't help but smile.

"Are you suggesting you could protect me?"

"I could alert you to danger. You're pretty old. I'm guessing your vision isn't 20/20."

"Only a nineteen-year-old could think forty-one is old."

"You look good for your age."

"I look good. Period. And you can stop calling me Uncle Lou, you make me feel disgusting."

"So you *are* going to acknowledge what happened."

"I didn't put that baby in you," I say to her with a blustering confidence that causes her face to fall instantly.

"Yes. You did."

"No. I wore a condom."

"You didn't wear a condom."

"Not even the first time?"

I'm not sure she can be right. I must have cared enough about her to wear a condom. She's so young. I couldn't have been that selfish, even back then.

"We were always in a rush. But that last time... you wanted to knock me up."

"The last time was when you left after Spring Break."

"No," she whispers, "the last night was... two months ago."

My stomach turns. If I hadn't seen more gruesome shit in my life, I would have reacted more. There's nothing more disgusting than what I've done. How I acted. Tisha doesn't deserve a monster like me.

"I don't remember that."

"You were drunk."

"I was always drunk."

"That doesn't excuse it," she blurts out.

I grab her so she can't avoid the question. She doesn't flinch when I hold her forearm, so I relax my grip. Her soft brown eyes turn up toward me. She's so much *smaller* than me.

"You were eighteen. You knew what you were doing."

"You knew you could never feel for me what I felt for you," she snaps.

I could never let her know how I felt. I could never tell her because of what it would mean. I have to let her go... Why can't she see that? She's too young for me to rip from innocence. I've done enough damage to her honor.

"Don't be coy. There were never any feelings between us."

"How could you say that?"

"I was drunk. Whatever feelings you have for me, Tisha, get rid of them."

"You expect me to carry your child for nine months, keep it a secret, and act totally stoic around you at all times? You have three kids, you know what pregnancy's like. See, this is why I want an abortion. We would be the *worst* parents."

"I am a wonderful father."

"You fucked your daughter's best friend."

"Some best friend," I shoot back. "You're screwing your best friend's father. That hardly makes you an angel."

She pushes me. I raise an eyebrow. You don't parent Carlotta and not adjust your body to a baseline level of physical assault. My eldest is a true Pagonis.

"I am not having a stupid baby for you."

"If I had my way, you wouldn't get the choice."

She struggles against me, and I push her up against the railing. She's getting me hard again, and talking about the baby inside her makes it worse.

"Is it really mine?" I snarl, pinning her against the railing, "Tell the truth."

Women lie. Women manipulate. I learned that from my grand-mother. She squeals and cries out, "Uncle Lou, you're hurting me!"

I spread her thighs apart, instigating another scream. I rest my hips between her legs, pinning her against the railing but separating our skin by the barrier of my trousers. She screams again.

"TELL THE TRUTH!"

I run my tongue along her neck after screaming at her. She's young. I know how easy it will be to unravel her once I dangle the promise of pleasure in front of her. She's younger. More sensitive. Softer and easier to bend in more ways than one.

"I never slept with your brother. We were fooling around... To make you jealous."

I put my hand to her throat.

"Don't make me squeeze."

"Loukas...You are fucking crazy," she hisses.

I could never properly hurt her, but she doesn't know that. I just want the truth. I want Tisha to stop lying to me. I want her to be something she can't ever be — mine completely.

"I'm serious, Tisha. We're out here alone. And you know what I do for a living. You know I could."

"The baby is yours. It's why I begged Carlotta to come back here this summer. She didn't want me to come. She said it would be better for your relationship if I didn't."

"Why the fuck did you come back then?" I say to her. "Just for money?To find the child's father? To taunt me? I want the truth."

I keep my fingers around her neck and whisper into her ear.

"Loukas," she says, struggling physically but giving me the fiercest look she can muster. "You're scaring me."

"Good. I want you scared."

For once. Tisha has always been... unshakeable around me.

"Uncle Lou..." she whimpers and I press her harder against the railing. I won't let her use her little terms of endearment to get to me.

"Stop whining and answer me."

"I came back to tell you about the baby and because I need money for the abortion. You're the only person I could trust."

There's a beat of relief. It's me she wants to see, not Gal.

"No other men?"

"No other men," she whimpers.

I release her neck, and she presses her head against my chest.

"I couldn't," she whispers, "not after you."

That hurts, but I can't tell her why. I can't tell her how much I fucking love her.

I hold her so close to my chest and admit my feelings only to myself.

At least she's stayed away from other men for me.

My Tisha. Sweet. Innocent. *Mine*.

TEN
I HATE HER

Loukas
40 Years Old
Tisha
18 years old

Tisha arrives with Carlotta again on vacation. It's colder in Greece, so wool cardigans and black denim replace tiny string bikinis. Carlotta failed her introductory economics exam, and she's depressed about it. She needs the course for her other studies, but she's never understood economics. Her depression hasn't helped. But I don't know why she's so... hurt.

Matilda fights with her in the morning over the alleged theft of a Chanel lipstick. Carlotta cries in her room for the rest of the afternoon. Matilda takes Tisha to get their bikini lines waxed.

When Matilda gets home, I know it's time. Break up with Matilda. If I do it while Carlotta's here, she'll know I'm serious about repairing our relationship. In the afternoon, while Matilda disappears for a session with her personal trainer, Carlotta appears in the kitchen.

She throws her arms around me.

"I hate her, papa," she whispers.

"Who?"

"Matilda."

Carlotta winces when I hug her. I wrinkle my brow and she shrugs me off. What else is she hiding from me?

"I'm sorry. If it makes you feel better, I want to end things with her."

"Papa..."

Tears fill Carlotta's eyes.

"What?"

"I don't think Matilda is faithful to you."

I grunt. I'm not faithful to Matilda. At least not in my private thoughts. It's easier when Tisha isn't in the house, when I can focus my attention between Matilda's pale legs.

"She's a decent woman," I whisper to Carlotta.

"She isn't. She slapped me because... I told her I would tell."

"Tell me what?"

"She's fucking her personal trainer, papa."

I thank my daughter for telling me, but I make the day about her and her friend.

I'll worry about Matilda later. It's not like I needed a *good* excuse to end things. Just an excuse. But this one... *cheating*? It's a noble reason to end things. No need to spoil their day to do it.

Perhaps I could have broken up with her on the spot, but I have my duties as a father too. I need time to come up with the words.

I take Tisha and Carlotta for a sunset cruise on the Catamaran. We're headed to Africa soon and when I get back, Tisha won't be here. I want to make memories with my daughter... and her. Carlotta makes me promise not to wear a Speedo, so I don't bother swimming. I watch the girls jump into the sea together in wet suits, shrieking hysterically at how cold the water is.

"It'll only get worse! Enjoy yourselves."

When they come up for air, I give them a little alcohol to warm up. I'm drunk. Nearly too drunk to get us home, which thankfully Carlotta doesn't realize. Driving a boat drunk is much easier than it seems. I'm distracted on the boat ride home. I have to break up with Matilda. *Tonight.*

Matilda lounges in our bedroom in a red dress. Our relationship has been too short for this much drama. She giggles as she scrolls through my cellphone.

"Loukas… your browser history?"

"What's browser history?"

"Is Galanos the only one who understands technology around here?" Matilda says through giggles.

"What?"

"Your pornography. It's… interesting."

"I don't watch pornography."

"Yes. You do. Pictures of… African women? Is that what you fantasize about? Would you like to watch me with one?"

Matilda makes everything about sex. It's her one reason for living and she doesn't seem to care about the emotional side of things.

"I fantasize about having a woman who gets along with my daughter," I tell her.

Getting along with Carlotta is one problem sex can't solve. Matilda scoffs.

"Your daughter? I think she's a lesbian. She seems like the type to be involved in disgusting behavior like that."

"She's not a lesbian. And there would be nothing wrong with her if she was."

"That's only because you enjoy watching them," Matilda says, licking her lips seductively. I roll my eyes. I don't want to entertain this. She's talking about something she set up for me one drunken night. That wasn't my choice entirely. That was all her.

"I like women. Sue me."

Matilda's single-minded in her intention to complain about Carlotta.

"You spoil her too much. She's having sex already. How do you know men haven't raped her? She dresses like she's asking for it."

This is supposed to be a breakup, not a lecture on my parenting.

I snarl at her, "What do you want me to do, Matilda? Beat her *more*? And she's not asking for anything."

"Yes. She's a bitch," Matilda says.

"Don't call my daughter a bitch," I snarl at her. My rage is instantaneous. I might put up with the sideways comments, but nothing as direct as this.

"You always defend her," she says, scowling and drawing attention to the lines in her face. *I can't be with Matilda anymore.*

"She's my daughter, what do you expect?"

"I expect you to be a man."

"Matilda," I say. "I don't want to have this conversation with you and I don't want to hear anything else you have to say about my daughter."

"Pussy."

"Get over here."

"Fucking pussy," she accuses me again.

She storms off. Fuck. Every time we talk about Carlotta, we fight.

"Matilda," I snap. "Get over here."

She comes around the corner, red-faced with rage.

"What?"

"We shouldn't be together," I blurt out.

Matilda sighs.

"I know. But we are together," she says. "We're stuck with each other for life, idiota."

She wraps her hand around my cock.

"I don't want this," I growl. She strokes me to attention. *Fuck, I'm so weak.*

Matilda drags me to bed and fucks me all night. In the morning, Carlotta complains about the noise. Tisha sits in the kitchen, eating a Greek yogurt while Carlotta takes a shower. I walk in with Matilda. She giggles and kisses me.

Didn't we break up? I don't remember what happened. Matilda kissed me. She didn't stop. I tried to push her off and then... *fuck.* So much for breaking up with her. I feel stupid and ashamed.

Tisha lets out a sob. Matilda casts a scornful gaze in her direction before grabbing my cock and whispering something filthy in my ear. I kiss Matilda and she hurries off to prepare herself for that *very* naughty morning activity involving a blue wig, peppermint schnapps and a silk ribbon.

"I hope you slept well," I say to Tisha.

Tisha doesn't look up from her yogurt. She doesn't respond to me. I walk over to her and touch beneath her chin, tilting her gaze up to meet mine. Tears run down her face.

"What's wrong?"

Her lower lip trembles.

"Please. Don't rub it in," she whispers.

"Rub what in?"

My voice is gruff and commanding with her. She always activates this side of me. Half-father, half-lover. I can protect her, I think.

"Matilda. You two are back together," Tisha whispers.

Her lower lip shakes. She's so young and she takes every love so seriously because it's her first. And your first is always the best because it's new. And you aren't heartbroken yet, so you live in the bliss of infinite potential.

"Tisha... we were never... apart," I explain.

I want to end things with Matilda but... some relationships explode and others fizzle out.

"You saw me naked," she whispers, "I thought you liked it."

It's reckless. My daughter or fiancée could walk in at any minute and watch me kissing a teenage girl. But I can't stop myself. I lean forward and kiss her. She tastes sweet. Using her? I could never. Everything I feel about her is protective.

"I did. I liked it. A lot."

"I heard you *screwing your fiancée.*"

"Tonight," I whisper, letting her scent intoxicate me, "I'll end things tonight. I'll take you away tonight. Leave the villa for the beach where we made the campfire last year. I'll meet you there."

I suck on her lower lip. She whimpers and I pull away. She's still sobbing. She wipes her eyes and then gasps as Matilda walks into the room, missing us by seconds.

"What's wrong, little girl?" Matilda intones in a condescending voice, "Is it boy trouble?"

"N-n-n-no," Tisha stammers.

"Men are worthless. Even your Uncle Loukas."

Tisha forces a chuckle. Matilda kisses my cheek and yells Carlotta's name. I wince as she disappears down the hall to tear into Carlotta for tracking sand from her flip-flops into the house.

I'm alone with Tisha again.

"You're not a good man," she whispers.

"No. I'm not. I want to sleep with you."

"I won't tell anyone."

"I know. Because you're a good girl, Tisha."

I lean forward and kiss her again. She gasps as I shove my tongue into her mouth. Successfully break up with Matilda. That's all I need to do. I wait until later. I heard Carlotta crying from their argument and remembered. I need to protect my daughter and I can't let sex get in the way.

"Matilda. It's over," I blurt out again.

She looks like she's going to slap me.

"What?"

"I don't want this anymore. The sex swing, the butt plugs, all of it... it's wonderful. But I'm done. We need to end this. I tried to end it yesterday. I'm finished."

"I don't care. I want you."

I speak slowly so Matilda can understand, "I don't want you."

"It's because of your daughter, isn't it?"

"It doesn't matter."

"Fuck you."

"I'm leaving for Africa tomorrow. By the time I get back... move out of the villa. Please. I love you, Matilda. But... you're right. It's Carlotta."

"She's been filling your ear with lies about me."

"Lies? What lies would she be telling? About Angelo?"

Matilda scoffs and raises her brows furiously, "What the fuck did Carlotta say about me and Angelo?"

"You're fucking him."

"Oh, so you're faithful to me?"

"This is toxic. I have *children*. I need to set an example for them."

"You're a drunk and a murderer. You set a horrible example," Matilda says.

She always throws my career at me when she's mad, like she didn't know I was a fucking Pagonis when she met me. Yiayia introduced us.

"If I'm all those horrible things, leaving should be easy."

She sniffs and holds her breath like the next words out of her mouth were difficult to say.

"Men aren't like you in the bedroom. Leaving isn't easy. Trust me."

"I'm a scoundrel. A scoundrel who has already lost three other women. Don't become the fourth. Leave before I return from Africa. Carlotta will let you know when I'm coming back. I typically can only get the damned device to make a single call once we're at sea."

I'm no good with technology. My daughter understands all of it, but I loathe it.

Matilda shrugs, "I still want my money. But I will go. If this is what you want."

"I expected more... fire," I tell her.

I've seen Matilda assault servers because they forgot the lemon for her water.

"I know you, Loukas. I've seen the way you look at that little girl. Carlotta's friend. She's the one distracting you, isn't she?"

I shift uncomfortably, raking my fingers through strands of hair that should be grey. I only have a few grey hairs and I dread the rest.

"She's a young girl. Fuck's sake, Matilda. If I'm looking at her, it's only because you make eye contact with people. Normal eye contact. This has nothing to do with her."

Matilda sticks a cigarette in her mouth defiantly. She knows I hate when she smokes.

She mutters as she flicks her lighter aggressively, "Did you sleep with the little slut?"

"I told you," I snarl, "She has nothing to do with this. And she's not a little girl. Whatever tale you're trying to spin, keep me out of it. We're done, Matilda."

"Did you ever love me, Loukas?"

This part hurts. Because I don't want to say it out loud. Helen always said I was the most sentimental of us all. Times like this, I believe her.

I run my hands through my hair and confess to Matilda, "I *still* love you. But I love Carlotta more."

I know this will hurt Matilda, although it shouldn't. Carlotta's my eldest daughter. I would kill for her. I would die for her. Just like I would for Zoe or Antonio.

I'd had enough romance. When the women keep dying, it's hard to keep too attached. Even if I love Matilda. What's the point if I know how she'll end up?

"Fine. But don't tell your family we're finished," Matilda says, "Not until after you get back. I want to pack my things and enjoy another week here. Plus, someone has to look after Carlotta when you're gone."

"Can you manage not to attack her constantly?"

"I will find a way with her."

"Thank you."

"You deserve it, Loukas. You always had the best cock."

She blows out a circle of smoke as I grunt in response.

Matilda reiterates, "I still want my money."

"Whatever you want. Everything wrong between us, I'm sure it's my fault."

"You're too controlling," she says, "And I'm too stubborn to be controlled."

Matilda approaches me and kisses me on the cheek.

"And you're thinking about someone younger," she hisses.

Like Angelo isn't half her age…

A GIRL YOUR AGE

"Sorry for yelling."

"You don't scare me, Loukas," she says, holding me beneath an extremely fierce gaze. She seems older when she looks at me with so much fury, like she has a lifetime of anger towards men that she's saved up for me.

That's my fault, too. Despite being impressed by her fierceness, I can't exactly let this go.

"I should scare you," I say to her, puffing out my chest and hoping to put a little respect into Tisha's mind.

"What happened to Matilda isn't your fault," she says reassuring me. It hurts me how innocent she is. And it definitely hurts me that I'm not as perfect as she thinks I am. I'm not a completely honorable man, at least I wasn't about her.

The guilt eats me up inside. I don't know why I confess this to Tisha. I just have to.

"I lied to her about us," I say to her. I kept my feelings for Tisha away from everyone. I've even hid them from myself at times. I've forced myself to see her as just a forbidden fuck, but she's more than that.

She's always been more than that and I've always been ridiculously guilty about how she makes me feel. Watching myself fall from grace in her eyes hurts like hell.

Tisha pulls away from me and wrinkles her face.

"A white lie," she says. "That's what you told, right?"

"That's still a lie. Where did you learn your morality, child?" I grumble. She will do everything to put me on a pedestal. How? I'm a monster.

"I'm *not* a child," Tisha protests. "I'm pregnant. I'm grown."

Pregnant. That's my fault too. It's terrible that she looks so beautiful pregnant. That only makes me feel worse for several reasons. I try not to let her words get to me, but of course I have a harsh response for her.

"Grown? Hm. If you were *grown,* you would have been smart enough not to come here."

"When are we getting to Carlotta's boat?" She answers, ignoring my gruff tone entirely as if I weren't a terrifying mobster but one of those stupid teenage boys she probably has wrapped around her finger.

"*Tomorrow* morning. Right after sunrise," I say sternly, implying that she ought to be patient.

She approaches the railing and leans over it, her breasts nearly spilling from her dress. I can't stop staring. I come up behind her and kiss her cheek.

"I'll pay you to stay pregnant."

"Stop it."

"€45,000 is a lot of money to a girl your age."

"You're lying. You'd never give me that much money."

"I want that baby," I snarl.

I glance at her belly and look for signs of change. She's still wearing that navel ring. She'll have to remove it. She'll have to change everything.

Tisha plays hardball, "My tuition for the rest of university is £90,000. That's a bit more than 45,000 euros."

A ripple of fury passes through me as I sense her negotiating. Money doesn't mean as much to me as family. I wish that baby meant as much to her. Still, it's Tisha. I'll do whatever she asks.

"That's what you want?"

"I'm taking out student loans to go to Oxford. I don't want them. But I don't want this baby either, Loukas. I'm too young to be a mother."

"No, you aren't. You're the perfect age. And if you want £90,000, you'll have it."

I lick my lips, inadvertently dropping my gaze to her perky chest and she scowls. Is it my fault her nipples show through her clothes so perfectly all the time? It's impossible to be around her.

She folds her arms over her breasts and glares at me with pure malice.

"Stop it," she insists.

"Stop what?"

She sees right through me. For a girl this young, she's terrifyingly clever. I suppose it makes sense, with Oxford and all. Though it's hard to imagine a girl made it to Oxford without hearing about the Greek Orthodox Church. I chalk it up to the American education system. Not like Greece has anything better.

"Stop staring at me like that."

"You're beautiful. You snuck onto this boat with me. It's hard for me to believe you didn't know how I'd look at you."

"I betrayed my best friend. She ran away because I've been a rotten friend," Tisha says. "I'm not going to make it worse."

Her eyes well with tears again. I close the distance between us, approaching her from behind and cradling her. I kiss her cheek and she breaks.

"I should have told you to stop," she chokes out. Then she bends her head over the railing and sobs. I hold her, wrapping my arms around her waist and pulling her off the railing, turning her body to mine.

"Don't cry," I murmur, running my thumb over the high-cheek-bones on her heart-shaped face, "Keep the baby and I'll give you the money. For everything. School. Clothes. Whatever you want."

I'd give her the money, even if she didn't keep it. But I don't want Tisha to know.

"What will I tell Carlotta. She thinks I'm still a virgin."

"She might think it's Gal's."

She pushes me off her. Hard.

"I *never* slept with Galanos."

"What is it you kids call it... *hooking up?*"

"We hooked up. Yes. But not sex. I'd never sleep with him."

I regain my grasp of her and press her back against the railing, cradling the small of her back in my palm.

"Never?"

She shakes her head. I kiss her neck and then murmur, "I can't let myself go with you again."

"I know, Loukas."

Her small fingers rake through my shoulder-length brown hair. My midlife crisis involves growing it out again. At least I still can... few Greek men my age have a full head of chocolate hair, but I'm lucky. Would she still want me if I looked wizened and grey? In ten years, when she's not even thirty yet and I'm... too old for her.

I clutch the small of her back with ardent desperation and will myself not to act. Not to *use her.*

"I want to know what he did to you. Details."

She squirms. She doesn't want to tell me about him. My gentle but firm grip on her tightens. Now I'm possessive. Controlling. *Demanding that she tell me the truth.*

"Did he touch what's mine?"

I reach my hands between her legs and she tries to get away, but there's no escape.

"No."

"Good."

I release her, and she relaxes, leaning forward and pressing her head on my chest.

"I told you," she whispers, "I couldn't... not after you."

"Why did you kiss him, then? And let him finger you?"

She struggles to push me off unsuccessfully and then complains about my line of questioning, "Were you always jealous, Loukas?"

I prefer when she calls me Loukas. I don't want to be her *Uncle Lou.* I don't think of her that way anymore. She's pregnant and the baby's mine. She's *mine.* For the next 39 weeks and forever, there will be a bond between us that neither of us can break because I want this baby and Tisha will have it for me.

"Answer the question, child," I whisper, "Why did you kiss him?"

My heart races. I know I might not like the answer she gives me, but for her, I have to risk not liking the answer.

"I kissed him because I had a crush on my best friend's dad. And because... he blackmailed me."

"Blackmail?"

I clutch her more fiercely. To protect her. And because I have a flicker of worry that my younger brother Galanos *knows.*

"He has pictures of me on this burner phone of his. He has hundreds of pictures of girls. I didn't know he was taking them."

"I'll take care of it when we get back."

"Uncle Lou, no! I don't want him to get revenge."

I hold her chin up to my face.

"Look at me, Tisha. I'm not afraid of my younger brother. And you shouldn't fear him either."

"What am I going to do for the next nine months?"

"What they don't tell you is its ten months."

"Ten months?!" She says exasperated, "I know nothing about having a baby."

"I can help. I will help."

"I have to leave in two weeks."

My heart thuds. I can't let Tisha out of my sight. I can't let her go back to school because someone could kill her. My daughter killed Matilda, but there were three others before Matilda. Carlotta certainly didn't kill her own mother. And I won't let Tisha become the fifth woman in my life to die.

"I don't want you leaving."

"Loukas."

"Hm?"

"I'll have the baby, but I'm going to school."

"What do you need school for, eh? Stay here."

With me. I could keep her here while Carlotta's at school. Make love to her. Feed her pancakes and strawberries.

"I *need* school because I'm becoming a professor."

"Professor of what?"

Young people. They're so ambitious. I like it. And I like she hasn't pushed me off yet. I have a chance of keeping her here.

"English. I'm going to move to Greece and teach English. That way when Carlotta marries some fabulously rich guy, we can hang out together."

"You have it all planned out, eh?"

She doesn't want to hear that I haven't spoken to a single person I went to university with since I left. Then again, I spent all four years drunk and when I wasn't drunk, I was fighting over women.

"Yes. We have a plan. And having a baby or staying here with you isn't part of it. We're graduating together."

"How am I supposed to look after you?"

"I don't need you to look after me."

I kiss her. I can't hold back anymore. She's pregnant with my child and for the time being, I've talked her out of an abortion.

TWELVE
CAFFEINE ITCH

7.5 MONTHS AGO

Loukas
40 Years old
Tisha
18 years old

Tisha never meets me at the beach. I tell myself it's because of Carlotta. Stupid. It was stupid anyway. The type of daring stunt I could get away with when I was younger. Not anymore.

I drink the rest of my vodka and stumble back to the house. My brother will be back with Helen soon if they don't kill each other on the return to Greece.

They're too similar — rash, mercurial, painfully Greek. The next morning, I stumble downstairs hungover.

"Morning, Carlotta."

Carlotta clears her throat. It's not my daughter. It's Tisha. She doesn't look up from her yogurt.

"Sorry. Tisha."

I scramble around the kitchen and yell in frustration, "Is there any FUCKING coffee in this house?!"

I'm not frustrated about the coffee. I'm frustrated about the tawny legs peeking out beneath short shorts and the nipples jutting through a silk top. I want to spend one moment around this woman without a raging erection.

Matilda emerges from our suite and wraps her arms around me.

"Good morning, Lou."

I grunt good morning and then realize she can get me coffee.

"Matilda. We're out of coffee. Here's €5. Go."

"If you give me 20, I can get croissants and get one for the girl."

"Fuck."

I give her €50.

"Now hurry. I have a fucking hangover."

"Would you like me to make you eggs, Uncle Lou?"

"No. No. I can make my own eggs."

Stupid. You've never fried an egg in your life. I had chefs with Carlotta. And nurses. And help. Until I caught one of them stealing Carlotta's toys and clothes to give to her children and I fired all of them. She notices me fumbling around the fridge.

"The eggs are up here. I'm here so much now, I figured it out."

She brushes past me as she grabs the eggs, and her ass grazes the top of my thigh. *Control yourself, Lou.* She sets them on the counter.

"Are you sure you know how to cook them? Carlotta's... sleeping in. I can help."

"Fine. Fine. I might as well admit I don't have a fucking clue."

She cracks a couple eggs into a bowl and whips them around with spices. Paprika? In eggs? I peer curiously over her shoulder. But I tower over her, and my eyes catch not only the eggs she's whisking around her bowl. Beneath her white dress, she's wearing a white crochet bikini.

I bite my lower lip as her hard nipples poke through the bikini top.

"My mom always added paprika to eggs."

"Why'd she stop?"

"My dad died last year," Tisha says, "she stopped doing much of anything after that."

I take the bowl from her.

"I didn't know that," I say, "You were here when he passed?."

"Yeah," she says, "I went home for the funeral but... I don't want to go back there anymore. My mom's not the same and without him..."

I feel guilty. And I feel like I should say something.

"It's difficult losing a parent."

"I know," Tisha says, "Carlotta talks about it a lot. I never thought I'd lose my dad."

But my daughter never talks about it with me. And I shouldn't talk about this with Tisha. We're getting intimate again. In the worst way. Where emotions get confused.

"It will hurt," I murmur, "Let me know if there's anything I can do."

"You're such a dad, Uncle Lou. It makes me feel better. Like there will always be someone looking out for me."

My heart jumps into my throat. My body says "yes" but my mind tells me to stop getting closer to her before I hurt her. She's emotionally fragile. And here I am, confusing her grief with lust for me. She's missing her dad. That's it. And I'm taking advantage of her.

"I can handle the rest," I grumble, embarrassed.

"I don't mind helping."

"Get Carlotta. We'll toss the entire thing and go out for breakfast."

I grab the bowl and hold it in place.

Tisha's confused, but she stumbles off to find Carlotta — or to think of a good lie about where my daughter might be. I move the bowl away from my crotch. *She didn't notice.*

I'm lucky. But I might not be so lucky next time. Tisha emerges with Carlotta. I'm just happy my daughter slept in the house last night.

"Late night?"

Carlotta ignores the question and immediately makes her demands, "Before you go to Africa, I want to go to that place Matilda hates."

"Matilda's not coming this morning."

I haven't told Carlotta we broke up yet. I want to. I want her to know that I'm putting her first. That I always will. Carlotta doesn't get my hint.

"Good. Does she have another personal training session?" Carlotta says.

I deserve the jab.

"No. Come, we're going to the beachfront."

The beachfront cafe serves Carlotta's favorite breakfast, so naturally Matilda hates it. She complains about all the calories in the food. I thought that was the *point* of food. We've never taken Tisha here before.

She orders the special, which is Carlotta's favorite. I order a green kale smoothie and a triple shot of espresso, which I'm convinced I need to make it through this breakfast. Tisha's eyes light up when she sees the food. She laughs at a joke Carlotta makes about one pickle being shaped like a penis.

I wish we were alone.

"Sweetheart, I'm going to Africa tomorrow morning. After Stavros returns with Helen, we're making the deal with Ofek and I'm leaving."

Carlotta ignores me and plops a tomato into her mouth.

"Did you hear me?"

"You always leave."

"I'm coming back before you head off to school. I know Tisha's heading back early, but at least you'll have Matilda here until I get back."

"I *hate* Matilda," she says, "she's a gold digger."

Tisha mutters a warning to Carlotta, which my daughter promptly ignores.

"What are you doing in Africa? Why can't you bring that annoying tramp with you?"

"Don't call her a tramp."

"She's a cheater, papa."

I hate when Carlotta gives me relationship advice. I feel like such a failure. Like I've cost her a mother and I can't get it right.

"That's none of your concern."

Tisha always tries to make herself invisible when we argue. I hate that I always snap in front of her, that I expose my weakness.

"Fine. Tisha and I will stay here and have lots of parties."

"No parties," I scold.

"We won't have any parties, Mr. Pagonis. Don't worry."

"Since when do you take his side?" Carlotta elbows her best friend.

Tisha bites her lower lip.

Carlotta giggles and then says rudely, "Now she's shy. Earlier she said you were a control freak."

Carlotta shrugs and then smirks. She knows I care about making a good impression on her friends. That I always try for her because nothing else about our life looks good upon closer inspection. I turn red and snarl, "Quiet, Carlotta. I'm too hungover to put up with your shit."

Tisha puts her hand on Carlotta's forearm. Carlotta shakes it off.

"Whatever. I don't want breakfast anymore."

"We can spend time together when I'm back from Africa."

"You don't care about me, dad. If you did, you wouldn't leave."

She storms off. Tisha tries chasing after her.

"Sit."

"She's my friend. I have to go after her."

I sigh and rub my forehead. Carlotta has a good friend.

"You can blame me for not going. She'll blame me for everything, anyway."

"She just wants her dad."

I grunt and answer, "She's too spoiled already."

"Mr. Pagonis… I don't want you to leave either."

My fingers tap impatiently on the table. This *girl* plays too many games with me. The teasing. The brushing up against me. The way she responded when I kissed her. But when I beckoned her, she didn't come.

"It doesn't matter what you want," I respond coolly, "Now eat. I'll speak with my daughter. Later."

Nothing more happens at breakfast. I don't ask her why she didn't meet me on the beach, and she never explains why she didn't come.

When we arrive home, Carlotta's gone. She answers the phone, laughing, and tells me she's going on a drive with Antonio in his new Ferrari. When did Antonio get another Ferrari? I hang up and Tisha sighs.

"I hate when she goes off without telling me."

"We can do something together. I won't have one of my guests bored."

Tisha grins.

"I could never get bored in this house. This place is amazing."

"Do you play tennis?" I ask her.

She smirks before replying, "Badly."

"Come on. I'll take you to the tennis courts."

Tennis. I can't go wrong with tennis. We'll be far apart from each other. But I can still watch her. I maintain I can look but not touch, even if all evidence points to the contrary.

Tisha perks up and announces her need to change.

"Carlotta ought to have some gear and a racket."

Tisha emerges, ready to go to the courts with tiny white tight shorts and a white sports bra that doesn't cover her belly button. The navel piercing draws my attention. Her hip bones jut forward a little, framing her perky teenage body.

I don't remember buying clothing this revealing for my daughter. Tisha has on white sneakers and her hair sits in two braids that hug the sides of her head. I could never figure out those braids on Carlotta growing up. She hated always having the ugly hair because I didn't understand *styles*.

"Ready?"

My voice comes out gruff and uneven. Right. Tennis. The perfect activity to get us gross. And sweaty. And unappealing. Except she's a curvy eighteen-year-old with breasts. And hips. And a navel that beckons. The little ring flashes in the light. I want to kiss her stomach. I toss the ball at her and she catches it.

We walk to the tennis courts without saying much. She's close to me and that's all I want from her. We get to the courts, surrounded by ten foot high hedges to block out the sun.

"Ready?"

She takes a position on her side of the court. I serve and she volleys. *Damn.* She doesn't hit like an eighteen-year-old. Or I'm *really* shitty at tennis. I lose the next three points. I approach the net and Tisha grins from ear to ear.

"What's your secret, kid?"

"I played varsity tennis in high school. I was unbeatable in the Tristate regionals."

Fuck.

"You tricked me. But... you should have warned an old man," I say, panting and wiping sweat onto my shirt.

She laughs.

"Old? Uncle Lou... you are *not* old. You don't even have wrinkles."

"Wrinkles don't make you old, kid. Experience does."

It takes everything I have to win a single point against her. She approaches the net and shakes my hand.

"Good game."

I can't breathe. My shirt's soaking and sticking to my chest. With each breath, the shirt gets heavier. I need to get it off...

I strip my shirt off and Tisha gasps. I drop it on the ground and then fall on my ass, lying on the ground.

"Uncle Lou, are you *dead?*"

"Christ, I'm not that old."

"You dropped like a stone!"

"You're the one tiring me out," I gasp.

"Tiring *you* out? My legs are *red, and* my legs don't change color. You've had me hauling ass across this court for like two hours."

I chuckle and tap the court next to me.

"Come then. Let's cool down. Lie here. Breathe through it."

She wrinkles her nose and tosses my shirt aside before lying next to me, panting. We look over at each other and laugh. I haven't smiled like this in ages. But I'm going to Africa soon. We won't have another moment like this. We shouldn't have this one.

She rolls over onto her side.

"Uncle Lou?"

"Hm?"

"I'm sorry I didn't come down to the beach," she whispers.

I shake my head.

"I was being impulsive. And inappropriate."

As usual, Loukas.

She reaches for my chest. I shudder when she touches it. She runs her hands down my ab muscles, going over each curve twice until she gets to the waistband of my boxers.

"I wanted to go," she whispers, "I'm sorry."

I turn to look at her. She's *so* young. And small. I can't kiss her. Or hurt her. I can't let myself.

"No, Tisha. I was wrong."

"I'm eighteen."

"I know. That's the problem."

"Uncle Lou," she whispers, "I won't tell."

That shouldn't turn me on. I roll on top of her, pinning her to the court. I have her in my arms. She's eighteen years old, my daughter's best friend, and perfect. I run my hands over her body, touching her breasts and hips and then sliding that white sports bra over her perfect breasts so I can touch them. Taste them.

Desire for her consumes me. Desperation. Waiting. I'm finished with it. Because I have Tisha pinned beneath me on my tennis courts. She's naked when I trail kisses down her stomach. She doesn't stop me as I reach her mound.

I've seen her naked. I know what to expect. But nothing compares to *this*. The bliss of having her.

My tongue eagerly searches between her legs for her untouched pearl. Tisha's uncomfortable at first, but it's expected. She's young. Uninitiated.

"Mister Pagonis," she gasps as my tongue plunges along her lips. She wriggles away from my grasp. Her glossy juices coat my mouth and I want more. I need more. She's young and perpetually wet. I don't remember younger women being that wet, but it's been a long time since I've had one.

"Am I going too fast?"

"No. My chest hurts. And... it feels... *tight*."

"Orgasm," I whisper, lapping at her soft outer lips with soft tongue strokes, "You'll have an orgasm."

She moans as I rub my tongue along her clit again and I lick her to a loud climax. She soaks my shirt with her wetness. And her thighs. When I pull away from her, kissing up to her navel, she's embarrassed.

"We should stop."

"I don't want to stop," she pleads with me.

"Uncle Lou..."

"Not your uncle. I'm an adult. You're an adult."

She casts a disdainful sideways glance. She's right. It's a stupid excuse.

"I can't call you *Lou*."

"Why not?"

She can't move now, and I can have her the way I want. I can pierce her. Claim her like I've wanted to.

"Loukas... you're getting my *pee* all over you."

"Pee?"

"The stuff that comes out when you... lick it."

"It isn't *pee*."

"It's wet. It comes from *down there* what else could it be."

I've heard horrors about the American sex ed program, but it can't be this bad, can it? I move off her. Holy fuck. She's too young. She's too young and I've nearly fucked her. On the tennis courts. She hasn't ever had sex before and my plan was to take her virginity outside like I'm a beast. I roll off her. My heart races. Guilt courses through me.

If I touch her, I'm a monster...

"I have to go."

"Loukas, wait."

She grabs my hand. I wrestle it away from her.

"No. No, I can't."

She takes my hand again, and I push her back onto the courts, pinning her body again. She squirms, and I put one hand over her mouth. Before I go...

"Listen to me, Tisha. You don't tell anyone about this. Nod if you understand."

She nods.

"You can't tell anyone."

"I won't."

I remove my hand and kiss her. She wrinkles her nose and pulls away.

"Is that what I taste like?"

I press my forehead to hers, trying not to let her scent overwhelm me. I want to fuck her. Badly. I don't care if she's too young. She's wet. Eighteen. Beneath me.

"Yes. Yes. And before I do something reckless, I need to leave you. But you keep your mouth shut."

"I won't tell."

"Good. Good. Tomorrow, I'll get you a necklace. Before I go to Africa."

"I don't need a *bribe*."

"But you'll take a gift. I don't want to hurt my daughter."

I kiss her again and I leave before I watch her get dressed. She'll be safe at the villa.

I was so stupid I let myself get this far. I let myself believe I could be her first. I let myself believe I could take her. She doesn't know how much of a monster I am. What I'd do to be with her.

THIRTEEN
I DON'T WANT YOU TO MARRY ME

Tisha pulls away from me and grabs my cheeks, running her fingers over the stubble.

"Do you remember the night we played tennis?"

My dick strains through my pants. The memory has been more than enough to make me cum for the past few months. Tisha. Beneath me. Half naked with immaculate brown skin and a face made for kissing.

"Yes."

How could I forget? I came so close to having her. So close to touching what I want more than anything. And then I gave her the ruby pendant afterward.

"Tisha. I shouldn't have done it. I shouldn't have touched you."

She kisses me, gently. Slowly. I feel worse. Guilty. And guiltier because her kiss finally satisfies a yearning in me that strengthens each time I'm close to her. When I pull away from her, she eagerly kisses me again. Quickly. Passionately. I force my lips away from hers.

"No," I growl, "Don't do this. I'm apologizing."

"You don't have to say sorry, Uncle Lou."

"You're pregnant. And unmarried. I would marry you... if I could."

Tisha scowls.

"Marry me? Loukas. I don't want you to marry me."

Now it's *Loukas* again.

"It's what's right," I urge, like I have any ground to stand on when it comes to what's right and Tisha, "And I ought to. But right now, I can't."

Carlotta killed Matilda but that leaves three other women dead inexplicably. I don't want Tisha to become the next victim. The horrible thought occurs to me that Stavros knows about us. He suspects, at least. I never admitted the truth but my brother knows me better than anyone. Even better than Helen.

"You aren't marrying me. And I'm not marrying you. I'm *never* getting married."

"You say that because you're in university. You'll see what the real world is like. You'll marry someone. Eventually."

She wriggles away from me and I let her walk to the other end of the boat where she watches the white wake foaming to the surface.

"No. I won't. I'm giving up my baby and then I'm focusing on moving to Greece."

"Hm."

I don't like the idea of seeing Tisha all the time. My child's mother wandering around Thessaloniki and the child never knowing.

"What are you going to tell Carlotta... that you're adopting my baby?"

"Yes."

"Don't you think she'll suspect when... you know."

"When what?"

"The baby won't come out *black*. Not as dark as me at least."

"Genetics are funny."

"They aren't *that* funny, Uncle Lou."

"We have months to figure it out then."

"At most ten months. I'm going to have to quit club tennis."

"Yes. And you'll have to quit partying with Carlotta."

Tisha folds her arms and snaps, "You don't get to tell me what to do, Loukas. This baby might be yours but my body is *mine*."

"Not for the next ten months if you want your money."

Teenagers. They only respond when you dangle what they want in front of them. Otherwise, good luck getting them to do anything.

"This isn't fair."

"What isn't fair is that you want to end a life."

"Don't give me that old school bullshit. I'm not *ending a life*. If you were worried about *ending a life* you wouldn't have knocked up your best friend's daughter."

I lunge for her and she shrieks, running around the to the other side of the deck.

"Tisha, get back here!"

"I'm not going to let you *whack me,* Uncle Lou."

"Whack you?! What are you talking about. Tisha. Tisha don't run down there."

Fuck... She scrambles below deck and I chase. I hear the gun click and she points it at me. When I stashed my weapons, I didn't account for annoying stowaways.

"Tisha, you don't know what you're doing."

"Don't kill me," Tisha whimpers, "Please, Loukas. I'll do whatever you want."

"I'm not going to kill you, damn it. Put the gun down. *Carefully.*"

She sets the gun down and takes a step back.

"If you lie to me..."

"I'm *not* going to kill you. Whack you? Where did you get such a ridiculous idea?"

I pick the gun up and make sure it isn't loaded (it was) and then turn the safety on. Tisha wipes her nose like a kid. *She's barely grown up. What the hell am I doing to her?*

"I know about your family. Carlotta told me that you... she told me what you did to Matilda."

"What *I* did to her?"

"You hired someone to kill her. I didn't believe her until... up there. You had a look in your eye."

Her breathing is heavy and quick. She may have put the gun down but the poor girl is still terrified. She's terrified of me.

"I would never hurt you."

"Carlotta thought you'd never hurt Matilda."

My daughter's lying to her best friend. I bite my lower lip to keep from telling her the truth. Carlotta needs me to protect her. She's still my daughter. She still comes first.

"Listen carefully, Tisha. I'm not going to hurt you. Not now. Never again. Do you understand?"

She nods.

"I don't ever want to hurt you."

"Fine, I get it."

"Will you come over?"

She shakes her head.

"Please? I want you close."

She relents and smiles. That makes me feel better.

"Fine. I want to go watch the sea before it gets too dark," Tisha says.

I might be able to sleep a little throughout the night, but I'll have to stay awake to keep the boat on its course. Carlotta's waiting for us and I don't want to keep her waiting. I have a lot to say to my daughter. Above deck, Tisha lets her hair down and it flits through the breeze. It's long. Curly. Thick. As much as I want to keep away from her, I can't stop myself. The sun sets in the west, where we're headed, giving us a perfect view of our star disappearing over the horizon. She shivers and clutches her shoulders with her palms.

"Cold?"

She nods and I take my wool jacket off, throwing it over her shoulders. Her fingers grab the lapels as she disappears beneath it. In a few months, her belly will extend so far she wouldn't be able to close the buttons. Pregnant. I want to hate myself for doing it to her but there's something about a new life that excites me. From the moment I found out I was having Carlotta, I felt the change. The realization that there was something *more* to being Loukas Pagonis than killing, fucking and drugs.

Becoming a father made me grow up...

I kiss Tisha's cheek. She mumbles something and wriggles deeper into my grasp. I pin her to the railing with both hands curved around the metal. She runs one hand over my forearm, ruffling the thick hair with her young fingers.

"I want you," I murmur.

She whispers, "I know."

"We shouldn't," I say.

In a few hours, we'll see Carlotta. And I'll have to keep a straight face around my daughter and her best friend, pretending that I don't want to make love to Tisha the moment I lay eyes on her in the morning. We're tempting fate.

"Why did you ask about tennis?" I murmur.

"That's when I fell in love with you, Uncle Lou. I don't love you anymore. So don't worry. I'll have the kid and I won't be a problem anymore."

I don't love you anymore.

The words shouldn't bother me, but they do.

What makes her think that I don't want her to love me? What makes Tisha West assume that I don't love her. I press my forehead against hers and kiss her. It doesn't matter what I feel. She's said it herself. She doesn't love me *anymore*. I'm a phase she's grown out of. We'll see about that.

"You don't have to love me to spread your legs, angel."

I force her thighs apart and lift her against the railing. She doesn't have to love me to belong to me.

FOURTEEN
EVERY WOMAN I TOUCH

7 months ago

Matilda's dead. Helen swears Stavros did it. She can't account for where he was last night, and she heard strange noises. He may have left the boat and returned — leaving Matilda dead. They found her in the kitchen. Slumped over. *Drugged.*

I hang up after Helen gives me the news over the phone and then I tell my family, "She's dead."

I whisper it, because I can hardly believe it. We were over. But… that doesn't stop it from hurting. No one knew we broke up except Tisha. I haven't seen her since the tennis courts. I avoided her, embarrassed by my lascivious actions. And aching for her. If I saw her before getting on this yacht, I might have kidnapped her and brought her along.

Yiayia sips her gin and tonic. My father stops rubbing her shoulders and puts his hand on my back.

"You can always have another daughter."

"Not my daughter," I snarl, "Matilda."

Grief. I turn it inward. That's what I did when my first girlfriend died. And then Carlotta's mother. Then one more lover, then Matilda. Every woman I touch disappears and Stavros is the one who has taken all this away from me. I scream and throw my drink into the sea.

"That was a Swarovski wine glass," Yiayia says, "What's the matter, Loukas? Did you like this girl?"

"I loved her."

It's not a lie. Even letting Matilda go, I loved her. But I loved Carlotta more. I always put my daughter first. For all my flaws, I did all I could to prevent my daughter from faring an even worse fate than her mother.

"Was she raped?"

"No."

"Hm."

She's referring to what happened with the others. I never told Carlotta what happened. But it happened to my first girlfriend too. The killer — or killers — raped them both. Violently. I found them all in blood. Rape is a horrible thing. To witness the result of it. A brutal rape. A worse murder. It changes you. It makes me drink. It makes me obsessive. I have to protect my daughter. Why the hell haven't I heard from her?

"We need to hurry home."

The next few nights blur together. I find Fallon Iverson in hiding. She's easy to bring along. I threaten her. Rage at her. Drink. Too much. I wake up naked and alone on my boat with sunburn across my neck. Then everything goes to hell. Typical Pagonis bullshit. Guns, drugs, jewelry, petty arguments, and a confession.

As my father and grandmother sail away, the truth about Carlotta surfaces. I handle it poorly. And then I drink even more. Two bottles of whiskey, a pint of beer. A shot of tequila. I leave my gun in the living room so I don't act too recklessly. Galanos steals it and gives it to a hooker.

And then there's the truth that emerged. Matilda. Dead by my daughter's hand. A mafia daughter who succumbed to her instincts and killed her enemies. I killed when I was her age, which means all my efforts to set a good example for her failed. I have to talk to her. To save her before I ruin her entirely.

"Carlotta."

I knock on her door. She sobs.

"Carlotta!"

I force the door open. Carlotta shrieks.

"I'm sorry, daddy! I'm sorry!"

She's squealing and hysterical, and even if I want to scream at her for killing my fiancée, I can't. I grab her and hold her. She cries and scrambles away like she thinks I'll strangle her. But she's my daughter. My world. Carlotta Pagonis. And I could never hurt her. Not even for this. By the time Carlotta stops crying, we're both covered in sweat. She doesn't have the air-conditioning on and her tears and thrashing warm up the room.

"Turn the machine on. I'm a pig," I growl.

She turns it on and sits on her bed next to me.

"Daddy…" she chokes out.

"Did you do it for revenge?"

She shakes her head.

"Carlotta. I need you to be honest with me."

"I never showed you what she did to me."

"What did she do?"

Carlotta sobs and leans forward, burying her face in her hands. I grab my daughter's wrists and pull them away from her face.

"Look at me. What did she do?"

"Daddy…" her blue eyes swim with tears and sink back into her skull. She looks tired. Weak. Have I missed something? Is there something more going on with Carlotta?

"Talk to me, child."

"I don't want you to be angry."

"I won't," I utter hoarsely, but I'm too drunk to guarantee it. Shit. I'm probably too drunk to muster up the effort of rage.

"I'm not a virgin anymore, daddy."

"What does that have to do with Matilda?"

I try not to show her I'm not angry with. It's not so bad to lose your virginity once you've lost it. As long as you meant to lose it. And I've known Carlotta has plenty of boyfriends, so I assumed she snuck around behind my back. But my daughter sounds ashamed. I put my arm around her and she sobs again.

"She was there two nights ago. When it happened. Tisha... she got rid of Tisha, but Tisha remembered her standing behind the guy who forced Tisha into the cab... and... then... when she told me... it all came back to me, papa."

My daughter's speaking in half sentences. But I can piece together what she means. What she's trying to say.

"She hurt me while you were gone," Carlotta continues, ignoring the details I want to hurry on to, "But I didn't want to show you, Papa."

"Show me what?"

She lifts her dress and pulls her underwear to the side, showing me her hips, back and buttocks, before hastily pulling her underwear up. Bruises. Cuts. Signs of abuse.

"She did this to you?"

Tears of rage prickle my eyes. Matilda's death was luck. Because for this, I would have killed her. My daughter knows that. She knows me too well. Carlotta nods and sits next to me. Why didn't she tell me?

"What happened that night, Carlotta? I need to know."

The details will hurt me. They'll kill me. But I need to know who else abused my daughter. Matilda couldn't have done this alone. She wouldn't have dared without protection from other guns.

"I don't want to talk about these kinds of things with my father," She whispers, tears in her eyes. My throat tightens. She doesn't want to talk about this with me, but I'm all she has. And she's all I have.

"If any of them are alive, I'll kill them."

"They're alive," she whispers bitterly, "but Papa, you can't kill them."

"Why didn't you tell me?"

I hate myself. I want more gin. More vodka. Anything I can get my hands on to black out what my daughter's telling me. That the woman I loved — because at some point, I'd loved her dearly — hurt her and arranged for men to rape her. I wrapped my arms around her and kissed her forehead, repeating, "Why not, Carlotta?"

"You deserved love."

My heart breaks. This is what my lust and my desire gets me. My child, the one who I swore I'd protect. I've failed her. And it's my fault.

"I'm sorry."

She shakes her head.

"It isn't your fault, papa."

"Yes. It was."

"I went out. I snuck out that night. She wanted to teach me a lesson."

"It's my job to protect you. I left you here with her! I failed."

"No, papa. I handled myself. I will handle the boys."

"You will not kill again," I say to her.

"I don't have to."

Carlotta touches my hand and kisses my cheek.

"I love you, papa."

"This can't be the end of our discussion. I have to do something. Please, Carlotta. I know I haven't been the best father. But…"

She watches tears prickle my eyes. My daughter. My beautiful daughter. A sob catches in my throat and I bury my head in my hands. She knows I'm weak. That she's my weakness. Carlotta sits on my lap and holds my head against her chest.

"It's not your job to comfort me," I murmur. I think about Zoe too. I have to send her away from here. Antonio will never leave, but my youngest... I can save her before it's too late.

"Papa, I'm sorry too."

"No. Don't apologize. And... tell no one. As far as anyone knows, I killed her. That's what I want you to understand. You aren't responsible for this. I am."

"Papa..."

"Don't argue. Let me do this."

My daughter rests her head on my shoulder. I cradled her there when she was young and barely rose to my knee. She had ruddy little cheeks and a crop of straight brown hair. And her eyes. I could see the ocean in them — her wildness. Her freedom. My feral Carlotta with her Pagonis temper and wiles like her mother. A lust for life and a lightness I hadn't felt long ago.

And I ruined her.

FIFTEEN
STROKE IT FOR ME

Tisha's legs wrap around mine. She doesn't cling to me tightly. She trusts me to hold her, even as the boat speeds along the water. Her hands run over my facial hair and my heart thuds in my chest.

Blood rushes past my ear as she kisses me. Her mouth is small and each kiss tender. It's like she's scared to be rough with me and unleash her passions.

"Stop me," I murmur, pressing my forehead to hers and running my tongue over her lips.

"I don't want to."

"I'm not a weak man," I whisper to myself.

She reaches for the waistband of my trousers and grabs my cock. Yes. I'm weak. Incredibly weak.

"Hold on to it," I whisper, "Stroke it for me, Tisha."

She's done this before. But this time feels better than the last. She's more experienced. She *knows* my body. As much as I want to deny it, I can't. She *gets* me. I groan as Tisha's hands wrap firmly around my dick and she strokes it. I'm hard. Long. And stiff in her hands.

"I want you," I growl.

"Take me, Loukas…"

I move her panties aside and touch her, hoping to get her wet and find that she's soaked. She's still young. And she's pregnant. Probably in a near constant state of arousal. I move my finger over her outer lips and she whimpers when I touch her rosebud.

"You're wet."

She gasps and spreads her legs wider, begging me to go deeper by shifting her hips forward, struggling to take control. I push another inside her and she cries out in surprise and then moans in pleasure, bucking her hips toward me. My fingers aren't enough. I need my cock between her legs. I need to feel her soaked and wrapped around me.

"More," she whispers, grasping madly at my crotch.

I release my cock from my trousers and allow her to grasp it and line it up with her entrance.

"I should taste you first," I whisper, knowing that I won't. That I can't wait to have her impaled on my erection.

"No," she whispers, "This. I need this."

I drive my hips forward and she cries out, leaning backward over the railing, safe in my arms as my thrusting buries my length inside her. She's so tight I have to pause, allowing her tightness to adjust to my size. She's so much smaller than me that the slightest movement at this point could hurt her. I kiss her on the lips as she whimpers.

It always hurts at first.

"Can I move yet?" I murmur.

She shakes her head. I kiss her lips again. And her neck. I can be patient. I can be strong for her. After a few more kisses, I ask again, "Ready?"

She responds by drawing me into her with her ankles. They hook over the muscles of my buttocks and draw my hardness inside her. Tisha cries out as I withdraw and slide back into her. She's soaking wet, but getting a cock this big inside any woman has always presented a challenge. Tisha submits eagerly to me. Her thighs stretch apart and she tightens around me as I thrust again.

My hair falls from its knot behind my head, thick brown locks cascading as I lose myself in making love to her. I need her. All of her. I suck on her neck so hard that she comes undone and I know my teeth will leave a bruise. As I'm thrusting between her widely spread brown legs, she grabs onto my shoulders and I squeeze her against me. I need her dress off. I tear at the fabric and press into her deeper. Tisha cries out and climaxes. Yes...

I love the sound she makes when she cums. The high-pitched moan drives me wild. I fuck her like an animal, rutting between her legs until she cums again. Her tightness contracts around me as she climaxes and I can't hold myself back. I grunt as I spill my seed into her. She attempts to scramble away as if she can stop the seed shooting from me between her legs, but I hold her steady, keeping her impaled. She gasps.

"You came inside me."

"Yes."

"How many other young girls have you cum in..."

I'm still inside her. And since when did she start worrying about other women. Or as she puts it... young girls.

"Tisha..."

I try to slide out of her, but she wraps her legs around me, holding me firm. Controlling me. If she keeps me between her legs like this, I'll get hard again. She has me under her spell.

"Don't move," she whispers, "I want answers."

"I'm not running around with other women."

"Uncle Lou, I get it. You're in your forties. You're a hot single dad. But I don't want my baby having a bunch of slutty stepmoms like Carlotta did. No offense."

"I ought to whip you for your sharp tongue."

She's not sure I'm joking, but she doesn't seem scared. Tisha's ankles hook over each other. I'm not leaving her until she gets an answer. Does she want a real one, or does she only want an answer she likes? I kiss her shoulder and she relaxes.

"There are no other women."

Her ankles uncross, but she doesn't seem less suspicious.

"You don't believe me," I murmur, withdrawing an inch. She's had me between her legs too long. I want her again. I want her badly.

"You came inside your daughter's best friend. Several times."

"I bought you birth control," I said, "You should have used it."

"So this is my fault?"

She presses her hands to my chest.

"Yes."

Tisha pushes me off her. Then slaps me, scrambling out of my arms and off the railing before stomping across the deck trying to dress herself.

"How dare you!" she snaps, hurrying back to me and flinging herself at me again. I miss her punch — easily — but this only enrages her more. She throws herself at me nails first again and I catch her.

"Damn it, Tisha!"

"This is not my fault!"

She pushes me off again.

"You *fucked* your daughter's best friend! Don't you get how that messed me up? I fell in love with a man who only saw me as a walking womb. I spent *six months* in love with a man old enough to be my father, and that is *your fault,* Uncle Lou."

I grab her arm and pull her close to me.

"Don't run off. Don't."

"I don't want to be near you."

"I didn't want to hurt you."

"But you did. Because you could never be in love with a teenager. You knew that, but you made me think..."

She sobs.

"You made me think..."

"That I loved you?" I finish. Her crying gets louder. And Tisha

West falls against my chest. She thought I loved her because I did. But I had to let her go. I just had to. Why did it seem so important to stay away from her? Now it's the last thing on my mind.

"You made me think you loved me," she whispers after her tears subside.

She's right. That was entirely my fault.

SIXTEEN
COCAINE OR XANAX

7 MONTHS AGO

Carlotta comes back every weekend now. I want her close after what happened. I know it's affecting her. She's had slipping grades. She's doing drugs. Antonio complains that she never answers her phone.

Galanos claims she's "off the rails" and doesn't want her screwing his friends.

But I'm trying to help her. Therapy. Rehab. Anything for my daughter. Tisha West struts down the walkway a few inches behind my daughter in practical sneakers while Carlotta stumbles in six inch heels, dragging her suitcase behind her.

"Papa!"

She throws her arms around me.

"Are you drunk?"

"No," Carlotta replies, giggling effusively.

"Yes, Uncle Lou. She's drunk. She's been like this the entire time. I think she needs sleep."

I stop Carlotta, holding onto her shoulders and looking into her eyes. Her pupils are so dilated I can barely tell her eyes are blue. Fear grips my stomach.

"What else is she on?"

Tisha bites her lip. Carlotta giggles and presses her finger to my lips.

"Quiet, Papa. I am an adult woman and it doesn't matter how much cocaine or Xanax I've taken."

"There's your answer," Tisha mumbles.

I hold my daughter upright. Tisha grabs the suitcase and I drive her home. She's slightly more sober once we enter the private villa. I don't want to be near my family right now.

"How much did she take?"

"I don't know, Uncle Lou. I'm worried about her."

"So am I. I'll call the family doctor. Let's get her to her bedroom."

With the phone in one hand, and another under my daughter's shoulder, we walk her upstairs. I should never have let her go back to school. And I mutter it under my breath.

"She's taking Matilda's death really hard," Tisha sighs. I grimace. It's more than that. And she hasn't told her best friend. It isn't my place to tell her and thankfully, we've arrived at Carlotta's bedroom. I had it painted last week. She was tired of the Caribbean blue she got when she was a little girl and she asked for a neutral taupe color. I liked the blue. But I have to admit that Carlotta's not a little girl anymore. And I'm getting older. And lonelier. So lonely that I put her life at risk. That I cost my daughter her dignity.

We get Carlotta into bed and I call the family doctor over.

"You can go downstairs and help yourself to some fried fish. I remember how much you enjoyed it last time."

"Thanks, Uncle Lou."

She runs off. The doctor arrives half an hour later. I don't leave Carlotta's side until he tells me she's *fine* and needs to sleep it off. I have him draw her blood so I can find out what the hell my daughter is doing to self-medicate. And then I reach for my flask. I tip it to my lips and let the burn sear my throat. Only it doesn't burn anymore. I drink so fucking much, vodka tastes like water.

"Why can't I stop hurting you," I murmur not sure if I'm telling my daughter. Or me. I shut the flask and throw it out her bedroom window. It lands on the beach, not the sea. But that's good enough. I lean forward and kiss my daughter's forehead.

"I'm done with the drinking."

I don't know how I'm going to stop. But I know that if there's any reason to stop, she's lying in that bed upstairs. And I owe it to her. The past few deaths hit me hard. Losses keep piling up. But how could I live if my own actions led me to losing her? Carlotta...

I walk downstairs, instantly regretting my impulsive release on my flask once I see Tisha sitting at the counter with her shorts riding up her thighs. The evening playing tennis flashes before me and I feel something I don't feel often as a man in his forties. *Shy.*

"Did you enjoy the food?"

"Uh huh."

"Good. The doctor says she'll be fine."

"Cool."

When did talking to Tisha get so uncomfortable? Have I ruined this already?

"What happened to Carlotta?"

"They think it's a mixture of Xanax and uh... some sort of stimulant. Possibly cocaine. Mixed with alcohol, it's a mess, but she seems to be fine. I'm to call if there are any problems."

Her expression becomes cold and indignant.

"That's not what I meant. What happened after I went back to school. I left early and next thing you know, Carlotta's back four days late from her weekend and she's different. She won't tell me what happened here and now, Matilda is *dead*. I want nothing bad to happen to my best friend."

"Neither do I. Espresso?"

At first she wrinkled her nose. But enough time in Greece and Tisha has become an aficionado of coffee made *properly*. She accepts my offer. I set the machine up and wait for the water to heat, leaning against the marble counters and taking in her expression, still noticeably upset.

"She's lying to me."

"About what?"

"She told me you killed Matilda. But you couldn't do that. You're not... you're not like that."

"I'd do anything to protect Carlotta."

Tisha's face loses its color. It's not an admission, and it isn't denial. If my daughter wants to keep the truth from her best friend, I have to respect that.

"You'd kill to protect her?"

"Yes. That's what any man would do for a woman he loves, whether it's his daughter or... someone else."

She gazes at her phone, and I'm not sure if she's bashful or distracted. Since she's still a teenager, I assume she's distracted. I hand her the espresso and sip it.

"Delicious."

"You make the best coffee, Uncle Lou."

"I've been told. And thank you, Tisha. Carlotta needs support right now. It's kind of you to be here."

"She's not the only reason I came," Tisha says.

Before I can ask her the other reason, my brother Gal struts in.

"I heard the ladies were back. Tisha! Holy shit, did you get a boob job. He takes his camera out as Tisha indignantly covers her chest with her hands.

"Don't act shy... show the nips," Galanos says.

Tisha scowls at him and sticks her tongue out. He gives up and slips the phone into his pocket.

He thumps me on the back before giving her a big hug. I don't stick around to see how she reacts. It's him. Of course it's him. He's her age, for one thing. I caught them kissing. They're friends. How could I have been so foolish to think Tisha would have been talking about me? A man old enough to be her father. The pervert who forced himself on her.

I return upstairs to Carlotta's bedside. She's sleeping. Peacefully. And I watch her like I used to. Every night for the first two years after her mother died, I protected my little girl and her little brother. Although Antonio doesn't act so little anymore and he handles things better than she does. Maybe that's my fault too. Maybe I'm overprotective.

I decided to stop drinking, but my body doesn't get the message and immediately expel the alcohol that I already consumed. I wander downstairs for a glass of water. Antonio's on the phone, but he hangs up the moment I walk into the kitchen.

"Up late?" I ask him. He snorts and shoves his phone into his pocket before answering. Antonio's darker than me, brown eyes and long black hair. His nose is straight, like mine, but without the curve because of his distinct lack of fighting in bars, which I'm grateful for as his father.

"Another late night," he says.

"Drunk?" I ask my son.

He shrugs and then answers, "No, papa. You're drunk."

He smiles. I hug him. Antonio yields to my hugs. My grandmother says I love him too much. He's less of a worry for me.

"I'm a horrible father."

Antonio chuckles awkwardly, "Papa, you need sleep."

"You're my first-born son. I don't care... I don't care if you don't have any heirs. I love you. I love all of you."

I choke out a sob, and Antonio pushes me off him, laughing.

"Papa, stop. Get some rest."

He strolls away and starts his phone call up again with an excited, "Ciao."

I strain to hear the voice on the other end of the line. Male or female? I make nothing out. Fuck. I barely know my kids, and the drinking is to blame for everything. I stumble back upstairs, but the door I lean against isn't Carlotta's room. I'm too drunk to make sense of what I'm doing, but I don't recognize the bed as my own either.

"Guest room…" I mutter under my breath as I drunkenly stumble forward against the post of our guest room's four-poster bed. The mesh canopy moves. I squeeze my eyes shut and open them again, attempting to stop the blurry room from spinning. I groan and land on the bed when I hear a squeak and then feel shuffling beneath me and the covers.

"Galanos, get out of here!" Tisha hisses, "I'm *not* doing that with you. I don't care what Carlotta told you…"

I groan again. Tisha wriggles again. I groan, but I can't move. She finds her way to the bedroom light and turns it on. She gasps.

"Uncle Lou!"

She shakes my shoulder.

"Uncle Lou, what are you doing up here!"

She races for the door and shuts me into the guest room. I should get up. And leave. But I can't. My head spins and I'm sick to my stomach with worry over Carlotta. And more liquor than I need. I can't forget the liquor. Tisha pushes my shoulders again.

"Uncle Lou, wake up!"

My eyes snap open, and I take in the vision standing before me. She's sleeping in her underwear. Tisha wraps her arms over herself because I'm watching her. She's only wearing a tiny red thong that slides between her mound, buried in a puffy set of lips, and a tiny white bra covers her breasts. Except for her nipples, which stick out. Luring me. I groan. Because watching Tisha like this instantly makes me hard.

I grab the poster and stumble to my feet.

"Sorry," I groan, "Wrong room. Sorry, I'm getting out of here."

I stumble forward and crash into her. Not into her. She dodges out of the way and I stumble forward against the wall. Fuck. Did I mix something into my drink? I can't remember anymore, but I know I'm making a fool of myself.

"*Loukas Pagonis.*"

She tries to catch me from falling. It barely works. Instead, I have her pinned to the wall, the only thing helping me keep my balance. She screams again, "Uncle Lou!"

"Yes... I'm standing. I'm standing."

"Your *thing* is poking into me!"

I pull back from her, sobering up just enough to realize that I'm hard. Harder than I've ever been. Worse than that, my erection poked into my daughter's teenager best friend. She pushes me away from her, but once I move, she doesn't.

"Loukas... Pagonis... This is..."

"Matilda," I slur stupidly.

"I'm not Matilda," she snaps, folding her arms and looking at me crossly.

And thank goodness for it. Tisha's beautiful naturally. Dark skin. Thick hair that smells like coconut oil.

"No," I explain, "I ended things with Matilda. Before... before it happened."

"Before you killed her?"

There's a pang in my chest. She doesn't seem scared. That I'm a murderer doesn't terrify an eighteen-year-old girl. I can't fathom why not. It's nice not to scare her. I nod and press her against the wall again. The distance between us closes, but this time, Tisha doesn't complain about the organ pressing into her.

"Loukas."

"I know what I'm doing," I whisper, trying to convince myself.

"You smell like whiskey."

"I'm drunk. And I'm hard. You can toss me out."

"Carlotta's down the hall," she whispers, bracing herself with small palms against my chest, "she could come in here any minute."

"You thought I was my brother," I accuse, "Did you fuck him?"

"No."

"Don't lie, little woman."

My cock is harder than before. Angry. Lusting after her. I've waited too long. And now I'm too drunk to listen to any sensible voice telling me not to make love to my daughter's best friend and claim her the way I wanted on the tennis courts. Her hand travels down my chest and my stiffness throbs. She gasps as it moves against her again.

"I didn't," she whispers.

"Good. Are you a virgin?"

"N-no."

I kiss her. The kiss is a test. She tiptoes and reaches my lips. I firmly plant mine against hers and spread hers open. She's tentative once I open her lips with mine. If my brother didn't fuck her, what did he do between her legs? Why do I hate that there's any chance she belonged to him? I tell myself I'm only here because I'm grieving and drunk and Tisha's my forbidden fruit. I hold her cheeks and kiss her firmly. When I pull away, I keep holding her.

"I'm not forcing you," I murmur, "if you'd rather my brother, I'll get you ready for him."

She winces and shakes her head.

"Galanos is cruel."

I'm worse. Because the words turn me on. And this was another test. She's too young to know how to lie.

My brother is cruel but I'm Loukas, a kindly single father. A man she respects. A man she'd never lie to. I kiss her and wish I could be the one to have deflowered her. I pull away from Tisha and she pauses, not in a hurry to rip her clothes off, too scared to touch mine. I move her hand to the first button of my shirt.

"Take it off. You're right about my daughter catching us. I don't think either of us would like that."

I'm too drunk to listen to my inner voice, which has now devolved into a series of animalistic grunts and raw desire. I'm hard and I need her.

She unbuttons the first button. She's quiet as she undoes the second. We don't have *conversations,* I've realized. And we're crossing a line here. I'm not her best friend's father now, I'm the man she's about to make love to. And she's... a woman. Not a little girl I can boss around or drive to the mall. I should say something. Make her feel more comfortable.

"I've thought about you," I whisper, "I've wanted you."

She reaches the last button before she answers, "For how long?"

My heart races. She doesn't want the answer to that question. She'll hate me if she knows it. Instead, I kiss her again. She opens up to me, so young and willing for my experienced hands. And lips.

"Long enough. Now come, get me ready."

I tap my crotch and she grimaces.

"What do you want me to do?"

"You aren't a virgin," I answer, "surely you know?"

I tell myself she's had plenty of time to get experience since the tennis courts. I wait, breathless for Tisha's touch.

She runs her hands on the outside of my trousers and reaches for the belt. She's so *slow.* If I had any sense, I'd push her onto the bed and have her. Ravage her. But around Tisha I'm part animal, part lover. I want her, but I want to caress her. She removes my hardness from my boxers and gasps, "It's huge."

"You've seen one before. It's like all the others... only bigger."

"And... more skin."

She runs her fingers along my foreskin and I bite on my lower lip to stop from groaning. I want her to stop touching me and *suck me.*

"Knees," I gasp as she grasps me. She obediently falls to her knees and wraps her lips around my member. At first it's rough. Her lips struggle to accommodate my size, and she doesn't have a clue what she's doing. At least she's experimental. And willing. I guide her until I'm ready to burst and wet enough to enter her easily.

I pull her off.

"Did you cum?"

"No," I say.

Can't she tell? I chalk it up to her inexperience. She may not be a virgin, but she's still young.

"I like to enter women from behind," I tell her bluntly, "Get on the bed."

"Uncle Lou..."

My cock juts from me, hard. Wanting her.

"What is it?"

"I don't want to have a baby."

"I'll get you birth control," I growl, "After I've fucked you. Do you have STDs?"

"No!"

She sounds indignant. I'm too drunk to notice if I've phrased it offensively.

"I don't either," I grumble to myself, because Tisha's panting too loudly to hear me.

A drunken, foolish response on my part. She unhooks her bra and lets it fall to the ground. I can't stop myself. I grab her from behind and kiss her neck. Her shoulders. She whimpers and leans into me. I lift her off the ground, pulling her body against mine.

"Let me have you. You perfect little thing..."

Her hands find my cock, and she guides me to her entrance. I cry out as I slide between her legs. She's tight. So tight that the first inch barely fit between her legs. She screams. So loud, I think my daughter might hear her. I clasp my hand over her mouth and move my hips slowly, giving her time to adjust to my length.

She's small and her tightness grips my cock so firmly that I nearly erupt inside her then. But I don't want this to end. I don't want to stop *having her.*

"It feels so good to be inside you..."

She gasps as I withdraw my hips and plunge into her again.

"You're tight. How small was the last man who did this?"

She moans again. I have my hand over her mouth, mercifully, as I withdraw and then thrust again with a smooth erotic movement. Tisha squirms and her body tightens and then releases as she moans.

Orgasm.

My hardness convulses between her legs, eager for release of its own as she squeezes me. I brush my lips against hers, teasing them open as I move between her legs. I drink Tisha in and make love to her, allowing her to cum several more times before rutting against her to stimulate my climax.

She grabs onto me, submitting to my conquest of her teenage body, small and pressed up against mine with an expression of fear and pleasure plastered over her face. It's too late for me to have regrets. I can only feel the pleasure of having her, the bliss of her tightness squeezing me.

I thrust into her deeply and erupt between her legs. She begins to verbally protest, but I clamp my hands down on her mouth and hush her, kissing her cheek and her neck and allowing my seed to spill into her. I kiss her neck and then her breasts again as I release her mouth from my grasp.

"You came inside me," she whispers.

I growl and spread her thighs apart, pulling them away from my torso, "Yes."

"Uncle Lou…"

"What is it?"

I withdraw my cock and kiss my way down to her navel. I flick my tongue over her ring and suck on her stomach flesh. I need more. She gasps as my tongue splits her lower lips apart and slides on her clit.

"I lied."

"About what?"

I'm too busy kissing her inner thighs to hear what lie.

"Mm."

"You didn't *hear me,* did you?"

I scowl and answer, "I heard you fine."

"What did I say then?"

I know my eyes must be wide and blue. And stupid. She rolls her eyes.

"I lied. I was a virgin."

My heart jumps into my throat and catches. She lied to me. There's anger. But then... I ruined her. She's my daughter's best friend. Her honor *matters*. But I jumped between her legs and stole from her. I will always be the man who stole her innocence.

"Uncle Lou... are you angry?"

I step away from her and massage my skull. She's a teenager. Teenagers lie. Of course they lie. I should have known. But I didn't want to know. I didn't want to see. All I cared about was getting what I wanted.

"Not with you."

"I don't care that I was a virgin. And don't worry, I won't be *falling in love with you.*"

The lump in my throat grows, nearly choking me completely. My ex just died. The last thing I should want is to crawl drunkenly between a teenager's legs. But here I am. Tisha curls her knees up to her chest, her soaked pussy exposed to me. I can smell her — sex, my seed, and her essence mixed.

My dick grows in her presence. Again.

"Love. Who said anything about love," I pant. I can smell her sex and it's all I want. I'm too drunk not to take another chance with her.

"What about Carlotta," she says, "We should tell her."

"No," I snarl, "We *can't.*"

If my daughter found out, it would break her.

"Lying is wrong," Tisha protests.

"You didn't think it was so bad when you lied about your virginity."

"That was different."

"Oh?"

She accuses, "You kissed me."

"I shouldn't have."

She snorts and mutters, "it's too late to take *that* back."

"Enough talking. I'm drunk. I'm hard... and I want you again."

I drag her by the ankle and spread her legs apart. She shrieks, "Loukas!"

I press her stomach into the bed and position my body on top of hers. My cock spreads her ass cheeks apart as I line the head up with her soaked entrance.

"Quiet," I murmur, as I kiss her neck, "give yourself to me... quietly. And I promise, little woman... I will make you cum... again..."

I kiss her neck and murmur, "And again..."

SEVENTEEN
YOU SOUND LIKE GALANOS

share supper with Tisha. She sits near me in the cramped space, careful not to allow her elbows to jut into me. She's pregnant, she needs food more than I do. I scrape half my plate onto hers.

"Loukas, you'll be hungry soon."

"I won't," I tell her, "Now eat. You're eating for two."

She scowls.

"I hate that."

"The truth?"

"No. How everyone will treat me differently when I'm pregnant. If I were going to be a mom."

"Treat you different?"

"Like I won't be a person anymore. Just a mother. I never wanted kids."

She says the last part like an accusation. My chest tightens. Maybe *this* is why I like Tisha. I can relate to her. She reminds me of myself when I was her age. Except I'm sure Tisha has killed no one. She's a sweet girl. Her parents let her run amok, but they mustn't have been so bad if she turned out like this.

I remember that she's lost her father and guilt surges through me again. I can't fuck a girl who sees me as a father figure.

"Neither did I," I tell her. And I'm not lying.

She seems surprised.

"You didn't want Carlotta?"

"No. You misunderstand. I love Carlotta more than anything. But I never wanted to become a father. My entire life was ahead of me. I wanted boats. Cars. Gold. Houses. Guns. And women."

She wrinkled her nose. Especially at the last two.

"You sound like Galanos."

I make a gruff sound in my throat (and tell myself it's a reflex).

"Yes."

She puts her hand on my thigh. Her touch drives me fucking wild. I am totally fucking weak when it comes to Tisha West. It's a cruel joke from the universe that a woman this perfect would come to me in the form of my daughter's best friend.

"I didn't mean it like that."

"You like Galanos. Why should it offend me?" I grumble, even if it obviously offends me. My brother is completely unrefined. We're nothing alike.

"I do *not* like Galanos."

"Tisha. I caught you with him on multiple occasions," I say accusatorially. I don't care if I sound like I'm jealous. She's my woman and that means I keep track of who she talks to, who she interacts with. I make sure idiots like my brother keep their hands off her.

I'm meant to protect her, but clearly this offends her somehow. *Sigh.*

Tisha slams her fork on her plate.

"I'm not hungry."

"You've barely touched the grape leaves."

"They're nasty."

"Tisha…"

She huffs and slams the plate on my lap before she spits, "I only hooked up with Galanos to make you jealous. I had a crush on you and I wanted you to notice me. Your brother has a tendency to let things go way too far."

"He knew?"

"Yes. Carlotta didn't. But Gal's my friend, too. And he wanted to help me."

"I didn't know."

"It's not like I announced having a crush on some forty-year-old guy."

"I was only thirty-nine back then."

She glares. Not the point. And certainly not the time for my Pagonis narcissism to rear its ugly head.

"And the baby isn't his."

She punches my side then, and it's harder than I expect.

"No. It is *your baby*, Uncle Lou."

"Our baby."

"No," she says fiercely, "Yours. I'm going above deck."

She ignores my protests and storms off. I take care of her grape leaves, grateful for the additional morsels. I trail behind her. She sits on the deck, her knees clutched to her chest as she cries.

"Tisha. Have I made you cry?"

"Go away!"

"I need to steer the boat."

"Go. Away!"

"If you wanted me gone, you shouldn't have climbed on this tiny boat with me. Now get up and tell me what's wrong."

"I hate being pregnant! I'm emotional. And stupid. And I..."

"What is it?"

"Horny," she whispered.

I reach for her hand and pull her to her feet before she realizes what's happening.

"Not tonight," I say to her sternly, "It's dark and we need sleep. There's not enough light to navigate. Come sleep next to me. It'll be your only good night of sleep on this voyage because we're facing a headwind back. It will take double the time."

She agrees to return downstairs. I anchor us down and follow her. She's on her phone, which she quickly hides once I've entered.

"Ready for bed?" I ask her.

She doesn't look at me.

"Uh huh."

"Good."

I flick the light off. A little nightlight turns on. It's otherwise too dark out to see. I pushed us as far as we could travel. As far as I know, my men still hold my position.

"Which would you prefer? Wall or door?"

"You can have the wall, Uncle Lou," she whispers, her voice all soft and full of her breath.

She gets up so I can crawl into the bed. It's barely enough space for both of us. But I'm getting old. I need all the sleep I can muster before I get my daughter back and I can't have my little stowaway sleeping on the floor. Not while she's pregnant. She slips into bed next to me and under the covers. I tense up as her freezing toes touch my shins. Jesus. Did she teleport to the arctic in the five seconds I closed my eyes? I grimace and clench my jaw as she sidles backward.

Her tiny rump presses against my chest and I thank heavens she doesn't find her way lower. Tisha sighs and moves her pillow from beneath her head, holding onto it in a tight hug instead.

"Good night," she whispers.

"Good night."

"I hope the baby gets your eyes. That will make being black in Greece easier, I think. If she looked like you."

"Hm," I grunt. She's so small and innocent. I want to hold her, but I can't. I can't touch her and hurt her more than I already have. Pregnant. What the hell was I thinking climbing into bed with her?

"I don't care or anything," she whispers, even if I've barely answered, "I just love your eyes. They're beautiful."

Everything she says makes me fall in love with her. I feel like a teenager again and it's fucking ridiculous that this loud little thing could have that effect on me. Half the time I think she's a brat and the rest of it I find her fucking mesmerizing.

She moves her butt down and finds the spot I didn't want her too. I suck in a sharp inhalation, struggling to muffle the noise. I bury my face in her hair and in the back of her neck.

"I love yours," I whisper. My fingers find her forearm and then slide down to her hips. And the front of her stomach. She gasps as I find the waist of her pants. I don't slip my fingers past. I love so much more than Tisha's body.

"And for what it's worth," I whisper, "Even if you aren't ready, I think you would be a wonderful mother."

"Thanks, Uncle Lou."

I kiss her shoulder.

"That won't change my mind, though," she whispers, "I'll give you the kid but... I'm not ready to be a mom. I'm too young."

And here I thought the problem was my age. Maybe it's hers. My yearning for her competes with my yearning for sleep. I can smell her scent so powerfully now, and my hand lingers so near the thing I want. She's still pregnant. And I still want her to stay. To be mine. My precious Tisha. I slide my hand into her underwear. She gasps.

"I'm sorry," I whisper, as I kiss her shoulders with urgency that makes them wet, "I can't stop myself."

Because I can't. Not with Tisha.

"Then don't stop," she whispers.

Here I am again. I always want to stop myself. Even then, I wanted to. I never can... not with Tisha.

EIGHTEEN
HE'S BEEN DRINKING

6 MONTHS AGO

"You shouldn't be here Loukas," she says sternly. This time, she's the responsible one. I don't care. I want her.

It aches how badly I want her. I'll kiss her and spread her legs until I lose myself enough in her to beg her to stay

I need her to stay. I need a woman... Loukas," she says sternly. This time, she's the responsible one. I don't care. I want her.

It aches how badly I want her. I'll kiss her and spread her legs until I lose myself enough in her to beg her to stay.

I need her to stay. I need a woman...

I'm drunk. Again.

"I don't care."

I climb into bed next to her and push Tisha onto her back.

Tisha pleads half-heartedly, "Carlotta will be back from bowling soon."

"My daughter is not bowling. I don't know where she is and why she's lying, but she isn't bowling. Now... will you spread your legs or will I have to take what I want?"

"You wouldn't," Tisha gasps in horror. She turns me into a caveman. All desire. No sense. I say whatever comes to my mind. Even if it's filthy.

I'm not sure I wouldn't. I wouldn't *want to.* Because hurting her would be wrong. And I've never done it before. I've always waited for the woman to beckon me.

"No," I tell her, "I would not."

"Lou, should we... use protection?"

I chuckle. Because I'm too drunk to care about that.

"Is that what I'm paying you for, then?"

She pushes me. Hard.

"What the hell, Loukas!"

I laugh and roll onto my back.

"Sorry. Not politically correct."

She stares at me, mouth agape and then finds the words she wants to yell at me.

"I'm not a prostitute."

"Then you shouldn't need a condom."

"Lou! That is so *rude!*"

I kiss her neck. And then her lips and then grab her hands and pin them above her head.

"Tomorrow," I tell her, "I'll give you birth control tomorrow."

I kiss her lips and enjoy the way her small body squirms against mine. I like the fight in her.

"What about *herpes?*"

"You don't have it, do you?" I growl.

She sounds terribly concerned. Is my reputation that bad, even with her? Carlotta has probably told her about all her stepmothers... or at least the women I called stepmothers. Fuck...

I'm not that fucked up. I just want her. I want her more than I've wanted anyone. It's easy to pretend I can stay away from her, but I just can't.

My cock rests between her thighs, ready for her. *Needing her.*

"No! But you might," she insists. I can't wait for her longer. I need her badly.

"You worry a lot for such a young woman..."

I run my tongue over her collarbone and grab a nipple between my teeth. Tisha moans. Good. I like when she's moaning. Her nipples harden as my tongue runs over them repeatedly.

"And... you're much better than a prostitute. First, you cost me nothing. Second, you're far more beautiful."

She pushes my chest again and groans.

"Get off."

I roll off her again and roll my eyes.

"Fuck, Tisha. I want to cum."

"You're too drunk," she snaps.

"I can make *you* cum when I'm drunk."

"That's not the point," she snaps, "Carlotta might not be bowling, but she's still coming back."

"That has nothing to do with me cumming..."

Her voice changes, like she's about to ask something she's been meaning to ask for a long time.

"So you never... hurt her?"

Sobriety hits me like a bus. (Although, realistically, my blood alcohol content hasn't changed).

"Who asks that sort of question? Christ. She's my daughter."

"When I was seventeen... you... I thought maybe you were attracted to..."

"Girls?!"

I'm repulsed. Sick to my stomach by what she's suggesting. Yet, I'm guilty. Of wanting her when she was seventeen. I'm guilty of wanting her now. More than that. I've had sex with her once and it's all I think about.

"Yeah. Kids. I thought you were..."

"A pedophile!?"

She nods. I lean over the side of her bed. And I throw up. Fuck. I'm drunk.

"Loukas," she shrieks.

Right. Perfect time for her to remind me I'm the adult and I'm drunk, in a teenage girl's bed where she confesses she thought I was a bloody pedophile.

"Fuck," I groan, spitting on the ground into the pile of sick, which is clear — like the vodka I dined on. I might have had vodka for lunch too.

"I can clean this up."

"No," I growl, "I'll go get a towel."

There's an en suite bathroom in the guest bedroom. I search for a towel in the linen closet when I hear my daughter's voice in the hall-way. Tisha gasps.

"Loukas Pagonis," she hisses. I climb into the shower and pull the curtain. Fuck. There's sick on the floor of the bedroom and I'm half-naked, hiding in the shower. This is it. This is the night my daughter finds out I'm fucking her best friend. Shit.

"Ew! Tisha... it smells disgusting in here."

Thankfully, Tisha closes the bathroom door.

"I threw up."

The lie comes to Tisha easily. Carlotta peers over the bed.

"Are you okay?! It smells like vodka."

"I had some earlier... from Gal."

"Fuck! Do you want a bump?"

"Sure."

I have to resist the urge to yell "A BUMP OF WHAT" and burst out of the shower. The thing about parenting is you can't be a lecherous bastard hiding in a teenager's shower moments before you do it. I bite my tongue and hope Tisha is smart enough to get her best friend out of here...

Carlotta continues talking, "I had so much fun tonight. It was the perfect first date."

"Yeah?"

"I almost fucked him," Carlotta giggles.

Rage courses through me. I have to stop myself from bursting out of the shower and finding every man she knows and killing him. I want to respect my daughter's wishes, but I can't let her keep running into harm's way. I don't care what a stupid therapist says.

"Carlotta! I don't want to hear about that."

I tell myself Tisha wants to spare me the anguish of hearing about my daughter's sexploits.

"You always want to hear. Or are you still on your 'older men' phase?"

"It's not an older men phase."

She giggles.

"You told me Marlon Brando was sexy the other day. I mean... he's dead!"

"He's still sexy," Tisha says, "And Ian Somerhalder isn't old. He's 42."

"Ew. That's older than my dad," Carlotta says, "That's so gross. I like guys from our generation. They're less old-fashioned. They don't care if I want to hook up with three other guys."

Loukas, don't lose your cool and stop thinking about the words coming from your daughter's mouth. Remember that you are a monster, hiding in a teenager's shower. I take a slow inhalation.

"Carlotta, I've gotta clean this up," Tisha says, trying to change the subject.

"Want me to get a towel?!"

The towels are in the bathroom. Fuck. I hold my breath.

"No!" Tisha yells.

Carlotta, naturally, doesn't listen.

She says, "Nonsense."

I'm holding as Carlotta opens the bathroom door. She sniffs and rushes to the closet, grabbing a towel and shutting the door behind her.

Carlotta accuses, "The guest bathroom smells like a man."

"There's no man in there," Tisha says with the guiltiest sounding voice I've ever heard.

I nearly scream. *Has she lost her mind entirely?!* I hope my daughter doesn't recognize her confession for what it was.

"I never said there was... wait... was there?"

My heart pounds. I can feel my stomach churning again. They don't speak for a little while. I assume they're cleaning up my sick.

"Disgusting. Please never vomit again?" Carlotta says.

"Promise."

They sit on the bed. Tisha puts on some music.

"I'm *so* tired," she says.

"Was it that man who came in here? Did he fuck you that good?"

"It does *not* smell like man in here!"

"You're a terrible liar. You fucked someone. Finally. I can't believe you were still a virgin."

"I am still."

That lie is her worst yet. Not even Carlotta believes it, because she asks, "No, you're not. Was it Alec?"

"No!"

My daughter guesses again.

"Homer?"

"No, ew!"

"Linus?"

"He ended up having a girlfriend."

My daughter's voice gets somber, "It wasn't Galanos."

"No. I *wish*."

"Ew!" Carlotta teases and hits her.

She wishes?!

Carlotta guesses again.

"Was it Dorian?"

"Nope."

"Eugene?"

"Hell no."

"I'm tired of guessing and properly rolling, so I'll head to bed. I need to send Kyle a picture of my boobs."

Boobs?! No. There is no way my daughter is sending pictures of her breasts out to men.

"Bye."

"Don't drink so much! And sleep well. Have you seen my papa?"

Blood rushes so loudly past my ears that I don't hear what Tisha says, and I nearly lose it when she flings the shower curtain open.

"Get out," Tisha hisses, "I told you she'd get back soon."

"Who were all these men? Are you talking to this many men? Dorian? Eugene? Linus? Homer? Alec? Are you building a fucking Olympic gymnastics team?"

"I haven't slept with any of those people. And you have no right to be jealous," she whispers.

"Right. Because apparently you are giving it out freely, eh?"

"You are so cruel, Uncle Lou," she hisses.

"Cruel? You knew I could hear you. You want to fuck Galanos? Eh? I could share you with him. If you want to be a slut so badly. I've shared women before, I just didn't think you were a whore."

She slaps me. Which I deserve. But I'm still drunk and I still want to throw up.

"Stop. Drinking," she snaps.

"I'm not a pedophile," I snarl.

Our eyes meet. She stares at me. At my lips, which are admittedly not in the best condition.

"And I'm not a *slut*."

"Good."

"You should leave," she sniffs, "Now."

Great. I've angered her. But I still want her. I still *need* her.

"Not until I get what I came for. Get in the shower, Tisha. And take your clothes off. I'll get you the morning-after pill tomorrow."

NINETEEN
ALL MINE

spread her legs apart and lower my face between them. *I'm still hungry.* Tisha makes a sound between a mewl and a gasp as my tongue dives between her legs. *Mine. She's all mine.* I tell myself this isn't hurting either of us and it's only what I'm doing to pass the time. But I know the truth.

It's a truth I won't be able to keep from her for long. My tongue finds her clit, and she cries out as I move my tongue in slow motion over it and then wriggle it until I find the spot that makes her moan the loudest.

We're stuck on this boat together. Tisha moans and pushes her fingers through my hair as I squeeze her thighs tightly and force my tongue between her lower lips and deep inside her.

As her hips buck against my face, my desire for her only mounts. I need her. And I love watching her cum. Her hips eagerly buck close to my lips and as my tongue traces the outline of her lower lips and sinks into her pussy, she makes perfect moaning sounds, goading me to kiss her and fuck her more deeply with my tongue. I pull my mouth away from her cunt after she climaxes and force myself away from her.

"That's all," I gasp, "I can't... No more..."

"You didn't cum," she says.

Doesn't she think I know that? I'm painfully aware of my tightening balls, eager for me to get the job done and bury all eleven inches inside her. It was a lot the first time she handled it. But she didn't complain. I'm her first. The only man she's had. And she'll never have another.

"I can't do this to you anymore," I whisper.

"Loukas," she hisses, "Can you stop giving me this old school bullshit?"

"You shouldn't use foul language."

I roll onto my back and close my eyes. Temptation lingers even when I can't see her. I can smell her, firstly. Her juices coat my lips and even after I've licked them clean, my upper lip smells like her pussy. I inhale deeply. Maybe I can survive the night with only her smell.

"That's exactly what I mean," Tisha complains, "I'm not a little girl. I'm an adult. I go to university. I can make my own choices. And I want... sex."

"Look at where sex got us."

"That was a mistake. And I'll have an abortion. It's no biggie."

No biggie?! I clench my jaw to stop myself from yelling at her. Thank goodness I gave up drinking. I couldn't make it through this conversation if I was drunk. I should sleep anyway.

"Your honor matters."

"I'm American. We have sex. The entire country is basically a giant fuck-pad."

I question the accuracy of her statement. She may be an adult, but I'm an *older* adult. An adult who should know better than to impregnate his daughter's best friend.

"When we get Carlotta back, I'll explain you are pregnant and as a father figure, I'm generously adopting the child. Then, we're finished. We have to end this. It's the responsible thing to do."

"I don't *care* about responsible. And why is that the only thing you care about?"

"I've been irresponsible, and it's cost people around me. It's cost their lives."

"You killed Matilda."

I swallow. She doesn't know the truth.

"Tisha," I growl, "We cannot have sex."

"Did you ever have feelings for me? Or were you always using me? I just want the truth."

The truth hurts like a thousand bullets grazing my flesh. The truth peels back my walls and layers, my indulgence in sex and alcoholism. The truth makes me look weak.

"I love you, Tisha. I have always loved you."

She rolls onto her side and rests her head on me. I sink back into the bed, allowing her to get close.

"Say it again," She whispers.

"I love you."

"I'm not crazy," she whispers.

Her words rip at my chest. No, she isn't crazy. But I understand why she thinks she might be. It's my fault that I never said the words to her before. I don't know why I'm saying them now. It will make things harder.

"Loving you is wrong," I say firmly, "And I'm only telling you because you asked for the truth. Loving you does not make what I did to you right."

"What did you *do* to me?"

"I fucked you. I... I raped you, Tisha."

She's so quiet that I consider I should probably stop talking. But I don't stop. Because I'm finally telling her the truth about how I feel.

I continue, "I kissed you when you were a child. I made you fall in love with me."

"You didn't rape me, Loukas. I was 18. And you didn't *make me* fall in love with you."

"I'm older," I explain, "It's my job to stop looking at you. It's my job not to kiss you. I'm old. I need to leave you for younger men."

Tisha huffs a little, warm breath spilling from her little nostrils onto my chest.

Then she argues, "So? Do you think because I'm young, I'm not a person? That I can't think for myself?"

"You have to admit, there's a difference in maturity," I answer.

I can tell my answer displeases her. But she's close to me. And if I can't have sex with her, I can at least hold her.

"Right. One of us runs around killing people when he's angry and the other one is a mature adult in charge of her emotions."

"I don't run around killing people. I usually walk."

She groans.

"That's *such* a dad joke."

"In case you've forgotten, I *am* a dad. Your best friend's dad."

I don't mean to sound so bitter, like I'm blaming her.

"And Zoe's dad. And Antonio's. But you're also... Loukas."

Her fingers run over the stubble on my chest. Her touch is electric. There's something special about when we touch each other, like the tension that always exists between us breaks just for a moment before my guilt or her outrage drag us apart again.

Touch is a language I much prefer to talking. I'm better with my hands and lips when I don't have to form any words. Tisha's touch communicates everything I need. She's soft. She's delightfully feminine. Her skin is this light, tawny color much less dark than Fallon's. She gets a little darker each passing minute in this sun, but I like her complexion the way it's gently toasted.

I like everything about her. That's the problem.

"None of the boys my age have chest hair," she whispers, "or beards... and none of the boys my age kiss like you do."

My throat tightens.

"So you've kissed others."

"Yes! Uncle Lou... I tried to stop myself being in love with you. It took a long time."

"And you were successful."

I can feel her nodding.

"Yes," she whispers. I have to keep myself from reacting. This is good. I love her and she doesn't love me. That will make this easier when I have my daughter back. For all of us.

"Then," I whisper, "If you have no feelings for me, there's no reason I can't make you feel good."

"No reason at all."

"Tisha…" I whisper, "I'm sorry."

"For loving me?"

I clear my throat and murmur, "No. For acting on it. For kissing you. I haven't felt so stupid about a woman in decades. Where I'd risk everything. The older I get, the more people I lose. The more regrets I have. I miss my youth."

She kisses me. Her kisses are urgent, as usual. Her hands rush to my face and her thumb brushes my cheek. I shudder. Her touch melts me and undoes my better judgment. My throat remains tight, so with each word I say, I nearly wheeze.

"You weren't stupid," she says.

I know she believes it, but I still don't. My hands are on her waist now. I feel her bones jutting out of her hips a little. Soon, she'll be plump and growing with my seed inside her. And I'll have to let her go.

"I've failed at love my entire life," I whisper, "So whatever you do, whoever you end up with, don't fail at love on my account."

"I won't."

"Promise me."

"I promise."

I spread her thighs apart and mount her, pressing my cock into her urgently with a swift motion. Her wetness surprises me. My hips join to hers as I'm fully thrust between her legs. She moans and I join my lips with hers. I have her. And I don't want to let her go. Even if it's the right thing to do.

TWENTY
A BIT OF SAG

Carlotta stomps into the kitchen with a cigarette hanging from her lips and a nicotine patch on her shoulder. Quitting isn't going well.

"Papa, I need €500."

"For what?"

"None of your fucking business."

"Carlotta..."

She ignores my warning tone.

"I need it," she says, but her voice comes out whiny.

"Give me your arm."

"Papa, stop acting like a freak!"

I take it and run my fingers over her forearm.

"No needle marks. But what's this."

She has a bruise.

"I fell."

"On your forearm?"

"Yes."

"You can talk to me if anything's wrong."

"Nothing's wrong, Papa. I need money, that's all."

I give her five notes. She counts them and stuffs them into her purse. I caved and got her the Prada.

"How are you feeling today?"

"Fine. Tisha's still sleeping. She spent all of last night crying."

"Oh?"

"She won't tell me. She's in love with this boy, but she has to keep it a secret. He sounds like an asshole."

Carlotta lights her cigarette. *He is an asshole.*

"Well, boys your age can get that way."

Carlotta snorts.

"Yes. They can. I wish she would give them up. Tisha's too sweet for guys our age. They take advantage of her."

"Lovely girl."

"Yes, Papa. Try with her. I think she fears you. She never wants to take the boat out if you're going to be there. Let her know that you're not some scary mafia guy."

I clear my throat and nod.

"Right," I mumble.

Carlotta shrugs, "I enjoy having her here. It's making me forget about Matilda."

"Hm."

"I'm sorry, Papa. You loved Matilda."

Carlotta's beyond forgiven. I don't punish vengeance. It's her right to have justice.

"Yes. I did."

My heart still skips a beat when she mentions Matilda. It's not terror exactly. Dread. Guilt. I should have protected my daughter. Matilda didn't need to die for me to do that successfully.

"What matters is your safety," I say, "Please… tell me you're safe."

"I'm fine."

"Good."

"Papa… what happened to my mother?"

I grip the countertop. Fuck. I need a drink. Only, after I *threw up* all over a teenager's bedroom before fucking her, I've officially hit rock bottom. I think. I'm not trying to find out if I can sink any lower.

"I never hurt your mother."

"I want to believe that."

"And just because she was my second wife doesn't mean I loved her less than the first."

"Papa, that's not what I want to know."

I don't want to tell her what she wants to know. I killed seven people trying to find out who killed Carlotta's mother. For a time, I believed it was Stavros. Not anymore. My brother might have a mental unrest, but he's not responsible for the women I've lost. Someone else is. I don't know who. Not yet.

"I've kept this from you to protect you."

"I'm not a child anymore."

What Matilda did to her… She organized my daughter's gang rape while trying to pilfer her inheritance. My feelings twist into complex knots and I want to forget that she was also a woman who massaged my shoulders after a long day at work. A woman who could take cocktail shrimp and turn it into a kinky night. But she hurt my daughter, and that meant her death. My only regret is that she never faced my wrath.

Good bye, Matilda.

"I know," I whisper.

But that hurts too. I remember holding this beautiful baby like it was yesterday. She was so small with such plump cheeks. Her eyes went on forever. I loved her more than I'd ever loved another human. When I first held her, I never wanted to let go.

"Whoever killed your mother raped and beheaded her. I found her when I returned from London. Yiayia had Galanos for the weekend. Papa was in Sicily. No one had been around to check on you. The two of you had been there for days. Antonio was sick from starvation. You were... you were trying to wake her up. You were so young... and so was she. It was horrible. The worst day of my life. And when I came into the house, you held onto me and you kept calling me *mama*. You hardly knew me."

Thinking about it makes me want to drink. Carlotta puts her hand on my shoulder.

"I don't remember."

"You must have seen whoever killed her. And whoever did never hurt you two. But they might want to. They might come back. I've failed to protect you once, Carlotta, but it won't happen again. It was an assassination."

"You really loved her?" Carlotta asks.

How could I lie? I might be a monster, but there's room for love somewhere in my metal heart.

"Yes. She was the mother of my children."

My daughter finishes her cigarette and wraps her arms around me. I hate that she smells like tobacco, but I'm glad she wants to be close.

"I'm sorry, papa."

"Don't apologize. But you must stay safe, Carlotta. Our family attracts enemies."

"You could train me to fight them."

"No. I couldn't. This isn't the life I want for you."

"But you'll let Gal go through it. Even if he hates it."

I snort.

"Gal likes guns but hates killing. What a bloody contradiction."

"I don't enjoy killing," Carlotta adds hastily.

"I know."

"I killed her because... I didn't know what else to do."

"And the others. Who was involved?"

"I can handle it, papa."

"No more killing for you," I murmur, "I'm your father. It's my job to kill for you and your honor."

Carlotta nods and kisses my cheek. I'm not convinced, but I promise myself to keep a closer eye on her. Tisha can help. I go for a long run with Stavros in the evening. He comes back to my private villa with a slightly pregnant Fallon, who entertains herself for the duration of our ninety-minute run by reading on the couch. Tisha and Carlotta lounge outside by the pool. Fallon's not exactly babysitting, but she's good with people in our family and she promises to watch Carlotta closely. Cassia and Sandros are on another trip to Las Vegas, and I think Fallon misses having people to fuss over.

Stavros runs through the door all sweaty and she wraps her arms around him without missing a beat. I forgot how disgusting love can make you. Stavros kisses her through panting and strips his shirt off. Fallon giggles as Stavros bends to kiss her neck.

"Enough," I snarl.

Fallon leans against the counter.

"Jealous?" She teases. Fallon enjoys poking fun a little too much.

"Disgusted, more like. He's sweating all over the marble."

"Calm down, Loukas. You should get some once in a while," Stavros teases, licking his own sweat off Fallon's neck. Does romance turn everyone into a disgusting sap?

Fallon swats Stavros playfully.

"Babe, it's too soon for him."

She's talking about Matilda dying. I grit my teeth and prepare to snap back at my younger brother, not noticing that my daughter and her friend have just entered the house.

"I don't need *you lecturing me about sex.* I get plenty of it whenever I want it."

Tisha makes a strange gasping sound. Carlotta laughs.

"Tisha, what was that about?" Carlotta giggles at Tisha's wild reaction, like she doesn't know what to make of it.

"Maybe she's grossed out hearing her best friend's dad talk about sex," Fallon suggests, swatting me with her romance novel.

She spends all day reading books about aliens impregnating human beings. Fascinating woman, Fallon. She claims pregnancy makes her fantasize about tentacles. Hmph.

Carlotta giggles, "Maybe."

Stavros mutters something else under his breath, "Or maybe she's the one fucking him."

Thankfully, nobody hears and I pretend not to until Carlotta and Tisha disappear and Fallon returns to her romance novel on the couch. She claims she was getting to the good bits, which normally means there's a blue erection "sliding into her tightness like a hot knife through butter". Don't ask me how I know. Or if I read the "good bits" over her shoulder once. In her defense, they were good.

I drag Stavros into the kitchen.

"What was that comment back there?" I snarl.

"No one heard. Relax."

"You can't ever bring that up."

"You aren't sleeping with her. We cleared it up. Relax. I believe you."

"She's eighteen."

"Not exactly a little girl," Stavros says, shrugging, "But on the young side. Do you really like breasts that young? I like mine with a bit of sag. More *real*."

I want to punch Stavros in the face, which I'm pretty sure he wants too. He's always *testing me*. That's younger brothers for you.

TWENTY-ONE
WE GOT A PROBLEM, BOSS

Tisha gets more sleep than I do. She *snores*. It's adorable. At first. I push her away and she wriggles her little butt right back against me. I pull her close to me and growl, "Hush, you little demon..."

She makes a cute little whimper and mutters in her sleep, "Sexy..."

It's early when I see the boats in the distance. My daughter. *Safe.* Tisha sleeps a while longer as I speed the boat along. Soon, we'll have to pretend. I've never been good at pretending with Tisha. I've always let myself go around her. But I've lost her sentiments for me. Her body responds to mine because she's young, sensual... gorgeous. But what I want from her will be impossible for her to give.

I want her as my wife. Not my third or fourth wife. My *last wife*.

I can't have that for several reasons. The biggest is sitting on the horizon, safe on a boat somewhere. I call Yiannis. He answers with a series of expletives.

"Good morning," I say gruffly, "Put my daughter on the phone, I'm an hour away."

"We got a problem, boss."

"What kind of problem?"

"Your family came and picked your daughter up two hours ago. They killed all the motherfuckers she was with. Boss, we're up to our fucking elbows in dead teenagers. One guy looked like one of Khalid's cunt hunters."

My chest tightens and then my heart races. Stavros and Fallon are at home. I didn't think Galanos knew where she was. And anyway, the little shit wouldn't dare cross me. He's bold, like any Pagonis, but he's not stupid.

"Which one of my family members?"

But I know who before I hang up.

"Mrs. Pagonis and your father show up with guns and say that you sent them. Boss, I tried to talk them out of it, but you know how they can get."

"I'll deal with you later, Yiannis," I snarl.

I hang up and impulsively (and stupidly) fling my cellphone into the sea. I scream out another expletive, realizing what I've done. Fuck. My swearing gets Tisha's attention. I stop the boat as she stumbles above deck.

"Uncle Loukas?"

"Yiayia has Carlotta."

Tisha's eyes widen. She's had her own experiences with Yiayia in the past. Tisha figured out quickly to stay out of my grandmother's line of fire. Her bitter cruelty had become legendary.

"Where?"

"I don't know."

"Call her," Tisha says, in that voice young people use when they think you're completely technologically stupid. Which I am. But that's not the point.

"I'm a fucking moron and threw my phone in the fucking ocean! FUCK!"

Right after I swear, a clap of thunder resounds over the water. Tisha points behind me.

"Uncle Lou. Please tell me those clouds are far away."

They are. But not if we stand around talking.

"Tisha, get below deck. I'll get us out of here. We'll stop in a cove village and I'll contact her."

"Could you use my phone?"

Tisha reaches for her phone. Naturally. She's a teenager. She always has a cellphone. I take her cellphone and search for Carlotta's number. Everything has these yellow face symbols all over it.

"Why don't you use names?!"

"Carlotta is Greek flag emoji, martini emoji and high heel emoji. Isn't it obvious?"

No. It isn't obvious. It's times like this when my guilt for sleeping with her reaches an all-time high.

"Carlotta's been ignoring my calls," she admits.

And she ignores mine.

"Fuck."

I punch in Yiayia's number. She answers calmly.

"Loukas."

I don't know how she knows it was me.

"Where is my daughter?"

"Your daughter is spending time with her grandfather and great grandmother. You shouldn't concern yourself with her well-being any longer. She's my grandchild and I can look after her."

I swear I hear my daughter's voice yelling "papa" in the distance. I swallow.

"Put her on the phone," I whisper, "Please."

My grandmother has the upper hand. She always gets it. We've been complacent. For six months, we assumed Papa and Yiayia were both content at sea. Naturally, my grandmother would have revenge. But I never thought she'd stoop so low to go after her own great-grandchild. I hand Tisha her cellphone. She takes the phone and then takes my hand.

"It'll be okay, Uncle Lou," she whispers, "We'll find her."

"I do not know where to look. There's a storm coming."

I'm so angry and rage makes me want to drink. Tisha steps up, mercifully. I'm grateful that she's here, even if I'd never admit it to her.

"I'll call the villa and talk to Stavros and Fallon. You decide what we do next. We'll find her. Together."

"I should take you back to safety."

"Uncle Lou..."

"No!" I snarl, "You're pregnant. And I'm the father of that child, whether you care to admit it. That baby is *mine*."

"That doesn't give you the right to control me!"

"Doesn't it? I'm paying good money for you to carry that child. Someone needs to keep you under control. Look at the danger you could have been in today. Look at the danger we're in now!"

I'm loud and gesticulating madly at storm clouds, which is probably a sign that I've nearly lost my temper. I always say things I don't mean when I lose my temper. The only thing I have on my side is that I'm not drinking anymore. So I have a chance of sounding like a sane person, eventually.

"Stop it, Loukas! You are angry and upset about Carlotta, but I'm not her and I'm not a child. You point that boat towards shore and let me call your family *right now*. And we will sit and think and figure out where my best friend is. Got it!?"

She's so forceful it surprises me.

"Fine," I relent.

I'm powerless against her, aren't I?

"Good," she huffs, "I'll call."

I turn the boat towards the cove. I know a spot with small hotels, where I can think and strategize without my family's people watching my every move. Sometimes, you need to get away from Thessaloniki to solve your problems. I hear Tisha talking to Fallon and then she hangs up.

"Fallon's mad at me," she sighs.

"Why?"

"She says I shouldn't have followed you."

"I'll never hear the end from Stavros," I grumble.

"About what?"

"He figured out I was sleeping with you. Months ago. I've been... lying to my brother to protect you."

"And Carlotta," she reminds me.

"Yes. But I am terrible at protecting my daughter. I try to then... this. The incidents with Matilda. I am not a good father, Tisha. You think I'm trying to control you, but I've had forty years of wrong in my life. You want to get rid of that baby but that baby... is my second chance."

I can feel my voice cracking and I feel so weak. She wraps her hands around me and whispers.

"Loukas. I won't have an abortion, okay? I can't be a mom, but... you can have your second chance."

I bury my nose in her neck. I can't hold her like this forever. I need to steer the boat. But holding her gives me hope that I desperately need. Her body, intertwined with mine like this, feels so right. Why did I push her away? When I held her love in my grasp, why did I force her to let go?

"I'm sorry, Tisha," I whisper, "For not loving you when I should have."

"You're forgiven, Loukas."

"And... I'm sorry for... knocking you up."

She shakes her head and pulls away from me.

"Every time you wanted me... I wanted you more. I know you think I'm a dumb kid who you manipulated, but that's not what happened."

TWENTY-TWO
DON'T FLIRT

5 MONTHS AGO

Carlotta's here to visit her therapist and for a weekend retreat. Tisha's staying at the villa to write papers for school. She's researching Maya Angelou for a paper and works daily on the kitchen counter. I hear her talking to Carlotta on the phone during one of Carlotta's breaks, and Tisha reminds her best friend that black American women are the fastest growing group of college graduates.

I have to work hard, Carlotta.

My daughter probably encourages her to have a tall glass of wine. But Tisha's so focused, she doesn't notice me walk into the kitchen.

"Studying hard?"

She lets out a little yelp.

"Sorry. You scared me, Uncle Lou."

"Sorry."

"Yeah. I am."

"Maya Angelou. I know little about her. I spent all my time in school... well... drunk."

Tisha peers at me over her screen.

"Did you have research papers?"

"Yes. And we didn't have those devices. In my day, you'd find a smart girl to write your paper for you."

"That's cheating," she says, seriously. But the corners of her lips turn up slightly and I realize she's teasing.

"Yes. It was," I said, silently reflecting on my younger days. I don't bother telling Tisha that my first wife died after our senior year of high school, careening me into the arms of Carlotta's mother.

"I have to write this paper myself."

"I could help."

"No offense, Uncle Lou, but I don't think you could."

"You're right," I groan, "You're much smarter than me."

"Don't do that," Tisha says, "don't *flirt.*"

She says it with disdain in her voice. Shame courses through me. Each time I flirt with her or think about her, my heart pulses with this funny mixture of guilt and desire. Even now... I want her.

"I enjoy flirting with you."

"That's the problem," she says, slamming her laptop screen shut, "It's confusing."

"What's confusing about it? You're a beautiful woman."

"I'm not, though," she says, softly.

Her voice catches in her throat. In what world would someone *not* consider Tisha exquisite?

"Yes. You are."

"No. Seriously, Loukas. I keep trying to date boys my age and they all think I'm too black, too fat, too skinny, too slutty, not slutty enough, too dumb, too smart, or *something*. If I was white and skinny like Carlotta, they'd line up out the door. Even my past dates prefer Carlotta to me. It's difficult being best friends with the prettiest girl in school sometimes. And she knows exactly what to say to guys. Guys don't even talk to me."

"Carlotta's beauty doesn't take away from yours. I love my daughter, but in Greece... we don't have many women like you. I like that you're different."

"Stop it."

"I'm not trying to offend you," I say, "If I've been racially insensitive, I-

"It's not that," she snaps, "It's... you make this *so hard.*"

For a man with my experience, women still surprise me.

"What?"

"I don't *want* to be in love with you."

Silence fills the kitchen. The poor girl. That's when it hits me. I'm abusing her. And confusing her. So soon after losing Matilda, I'm not ready to put another person at risk. Especially not my daughter's best friend. What I've been doing with her has been reckless and impulsive. It's not the love that Tisha West deserves.

"Listen, Tisha. What you're feeling isn't love. It's a passing fancy."

I sit across from her and her lip bunches up into a childish pout.

"I knew it. I'm coming on too strong and scaring you off... *again.*"

"Again?"

"On the tennis courts?" she whispers, "I... I thought you were... I wanted... it's stupid."

"Your feelings are not stupid. Even if they are fleeting, that doesn't make them foolish."

"I *love* you," She insists, "It's not fleeting. I want to be with you, Loukas."

"No. You're mistaken, child."

Tisha sits up straight.

"Don't do that. Don't call me a child."

"You *are* a child. Look at us. How ridiculous would we look? An old man with a woman young enough to be his daughter on his arm? People would think you were a prostitute."

A pen comes flying at my head. Tisha's aim has improved.

"You always make comments about my sexual agency," she snaps, "And even if you're a total pig about it... you have a big heart. Stop being such a sexist old school freak and listen to me!"

She slams her book and storms off. Fuck. That's one thing about teenagers that I won't miss. The tantrums. Toddler tantrums have a place in the world. Toddlers have no way of communicating. Teenagers can trick you into thinking they're adults. And then they storm off in a huff, leaving you feeling like a foolish old man in your own home!

I follow her and knock on the guest room door.

"Busy!" Tisha snaps.

"Tisha. Let's talk. Please. I won't call you a child. We'll just... talk."

I doubt I'll let her talk. I've spent too much time around her to avoid the consequences of doing so. A raging hard-on. She may rage with hormones, but I'm burning with desire for her. Love or not... she's beautiful. The most beautiful woman I've ever pursued. That's why I couldn't stop myself with her.

"Tisha... please."

"Apologize!" she yells from the other side of the door, "For once in your life, *apologize!*"

"I'm sorry."

"About what?"

"For insinuating you were a prostitute again. And for calling you a child."

"Good."

"Can I come in now?"

"I haven't decided yet."

I try something that normally works wonders on my daughter.

"I'll... take you out for gelato? Or out on the boat?"

"You can't buy me off the way you buy off Carlotta!" she yells.

Fuck. None of my tricks work on her.

"Fine. Talking then. And wine."

"I'm not drinking with you," she snaps.

I shouldn't be drinking at all. I promised I'd quit getting black out drunk and I've been good for most of the month. I was only tipsy at Stavros' last party. He's obsessing over becoming a father and I couldn't listen to him asking for advice for another moment.

"I'll have half what you're having. That will... keep me in line."

She opens the door.

"When you're drunk, you want sex."

"Yes."

I want sex now.

She grabs my collar and yanks me into the room.

"Screw getting drunk then. Fuck me, Loukas."

"What?!"

I thought we were arguing.

"I love you," she says, "I want you. And if you don't believe my feelings are real... adult... I'll prove it to you."

She reaches for my cock and takes control of me in her palm. She works her hands down my pants and wraps her hand around the growing member. It's hot and throbbing in her grasp.

"I can't do this," I whisper, "I have to stop."

"Don't," she commands, "Because I want this."

"Tomorrow," I murmur, "The morning-after pill... tomorrow..."

TWENTY-THREE
SHE'S MY DAUGHTER...

We get to the cove. I know an inn there — one that not even Stavros knows I frequent. During my younger, more single years, I enjoyed the pretty ladies in this town.

All of them will loosen their morals for a night with a Pagonis. Word of my family's sexual prowess has spread along the Greek coast.

It helps that we're all dashing, dark-haired and blue-eyed. Except Gal. He's blond. But his eyes are just as blue as ours... As blue as the Aegean, Yiayia said.

My chest tightens when I think about what she might do to my daughter. Beating her? Marrying her off? I can't imagine how we're going to find her. I forget momentarily that Tisha is right here. She slips her hand into mine and warmth spreads through me. I feel guilty being happy that she's here. My daughter isn't here... that ought to overwhelm this.

Carlotta has been through too much for me to leave her fate in the hands of her grandmother. I squeeze her hand. She might not have romantic feelings for me, but... *she cares.* I'm so used to taking care of people that I've forgotten what it's like for someone to take care of me.

I take her into a small inn. A thin woman with a sour face glances over my shoulder.

"Is that one of Khalid's girls? I won't have men bringing whores in here," she says, in Greek, thankfully.

Tisha wrinkles her nose, but I don't think she knows many of the words. She probably recognizes *whore*.

"She's not. She's…"

I take my hand out of hers.

"She's my daughter."

The woman snorts and glances at Tisha in disbelief. I pay in cash and take her upstairs.

"Did that woman call me a whore?" she hisses.

"No," I lie.

"Yes," Tisha said, "She did. I've been doing Greek lessons, you know."

"Have you?" I grumble.

This girl is always doing the unexpected. Fuck. You can't *fool* younger women. They grew up fooling our generation so they could sneak out and go to parties. I'm more vulnerable to her than she is to me.

"Yes. And you told her I was your *daughter*."

"I didn't want to tell her you were my lover," I snap as I push the door open. Tisha refuses to enter the room. She folds her arms.

"Why not? I'm pregnant with *your* kid."

"That doesn't make you my lover. We made a mistake. I will take and raise the child but I won't run around damaging your reputation."

"I don't *have* a reputation. I'm not Greek. And if I had one, I wouldn't care."

"Get in the room, Tisha."

"Not until you tell me you don't see me the way you see Carlotta."

I snort, and then my snort turns into a laugh.

"Trust me, Tisha. What I feel for you is not fatherly. It's different."

"Uh huh."

This doesn't satisfy her.

"And for the time being... I suppose you are my... *lover.*"

She enters the room, and I shut the door. Before she can stomp off, I grab her arm and pull her close to me.

"Little woman," I mutter, "You are the most infuriating creature."

"Loukas Pagonis, I demand—"

"Shh," I whisper, "You don't want the woman downstairs hearing you scream, eh?"

She pulls herself away from me and flounces off.

"I don't care. I'm hungry anyway. I want ice-cream, watermelon, pecans dipped in caramel and then a big chicken sandwich from Chick-Fil-A."

"I don't think I know half these foods."

"Pregnancy cravings, Loukas. I can't help it."

She flops on the bed with the infuriating sluggishness of a teenager.

"You'll wait until supper. I'll find some fish and fries on the wharf for you."

"I'm hungry... *now.*"

"Tisha..." I warn her sternly. This doesn't affect her in the slightest.

"Fine," she says, giggling and bounding over to me, "Don't help."

She reaches for my cock and grabs it through my trousers.

"Tisha... what are you doing," I say as she works the zip down and sticks her hand down my pants.

"If you won't satisfy one craving," she says, "Satisfy another."

"We can't keep doing this," I say, "We can't."

Tisha presses her body against mine, keeping her hand wrapped around my cock. She's a teenager and I remember what my hormones were like back then. It only gets worse as you get older.

Sex runs constantly in the back of my mind and when she's around, I'm always seconds away from an eruption. I'm powerless against her grasp on my cock. She moves her hand up and down my shaft.

"You taught me this," she whispers, "You taught me how to please you."

I bite my lower lip and close my eyes, shaking my head. Fuck, she's good. She grips with the correct amount of pressure and she moves my foreskin over my thick member. Her hand can't make it all the way around my shaft and she rubs me perfectly.

"Tisha," I murmur, "Stop…"

"No," she whispers, "Not until you give me what I want."

She's fucking good. I groan and she strokes me faster.

"Which is what?" I gasp.

"A chicken sandwich. Ice-cream. Watermelon."

She removes her hand from my cock and zips me up. I'm red in the face and shocked at how utterly devious this pregnant teenager is. My brow knits together in fury.

"You think rubbing my cock will get you whatever you want?"

"Yes," she says smugly.

"Think again, child."

"I've told you not to call me *child*," she snaps.

"If you keep playing games, I'll call you what I like."

"OH YES," Tisha screams, "I LOVE YOUR BIG DICK. OH YES, GIVE YOUR DAUGHTER THAT COCK DADDY—

I jump over the bed and clamp my hand over her mouth. Tisha kicks… *hard*.

"Are you crazy?" I yell, "Everyone downstairs can hear you? The walls are paper thin."

"Sandwich," Tisha hisses.

"No," I snarl back. But I'm only arguing with her because I hate losing.

"YES! OH MY GOD, DADDY, YES!"

I catch her again and press her against the bed with my hand over her mouth. My weight captures her, still for once, on the sparsely blanketed Queen-sized bed. I run my tongue over her neck.

"You'll be quiet," I snarl, "Or I'll make you scream in earnest."

I muffle Tisha's response, but I'm sure she's dripping with her signature attitude. I graze my teeth over her shoulder.

"Little woman... I will obey you... but I'm going to have your cunt first. If everyone downstairs already thinks I'm fucking you."

Tisha wriggles and makes muffled sounds that are probably "chicken sandwich first" but I don't care. I pull her underwear aside as I lift her dress and take my pants down, uncovering her mouth as I guide my shaft to her entrance. The tip of my cock jerks as I glide between her thighs. She's *soaked*. The little minx is playing a game with me, and it's a game she enjoys. Turning me into a hunter. Allowing me to take her.

A low, lusty growl emerges in my throat as I kiss her neck. I grunt as I push the head between her lips. Tisha moans.

"Loukas..." she gasps.

"You want me to stop?"

"N-no," she whimpers, "Don't... stop."

I thrust into her with one swift motion. She moans... but with none of her humiliating screaming. Just a pure moan of pleasure as I bury my dick in her tightness. Pregnancy hormones make sure she's nearly always ready for me. Maybe we experience the same effects around each other. Constant arousal. I groan as I bury my shaft inside her and guide my hips out slightly.

I grunt and I enter her again. She moans louder.

"There," I murmur, "Much better than a chicken sandwich."

She moans.

"It's pretty good," she whispers, "About as good as Chick-Fil-A."

I rake my fingers through her hair and wrap some of it around my wrist. I tilt her neck back and drive my cock into her deeper.

"Careful, little woman," I whisper, "You don't want to make *daddy* angry..."

TWENTY-FOUR
MORNING-AFTER-PILLS

5 MONTHS AGO

I wake up and she's there. *Fuck.* I shouldn't have this woman in my bed, but I couldn't stop myself. And I promised I'd get her the morning-after pill, but as I watch her sleeping next to me... I don't want to get her any pill. **I want her pregnant.**

She rolls over onto her back, exposing her navel ring. My cock rises. I could have her down. Again.

I want to fill her fertile womb with Pagonis seed and *keep her pregnant.* It's my biological urge to have her. I thought I finished with children. With women. Matilda would have made a horrible mother. I can see clearly now what I couldn't before. I made a mistake with her.

I run my fingers over Tisha's navel and stop above her mound. I'd love to finger her awake and watch her mewl as she came to. Fuck. Why are all my fantasies about this young woman so utterly filthy?

Guilt catches in my throat, and I make a strange noise against my will, waking Tisha. She yawns and sits up.

"Good morning, Loukas."

"Good morning."

"Carlotta's coming back tomorrow," she whispers.

"I know."

I take her on top of me and kiss her. Tisha's tiny breasts poke out of the white t-shirt she stole from my closet. I run my hands over her back and grab onto her butt. She's so *tiny* compared to me. And she makes me feel old. Her little breasts tickle my chest and then she kisses me, hair falling in front of her face in thick curly tresses. She smells like the sea. I kiss her back.

"I don't want to leave," she whispers, "I never want to go back to school when I come here."

"You *must*," I tell her.

I grab onto her lower back and pull her close to me. She kisses me more. My tongue finds a way into her mouth and dick stiffens in my pants again. *Fuck.* Everything feels serious. It's the worst time for me to get a boner.

"I love you, Loukas."

"Stop," I murmur.

"I love you," she says again.

"Tisha... stop."

"No," she snaps, "You can't tell me how to feel."

"Yes," I respond, "I can. I'm old enough to be your father."

"You're older than my dad," she snaps.

Great. Like I didn't already feel like a terrible fucking person.

I kiss her some more and push her onto my back, taking a position on top of her. I'd rather mount her and fuck her than talk about how old I am. Or talk about her feelings. She has feelings I can't return. She wants something I can't give her.

"Think about Carlotta."

"We'll tell her," Tisha says, full of hope. And naivete.

"No," I say gruffly, forcing her legs apart, "You can't."

"Then you can't fuck me," she says.

I raise an eyebrow.

"Yes," I reply gently, "I can. And you will let me."

"No," she hisses, "You will *not*. I won't have sex with a man who doesn't love me."

"You've done it before."

She slaps me. Hard.

"Fucker," she snaps.

"What did you call me?"

"Fucker," she hisses, "Or maybe I should call you what you are... a fucking... predator."

I roll off her. Fuck. I grab a pillow and cover my face. Shame. She knows exactly how to hit me where it hurts. I'm *not* what she thinks I am. I've never felt attraction to a woman so much younger than me. But I'm not... a monster.

"Hurts, doesn't it?" she snaps, "You took my virginity. You took my heart. You want to take everything from me and give *nothing*."

She grabs the pillow off my face and throws it across the room.

"Leave then," I say to her, "I'll stop."

"No," she snaps, "You won't. The next time you get drunk, you'll come here and fuck me like you always do. You think I'm a stupid little girl or an easy fuck, but I'm a grown woman and I know my heart. If you weren't a pedophile, you'd take me seriously."

She blubbers and cries. Blood rushes past my ears. My heart beats so fast, I can't hear myself think. A monster. This is what she thinks I am. And I've done nothing to prove her *wrong*. I act like a monster every time I drink. Every time I slip my cock into her tightness, I take a woman who was *born* when I was twenty-two years old. She's my fucking daughter's age.

I sit up and grab another shirt.

"Maybe you're right," I snarl, "I'm a dirty old man. Fine. But think for one moment what it would do to you to be with me. You think you love me? I'm forty. I'll get OLD! I'll go gray! And you'll be a YOUNG WOMAN. You think I'm a pedophile? Fine. I don't care what you think. But you don't know love if you think you'll love an old man when you're beautiful. When you could have *anyone*."

"I don't want anyone!" she yells, "I want YOU."

"Stop fighting with me!"

"You stop fighting!"

We glare at each other. *What am I doing?*

"Fine," I relent, "I'm sorry."

"For what?"

"For diminishing you. But I'm right. You will not love me. And I'm too old to be a young woman's fleeting fancy."

"I'm too caring to be an old man's experiment."

"Good."

"But I still love you. And I can't stop," she whispers.

"You'd love an old pedophile?" I snarl.

"Sorry for calling you that."

She flops back, and my shirt rides up to expose her stomach. I join her on the bed and kiss the bare spot. She whimpers. I kiss her again. I kiss around her navel and move my lips to her underwear.

"One more day," I murmur, "I have one more day to taste you. So come on…"

"Loukas…"

"Yes," I grumble, "It's a horrible idea. But… I can't stop myself when your cunt smells so sweet…"

I pull her underwear apart and slip my tongue between her legs. She cries out and I push my tongue all the way to her clit. She whimpers and runs her fingers through my hair. I can't stop myself with her. My tongue licks and sucks her lower lips until she cums. With her juices on my tongue, I get her completely naked and eat her out until she cums again. I lick my lips and dive between her legs, licking her to five orgasms. That calms her down nicely. I groan and lie next to her.

"I love sex," I whisper, half to myself. She whimpers and peels her sticky thighs apart, wrapping one leg around me and holding onto me.

"We should stop," she says.

"I know."

Tisha runs her fingers through my chest hair.

"If you can't love me, Loukas... I can't be with you. I should move on."

"And I should let you move on," I say, "But it's hard."

She sees her opportunity to get the truth out of me. But the truth will break her heart. Because I'll age and die — and one day, I'll leave her. I can't do that to Tisha.

"Why? If you don't love me... it should be easy."

I spread her legs and roll my body on top of hers. Nothing about her is easy. She drives me mad with lust... desire... and something more. The need to keep her.

Am I just another crazy Pagonis man, desperate to hold onto a woman he shouldn't? Or is this... *love*. With a girl my daughter's age. I kiss her neck until I'm breathless before replying, "After this, we'll be done," I murmur, "One... last... time."

"And then I'll get birth control," she whispers.

"Yes."

"Go slow," she pleads, "I don't want this to be over."

But everything must end. Especially us.

TWENTY-FIVE
PANTIES & CHICKEN

Tisha delightedly eats a chicken sandwich in her panties and a thin tank top that barely covers her breasts. I'm smart enough not to point it out to her, but she's showing.

I like that part of pregnancy, when the stomach stretches as an incredible woman grows another life.

"You're looking at me, creepily, Loukas," she mutters.

"Hm."

"How are we getting Carlotta back?"

She sticks her finger between the bread and chicken and licks mustard off it.

"Yiayia wants me to come after her, which means... she wants something else. I don't know what."

"She's scary."

Even Fallon fears Yiayia more than anyone else in my family. Thanks to Fallon, we've had a break from my grandmother's blood lust. But she's back. And she has my daughter.

"I tell myself she wouldn't hurt her own great-grandchild. But she would."

"She hurt Cassia," Tisha whispers.

So Tisha remembers the incident with Ofek. What a charming introduction to my family of sociopaths. It's a miracle she stayed around.

"Yes," I grumble, "She did. And she and my father are both devious. I suspect they may have brought her to Italy. Or they're on the way there."

"Why?"

"Because... my cousin's Geo's a pig and Yiayia's his godmother. It's possible she wants to marry Carlotta off. I've refused her each time she offered."

"To her cousin!?" Tisha wrinkled her nose, "That's incest, Uncle Lou."

"It's worse than incest. Geo's a monster."

Tisha finishes her sandwich and prances over to the inn phone. I doubt it's connected, but I can't focus on the phone when Tisha's ass cheeks are practically hanging out of her panties. When did women's underwear get so *insanely sexy*?

"What are you doing?" I ask her. I know what I wish she was doing.

"Give me your cousin's number. I'll get the intel."

"The intel?"

"The tea. The gossip. Or do people still say... the 411?"

"Careful," I grumble, "More of your age jokes and I'll show you just how much of a curmudgeon I can be."

She drags the phone off the hook as she approaches me and plants a kiss on my forehead.

"You're already a curmudgeon, Uncle Lou."

I lunge to catch her. Tisha shrieks and returns to the phone, sashaying out of reach. I give up and lean back before reciting the numbers. Tisha calls and puts on a convincing "dumb girl" voice, telling Geo that her friend Carlotta *promised* this was her number. Geo's English isn't perfect, and he seems to think getting louder makes his English more comprehensible.

"Three days. I have Carlotta. Three days! Enough on the phone!"

He hangs up on her. Tisha shrugs and sticks her thumbs into the waist of her underwear.

"There you have it."

"Fuck," I snarl, "it takes days to get a boat ready to go that far. Mine are all tied up in... business."

I think better than telling an eighteen-year-old too many details about what my family does.

"We could drive."

I stiffen.

"What?"

"You know. We could take a car."

"I can't *drive* to Sicily. It's a twenty-hour drive."

Tisha rolls her eyes. I hate when she does that.

"I could drive twenty hours," she says.

"That's ridiculous."

"Um... I'm American. We drive three hours to go to a better Target."

Half the words out of Tisha's mouth confuse me.

"Target?"

"It's a store."

"Hm."

She brags, happy to be useful and adorable as she smiles, "Give me a car, I'll drive it."

"I can't make you drive twenty hours to Sicily."

"Why not? Have Stavros and Fallon meet us there by boat. Sure, they'll have a delay, but at least we can save Carlotta from your freak cousin."

I snort.

"You would make good mafia."

"I know," Tisha says proudly, "I always wanted to be a mob wife."

I glare at her.

"What the hell is a mob wife, Tisha?"

"Um... it's an amazing reality show. I always imagined a rich mob husband..."

"Most girls dream of Prince Charming," I mutter to myself. Carlotta dreamed of hanging her Barbie dolls and boiling them alive. I suppose I shouldn't have let Yiayia babysit her when she was in preschool.

Tisha's voice gets soft and I yearn to get close to her, "I dreamed about you, Uncle Lou. From the first time I saw your picture on Carlotta's desk. I thought you were her boyfriend."

I freeze as she rests her hands on my shoulders. I want her body against mine. I want to join with her. I want to hold her.

"We should go," I murmur. Fuck. Why do I always have to be the responsible one?

"I know," she says softly, "But I wanted you to know that you had the most hypnotic blue eyes. And I wouldn't care if you were my age or a hundred. I'd still have fallen for you."

My heart cracks into a million pieces. She wanted me. Right when I had my chance with her, I blew it and now this beautiful woman will slip from my grasp and all I have left of her is the child from the pregnancy I purchased. A lump catches in my throat and my voice emerges like a croak.

"I'll call my guys downstairs in the lobby and keep a lookout. Will you be okay up here?"

"Yup."

"Great. You can watch the television."

"I wonder if they have mob wives re-runs," she says, flopping back on the bed and letting her shirt ride up. The pulsing in my chest quickens as I notice the tiniest baby bump. I walk outside, gasping for fresh air as I call Stavros. Fallon picks up, giggling.

"Hello, Loukas. Stavros can't come to the phone right now."

I groan. They're always busy. Stavros is fussy about this baby. He built a crib with his bare hands after an anxiety fueled night panicking over dropping a baby Fallon hasn't given birth to.

"I need to talk to him."

I hear Stavros bellowing in the background, "Pregnancy sex, Loukas! Can't get enough of it."

"Stavros!" Fallon chides. I hear her whacking him with something. Unfortunately, it isn't enough to render him unconscious as punishment for making me think of him having sex with his pregnant fiancée.

"It's serious, Fallon. Carlotta's gone. Yiayia has her and I think she's taking her to Geo."

Stavros makes an enraged sound like a growl.

"She did *what*?"

"Tisha stowed away and I have her. She's safe for now, but we don't have time to get the boats ready for a trip to Sicily. Tisha's going to drive. I need you to meet me there by boat. As fast as you can. And have Sandros get a car ready for me at the villa."

"We'll do it!" Fallon yells, "I'll call the docks to have the boat ready."

Stavros snarls and snatches the phone from her.

"My *pregnant* wife won't be coming. But I'll be there. She could pop at any minute. I won't have my baby born in fucking Sicily."

Fallon protests, her favorite hobby aside from her "case study," of our family, and says, "Pop at any minute? I'm not a rump roast, Stavros. I'm going to Italy."

"No, you're not, woman!"

I hang up. I don't have time for their petty arguments. Tisha's still upstairs and we need to leave. I hurry upstairs and get Tisha ready to leave. She's quiet on the boat ride to Thessaloniki. I don't know how I'll act with her once we get home. I don't know what my brother or Fallon will say. I pull her close to me and she rests her head on my chest. Holding her close feels better than anything. I don't want to stop holding her.

"I'm such a little kid," she whispers.

As I hold her, the last thing I'm thinking is how similar she is to a child. She's a woman. And she's growing another human being inside her. My baby. A lump catches in my throat again. Fatherhood chokes me up. It's that way for most men. Except Papa, who never had much of an instinct for anything that involved movement.

"You are not a little kid," I murmur, pushing hair away from her face and kissing her. I don't want to hurt her again, yet holding her against me only makes me want her. Wanting her makes me hard and... I ought to listen.

Tisha's hands tease my shirt open and she rests her bare palm on my chest before saying, "I always do something immature to push you away," she says, "I'm sorry."

Tisha rubs her body against mine. I tell myself that this time, when we walk off the boat, I'll tell people we're seeing each other. I won't keep her a secret any longer. I can't protect her from everything.

"What on earth are you talking about?"

"Telling you all that stuff about your picture and your eyes. It was stupid, sentimental bullshit. You're forty. You don't want to be a part of my teenage love story. It's the reason you ended things with me before. I'm not grown up enough."

Her voice cracks. And her heart breaks in front of me as I realize the truth. Tisha West never stopped loving me. And I've never stopped loving her. But I hurt her. The last night I had her in my arms, I hurt her so much that she can't let me in again. I've ruined things.

TWENTY-SIX
MY SINS AGAINST HER

3 MONTHS AGO

My routine when she arrives fills me with lustful anticipation. I know it's wrong, but I enjoy the hunt. The girls separate at night and when my daughter's bedroom door locks, I sneak into Tisha's room. It's not sneaking, really. She knows I'm coming. When she wants me, she's naked. And wet.

When she's pulling away, she wears a satin pink nightgown that clings to her. I beg her. Or command her. And Tisha obeys. Tonight, I'm clearheaded for once and when I wait for her to go to bed, I don't hurry in to have my way with her because this will be the last time.

It's like she knows. When I push the door open, she's standing there, fully clothed with her arms folded. I stick my hands into my pockets and shut the door behind me, turning the lock.

I say simply and quickly what I mean to say, "We have to stop. *I* have to stop."

"I love you, Loukas. I don't want you to stop," she says, like life is that simple.

We don't always get what we want.

"Listen, Tisha. I'm your best friend's father. This could never work. I don't care for you the way you care for me. You were right about me. I had monstrous thoughts about you and I waited to act on them. I'm exactly as terrible as you think."

"I don't believe you," she says, pouting.

I'm weak every time she looks upset, but I have to steel myself and commit. This is the last thing I want: to lose her. But I'm an old man who has already failed all three of his children. I don't want to risk having another child with her and fail that child too. I've been mostly sober for the past four weeks. I quit wine a week ago. And I see with perfect clarity that even if I don't want to believe the words I'm saying to her: they're true. I'm a monster for caressing her and spilling my seed between her legs.

"I don't care if you believe me. You will obey me. Has my daughter told you what I do?"

She shakes her head.

"I kill people. I've killed men. I've killed women. My family is dangerous and I'm the worst. Fatherhood has settled me, but I am not interested in an Oxford graduate with a bright future ahead of her. You're young. You're beautiful. Find another man."

"I don't want to find another man," she argues.

"Damn it, Tisha. I'm trying to do this. We are over. Done. Understood?"

"I hate you," she seethes.

"Good."

Her eyes well with tears.

"How could you treat me like this? If you were going to break my heart, you should have never kissed me!"

"I kissed you because you were there," I lie, "And because I knew you'd let me."

Her face falls. I've hurt her because I've verbalized her biggest fears. That she isn't special to me. But of course, she's special. Every time Carlotta needed her, Tisha took care of her. She never let my daughter down. And when my daughter strayed too far, Tisha was always there for me to help me get her back. She's the only woman I've ever met who genuinely loves my daughter. She doesn't care what Carlotta does. She'll never abandon her friend. And to me, that makes Tisha the most beautiful woman in the world. It's not about her age. Or her body. And it's not about her skin color either.

She's got the biggest heart of anyone I've ever known, heart sorely lacking in my family of murderers and psychopaths.

"That's not true. You *like* me. You... *love* me."

"You're a foolish little girl," I snarl, "I would never fall in love with someone so childish. I want you to grow up, Tisha. Stop coming here and waiting around for me to love you back because I won't."

She strides across the room and slaps me. Hard. I grab her forearm and whirl her around, pushing her up against the door.

"Never hit me again," I whisper, "Or else..."

"Or else what?"

My heart pounds. It's over. I have to make myself Loukas Pagonis, a terrifying killer from the Pagonis family.

"Or else, I will fuck you and put you on a plane back to London. You will never see me again."

"I hate —

I stop her from finishing her sentence with a kiss. She's trembling when I pull away. I want her. More than anything.

"Tell me, little woman... what do you hate?"

Her thighs clench together, and I imagine the moisture between them and get hard. Extremely hard.

"What do you hate?" I repeat.

"You," she sneers.

"That's the problem, isn't it? You don't hate me at all. But after tonight, little woman... you'll hate me a lot."

I kiss her again and let go of her wrist. Instead of pushing me off or pulling away, she wraps her arms around me and digs her fingers into my hair. Her jewelry catches on my hair, tugging it as she kisses me madly. The pain makes me want her more. I lift her off the ground and instinctively, Tisha wraps her thighs around me. Her hands move to my shoulders and she braces herself as I slam her against the wall, holding her still with my hips.

"Give me your ass," I say, "*Willingly.*"

Tisha's brown eyes widen like a doe's.

"My ass?"

"I want to fuck it."

She squirms uncomfortably but only ends up grinding her damp crotch into the member growing erect in my trousers. Her breath is warm as she pants nervously before whispering, "You can't fit that in there."

"I can," I snarl, "And I plan to."

"Loukas... I've never done that. People don't do that."

"I'll go slow," I murmur, "Start with a finger."

"You're going to put your finger in my booty hole?"

"That's all I want from you tonight," I whisper, "Your ass... and your obedience."

I watch the hairs on her neck stand up as I whisper. I kiss the gooseflesh until it subsides into her smooth walnut-colored flesh.

"I love you, Loukas," she whimpers, "I love you."

I press her harder against the wall and sink my teeth into her neck, just enough to exert pressure and control, but not enough to hurt her. She freezes like a hare, but can't still her racing heart.

"No," I say to her, "You don't. Tell yourself every day until you make it true. And remember..."

I grab her ass cheek until she screams, "Remember how I used you tonight... mercilessly."

She's heartbroken. I close my eyes and kiss her to stop myself from witnessing the heartbreak on her face and knowing I caused it. I raise the pink nightgown over her hips and flick her piercing with my thumb. I'll have her ass tonight, but then I'll cum inside her one last time. I've never been good at goodbyes.

Using my fingers, I get her wet, forcing Tisha to orgasm repeatedly as I ready her for my cock. I slowly slide between her legs, fucking her against the wall until she's soaked with her own juices as they dribble down her thighs and create a darkened damp spot on her nightgown. She screams and grabs onto me, her tiny fingers grabbing onto lengths of my chocolate brown hair as I plunge into her eighteen-year-old tightness. Her breasts press against my chest as I thrust even deeper into her. Those small nipples rubbing against my muscular chest nearly push me over the edge. I withdraw my cock and she wraps her ankles around me, keeping me still. No. I can't cum inside her... not yet.

I set her down when I'm ready to burst... *and ready for her ass.*

"Loukas," she whispers, "I can't... it's too big for my ass..."

"Turn around," I snarl. I push her up against the wall. She braces herself with her palms as I hurriedly raise her nightgown and slide a dry finger between her cheeks to touch the outside of her hole. She squeals in terror, thinking I'll shove the entire dry digit into her virgin ass. Once I've found the tiny hole, I'll slide my cock into, veins bulge eagerly from my erection. I need to get her ass wet... *now...*

I spread her ass cheeks apart and slide my tongue between them. She yelps and presses her body against the wall. I lick from her puckered back door all the way back to her pussy. Fuck. Every bit of her smells good. Her cunt drips like a fresh pomegranate and she shivers as I run my tongue up her thighs until I find her folds again and lick my way around those. My lips fasten around her lower lips and my tongue juts out, tasting her and licking her to a heady climax. She's whimpering and soaked, at my mercy in every sense of the word when I stand and squirt more lube onto her puckered asshole. My finger dives into the hole, slowly stretching her.

Tisha yelps. Her ass accepts my finger easily after the first thrust forward. She's frozen, uncertain what to make of it and whimpering. I press my body against hers and kiss her shoulder.

"Does it feel good?"

"Y-yes…"

"I love fucking a woman's ass," I whisper, "That's what I am, little woman, a monster who enjoys fucking your tight ass with my finger."

She moans and her cunt dribbles over her thighs more as I move my finger around in her satiny heat. It's *so tight*. She's right to fear how I'll get my cock in there. Tisha squeals as I withdraw my finger slightly and then press it into her ass, taking her deep.

"It's… *big*."

"And that's only my finger," I growl into her ear, "Spread your legs for my Tisha. I want to watch it disappear into your tight hole."

Her cheek presses harder against the wall. She sticks her hips out so my finger gets a better angle to move inside her hole. She's nearly ready. I drop to my knees again and lick her dripping rosebud to another orgasm while I take her perfect ass with my finger. She moans as I run my tongue over her clit and work her to the end. I slowly slip my sopping finger out of her. Her smell fills the room. If this will be our last night together, I'll make it worth both of our time. My hardness strains from my trousers, hard and angry with lust for her. I rip my pants down just beneath my ass and press the tip of my cock between her cheeks. The enormous mushroom head presses against her puckered hole.

This is her last time to plead with me for mercy. But I don't know if I'm capable of mercy at this point. The wetness and the heat pulsing from my dick enslave me entirely to my desires.

"Was this part of your teenage love story?" I snarl at her. Tisha squeezes her eyes shut.

"Do it," she whispers, "I trust you."

Fuck… she knows how to toy with me. Just when I'm trying to prove to her how monstrous I am. I brace myself against the wall, squeezing her body against it as I slide the first hard inch into her forbidden hole. Tisha gets incredibly wet from my first movement, but she cries out because... well. It's an eleven inch cock. All the preparation in the world can't *fully* prepare any woman for the filling experience of a giant eleven-inch Greek dick sliding into any of their holes.

"It hurts, doesn't it?" I snarl, "Loving me?"

She nods and whimpers, "More..."

I slide another inch inside her. Tisha cries out. This connection is more forbidden than any we've had. My heart pounds with anticipation of filling her with my cock, giving her every inch of pleasure and taking all I can from her before I let her go. A goodbye to remember. I kiss her neck, slowing down as my cock stretches her ass with the first few inches, preparing her to take the rest of the rigid staff. She tilts her head down so I can kiss more of her neck. I use my teeth and she cries out, "Uncle Lou!", mostly from surprise.

Hot shame courses through me... she's calling me *that name* with my dick nearly buried in her ass. I submit to my desire for her and grunt as I plunge the remaining inches of my dick deep into Tisha West's perfect, round ass. She cries out loudly and for a moment struggles to get away.

I hold her.

"Shh," I murmur, "The pain will go away. Let me pleasure you, little woman, while you wait."

I reach forward and rub her clit as I hold her, sending surges of pleasure through her young, tight body as I wait for her ass to adjust to the dick buried in it. With each breath, I feel her body moving and I'm *inside her.* Every shallow breath and movement she makes travels up the length of my shaft. She tilts her hips backward and I nearly erupt inside her. The tight backdoor grasps my cock firmly. I withdraw my hips slightly as I kiss her.

"Feel better?"

"Yes..." she whispers.

"You're going to cum," I tell her, "But tomorrow, it'll hurt."

"I don't care," she whispers.

I plunge into her again. She moans. I can't control myself anymore. I'm done going slow with her. My hands grip her waist, firmly controlling her movements as I use her ass. It's so tight that each thrust threatens to draw out a deep orgasm. Within a few moments, Tisha responds to the pleasure coming from her ass. As my cock moves between her legs, her thighs spread apart lewdly, and she moans *differently* with each thrust, yelping loudly. When I move my hips and plunge even deeper, her cries get louder. She cums — hard. I groan and collapse my weight onto her, pumping my hips faster.

My cock in her ass drives her mad. She lets me *use* her and cums every time I push harder and deeper into her. When I feel myself about to burst, I push her against the wall and finish inside her. She cries out louder as my cum fills her ass. Thick spurts of cum drip from the hole once I remove myself. She whimpers and settles from her tiptoes onto flat feet. She touches her ass cheek and winces as even contact with the soft cheek aches. I'm not finished with her.

"Get on the floor," I snarl, "I want you on all fours."

She obediently positions herself on the floor and doesn't dare look up at me. I touch her ass from behind and groan. This is... *tempting*. I want to have her ass again as my cock grows to another impossible level of arousal. It's about time I learn about denying myself my darker fantasies. I slide into her wetness and she collapses. I fuck her against the floor until she cums several times and then I cum inside her young pussy, watching cum drip from both her holes as I get up, too quickly, leaving her on the floor to catch her breath.

"That was..." she struggles to find the words as she stretches her body and rises to her feet.

"That wasn't love," I snarl before she can finish, "that was a reminder that I was never your teenage fantasy. I've always been a monster. It's over, Tisha. You're too young for me, and that's final. I'm leaving you here tonight. Don't follow."

"But Loukas..." she pleads, "I let you do... I *love* you."

I draw myself up to make eye contact with her. *To lie to her.*

Because this is the only way to set her free. Lying to her and pushing her away so she has a chance at happiness with someone *normal,* who isn't a murderous mobster.

"I don't love you," I tell her, "I never did. You were always my prey and now there's nothing left for me to chase."

I leave her room and pretend I don't hear her burst into tears.

TWENTY-SEVEN
FISH SANDWICH

We sail back to Thessaloniki. The water's a perfect shade of blue and the breeze catches in my hair. It's a perfect day for fishing. I've never taken Tisha fishing. She stands at the bow, letting the rocking guide her movements.

I'm half-scared she'll fall overboard, but she doesn't seem nervous. The wind whips her hair around her beautiful, brown-skinned face. She has the *cutest* heart-shaped face. Wanting her always made me feel so dirty. Breaking her heart feels worse. And that's what I did. I broke her heart so badly and she *still loves me.*

I don't deserve this young woman's love after what I said to her... after the things I did to her bottom.

Tisha's starving again by the time we get back to Thess. It's only been an hour, but she claims her stomach is growling.

"Loukas," she says, tugging on my shirt sleeve, "I need something to eat."

"You just ate."

"I'm pregnant. I'm eating for two. And *our* baby wants a fish sandwich."

"Oh, it's 'our baby' now, is it?" I respond gruffly.

"Yes," she snaps, "Until I get my fish sandwich. Then it can *shut up* and go back to being your baby."

"I think that baby is far too small for you to feel it moving," I mutter.

Tisha pats her stomach and hisses, "Mama. Needs. Fish. Sandwich."

I glare at her and she winks. I ended our conversation briskly last time and she's still uncertain. I realized that she still loves me, but I'm acting like I don't know. Like I can't tell. She's young and naïve enough to think she can fool me. That she can hide it. Deciding my next move would be easier if she didn't care for me like this. I remind myself that feelings don't matter. There's one good reason we can't be together. My daughter.

I stop at the first café off the docks and pay €13 for a fish sandwich thanks to Tisha whining in her American accent and accruing an unofficial 'foreigner tax' on the slab of fish in moist bread. As I gruffly hand over the change, she kisses me and whispers thank you. My chest tightens. This little woman has utter control over me. But not complete control. She eats the sandwich while I walk back to the docks. It's hard for Tisha to keep up with my long stride, but she's getting faster. Not one to let the source of her endless sandwiches wander out of sight.

Sandros ought to be here with a car by now. I sit on a bench and Tisha sits next to me. She's close. Too close. I lean over and nearly kiss her when I hear the vehicles pulling into the parking lot. I move a few inches away from her and Tisha scowls. Sandros gets out of the driver's seat and tosses me the keys. Fallon and Stavros emerge from the back, arguing. What the hell are they doing here? My heart pounds as I reckon they've figured out that I've... been with Tisha. If Fallon knew I got her pregnant, she'd drag me out to sea and shoot me herself, most likely.

I'm impatient with my brother and his bursting fiancée, telling them, "What are you doing here?"

"We're getting the boats ready," Fallon says.

Then she lets out a groan and bends her back in an odd stretch, like she's ready to burst. The weight of her stomach nearly topples her over. Is this woman certain she isn't having twins? Stavros' eyes nearly pop out of his head. He rushes to grab the small of her back.

"Is the baby coming?"

"For the *last* time, the baby isn't coming. I ate too many pepper wings."

Stavros snarls, "I told you all these spices would hurt the baby."

"The baby is the one who wants the spices!" Fallon yells, perhaps louder than the situation called for, "And ghost peppers aren't even that hot! We need Trinidadian food."

"What do you want me to do? Sail to Trinidad?!"

"Maybe!"

"Spoiled woman," Stavros grumbles, but there's a hint of his smile on his face. Love. Bliss.

Stavros kisses his wife's forehead and leaves her to amble forward with Sandros' help. Tisha continues eating her sandwich. My brother approaches me and puts a gun in my hand, "Take this in the car. Four bullets. Use them well."

"Four bullets? I didn't realize you'd implemented rations."

"You won't get over the border by car if you're too heavily armed. I doubt your cottage has ammunition after your last weekend there."

I got drunk and fired all my rounds at our gun range. He's right. I'm dangerously low on ammo. Stavros pats my shoulder and turns his attention to Carlotta's friend, "Twenty hours of driving? Up for it, Tisha?"

Tisha's *terrified* of Stavros. The fish sandwich forms a large bolus in her throat as she nods nervously and then swallows, nearly choking. Stavros chuckles and pats me on the back.

"Look after your daughter's friend."

I grasp Stavros' forearm. *He knows.*

"Keep this between us," I murmur, "Fallon will kill me."

Fallon hobbles over to me and pushes Stavros out of the way. She leans in and hisses into my ear, "I know what you're hiding, Loukas. Shame on you."

Great. So much for keeping a secret from her. Those two are obsessed with chittering away their little couples' gossip. I want to gag, but they're... cute. If you're into romantic couples who can't keep their hands off each other. But Fallon gets me. Sometimes.

I tell her, "We should talk, sister."

"Let her go," Fallon whispers, "She's too young."

My cheeks burn and I pray Tisha didn't hear a word. How would it hurt her for people to look at her with disdain? For me...

Sandros helps Fallon over to the boat so she can guide the men to prepare it. Stavros salutes as he follows her, yelling at Sandros over his improper grasp of his wife's waist. Tisha licks her fingers from the chicken sandwich.

"What did she say to you?"

"Nothing."

"It didn't look like nothing," Tisha grumbles.

"Not everyone will approve of a man my age with a woman like you. People will say things. Every day for the rest of our lives. They'll talk. You might not understand what impact that will have. But it could cost you. Friends. Respect. They'll judge you."

"I don't care what Fallon thinks," she snaps, "You're the one who cares about that."

"What do you care about then? Because you don't care that baby. You don't care about anything except partying and sex. And you're young, I understand. But I can't look at a living creature and abandon it. That's the difference between our ages. You aren't ready for a child and I would do anything to relive fatherhood from scratch..." I can feel my voice shaking with rage, "I could start over and do it right this time. And then my daughter or son wouldn't gallivant to the ends of the earth because I would have been ready. This time... I'm ready."

Tisha stares at me and I put the keys in her palm forcefully before storming over to the passenger seat. The gun burns a hole in my pocket. I want target practice. Or hunting. Something to take my mind off the rage. The embarrassment. And my selfishness for putting Tisha in this position. They'll all think I *bought* her. That I purchased her for pregnancy or worse perversions. But at offering to pay her tuition, that's what I did. She's here for money, I remind myself. My scowl deepens.

The backseat has duffel bags packed from Tisha's room and mine. I scowl and face the windshield as she enters the car.

"Ready," she says softly, "I'm ready to go to Sicily and get my friend back."

"Have at it."

She glances at the GPS before pulling out of the driveway and onto the narrow streets. She's used to getting behind the wheel here when Carlotta's too drunk to drive, I realize.

She navigates the streets of Thessaloniki like she belongs here. But for the first five minutes, she's crying. After we leave the city for the highway, I ask her, "What's wrong?"

She whispers, "I don't want to give up my baby, Lou."

TWENTY-EIGHT
100 KM/H

want to *hold* her, but she's driving and nearly hitting the 100km/h speed limit with ease.

"Careful," I mutter, "Try not to kill us all."

She wipes tears from her eyes and swerves. My heart jumps into my throat.

"Sorry," Tisha whispers, "I'm acting like a big baby. This is why I shouldn't have a kid. I'll give it to you and he or she will be rich and fabulous... and I don't need to be a part of that."

But I want her to be a part of that. It's what I've always wanted from her. To keep her here.

"It's not foolish," I tell her, "Every mother goes through something like this. You feel you aren't ready. I have three kids. Trust me."

"That's the problem," she whispers, "you're an expert at parenting and I... I'm selling my baby to a Greek man in his forties."

She sobs in only the way pregnancy hormones can stimulate, her eyes precariously darting from the road. She can keep this up for twenty hours, but I'm not sure I can. Her driving scares the shit out of me, but when I offer to drive, she puffs out her chest and gets much scarier than an eighteen-year-old should.

"We'll stop in a couple hours," I tell her, "To stretch our legs and to check my pulse..."

"Everyone drives *so* slowly here," Tisha complained. Never a complaint I've heard about Greece. The young woman's mad. She stops crying when I put on that teenager radio station Carlotta loves so much. I still worry constantly about Carlotta and what Yiayia has planned for her. And as for Stavros... I ought to blame him. Only Fallon's the best ally against Yiayia because Yiayia respects her. Fallon nearly *shot* her, which surprised me. What surprised me more was the lack of subsequent assassination attempts. To us, she's our wicked grandmother, but to our Italian cousins, she's their sweet Greek great-aunt. In a world where my grandmother's sweet, I'd hate to find out what counted as bitter.

We stop after a couple hours. I try not to nod off, but fail miserably, prompting Tisha to experiment with her vocal abilities while driving. She's a beautiful woman, but her voice is anything but. After screeching like a horny tom cat to *Halo* by Beyoncé, I clear my throat and open a warning blue eye. At our stop, Tisha yawns.

"Phew! I need some *coke!*"

"*Drugs* while pregnant?"

I can feel heat rising in my chest. I'm ready to overreact.

"Like... the soda," she says slowly, like I'm stupid.

"Right. Well, that's not great for a baby either..."

"Whatever. I'm going into that shop."

She struts away with her perfect legs and her even better ass. She's... *everything*. I bite my lower lip and stare at her as she enters the store. There's a man selling jewelry at a table a few feet down. He has some bagged fruit on a stand. I approach him and point to a blue evil eye necklace.

"How much for that one?"

"Pagonis?" he asks.

Even two hours outside of Thessaloniki, people recognize us. I wave him off.

"Never mind."

I'm not in the mood to inspire fear today.

"For you, €50. I lost a bet to your fucking father back when he played cards. Lost everything, now I sell jewelry. So for you, double."

I have my doubts about the truth of his story, but I grin and give him €50, which seems overpriced for a bit of glass on leather. He'll probably brag about it to the men at the bar later and buy them a round of vodka. Tisha hurries out of the store and comes over to me.

"I got you something," she says.

"Oh?"

I clutch the necklace in my hand and hide it behind my back as she drags her cloth bag of road trip essentials to the vehicle.

"Fresh pomegranate."

She sticks it out to me and says, "Here you go, Hades."

"Hm," I mutter gruffly, "And I suppose you're Persephone, allowing me to drag you down to hell?"

"I've always hated Italy," she teases. Maybe she'll fit in with my family fine. Stavros hates Italy too. And after the incident when he was fifteen, Galanos has a lifelong ban from the country which he flagrantly disregards when traveling by sea.

Once we're back in the car, I hand her the necklace.

"I got you something too."

She takes it without looking and then gasps when she opens her palm.

"It's *so* pretty."

"Maybe I'm the evil you need protecting from, but... I figure you could use some protection."

Tisha glances over at me and starts the car. She takes the necklace off her thigh and slips it around her neck, adjusting the pendant.

"You're not evil, Loukas," she says, "We're just in a *really* weird predicament."

"I know," I murmur, "And your baby... you can see your child whenever you'd like. Our child. It's not my right to stop you from living the life you want so I can be a father again."

"I don't want to do it alone," Tisha says softly, "But you made it clear how you felt about me. Even if you say you've changed... you broke my heart."

"I did things to you I'm ashamed of."

"The sex stuff?"

Yes, the sex stuff. I used her. I was rough and crude.

"Yes."

"Loukas... you made me realize... maybe I like it rough."

She steps on the gas and I clear my throat, covering my crotch with my palms in a manner that may not be as entirely subtle as I think.

"No," I say, trying to be responsible, "You can't know that. I broke your spirit, and I broke your heart. And you're right. It doesn't matter if I love you now."

"Or if I love you," she says.

We glance over at each other and then Tisha hastily turns her attention to the road.

"But," I say, giving in to how much I feel for her, "If we wanted to end up together, we'd have to tell people."

"Carlotta would find out anyway," Tisha admits, "But when she does, she'll never talk to me again. You won't choose me over your daughter."

"Both," I say, "Why can't I have both?"

We both know the answer. I'm hoping love will change, but it won't, will it? Love doesn't mean your responsibilities vanish.

"We're best friends, Uncle Lou. I know Carlotta won't accept us. Because we lied. We betrayed her."

"What was I meant to do? Tell her I kissed her seventeen-year-old friend? Honesty hasn't been easy for me because it exposes me for what I really am."

She responds to my bitterness with silence. Tisha's smart — nearly an Oxford graduate — and she considers every word that I've said.

"I kissed you back," Tisha says, "And I'm her best friend. I know how protective she is of you. And I know something else I haven't mentioned... something Carlotta wouldn't want me to tell you."

I don't want to probe her because a part of me has no wish to know my daughter's secrets. I know too many of them. And they all expose my failures as a father.

"What is it?"

"She told me she killed Matilda. I just... I wanted to see if you'd tell me the truth. And Carlotta wanted to know if you'd keep her secret."

They *conspired*.

"Is there anything else you're keeping from me?"

"Listen, I'll take Carlotta's secret to the grave. And so would you. That's why I know, you'll never tell her about us. And I can't either. We love her too much."

"We also love each other. And this child..."

"Please, Loukas. Do right by our kid. When I'm far away from here, that's what I want. Because I won't turn your life upside down again. I won't hurt my best friend."

TWENTY-NINE
VLORË, ALBANIA

We make our next stop at dark in Vlorë, Albania where we'll catch the ferry in the morning and drive the rest of the way. Tisha's exhausted. I park the car at a fancy hotel right on the water, *Hotel Vlora International*.

The place is modern, but simple accommodations right above the water. Once we're there, Tisha begs to climb into bed, but I insist on dinner. She's hardly eaten and her 'snacks' aren't enough for eating for two. We order fruits toast with warm honey and butter, which Tisha willingly eats.

"We can only sleep a few hours. Four hours until the next ferry."

"So no sex," she says, stuffing a kiwi slice into her mouth. Her tongue sticks out, running over her full lips and giving me an instant boner. It's like being a teenager again around her. Hard. Always. She sucks the kiwi juice off her fingers. I clear my throat and struggle to remain focused on anything that's not Tisha's lips. Or her cheeks. Or her body.

I take fatherly responsibility and say to her, "You're far too tired, you need to sleep if you're going to drive."

"I can sleep on the ferry. Stop acting like my dad."

She's tempestuous when she's tired. Another teenage trait. I put my hand on her lower back and lean over to kiss her.

"Sex," I whisper, once I've planted a wet kiss on her cheek, "Is that what you're thinking about?"

I kiss her on the lips, and she pulls away.

"Stop it, Loukas," she hisses. I think my sudden change in behavior takes getting used to. She's nervous, having me claim her. I kiss her again. An old woman tuts. I put my hand on Tisha's thighs and kiss her like I mean it.

I'm taking her upstairs after this, and everyone will know with no doubt that this is not my daughter. I kiss her neck and murmur into her ear, "If we're going to make this public... we ought to get used to staring."

She rolls her eyes.

"Sleep," she says, "I'll sleep."

I take her to the room and in the end, we're both too tired to do much but sleep. She curls up in the crook of my arm and I wrap my body around hers, placing my hand possessively on her stomach, which protrudes gently. I set an alarm so we can get to the ferry on time, and we catch critical sleep before the evening ferry. I pay our bills and Tisha drives. We unload the car and walk above deck. There's another ferry to Sicily after a few hours of driving across the Italian coast. We find seats eventually and Tisha leans her head on mine. She eventually falls asleep again.

The ferry across the Ionian sea rocks and sways. I used to get seasick when I was a boy — before any of the others were born. Papa taught me how to swim by throwing me into the Aegean sea in November. The story goes, I swam back to shore and didn't show up at the villa again for another five days. I don't remember five days. I remember wanting to scare him and teach him a lesson. He tanned my hide. I still have scars on my lower back. Tisha wakes up after a few hours and kisses my cheek.

"G'morning."

"Not quite," I grumble. It's dark out and lights from the ship reflect off the water. I love the smell of the sea and I want to wrap my arms around Tisha as we watch the waves together.

"Let's watch the water," she whispers.

She slips her hand in mine and we walk to the railing. She inhales sharply and turns to me.

"I love Greece, Loukas. I could live there forever."

"Then live with me. We'll tell Carlotta. And I'll protect you."

"She won't forgive me," Tisha says. My daughter burns with the fire of Pagonis rage. Tisha has a point there. We aren't a forgiving sort. We hold on to grudges, exact revenge, and kill anyone who gets in our way. Carlotta killed my last girlfriend.

"My daughter loves as hard as I do. She's never had many friends aside from Antonio and Galanos. She doesn't trust people outside of our family. But she trusts you," I say, "She'll trust your judgment."

"We *lied* to her," Tisha replies.

"I know. And we'll live with the consequences of that lie. But Carlotta... this will be her brother or sister. Blood is more important than anything."

I pull Tisha close to me and kiss her. She kisses back. She's soft and incredible. Her skin is brown and soft and her stomach touches against my softly.

"I have to finish school, Loukas. That's my only wish."

"I only hope that when you're finished, you let me marry you. If we do this together, I won't have you unmarried."

"Don't I get a say?"

"No," I say, "I'm forty. I can't have a girlfriend who is... an actual girl."

She wriggles away and rolls her eyes.

"That's old-fashioned."

"Exactly," I say, "I'm *old school*. Surprised it hasn't turned you off me yet."

She groans like I've said something embarrassing, but then she draws me close again. Her hand touches my chest and the other drapes over my trousers in an undaughterly way.

"Carlotta's going to kill me," she whispers.

"No," I murmur, "I won't let her. If I can protect Carlotta, I can protect my unborn child too."

"Do you regret this?" she asks.

I force her to look me in the eye.

"I could never regret you."

"That last night," she whispers, "the way you used my ass... I thought... I thought you were punishing me for tempting you."

"How on earth did you tempt me?"

"I *tried* to seduce you," Tisha says, as if this had been obvious, "I always wanted to wear the skimpiest bikinis. I never dressed like that at school."

My throat catches. Those skimpy little bikinis worked. But she'd still been seventeen when I wanted her. I shouldn't have even *looked*.

"You didn't tempt me," I tell her, "I'm responsible for my actions."

"But you looked," Tisha says, confident in her analysis of me, "You enjoyed looking at me. I didn't know men could genuinely like looking at you without comparing you to some model on Instagram or some airbrushed actress. You aren't like guys my age. You don't look at me and compare me to every other girl my age."

I chuckle.

"I'm no angel, little woman. You weren't mine to touch, but I'm entitled, rich, and I've always had exactly what I wanted."

Tisha shakes her head.

"And you're so much more," she tells me, "You're a father who's lost every woman he loved. Carlotta talked about you all the time. You're her beloved *papa*. I think I fell in love with you before I met you because of how much she told me."

"I'd like to know what else my daughter reports about her *beloved papa*."

I often have a hard time believing Carlotta thinks of me as anything other than a bank account. But we have genuine moments. And I would die for her. I'd give up everything for her. I hope she doesn't ask. Because if my daughter asks me to give up Tisha... I try not to think about it because Tisha recounts Carlotta's favorite stories about me. She told Tisha about my bank robbery arrest when I was fifteen. Those mugshots are on Yiayia's wall.

My daughter told her friend about my first wedding. My best friend Antonio died at the altar because my Italian cousin Vinnie poisoned his vodka flask for sleeping with his wife. We didn't call the coroners until after the party and supposedly was the night everyone single in Thessaloniki got lucky because Antonio was fucking half their wives. Man, my youth was crazy.

Tisha reminds me of the trip Carlotta and I took to Moscow, where the Russian mob tried to kidnap her and her brother. Antonio stole the guy's wallet, and they got away. The next day, I brought her every ring on the man's fingers and took her for ice-cream. That story didn't make me come out particularly well, but I'd been furious that they'd harm my children. By the time we get back into the car in Italy, we're better rested. And closer. We're committing to this, ultimately. We both want to end up together and it's what we'll fight for.

"We still have a long way to go," Tisha murmurs, talking about our road trip to Geo's Sicilian summer home.

"Together," I say to her. She slips her hands in mine, in agreement. Tisha rests her head on my shoulders and I never want to leave the moment because this is the first time we've admitted we feel the same way. And I can do nothing about the rush, but hold her and love her right here.

THIRTY
NO POLICE!

We arrive in Sicily in the late afternoon. We don't have long before someone reports our arrival to the Doukas family. I get Tisha out of the car and down to our cottage.

I've always kept a cottage in Sicily for emergencies like this, but one of my last nights here was the bender Stavros referenced. A difficult week of drinking indeed. I don't miss binge-drinking as much as I thought.

Helen liked to come here when she was younger so she could have her dalliances with Italian men. Thankfully, she's moved on from the bastards and spends most of her time smoking and bitterly barking out orders to the rest of us. I wonder what trouble she's been up to in Thess.

Tisha immediately opens the fridge, and she's about to plead for more food when she notices the grim expression on my face.

"I don't want you following me tonight."

Tisha closes the fridge and then opens it again before asking, "Why not?"

"Because, I might have to kill people, Tisha. And despite my daughter's confession, I hold no sympathy in my heart for those who die by my hand. You love me. You care for me. I don't want you to change that. Once Carlotta's here safely, we will tell her the truth and spend nights in bed together."

"Okie dokie," she says, sounding painfully American, "Does this place have cable? Do Italians have cable?"

She's fooled me once before I let her know I'm onto her... in case.

"Are you changing the subject so you can sneak out and commit a hare-brained rescue attempt?"

"I know what you do. I'll never rat, never snitch, I'll stay loyal. You get Carlotta back. Plus, my bones feel *raw* from sitting in the car and my tummy hurts."

Our baby... My protective emotions surge.

"Okay. I'll call the house when I have news. Don't leave. Don't unlock the doors. Can you shoot?"

"No!"

"You're American," I respond, confused again.

Tisha's eyes bug out, "That doesn't mean I know how to use a gun."

"Fine. Stay here. Don't open the door. If anything bad happens, you take that phone and hold down the number 3."

"The police?"

"NO!" I roar, perhaps too enthusiastically, "No police! But... there will be help."

"Damn, I didn't realize you hated the cops that much."

"Never cops," I hiss.

"Got it. When should I worry?"

"Don't. There's plenty of frozen food here. Just don't watch any of the VHS tapes."

"VHS tapes?"

Fuck. She's eighteen. She probably doesn't even remember cassettes. She may not have a clue what they are at all. I'll never tell her about the time I received a floppy disk of grainy scanned nude photographs. She'll laugh.

"They're videos. And don't watch them," I snap, "That's an order."

"What's on them that's so secret?"

"Nothing for your eyes."

Tisha shrugs and says, "I'm watching them the second you walk out of here."

"I'll tie you up," I threaten, cleaning the filthy gun Stavros loaned me on the counter as Tisha pops a frozen vegan burrito into the microwave. Another habit that reminds me of Carlotta. My throat catches. I need to get my daughter back. And fuck Stavros and his shitty gun. Tisha watches me clean the weapon as she waits for the burrito.

"You can't tie me up," she says, mesmerized by the weapon, "what if I pee."

"Then I guess you'll spend a long time sitting in your pee."

"That's *gross*."

"I've had three kids. You don't know gross until you experience projectile diarrhea for the first time."

"Ew!"

"Get used to it," I tell her, grinning, "When we're parents, we'll be starting from scratch. It's been years since I've done… baby stuff."

She reaches for a bullet and I swat her hand away.

"Ouch!"

"These aren't toys, Tisha. They're weapons. Be careful around guns."

"Yeah, yeah," she says, leaning on the counter peering into my eyes.

"Hm?"

"The tapes. They're sex tapes, aren't they?"

My cheeks darken.

"Yes."

"Aren't you worried about Carlotta finding them?"

"My daughter, unlike you, minds her own business with my personal possessions. And I've never brought her here. Not when she can remember, at least. We stay at the family home or on the boats."

"Wow. So it's your secret fuck pad with sex tapes and all. The mafia is *awesome*."

"We are *not* awesome," I grumble, "And you'll stay far from the tapes."

Her enthusiasm for my lifestyle worries me.

And as for the tapes. I brought them up because they're not exactly hidden. I'd forgotten until we got there. Right on display in the bedroom with the different dates. I come to the cabin alone, usually. Hence the tapes. Reminders of when I was younger and wilder.

"Can we make one?"

"Do you have a 90s camcorder lying around?"

"That was before I was born," she says, "so no."

"I'm going to hell," I grumble, replacing the four bullets Stavros sent me over the border with. I can't bring a shotgun. Geo's men will overreact, so I'll take the pistol and leave Tisha here with a shotgun that's mercifully unloaded. I'm not entirely wrong since I need to appear on Doukas property without rousing suspicions. We're family, after all. Distant. But still family. Stavros and Fallon will get here in another 12 hours, so if everything goes wrong, my brother can find Tisha. Tisha sidles up to me and kisses my cheek.

"Don't hesitate," she says, "I can handle myself. And trust me, I won't follow."

"Okay. But leave the tapes alone."

"Promise," she says.

I kiss her, fiercely.

"Tonight might be more nerve-wracking than this. We're telling Carlotta."

"Remind me to hide your guns."

"Good bye, little woman."

I kiss her, and then I leave, locking the door. She shuts the curtains as I get into the car and drive half a mile away from the

Doukas villas. They own an entire country club resort that covers over 300 acres of land. Their houses sit in the middle and they rule with impunity. As I walk onto the golf course, a friendly gardener tips his hat to me. A warning. I approach the big house and enter. There are no guards, no cause for concern. No one comes here without an invitation or a death wish. I have neither. When I open the door, there's a lazy Italian oaf on the foyer couch, a tipped bottle of tequila spills alcohol onto his bare chest. He's too drunk to notice the pool or the stench.

"Get up," I snarl, "Where is Geo Doukas?"

"Party on the patio," the boy murmurs in semi-fluent Greek. Perhaps one of my idiot cousin's children. Or nieces. Or nephews. I can't keep track of them. The Catholics have too many kids. I walk toward the patio without coming across anyone else. As I get closer, I hear that there's music. *Wedding music.*

I push the doors to the patio open. Everyone turns to look at me and they gasp. At least everyone who knows Loukas Pagonis' reputation gasps. Geo's wrapped up in himself and doesn't notice me. He stares at Carlotta, holding her body up. Her feet have no stability on the ground. She's unconscious, or near it. My chest tightens.

Geo dips my daughter Carlotta and kisses her on the mouth. Not a party: a wedding. I pull my gun out and I don't think before wasting all four bullets on Geo Doukas, who drops my daughter. She falls easily to the ground, as if she wasn't standing up on her own at all. She's immobile.

I want to run to her, but I just *killed a man.*

There's screaming, but the screaming quietly hushes when two men draw guns and point at me. The screamers either run or crouch beneath chairs. There are only two armed men here, which might have been an advantage if I had any bullets left. I didn't think before killing him. I told my daughter I'd do anything to protect her, and I mean it.

Yiayia's not here, my father's not here. They're gone. It's bittersweet. I can only hope they'll run into Stavros and Fallon, but I have bigger problems than my grandmother. I'm the lone Pagonis in a sea of vengeful Italian cousins, and I just shot Geo Doukas, related to us through Yiayia. The blood gurgling in his throat chokes him to death. He'll be dead in minutes. Carlotta's still silent. Sleeping and pale beneath the veil that fell just over face. I fight the urge to run to her.

"I have men surrounding this place," I snarl, "You shoot and this place will evaporate. I'm not here for trouble, only Carlotta."

The taller man lowers his gun and says, "You don't recognize me, Loukas?"

I shake my head. His eyes are familiar but the rest of him... he's covered in scars with a glass eye. And tall. I don't remember any of our Sicilian cousins towering over me like this.

The man holsters his gun and reintroduces himself. "Van. Giovanni Doukas. You saved me the trouble of killing a man I already wanted to kill. Guns down, everyone be calm. Everyone, welcome our Greek cousin."

Van claps and the confused guests and family clap along too because they fear Van. Everyone with common sense fears Van Doukas. He hasn't returned to his home country in over a decade for good reason. It took all the powerful mafia families to keep him out. But there must be cracks in Italy, and Giovanni Doukas slipped through.

I push past Giovanni now that I know he will not shoot, and I race to Carlotta. She's cold, but she has a pulse. She's also unconscious. Van's henchman lowers his weapon and my cousin approaches me, putting a hand on my shoulder. He's not the comforting type, last I remember. Several people died the last night I saw Van. I'm not eager to recall it.

He speaks in soft, but perfect English, "He couldn't drag her out here without copious amounts of heroin in her blood. Sal, Vinnie, Giac, get her upstairs."

I don't want them to touch her. She's fragile and lying there, unconscious. She was *barely* conscious as he held her. And *married* her. My heart races.

"What else has he done to her?"

I touch the side of Carlotta's head and wince. It's *soft*. They hurt her head and it looks bad with blood clotted in her hair and hair matted to the side of her head. This is serious. I've failed her again. *No...*

"Get her upstairs, boys. Mister Pagonis, we have much to discuss about your daughter. Marina, get the guests onto the dance floor. I want my money's worth from the D.J. Come, Lou. It's been too long."

He's right. It's been *fifteen years*. He was only a boy when I last saw him, and he's not a boy anymore. Not by a long shot.

THIRTY-ONE
CAPTIVITY

"He's had her in captivity here for two nights. He tortured her. His men beat her. I found out about Geo's wedding and came here to stop him. I wasn't far, mind you. He thought I wanted to make peace, but I'm back. Sicily will be different now."

I believed him. Giovanni could control the Doukas family. He's the only one who could. Their family has power across the Amalfi Coast all the way to Long Island. They're old Italian nobility and they look the part despite their constant trouble with the law.

"Are the police after you?" I ask him. I want to know what we're dealing with.

"They'll always be after me," Van replied with a coy smile, "But Geo has gone too far. I had to do this before heading back home. Clean up job, you know?"

Van's smile disappears as he loses himself in the past, "He *killed* the first woman I loved. I knew if he married another, he'd do worse. And I'm sorry, Loukas, but that's what he's done. Carlotta may not recover."

"I want his body," I snarl, "I don't want him to have a Catholic burial."

Van smiles again. He's a Doukas, so he's still more sociopathic than even my comfort levels allow. He agrees eagerly to give me the body.

Giovanni shrugs, "Have his corpse. I don't love Geo. He was only family until he chose to betray us. After that, he became nothing."

They live by the old mob rules. We don't need to explain what we both understand about each other. I nod and feel a strong craving for liquor that I must deny myself.

I have to check on my daughter. Giovanni takes me to her.

I glance at Carlotta, lying in the bed upstairs, her chest heaving up and down again. Yiayia did this to her. I touch her forehead through the veil and peel it back. Her eyes are closed and the bruises on her face are horrendous. Her wedding dress slips off her shoulder. One day, my daughter will have a real wedding.

"She's blind," Van says, "Geo hit her on the head yesterday and she hasn't been able to see. She's still the same person, but she lost control. I'm sorry I had to wait to ask. I remember when she was three years old, the last time I saw her."

"I'll take her back to Greece tomorrow. But call off your brother's people."

Van chuckles.

"Don't worry, Loukas. They'll fall in line or they will die."

He's an unnerving man, but I'm glad for his help. The men loyal to Geo disappear from the party, and I don't ask what happened to them. I get help to carry Carlotta to my car. Once I get her buckled in, she stirs. I freeze before starting the car. Blind. I don't want to believe it. When she opens her eyes, I'll take a proper look.

I'm still waiting for Fallon and Stavros to get here. I promised Tisha I would call, but how can I bring myself to call her and explain what's happened to my daughter? Carlotta's blindness will need more than medical attention. She doesn't know how to do anything blind. She'll need me. And then I think about Tisha. My chest caves and I want to hit something. I want to make someone else bleed. I mutter something bitter about deserving painful death. Carlotta mumbles.

"Papa… I won't do it… I need Papa!"

I reach over and touch her. She screams and scrambles away, feeling madly at the door to the car as her blue eyes gaze at nothing. She doesn't focus them because she can't see. I realize they weren't lying. My precious daughter's blind.

"It's me. It's me. I've got you."

She lunges over, her seat belt yanking her back. She scrambles for the buckle and then throws her arm around me. Carlotta cries.

"I'm blind… I can't see you… I can't…"

She collapses on my chest, and I hold her.

"I've failed you again."

"No," she whispers, "No, Papa. I always know you will be there. Am I married?"

"No," I tell her, "Geo's dead."

"Papa…"

"He hurt you."

"No," she whispers, "this is my fault."

"What?"

"Yiayia told me she would kill the men Matilda sent after me if I did her a favor."

I pull her close to me again. My breath is rough and agitated. When I see my grandmother again, it won't end well.

"Are they dead?"

She nods and whimpers.

"I didn't know how much he would hurt me. He promised not to do it. He promised it would be a marriage on paper…"

We stay there for a while until Carlotta's calm. She pulls away from me and I try to see the light in her eyes, but it's gone. Her eyes are unfocused again. Still blue, but empty. She leans back and wipes her nose.

"Tell me you didn't leave Tisha behind."

"You expected me to drag her to Sicily?"

"You're the host," Carlotta explains, "You have to take care of her."

By that my daughter means feed her and send her shopping, not what I've spent every night doing since the little minx snuck on my boat.

I sigh and tell her, "Tisha's here. At the cottage."

"What cottage?"

"My private cottage," I tell her, "You've never been there."

She'd been there as a toddler, but I didn't see the point in telling her. I didn't want to tell the complete story and think about her mother. Tisha peers out the window when she hears the car and races out, opening the door to Carlotta's side. She nearly drags Carlotta out and she hugs her tightly. *So* tightly. When she lets go, she notices.

"What happened?"

"I'm blind," Carlotta answers simply, "And I'll have to drop out of Oxford our last semester. No skinny dipping. No senior streak."

"No," Tisha says, refusing to believe it, "They didn't do that."

"*Yes,*" I say, "they did. Help me get her inside."

We help Carlotta inside and put her on the couch. She closes her eyes and leans back.

"It smells like you, Papa. This house..."

Tisha and I exchange worried glances. She didn't expect the blindness. Carlotta's condition will change things. I give Tisha a pleading expression, but she clears her throat and ignores me.

"Are you hungry?" Tisha asks her best friend.

"Yes. And sluggish. I think they've drugged me, Papa."

"They have," I murmur, "but it's worn off a bit. Should be fine once you get through the night."

"I can make a frozen burrito," Tisha says.

"No," Carlotta answers, "I want something Italian. Takeout. Please."

She's woozy and not making sense, but Tisha rushes to her aid.

"I'll go out and get it," Tisha says. She hurries outside.

"She forgot the car keys," I mutter to Carlotta, "wait here."

I burst out of the house behind Tisha and shut the door. Tisha turns to me, tears in her eyes.

"We can't tell her," She says, her voice trembling, "Please, don't make me tell her now."

"She's blind. But she's the same person. We can do it."

My voice is weak because I don't believe what I'm saying. Tisha and I can't fall in love while my daughter's world falls apart. It's not fair to Carlotta.

"Look at her! They tortured her, Loukas. Carlotta doesn't deserve that. She needs you. She needs you now more than she's ever needed you, and I'm a distraction. I can get through life on my own, but Carlotta can't anymore. She's *blind.*"

"You're carrying another one of my children," I tell her, "All my children matter to me."

"This is a fetus, Lou. Carlotta's a breathing woman and she needs you. Nothing has to change. I'll take the money and give you the kid. You don't have to choose. I'll be the responsible one. For once."

Her words hurt. I haven't been as responsible around her as she thinks. I impregnated a teenager — not exactly "careful" of me. I know she's right about ending things. We had a plan and we don't have to change it. But it's my form of denial. I don't want to face it. Geo Doukas hurt my daughter and my worst fears have come true. Eventually, I'll get old and die, and there will be no one to look after my little girl. She'll be *blind* and she won't have anyone. A lump forms in my throat.

"I love you, Tisha."

"I love you too. But we both know this isn't right. We can't put her through this now."

A pickup makes its way slowly down my driveway. Tisha wrinkles her nose.

"Who's that?"

"It's Geo Doukas' body," I grumble, stuffing the keys into her hands, "Get her the food quickly. I'll deal with the body... later."

Tisha casts a disapproving look in my direction and then disappears to get Carlotta some Italian food. I return inside to find Carlotta sleeping already. She stirs again once I come in.

"Tisha? Papa?"

"Only me."

Carlotta giggles, "Is she still scared of you?"

"I think not. But I'd rather talk about you. Does your head hurt?"

"Yes. It hurt since he slammed it into the wall. I feel like aunt Helen... I'm starting to hate men in the mafia."

I can't blame her for that.

"I hope you don't hate me. I came as soon as I could."

I sit across from her and fight powerful urges to bury my pain with copious amounts of whiskey. But I can't drink and work. Burying a body takes all your faculties, and once my daughter's fed, I'll have to handle the painful demands of that work. Doing anything that involves your back gets harder once you hit your late twenties, and it's all downhill from there.

"I know," she says, "You always do what you can to protect me, Papa. You deserve a better daughter."

"You were always so wild. I tried to tame you and it didn't work."

I touch the side of her face. Her eyes flutter shut and then open again. My beautiful daughter's lashes are long and brown. I can't help but stare at her in admiration. My baby girl... I held her. I changed her diaper. I soothed her tantrums. She's all grown up now.

"I've had time to think," she says, "I blamed you for everything. But you were the only parent I had. Mama might have been lovely, but she was always dead. You were always there. My beloved papa. You accept Antonio. You protect Zoe. You follow me to the ends of the earth when I've hurt you and betrayed you. I killed someone you loved and... I don't deserve you."

"Nonsense. You are mine to protect."

She takes my hand.

"I miss my siblings."

"I miss all of you when you're away. I miss Zoe now."

"Then get her back. I never realized why you wanted to protect me so much until now. I was foolish. But I can explain to Zoe. And you don't have to worry about me running off to party anymore."

There is a hint of sadness in her voice. And maturity.

"What about your studies?"

"I'll put them on hold. Tisha will have to go alone," Carlotta says, betraying her sadness for the first time. She can't imagine a world without her best friend. Neither can I...

Tisha returns with the food a few minutes later. Her face is red like she's been crying. When I try to put my hand on her shoulder, she brushes me off. I feel embarrassed. Carlotta can't see, but that doesn't mean I can touch Tisha in front of her.

"Tisha," Carlotta complained, "Why so quiet? I'm blind now, not boring. Close your ears, papa. Tisha, kissed any new boys?"

A sob catches in Tisha's throat.

THIRTY-TWO
PERSONAL SHOPPER

"'m sorry, Carlotta," Tisha whispers, holding my daughter's hand. Carlotta laughs. Her hand reaches out for Tisha's head to comfort her.

"Please, stop crying," Carlotta whispers, like she's comforting a kitten, "When we go out, you'll have to tell me which boys are the cute ones now."

"Right," Tisha mutters, "I'm like your personal shopper for boyfriends."

There's a hint of bitterness in Tisha's voice.

I want to tell her that there will be no more going out. But Carlotta knows that. She just doesn't want us to worry. She's made Tisha worry too much, and she knows it.

"I ought to have heard from Stavros and Fallon by now," I tell them, "I'd better go. Carlotta, Tisha will get you the phone so we can have a trustworthy doctor examine your head tomorrow. I'll check on your uncle and his pregnant fiancée. Understand?"

Carlotta makes a face at me. At least *that* hasn't changed.

"Tisha, get me a cigarette, please."

Really, I need to get rid of Geo Doukas and I don't want my daughter to trouble herself. She seems fine. I don't know how smoking will help her head injury, but I'm too guilty over what happened to my daughter to deny her anything. Tisha gets her a cigarette and Carlotta lights it. Tisha hurries to find an ashtray before she drops a smoking ember onto the couch.

I ask them again, "Will the two of you make it?"

"I'll look after her, Lou," Tisha says, "And we'll stay out of trouble."

She casts me a glance and my heart breaks for her. For us. For our child. I get Doukas into the car. He's fucking heavy and I ought to do this with help, except burying Geo Doukas is my punishment. I know the Sicilian countryside well and fifteen acres of land around the cottage. There are roads that only SUVs can travel on surrounding the property and thick forest growth. I planted those trees twenty years ago when I bought the land. I imagined the land filling with wildlife and bringing my children here to watch the birds. Carlotta may never see birds again. I drag the idiot's body out of the car and rest him on the ground as I dig.

I'm covered in sweat and dirt when I have six feet. Fuck. I spit in the grave and snarl, "Fucking Doukas scum."

I push the man who hurt my daughter into the grave and spill the first shovel full of dirt over his face. Stavros would pray right now if he were here. But he isn't. As I stare at Doukas, lying obscenely in the grave's bottom, I notice something hanging around his neck. It's silver and I've seen it before. I gave that necklace to Carlotta's mother the week before she died. Yiayia insisted the maid stole it. I fired her. And her legion of sons who worked in the gardens and kitchens. I'm a madman, standing in a grave with a man I've killed, ripping jewelry off his neck. I don't think, I just rip. I hear a crack in his neck and grimace as I stare at the loosened chain.

It's her pendant.

"He killed her," I murmur, "he killed Carlotta's mother."

I scramble out of the grave and kneel beside it. I failed her. I failed her mother. And this monster here died within minutes, without medical attention. With dirt-crusted fingers, I rub the silver, struggling to clean it when I notice an inscription.

From your great-aunt.

Geo's great-aunt is Yiayia. To add insult to the man's injury, I vomit. I didn't mean to desecrate him so thoroughly, but I can't hold back. My grandmother had a hand in killing her own daughter-in-law. I don't understand what role she played, but it was her.

At 24, when I drank myself into a stupor and they found me in the Czech Republic prodding a dancing bear with a hot poker, my grandmother was the one who promised that my life would get better. And then I remember. The next week, she handed me an AR-15 and a list of five Israelis living in Argentina. I left my daughter with her on the trip... her mother's killer.

I throw up again into the dirt, avoiding Geo's already tattered corpse. I have to close this hole. And then I need to find my grand-mother and *finish this.* I pull my phone out and call Stavros, but he doesn't answer. Maybe he has her already. Or worse, maybe she had him and Fallon. I shudder at the thought of Yiayia finally getting revenge on Fallon Iverson. I have to hurry and find them. I cover the hole. I smell like sweat, vomit and death, but I don't have time to shower. I strip my shirt off and blast the air-conditioning in the car over my bare, sweaty chest. Goose flesh prickles over my skin.

I stick the pendant in the glove compartment and drive to the docks. Stavros's boat has just docked, and it looks... horrible. He runs off and shakes his head.

"Our fucking grandmother wants to kill us all!" he snarls.

"So you don't have her."

"Have her? She threw a *grenade* at our boat. Thankfully, Fallon's better with an AR-15 than I could have expected."

"I wasn't trying to kill anyone," Fallon adds quickly. I grunt. She wrinkles her nose. Fallon's so much more observant than Stavros. With the voices, perhaps Stavros has more to *observe.*

"Why are you shirtless?"

Stavros covers her eyes dramatically.

"Don't look upon his horribly offensive body."

Stavros peeks between his fingers anyway, "Loukas, when were you going to tell me you had a six-pack?"

I grunt and Stavros scoffs. Fallon elbows him and he kisses her.

"I'm shirtless," I answer once they finally stop kissing and touching each other, "because I just put Geo Doukas' body six feet under and I'll be doing the same to our grandmother."

Fallon stops kissing Stavros, instantly attentive once there's talk of murder. She didn't marry into this family for the murder. But... death is a part of life.

The news of Geo's death stuns Fallon, but I can't imagine why she wouldn't immediately jump for joy. They met once, and he nearly hurt Fallon — the way he hurt every woman who crossed his path. His actions were his own undoing. A smart man would have never interfered with a Pagonis woman.

"You killed him," she whispers, but I'm not keeping it a secret. I did it in front half his family.

"Van's back," I announce to my brother.

Stavros scoffs, "Van? He's not running from the law?"

Van will run from the law until his dying day. Our family has always found two sets of books helpful. Giovanni Doukas never cared about hiding his criminal actions or intentions. So far, it's worked for him.

"He's lying low here, and he's more than happy to have Geo gone."

"He can keep the Doukas family in line," Stavros agrees.

Fallon pushes Stavros out of the way and interrupts us, a hand on both our chests.

"Stop!" she scolds, "What's this about *killing* Yiayia? Stavros... you can't *agree* with that."

Stavros shrugs coolly and explains to his wife, "She probably had it coming."

"She killed Carlotta's mother."

Stavros' body tenses visibly. He's lost women before. And he's taken the blame for this death. I can't imagine how it feels to hear the truth and to hear me saying it. I accused him before. But I was wrong.

His voice comes out hoarsely, "She did *what?*"

I take them to the car and show them the pendant. Stavros turns white.

"You all have blamed me for years," he snarls, "look at this. It turns out I wasn't the monster."

"You can't blame us," I grumble, "You skulk around like a gigantic depressed idiot all the time. I figured you had blood on your hands."

"You're one to talk," Stavros snaps, "You stink of shit. And death."

"Boys!" Fallon hisses again, "Stop fighting. Where's Carlotta?"

Right. We have a lot to catch up on.

"My daughter's safe at my cottage. But injured. They blinded her. And everyone responsible for this will die."

"What about Tisha?" Fallon asks.

I groan, "Fuck's sake." I get into the car, but Stavros holds the door open. I try to force it shut, but Fallon helps him.

"Cut the shit," Stavros says, "We know you're fucking the girl."

Why do they want to talk about this? It's my business. The girl is over eighteen. She can make her own choices. And right now, our choices don't matter. We both know the right thing. If we don't end this, someone else could get hurt.

"She's pregnant," I snap, "Yes, I fucked her. But what do you want me to do? I need to look after Carlotta now. I'll send Tisha back to Oxford and get on with parenting and I don't need either of you giving me your *psycho-babble* advice!"

I yank the door shut and Stavros lets it close. Fallon's smarter and works her way readily into the passenger side of the car.

"Not so fast, Loukas," she says, "We're here for you. We want to talk."

A shiver runs down my spine. Pagonis men don't *talk*. We shoot first, ask questions later. At that point, you've already shot, so there is no need for questions. I close my eyes and sigh as I expect Fallon's lecture.

THIRTY-THREE
DARK COMMENTS

"Don't say a word," I snarl before Fallon speaks, "Yiayia killed Carlotta's mother. She's the reason my daughter's blind. And Tisha can't stay here."

Fallon's interested in the Tisha subject. Her accusing voice grinds my nerves, "You got her pregnant, Loukas?!"

I hate how judgementally Fallon looks at me. This is how the world will look at me if I stay with Tisha. If I allow myself happiness, I'll bring this on her: loathing.

"Yes."

"When was this happening? How did you hide this? Did you screw her when she was a teenage girl?"

"She was eighteen."

Fallon scoffs miserably, "Right, like lying in wait makes it better."

"I didn't lie in wait," I snarl, "And I don't need you judging me when my brother bought you off an auction block."

Fallon punches me. Hard. Pregnancy has made her vengeful, at least according to the scowl on her face. I sigh and rub the area where she hit me. It doesn't hurt much.

"Slow down," Fallon says sternly, "We need you to explain."

Stavros pokes his head between us from the backseat.

"Yes. Listen to Fallon... or I'll gut you," he says.

"Those threats don't work on me," I snap.

"I had to try," Stavros says, shrugging and stroking his beard, "Now relax. It's not a big deal that you knocked up an extremely young girl like a creepy pervert."

"Stavros... I'm going to *kill* you," I snarl and I fumble for a weapon which I don't have in reach. I'm not as paranoid as Stavros.

My brother laughs as Fallon shoots him a pointed glare. The point is, she wants the truth out of me. I explain everything as best I can. Stavros is calmer as Fallon grows more frantic.

"This is serious. Stavros, what are you going to do?"

"It's simple," Stavros says, "We man up and kill Yiayia."

"What?!" Fallon squeaks, "That's your take-away here? Kill your grandma?"

"She is not a regular grandmother. Carlotta's blind. I warned them not to interfere with our business. If I don't follow through on my word, they'll think I'm weak. Yiayia's had a long life. It's time she meets a peaceful ending," says Stavros.

"No!" Fallon yells, "Stavros! I'm about to have a baby. You can't hear voices when we have a newborn, and you know that's what will happen if you kill again."

Stavros. He hasn't heard voices since Fallon. She got him to stop killing, chased away the cursed demons that follow my murderous brother. I'm lucky my demons don't follow me. But then again, maybe they have. Carlotta's blindness is my fault.

"I will help you, brother," I say, "However I can. This time Yiayia can't feign ignorance and she can't run far or fast."

"Papa will help her escape as best he can," Stavros murmurs, but we both know our father is cartoonishly incompetent at anything that's not spending money on liquor, gambling or prostitutes.

Fallon pushes Stavros' head, so he's thrown against the back seat.

"Focus! Loukas. What about Tisha? You got her pregnant, are you going to abandon her?"

"It isn't any of your business, but we had an arrangement and we'll go through with it. She'll leave here and when she has the child... I will take it and adopt it."

"Adopt?" Fallon sneers, "it's your kid."

"What would you have me do?" I snap bitterly at her, "Ruin Carlotta's life even more by admitting that I made a mistake with her best friend?"

"That's all it was then?" Fallon asks, "One mistake?"

Does this woman fancy herself a goddamned private investigator? I fight the urge to make her find out what happened to the *last* private investigator to bother me. But Stavros is right here, and Fallon's... well... I've grown used to her. I'm *fond* of her, you could say. Even if she's irritating.

"Not one. Several."

"Fuck!" Stavros laughs, "Have you always liked them young? I never noticed."

"Shut up, Stavros!" Fallon and I say together. At least we can agree on something.

"She's only a kid. She probably loves you. This could break her heart."

Fallon explains it to me like I'm three years old.

"I understand feelings," I say, "I know I've been an idiot."

"What were you thinking?" Fallon continues.

"She's beautiful," I murmur.

Stavros nods and agrees, "He has always liked beautiful women. But with brown skin? That's new."

Fallon glares at Stavros again and then asks again, "What about your agreement? Is Tisha really going to go through with giving up her baby?"

Fallon clutches her stomach. Motherhood is precious to her. But Tisha... Tisha didn't even want the baby. She didn't want our baby.

And maybe she was right to have wanted her abortion. But my tongue grows heavy in my mouth at the thought of ending a Pagonis life. Those babies are mine. And Tisha's mine too.

"She's agreed to it," I say, mimicking a calm I don't feel, "And she's not a kid. She's returning to Oxford and I'm going to pick up the pieces of my life and try my best to be a good father to the children I already have."

Stavros sighs and pats me on the shoulder.

"If my children are half as wild as yours, I'm bringing back the wooden spoon and the strap."

Fallon scowls disapprovingly at him, but I can't help smirking. Stavros got the worst of the beatings when we were kids. He was impossible to tame, even for Yiayia. He makes a good man in charge. A better man than I would, since I can hardly keep track of my children.

"Thanks for the fatherly advice," I mutter, "But that won't work with my *blind* daughter. I'll need to care for her. And I'm sending for Kayla. Tisha will have no choice to move on from me because... there's no room for her in my life."

Fallon notices my voice break as I say it. Stavros might notice, but he doesn't care. Fallon's face softens and she whispers, "Are you in love with her, Loukas?"

Stavros scoffs, "My brother doesn't experience love."

"Get out," I snarl at both of them, "Get out and drive back to the cottage. Say nothing."

"You do, don't you," Fallon whispers, ignoring my protests. Stavros leaves, uninterested in my love life and eager to get some food into his impossibly tall and muscular body.

"Yes," I confess to Fallon when my brother's out of earshot, "I love her more than I've loved a woman in two decades. But if I want her alive, I have to let her go. That's what you do when you're in the mafia. I only hope my brother doesn't come to regret keeping you around my twisted family."

I think I scare Fallon off with my dark comments, and she lets Stavros drive her away toward the cottage. We're all sleeping under one roof tonight, which means I don't get a last night with Tisha. I'm putting her on a plane in the morning and returning to Greece without her. When I get home, I'll tell her and we'll sleep in separate beds. We'll have to get used to the separation, because we can't ever be together. I don't know what I'll do about the child she carries.

When I get to the cottage, I book Tisha a plane ticket from the driveway. Stavros and Fallon wander inside. Tisha flings the door open and leaps into Fallon's arms, eyeing Stavros cautiously. I wonder what she tells Fallon... if they have *secrets*. I scoff. Women always have secrets. Especially my grandmother. I call Zoe and tell her she's coming home in two weeks. Once I'm finished with Yiayia, Greece will be safe and I will have reunited my family.

I approach the cottage. Tisha's waiting outside, sitting on a stone bench in the garden. She pats the seat next to her.

"Hey," she says, "Stavros and Fallon are with Carlotta."

I sit next to her and she wraps her arms around her shoulders.

"I'm sorry," I murmur, "but I booked your flight. I'll take you to the airport tomorrow morning. I'll send the rest of your things in the mail. It's time, Tisha."

"I know," she whispers, "But it hurts. A lot."

"Let's risk it," I tell her, "Let's tell her."

"We can't, Uncle Lou," Tisha whispers, "She needs you. Carlotta needs you."

"How did your heart get so big, Tisha?"

"I fell in love with a single dad. No one has a bigger heart than you, Loukas Pagonis. You hide it well with that scary, grumpy old guy stuff."

"Grumpy old guy, eh?"

She sighs and rubs her shoulders again.

"I want to kiss you," I tell her, "But I can't."

Something catches in my throat. The end of us. The painful goodbye.

"I'll tell you when I have the baby."

"I'll send money," I promise her.

"You go inside first," she says softly, "I want to be alone."

But I don't want to be alone. I want Tisha. I don't want to let her go...

THIRTY-FOUR
I NEED TO BE SOBER

enter the house. Stavros has a stiff drink poured for me. I've stopped drinking. I need to be sober: for Carlotta, Tisha, and all my future children.

"I'm not drinking anymore, brother," I tell him. It's one of the rare occasions that I feel affectionate and not angry with Stavros. At least the two of us get along better than me and Galanos.

"More for me," he mutters, "I'm drinking so I don't experience the sheer terror of my son being born Italian because Fallon won't listen."

Fallon sits across from Carlotta and snaps, "I can *hear* you."

"Yes," Stavros mutters, "And I'll pay for that later."

"Women," I mutter.

Stavros lowers his voice, "What do you know of women? I thought your latest was a *girl*."

"Not you too, on that moral high horse."

Fallon's one thing, but Stavros has his share of sins and his share of guilt. He need not worry about my guilt. Or my sins. My lust for a teenager is none of my brother's business.

"She's pretty," he admits, "But your daughter..."

"Don't you think I know that?"

"My approach differs from Fallon's," Stavros replies calmly, "You're a man. I understand that. But now she's pregnant. That changes things, doesn't it?"

"What's changed is Carlotta's needs. Once she's safe in Greece... I'll figure it out."

Stavros puts his hand on my shoulder, "I'm always here if you need me. I love you, old fool."

"Hm. Idiot," I mutter, "I suppose I feel a brotherly warmth toward you, not dissimilar to affection."

After we all eat, Carlotta's exhausted and Fallon helps her shower and gets her into bed. Tisha retires to her bedroom. Fallon and Stavros take the room across from Carlotta's. I sit in the living room late, contemplating polishing off my secret stashes of vodka. Three bottles of vodka would get me through the night. Maybe if I drank, I could find Tisha. I could *have her again.* It's impossible. I quit drinking and I need to quit Tisha.

I head to bed, because it's the only way I'll win the battle against the liquor. Sleep. As my head hits the pillow and I lie in that in between space, I hear footsteps in my room.

"Who is it?" I say calmly.

"It's me, Uncle Lou," Tisha's voice says, "I came to say goodbye."

"You shouldn't be here," I whisper, "they know. My brother and Fallon know."

"But Carlotta doesn't yet. And this will be our last night together. So please... don't push me away."

I relent and move aside, allowing Tisha the warmer part of my bed. When she gets in here, I won't want her to leave. But I will handle that hurdle when I come to it.

"Come to bed, little woman."

Tisha slides beneath the sheets wearing a sheer, lace nightgown which feels incredible against my skin. I wrap my arm around her and she nestles her little bottom against my crotch. I touch her stomach. It's growing.

"Do you promise to be good when I'm gone?" I whisper.

"Yes."

"Maybe," I tell her, emotion catching in my throat, "Maybe there's a chance for us in a few months."

"No, Loukas," she whispers, "there isn't. We put ourselves first and look what happened to my best friend."

Her voice sounds pained. Fallon's right. I broke her heart by following mine. I'm the grown up. I should know better. Tisha may be an adult, but she's still... inexperienced. I want to kiss her, but I'm scared to let myself go. Whenever I touch her, I lose my sense. I become young. And wild.

"I don't want to let you go," I tell her, "I love you more than I've loved a woman in decades. You're..."

"A second chance," she whispers, "I know. But you're my first."

"I'm old," I tell her, pinning her hands above her head, "and you can't be my first anything. I'm sorry if I stole that from you."

She kisses me, and I tighten my grip on her wrists. I want to take her again. She's right. One last night. I can *have* her.

"You didn't," she whispers, running her hand over my back and then removing my shirt. Her fingers linger over my chest hair and then return to my stubble. Tisha grabs my cheeks and kisses me, her tongue parting them open as she kisses with youthful vigor. I kiss her back and hold her against me. I want her.

Her thighs wrap forcefully around me as she hooks her ankles behind me and pulls me into her. Deeper. My crotch rests against her as my cock yearns for freedom.

"When the baby's coming, call. I'll be there," I say to her. But it's weak. I shouldn't be a phone call away. I should be there for her.

"Carlotta hasn't noticed I'm pregnant. I'll tell her once I've been at Oxford a while," Tisha says.

"I understand."

"She still won't know it's you. Your secret will be safe."

"Meet another man," I tell her, "Please. Don't wait for me."

I have to command it. I have to make her fall in love with

someone else. And I'll heal my heartbreak alone. When I have our daughter, I can pour my love for Tisha into that little girl and be the best father. One day I'll tell her of my mistake: not waiting long enough for her mother. And how it cost me. Because after Tisha West, there will be no other women.

I can't imagine another. Not after her.

"Not now, Loukas..." she begs, equally terrified of the future.

"Take my pants off then," I whisper, "I need to feel you around me."

I free Tisha's arms so she can perform the task I've commanded. She pulls my pants down and slides my hardness out, gasping at its size in her small grasp. Tisha guides my hardness toward her entrance. My bulging head nearly erupts upon contact with her soft and soaked thighs, parting slightly to give me access to her depths.

I've never had much talent for resisting *this moment*. She grabs onto my hair as I push the bulging head between her lips, forcing her apart. Tisha lets out a noise between a moan and a yelp. I grunt and push more of my cock between her thighs. She's soaking wet, but still ridiculously tight.

"Harder," she breathes. I groan as I bury myself in her to the hilt. She's soft. And *tight*. I've never had her cunt so hot and yearning for me. I can't go slow. This is our last night and joining sends my heart into a furious pounding. Anticipation. Desire. Pain. A last night together. I withdraw and slam into her. She cries out and my hand clamps over her mouth as I withdraw and thrust into her deeply again.

She can't be loud, but I *need to fuck her hard.*

The bed moves with each thrust and with one hand on my hips, I hold Tisha steady so her pregnant teenage body can accept the full length of my cock plunging into her depths. Each pumping movement drives her wild and she can't stop cumming. Her juices squirt from her tightness and I can't stop myself. I'm nowhere close to cumming. I need her. *All of her.*

I pull out and flip her onto her stomach. Tisha buries her face in the pillow as my cock slides all the way inside her and I bounce against her deliciously soft ass. I take her from behind and then I roll her on top of me. Her small breasts are *growing* from her pregnancy and the dark brown nipples have changed so they're larger, darker and more succulent. Before impaling her on my cock, I kiss her as she straddles me.

Her soaked cunt gets my crotch wet as she grinds her little hips on me, begging for my enormous Greek cock to enter her again.

"Please," she whimpers, "more..."

I grab her hips and balance her on me so her ass and cunt spreads and the tip of my cock can find her soft, welcoming opening. She kisses me and grabs my face, covering me with messy, inexperienced kisses. My cock stiffens with veins bulging around the strong shaft as I slide it against her entrance and tease her clit without sliding inside her.

I take her lower lip between my teeth as I push the first inch inside Tisha's spread lower lips. She moans into my mouth as I push another inch inside her. I slowly bury myself in her cunt, which squeezes the dear life out of my cock. My heart races. Tisha sitting on my cock feels *incredible.* She's unlike any woman I've had, and my ragged breathing and heightened arousal keep me joined with her. She brings the Greek stallion out of me... Stamina. Desire. Lust.

Holding onto her hips, I move Tisha back and forth slightly. She moans as my giant cock caresses her inner walls, building her slowly to a powerful climax.

As I hold her and move her, the door to my bedroom thrusts open. Tisha and I look over. She nearly screams, but I press my hand to her mouth and hurriedly flip her off me.

"Papa?" Carlotta whispers, "Papa, are you awake?"

Fuck.

THIRTY-FIVE
YOU SMELL SWEATY

keep my hand clamped forcefully over Tisha's mouth as I try to steady my breathing.

She's blind, I remind myself. She can't see and she's not freaking out, so she mustn't have known.

"Y-yes," I say, "I'm... up. I was reading."

"I... Can you help me come into the room?"

I glance over at Tisha, who is crawling out of bed, trying not to alert Carlotta to the fact that she's in the room with me. *She doesn't want her best friend to know we were just fucking like animals.*

"I'm coming," I say to her.

"You sound tired, papa. I hope you were really awake. Don't wake up on my account."

"I was." Tisha's out of the bed now and has her back pressed against the wall. I approach Carlotta and flick the lights on. Tisha holds her breath as Carlotta turns her head, looking right at her. But seeing nothing.

"Did you just turn the lights on? I thought you were reading. In the dark, papa?"

I clear my throat and glance over at Tisha. I can hear blood rushing past my ears. I link arms with my daughter and pull her a few steps away from Tisha. All my little snack-lover has to do is sneeze, and this will all blow up in our faces.

"Why don't we go to the kitchen," I say, "Perhaps you're hungry."

"No. Please, papa. I want to stay here. I'm... having nightmares. About Geo. And Matilda."

Tisha presses her back against the wall and presses her finger to her lips as I guide Carlotta to sit on the edge of my bed. She rests her hands in her lap. No phone. My chest tightens and I sit next to her. Tisha tiptoes around the edge of the room.

"Nightmares aren't nice."

"I know. I tried to wake Tisha up, but she must be in the kitchen. I stopped here on the way."

Tisha's close to the door.

"I don't know where she is," I *lie to my daughter*, "Perhaps we'd better look in the kitchen."

"No," Carlotta says, "We need to talk about you."

"Me?"

"I worry about you, papa."

Tisha's at the door. She mouths a heartbreaking goodbye and disappears. *I never came.* I never came inside her one last time. Not like that's the most important thing, but I wanted to. I've always wanted to. From the moment I saw her, I wanted to cum inside her. That was how it started. But I couldn't have her, so I fell in love instead. That'll make it worse.

"You shouldn't worry," I murmur, turning my attention to Carlotta.

"Papa, you smell sweaty."

I roll my tongue into my cheek, trying to avoid giving myself away, a task I've nearly failed at.

"Carlotta, I am not sweaty."

"Just because I can't see doesn't mean I'm stupid. You smell terrible. Maybe you have nightmares too."

"I don't," I say, "Don't worry your pretty Pagonis head about it."

"I worry about you because... I took away Matilda. The woman you loved. And I feel you must be lonely."

"I'm not. As long as I have my children, I am never lonely."

Carlotta giggles, "But papa, we're horrible children!"

"No. Never horrible. You're mine. And I love all my children. Especially my first."

"You aren't supposed to have a favorite," Carlotta protests.

"And you aren't always my favorite."

Carlotta stands up and reaches out for my hand, off by about six inches, and says, "Will you help me to the kitchen? Tisha's probably snacking. That girl eats so many snacks... It's an American thing."

"Let's find her then, since you're up early. I'm taking her to the airport in a few hours, sending her back to London. Our family needs to get closer now. You need us."

I help my daughter to the kitchen. She talks to Tisha. I make an excuse to leave because they don't need me hanging around. I close my bedroom door and lock it. My stomach twists into knots. Our goodbye felt so... *incomplete.*

At eight in the morning, before Carlotta reawakens, I load Tisha's duffel bag into the car and drive her to the airport, a few minutes away. I park the car and lock the doors.

"She doesn't know," I tell her.

"I know," Tisha says, "We got away with it."

She sounds sad. Maybe she didn't want us to get away with it. Maybe if Carlotta caught us, we could be together.

"The baby..."

"I'll tell you about the baby," she promises.

"I never... finished."

"I know," Tisha says, "But this is it, Loukas. I'm going to graduate from university next year and you'll be a father again. Your second chance."

"I'll miss you."

"I'll miss you too. No matter who comes next, you'll always be my first."

"And you'll always be my last," I tell her, "Because there can't be anyone else, Tisha West. I'll remember what we had and when I'm old and dying, I'll think of the young woman who saw so much in me worth loving."

"I don't want to miss my flight."

"One last kiss," I say to her.

Tisha leans over and kisses me. I grab her cheeks and pull her close. I don't want to let go of her, but I must. I watch her walk away, dark walnut legs sticking out of a pair of short-shorts as her stomach protrudes slightly from her hoodie.

"Goodbye, little woman," I murmur. I don't leave the parking lot until her flight takes off. When I drive back to the cottage, her absence hits me immediately. She was *life* breathed into everything and I let her go. *With my child.* Fallon and Stavros have Carlotta sitting up at the kitchen counter eating breakfast.

Stavros is telling her a story about me, which I hate.

"Your father was an excellent surfer. He punched a shark off the coast of Aruba and swam back to shore laughing the entire time."

My cheeks darken. The shark wasn't exactly *enormous,* but in Stavros' version, the shark was the size of a blue whale. He once told people I *bit* the damned shark. Fallon smiles when she sees me enter the kitchen.

"Loukas! How was the drive?"

"Fine," I snarl, feeling bitter. But mostly sad. Heartbroken.

"Tisha must be so excited to get away from our crazy family," Carlotta says, "Come on, papa. Have some of my eggs."

I have a bite and sit next to her. Fallon pours me an espresso.

"When is the doctor coming? I want us out of here tomorrow. We need to find Yiayia."

Now that Tisha's gone, I have other business to attend to. This is half the reason I asked her to leave. I already had to bury one body, but Geo Doukas won't be the last person to pay for killing Carlotta's mother. For doing this to her.

Stavros puts his hand on my forearm.

"I'll look into Yiayia. Fallon will help you prepare Carlotta for her doctor's appointment. Relax, brother. You did the right thing."

He's talking about Tisha. If Carlotta recognizes his secret communique, she says nothing. Fallon distracts her by talking about her baby's cravings. I can't listen to her talking about babies. Not when mine is sitting on a plane somewhere. With Tisha.

When the doctor arrives, he hovers around Carlotta with implements and asks her questions that appear useless to me. Fallon insists the idiot doctor knows what he's doing.

I'm the only one with the sense to ask the one question that matters.

"Will she ever heal from this injury? Can you tell me that or will you continue fooling about!"

"Papa, relax!" Carlotta argues, "You're embarrassing me!"

The doctor clears his throat.

"I can tell you, Mister Pagonis, with no doubt... there is no way to predict whether her blindness will disappear with time. Observe daily."

I want to kill this man. Badly. Fallon stops me from reaching for my pistol.

"What can we do to help her?"

"And," Carlotta asks, "Can I return to school? I go to Oxford. My last year starts in a few weeks."

"Oxford, you say?" The doctor says, "They have impressive accommodations for blind students, but typically, they have a lot of help. You might not have the independence you're used to."

"What would I need to do?" Carlotta asks, "I want to continue my studies."

THIRTY-SIX
GREEK WATERS

Carlotta and I spend the night arguing as Stavros sails the super-yacht away from Sicily, across the water and back home. I refuse to let my daughter return to university. At first. We argue about the matter for three tense weeks in Sicily while Carlotta arranges the accommodations and catches up on her work between our arguments.

She wants to return to Oxford, and continue her studies with their accommodations for the blind, but it's too soon. I can't let Carlotta out of my sight yet. My grandmother's still lurking around. Yiayia could *find her*.

The woman who killed her mother and sold her to Geo Doukas might kill her next. But why? Why would my grandmother do this? Why doesn't matter. The point is, Carlotta's safety is my first concern. It's why I sent Tisha away.

Plus, Carlotta went through trauma. She needs therapy. Carlotta screams at me she needs school, not therapy. She has friends at school. Then she devolves: she hates Italy, she hates Greece, and she hates me. Not necessarily in that order. My daughter stomps off to bed and slams the door.

I head onto the deck where Fallon stands against the railing, letting the cool air blow her hair around her. She inhales deeply.

"Stavros sails so beautifully," she whispers as I stand next to her. I make a strange grunt in response. Fallon looks over at me, holding her protruding belly.

"Having a baby changes things," she muses, letting the wind whip her hair around her face. Fallon has gorgeous features. Stavros claims he fell in love with her at first sight. I think she took longer to come around to him. And a child... well, a child is a beautiful symbol of their love.

"I have *three* children," I remind Fallon, "I understand how babies change things. Trust me."

Your children always come first.

"And a fourth," Fallon mutters, "What are you going to do about that?"

"Did my brother put you up to this lecture?"

"I can get involved in Pagonis business *without* Stavros."

"Carlotta's angry," I mutter bitterly, "But sometimes you have to get your children angry so you can do what's best for them."

"Is staying away from school best for Carlotta or is it best for you?"

"I don't like your insinuations," I snarl at Fallon, reminding her that although I'm Stavros' brother, I don't have to obey her.

Fallon shrugs and says, "You don't scare me, Loukas, so you can cut the grumpy old guy shit. You don't want to let Carlotta go to Oxford because you'll have to be with her. You'll have to give up Greece and your family until she finishes school."

"I would give up anything for Carlotta. She's not ready for this. She's been blind a few days at most."

"But she wants this," Fallon says, "This is her trying to get better, and she needs you to support her, not control her. Look at how trying to control her ended up."

I grunt and glance down at Fallon's stomach.

"Hm," I grunt, "When you have my brother's mischievous brat

bouncing off the walls, you'll understand the desperate need to control the Pagonis temperament."

Fallon pleads Carlotta's case and then begs, "Give Carlotta a chance."

"What would I do in England?"

"You could bring Gal," Fallon suggests.

I snort.

"Are you trying to pawn the troublemaker off?"

"He needs guidance," Fallon says. She makes a good point about Galanos. I never considered enlisting his help. But he's close with Carlotta. *And Tisha.*

Fallon holds her stomach and groans for a moment as she leans on the railing and the boat rocks. She continues, regarding Gal, "Bring him to England and he can help with Carlotta too. You have a big family, Loukas. You're there for everyone, especially your kids. But you don't have to do it all alone."

"Do you think this would help Carlotta?"

"Yes," Fallon says, "100%."

She groans again. And then gasps. Her eyes bulge out of her head and she whispers, "Loukas... we have a problem."

"What? Is it the child?"

Fallon gives me a worried expression. We're in the middle of the Aegean Sea on a super-yacht with no doctor and no chance of getting to a hospital.

"I think my water broke," Fallon's voice wobbles.

"What? No... that's... water... from the sea..."

Fallon goes into panic mode, "LOUKAS! Get your brother over here!"

Fallon lets out a loud, primal groan. I race to the helm where Stavros lazily adjusts the steering wheel but mostly appears to be glancing at pictures of Fallon in her bikini on his cell phone. I snatch the cellphone away from him and throw it.

"You idiot! Wake up!"

"I'm awake! What the fuck? Are you drinking again?!"

"It's Fallon!" I grab his shoulders and Stavros' eyes go from blue to black.

"Did you kill her?!" Stavros asks, ready to pluck my eyes out with his index fingers.

"No, you moron! She's having the baby! Her water broke!"

"NO!" Stavros yells.

"No?!"

This isn't the celebratory stance on fatherhood I expected from him.

"We're in *Italian waters,* Loukas.*"

"I'll get Giorgio at the helm. Go to her. Now!"

Stavros sprints away and I wake his co-captain, who reluctantly agrees to steer and doesn't seem to care about the possibility of new life exploding into existence on the boat. I race back above deck. Stavros holds onto Fallon, who death grips his arm and screams.

"The baby's coming!!!! Ahhhh!"

"Can you hold it until we are close to Greece!" Stavros asks.

Fallon glares at him and screams again, "I can't hold it, Stavros. It's a damn baby!"

"Loukas," Stavros says, sheepishly accepting his fate, "Can you help me get her inside?"

"NO!" Fallon yells, "You touch me Loukas Pagonis and I will *circumcise you!*"

If Stavros wants to get this she-beast inside, he can do it alone. Which he does. Fallon screams as Stavros throws her over his shoulder and drags her inside the yacht.

"Loukas, get her some water!!"

"The contractions are closer together!" Fallon squawks, "Holy shit... Holy shit!"

She screams again. Stavros makes an anguished sound. I race off to the bar to get water and return. Stavros is red-faced.

"Tell Giorgio if my baby isn't born in Greek waters, I will shoot him. Now!"

Stavros is nearly as scary as Fallon. I give Giorgio Stavros' message and the boat speeds up — but not by much. Fallon's labor lasts nine hours.

We crest into Greek waters ten minutes after the baby's born.

Stavros holds Fallon in his arms. They're both covered in sweat (and several more unsavory fluids). Unfortunately, I didn't get through the process without catching an eyeful of Fallon's distended body pushing a watermelon sized child through a tiny hole... but I had to do my part to bring the child into the world.

If only the boy didn't have Stavros' colossal head...

Fallon holds him against her chest. Whimpering. She's covered in sweat, but the hormones raging through her have stopped her pain for the moment. There's only bliss. And her newborn.

"I'm here," she whispers, "I'm here."

"He's Italian," Stavros murmurs, "And I don't even care. He's... beautiful."

"He's pale," Fallon whispers, a smile cracking across her face. Stavros pulls her close, his protective arms encircling her. Their new family.

The baby makes a crying gurgle and Fallon wraps the blankets tighter around him and pulls him to her chest.

"I don't want to let him go," she whispers.

Stavros holds them both. It's nearly sunrise, and he's a father to a baby boy. Stavros kisses her forehead. I sit against a chair across from them.

"I'm sorry I had to look at your..."

"Shut up, Loukas," Fallon giggles, "It's hard to care about that when we have a son."

She kisses the baby's forehead, and his eyes open. They're blue. A beautiful shade of Pagonis blue against the newborn's mocha-colored skin. Fallon giggles.

"We are *disgusting* right now," she whispers, "I don't even care."

"Let me hold him," Stavros murmurs, "Please..."

Stavros holds the child against his chest after Fallon reluctantly lets go. He prays over him and kisses his forehead. I recognize the

Greek words. Papa said them to Galanos the day he was born. And I recited them over Carlotta when I held her for the first time. It's a Pagonis prayer for protection. For wealth. For strength.

They get cleaned up and I take a much needed shower. Carlotta's still asleep when I check on her, and I don't bother waking her. She'll learn about her nephew in the morning. We still have another day before we arrive at the Thessaloniki port.

Once we're all cleaned up, Fallon holds the boy against her chest while Stavros pours her a glass of water. She's exhausted, visibly.

"I don't want to sleep," Fallon yawns, "I don't want to miss a moment of him."

"You need rest, my love," Stavros insists, "Take him with you. Have one of the staff help with a makeshift cot."

Fallon agrees and walks off. Stavros slams his fist on the bar once she's gone.

"Loukas," he hisses, once Fallon's safely out of earshot, "We have a problem."

KIDNAPPING MY BROTHER'S WIFE… AGAIN

"Problem? Is the child not clearly yours?"

Stavros' expression changes into pure loathing.

He snarls at me, his hand dangling over his handgun, "Make another insinuation about Fallon and I'll kill you."

"Relax. It was a joke," I say. A joke that doesn't feel nearly as good as a drink. I miss vodka. I miss losing myself and finding Tisha's bed. She was so tight… So perfect… Every moment I'm not touching her is miserable.

I don't want to sit here torturing my brother to make myself feel better. I want alcohol. And I want to help my daughter, who still won't talk to me.

"Enough of your stupid jokes, Loukas. Dice called. Yiayia's in Thessaloniki. Alone. The woman has no shame. We don't know how long she'll be there. Gal's fucked off to Albania for the week, apparently, and Antonio returned to England for school. But… I haven't told Fallon."

"Tell her and then get her to safety," I say, "We'll handle this."

"You don't understand," Stavros says, "She won't listen. I'm thinking… you kidnap her."

Stavros wiggles his brows and widens his insanely blue eyes —
the same blue eyes he passed down to his son.

"What? I'm not kidnapping your *fiancée*."

Stavros runs his hands over his messy hair in frustration and
hisses, "Do you trust me to handle Yiayia for you?"

"No," I snarl, "She hired Geo to kill every woman I've ever loved.
Why on earth would she do that? I need to know why. I need to be
the one to find out."

Stavros puts a meaty hand on my shoulder, "Brother. We need to
make decisions that may not be popular. And we can strike a deal.
You keep Fallon and my son safe, and I'll handle our family."

"That's your brilliant idea? I risk my life *kidnapping* Fallon and
take her to Oxford?"

"Yes. I've been working on it since we got to Sicily. Fallon's...
malleable."

I grunt gruffly, "And what happens to you?"

My brother might not be as tough as he thinks. I hope I'm wrong.

"Suicide mission," Stavros says calmly, "I *handle* both Yiayia and
our father."

"Do you remember what happened the last time I attempted to
kidnap that woman of yours?"

"This time you'll have my help," Stavros says, "We get her to the
airport and pretend I'm going on the plane. At the last second, you
just need to keep her from running off. That's it."

He makes it sound so simple. The only chance we have at success
is Fallon's exhaustion. She just gave birth, and she needs rest.

"Plane? Since when do we have jets?"

"I opened the Cayman account," Stavros says calmly, "Don't you
ever check your private-server email?"

"No," I snarl, "I don't. And you bought a jet?"

"Discount," Stavros says, winking, "And it's expensive to fly,
which is why I've saved it for this special occasion. You take Fallon
and Carlotta to London, drive out to Oxford. I'll have a car waiting
for you. Maserati with a full tank of gas."

"What about Galanos?" I ask him, hiding my thrill at the idea of a Maserati, "When he returns from Albania, he'll take Yiayia's side. He's her favorite. I wanted him in England."

"I can handle our little brother fine," Stavros says, "Trust me, Lou. I'm not a stupid little shit anymore."

He hands me a piece of paper with perfect penmanship, folded into a letter.

"Give this to Fallon once you arrive in England. Don't speak of this. We'll be in Greece in 24 hours and the plane will be ready to fly."

"Fallon won't like this," I warn him, "Will she forgive you?"

"She may not forgive me, but she'll survive," Stavros whispers, "That's what matters."

I ask him an important followup question, "Will you survive?"

"Yiayia forgets I run this family now," Stavros says calmly, "I will remind her. And if Fallon has taught me anything, I won't have to fire a single bullet."

"Let's hope Yiayia feels the same. Unlike you, she has no qualms about murder."

Stavros kisses my cheek, "Relax, brother. And let's shake on this deal before Fallon weasels out what I'm up to."

We shake hands and seal the deal. Our plan is simple: I kidnap Fallon again and agree to my daughter's demands. I'm sure the news will cheer Carlotta up. Except for the part where we live together. Carlotta awakens and Fallon helps her wash and change into a pink dress. Fallon braids her hair and Carlotta has a small breakfast. She seems... depressed.

"I've changed my mind," I announce, in front of Fallon and Stavros, "I'll take you to England as soon as we return to Greece. By plane. You can contact your teachers and tell them you're returning to Oxford and you'll have their accommodations."

Carlotta grins, "Tisha will be so excited!"

"There's only one thing. You'll need extra support. Stavros has generously allowed me a stipend from the family accounts to cover our living expenses. I'm moving in with you to help. Antonio's already in England and I'll send for Zoe. We'll be together until you finish school."

Fallon wrinkles her nose suspiciously at first, but Carlotta's beaming smile eventually infects her. This is *good news.*

"You would do all this for me, papa!?"

"I would do anything for you. Stavros has already called a realtor on my behalf to find the perfect accommodations. You may even have friends over whenever you like."

"I can't wait to tell Tisha!"

"I'm sure your friend will be excited," I say, trying my best to sound disinterested. But I haven't stopped thinking of Tisha since Stavros enlisted me to escape to England with all of them. I don't know what he has planned for Yiayia, but if he trusts me with Fallon and his newborn, I can trust him with this.

After breakfast, I retire to my bedroom alone. Fallon nurses her son and Stavros discusses baby names with her as I shut the door. Tisha. Thinking about her hurts. I can't show this pain to anyone or let them hear it in my voice. I slide my phone open and look at pictures of her. She had a gorgeous heart-shaped face and a sharp little jawline. And that body of hers... so *tight* everywhere.

Even her little protruding stomach barely betrayed her love of constant snacking.

"I miss you," I whisper to no one in particular. Heading to England doesn't change things for us. It's not like I can show up at her *university* and expect her to take an interest in me. An old man is a holiday fantasy come true. Compared to the boys her age... I'm *saddled.* Three kids. A murderous family. Trailed by death.

Whenever I think of Tisha, I remember how wrong I am for her. But as I close my eyes, I can almost smell her skin. I can feel her soft touch. It's easy to remember how pleasant her inexperienced lips felt against my neck, or her legs straddling my torso, small hands sinking into my broad chest.

I fall asleep, and I dream of making love to her. When I wake up, it's dark and we're still hours away from shore. Carlotta and Stavros play a game together, which involves Carlotta guessing the contents of various bowls based on the textures she feels. Stavros is a good uncle.

Fallon holds their baby and cheers up when I enter the room.

"There he is!"

"We picked a name!" Stavros announces, "Want to hear it?"

"Sure," I grunt.

"Adrian Loukas Pagonis."

They've named the child after me. I remind myself to pray for the poor boy.

"Are you serious?"

"Would you like to be the godfather?" Fallon asks, grinning. She's beautiful when she grins. My brother has excellent taste.

A mafia godfather. Tisha would get a kick out of this.

"Godfather? Yes. Of course."

"There you go. I told you he'd say yes," Fallon says.

Carlotta giggles and tells me, "Helen's the godmother. She's excited. Especially when she heard the boy had *blue* eyes."

"Well. Aren't we a happy little family then?"

Carlotta gushes as Fallon adjusts a nicotine patch on her shoulder, "I'm so excited for Oxford, papa. I never knew I could appreciate school this much."

"Until you graduate, I'm here for you."

"Thank you, papa. You always do so much for me."

"Loukas is my inspiration," Stavros says, and I feel shame that he looks up to me. I'm the furthest thing from perfect.

I'm not the best father I could be. I still slept with my daughter's best friend. And now that we're going to England together, I might see Tisha again.

The worst part is — I want to see her. The worst part is that even if I should regret falling for her, I don't. She made me happy. *Very* happy. And I don't think I'll ever be happy again without her.

THIRTY-EIGHT
MAFIA SISTER

When we arrive in Greece, we put our plan into action. It's time to kidnap Fallon and her newborn, Adrian Loukas Pagonis. But Fallon's suspicious. Carlotta's overjoyed and relaxes her, which makes my task easier. Stavros leads Fallon onto the plane and then returns to the landing strip, pretending to help me with Carlotta's suitcases.

"Hey," he says, "look after her. You get on the plane and shut the doors."

"Promise me you'll survive? I don't want Fallon to kill me next," I grumble.

"I'll come back for her. I promise. Look after Adrian."

"If he's anything like you, he'll be impossible to tame."

Stavros grins and mutters, "Fallon managed."

"I'll look after her, Stavros. I promise. If she claws me to death, look after my children."

"And Tisha?" Stavros asks.

I clench my jaw. I don't want to talk about Tisha.

"I've ruined things with Tisha. It's over."

"It's not like you to give up on a woman, Lou."

Stavros might be right about me, but I was younger. And I've pushed Tisha away. I can't possibly ask for her to come back. The next time I see her, I'll take our child away and never see her again. She'll move on. That's what's best for both of us.

"Maybe it's time I do it. If anything happened to Tisha... I'd never forgive myself."

"And the child?"

"I will provide for Tisha's child like all my others."

Stavros tenses his lips in a thin line, "I'll look after her if misfortune falls upon you. Stay safe. And be grateful that Galanos didn't father Tisha's child."

I blame Fallon for Stavros' sudden awareness of family gossip. He didn't know how far his nose stuck out before she pranced into his life.

"Goodbye. Get ready for hell."

I walk back onto the plane with a suitcase and shut the door behind me, preparing for hell. I hope Stavros warned our pilot to shut the cockpit.

"Why isn't Stavros here?" Fallon asks, clutching Adrian to her chest, "You just closed the doors."

"He can't. He's not coming, Fallon."

"What? Let me off this plane, Loukas. Stavros is coming to England with us. He promised."

"No. He's not. We are going to England and he's going to handle Yiayia."

"You let him handle Yiayia alone!?"

"Fallon, enough," I say, "Adrian needs you."

"He lied to me," Fallon says, and her heart sounds... broken. I dry swallow. I hope my idiot brother knows what he's doing.

"He wanted to protect you."

Fallon snaps, "He lied. It doesn't matter what he wanted."

"It's okay, Fallon," Carlotta says bitterly, "That's what Pagonis men do. They lie."

Her voice makes the hair on the back of my neck stand up.

Women. They don't know how terrifying they are. Fallon leans on Carlotta, who reaches her finger towards Adrian. Fallon puts up less of a fight than I expected. She's tired from having the child.

It's difficult to give birth to another human and keep walking around. She wants to be strong for Stavros, but I can tell that Fallon needs rest. We're not in the air for long. When we land in London, Fallon needs to change Adrian first before we get into the Maserati. I don't miss Tisha's driving, but I miss sitting next to her. Watching her.

Fallon and Carlotta fall asleep as I navigate. Our new address is a few kilometers away from the university — a large old manor with a study for Carlotta and a music room where she can practice cello. Carlotta wants to pick up her instrument again, which surprises me.

I can't wait to see what Stavros has done with the place. He loves real estate nearly as much as I do. Fallon's nearly exhausted by the time we arrive. Carlotta holds Adrian on her lap. When we get to the manor, I carry the little boy. My nephew.

"They named you after old uncle Lou," I murmur to him, "What on earth were they thinking."

Fallon takes him once we're indoors. She had to run inside for the restroom, and Carlotta held my forearm on the way in. The manor's cold. No one has been here for months and the rental furniture looks ancient. At least it's clean, the fresh smell of bleach contrasting with the marble everywhere. And it's close to her school. Fallon takes Adrian to her bedroom, furnished with a crib. For short notice, Stavros did well.

I lead Carlotta to her bedroom, and she sits on the bed, sighing.

"Papa, thank you for this. The bed feels nice."

"How is your head? The doctor warned flying may aggravate the injury."

"I'm fine," Carlotta says, but she doesn't sound fine. My precious daughter sounds *hurt.*

"Are you hungry?"

"No. Papa, can Tisha visit?"

"Yes. Why wouldn't I want her to visit?"

"Because she's bringing her boyfriend."

"Why would I care Tisha has a boyfriend?"

"You said no boys!" Carlotta reminds me, "Why are you being weird?"

My heart thuds in my chest. Right. I forgot about that rule. Carlotta *always* had too many boyfriends, and I hoped that while she focused on her studies, I would have a few moments with her without having to chase off whichever Mario or Dominic she's fallen in love with for the weekend.

"I'm... a weird old man. And right. I said no boys. I suppose if it's Tisha's boyfriend, I trust her judgment."

"Thank you, Papa. You are so good to me."

"Get some rest. I need to talk to Fallon."

I have to give Fallon her letter. I wonder what it says, but I never read it.

"She's angry with Stavros."

"I know," I say, "But he did what he had to. He loves her. And when you love a woman, you protect her."

I kiss my daughter's forehead and offer her help to get ready for bed, which she declines. She's figured out how to make do on her own. And so quickly. Only a couple of days and she's worked it out. I grimly consider that soon she might be ready to sneak out again and party. I hope not. Not soon, at least. I just want her to be happy. She's blind. She will always be blind because I failed her as a father. The least I can do is try to make her happy.

I return to Fallon's room. Adrian lies in his crib and she strides across the room and slaps me across the face.

"Ouch..."

I grab my face, and Fallon puts her hand on her hips.

"How dare you do this with him?"

"I had to protect you."

"That's not your job, and it's not his either. I look after myself."

"He loves you. He would die if our enemies or our family hurt Adrian. Or you. Yiayia is… racist. As you know."

"He might die now!" she yells.

"Stavros will not die," I make an attempt to comfort her but I don't sound convincing.

"You can't promise that."

"I can't," I say, "But I can promise that you and Adrian will have a safe place to rest your head tonight."

I give her the letter. She unfolds it and scans it before folding it and sighing.

"Stavros… it's hard to stay mad at him."

"That's it?"

"I can't stay mad at him for long. I love him."

I glance over at the baby.

"Adrian appears to be sleeping well."

"Yeah. He looks like Stavros. He has his eyes."

"You miss him," I say to her and Fallon nods.

"Just like you miss Tisha," she says.

"No," I murmur, "Tisha was… a mistake. I've let her go now."

And now, she has another boyfriend. I wonder if he's older. I wonder if he knows she's pregnant.

"Was it my guilt trip?"

I don't think Fallon feels entirely guilty. But Fallon is still a hopeless romantic.

"Not only that. Because it was best for her. I love her, Fallon."

"You Pagonis men," she sighs, "You always try to be so strong."

Fallon always makes me want to open up. She listens. And she listens so well. Fallon will be a perfect mother.

"You had to be strong in my family."

"Carlotta's lucky to have you as a father. And Adrian's lucky to have you as an uncle."

I snort and mutter, "I don't feel lucky."

"Go on, Lou. Get some rest. Carlotta will need you in the morning."

"Forgive him," I murmur, "Please. No matter what happens, forgive Stavros."

Fallon sighs.

"I love him. I love him so much it hurts. But I hate how he runs off without me. I hate worrying."

"Mafia, sister. That's what it's like."

"Good night, Lou."

"Good night, sister."

THIRTY-NINE
STALKER

Carlotta's tutor arrives in the morning. He seems competent, and he's not too handsome. He's Greek but doesn't speak the language. Marco's parents immigrated to London fifteen years ago. He's a pleasant chap and smitten with my daughter. Clearly. He takes her by car to her first class. Carlotta makes pleasant conversation with him and gives all the appearances of a serious university student. She kisses me goodbye and for once, we don't fight.

Fallon and Adrian spend most of the morning on Fallon's side of the manor. I don't want to bother her much. She has attendants and maids hired by Stavros, most of whom she chases off. Fallon's inseparable from the baby and she doesn't care for help. She holds Adrian so lovingly, appreciating every moment with her son. I know Stavros wishes he were here. He sends a text shortly after Carlotta leaves. He's tracking Yiayia. She left the villa, and he has his men on her.

I can't sit around the manor doing nothing for long. I attempt conversation with the housekeeper, but the British lack in both warmth and manners. I give up quickly. I go for a run instead. It's always damp in England, and I don't know Oxford well. I know where the university lies, but we're a few minutes away. It would be a relatively long run.

I change into shorts and a black shirt and warn Fallon I'm leaving her alone. She's safe out here and spends so much time with Stavros that she probably knows where all his guns are stashed in this place. He wouldn't rent a place without guns.

"Careful out there," she says, "I know you boys have a way of getting into trouble."

I plan a hard and fast 10 km. Since I was a young man, I could never stand sitting around idly. Without Carlotta to care for during the day, and few friends this far out from London, I have no choice but to look after my physique. I run a fast first mile. I'm in incredible shape. Muscular. I *could* have another woman. But I don't want another. I want her. I run harder. And harder. Before I know it, I'm downtown. Fuck. Where *am* I?

I stop running, dripping in sweat.

"Easy, tiger," a blonde woman teases as she walks past with a friend, giggling. I wave at them and they both smile. Loukas Pagonis, you've still got it.

I'm still catching my breath when I stare across the street at the campus. If I had any idea what class Carlotta had, I could find her. And then... *I see her.* Not Carlotta. Tisha. She's walking next to a man, her age, dark skin. Muscles bulging from his shirt. She turns down a residential block and I want to call out to her, but I freeze.

She knows I'm in England. If she wanted to get in touch with me, she could find me. What am I doing, anyway? I can't hang around her university like a perverted forty-year-old stalker. My heart pumps blood faster. Home. I need to go home.

I turn around and run home. Faster. I strip my shirt off as I step through the foyer. Fallon's eating ice-cream at the kitchen counter.

"Fuck," I mutter once I notice her.

"Calm down, Magic Mike. How was your run?"

The sopping wet shirt stinks of sweat. I throw it over my shoulder. Fallon wrinkles her nose in disgust.

"Fine. Sorry."

I jog past her to get a dry t-shirt and then come back to the kitchen where Fallon's drowning her feelings in some disgustingly American ice-cream flavor.

"Adrian's sleeping for five minutes. I'm eating my feelings."

"Is it helping?"

"Yes. Want some?"

"I think I've earned it."

Fallon grabs a spoon and hands it to me. I eat from the tub after her. The ice-cream isn't terrible, but it's far too sweet. That's how I *really* know I'm not a young man anymore.

"I haven't done this since I was twenty."

"You grew up fast. Young dad."

"That's what I get for being a... man-whore, as Stavros says. Babies."

Fallon snickers.

"Stop. You aren't a man-whore. You're..."

"I'm hopelessly in love," I blurt out, "It's embarrassing."

There she goes again with her psychiatric nursing stuff. It sneaks up on you...

"Hopelessly in love? That's new."

"Don't psychoanalyze me," I mutter.

"I'm not. After Matilda... I didn't think you were *loving* like that."

"Matilda and I were... not a suitable match."

"Tisha's a better one?"

"I saw her today," I confess.

My heart pumps faster as I think of her. And that man. She listened to me. But that hurts too.

"Where?"

"On my run."

"You ran all the way to the campus?!" Fallon says, sounding surprised.

I grunt and stretch my arms, "I'm not an old man, you know?"

"Right. And you *stalked* Tisha?"

"I saw her. I didn't stalk her. I ran away."

I realize how pathetic I sound. But what right do I have to approach her again? She was still pregnant when I saw her. Pregnant with my child. Fallon stares at me expectantly.

I gruffly respond, "I suck at women. Are you happy?"

Fallon grabs the ice-cream tub from me and teases, "I'll be happy when you stop smelling like sweat."

"I'll shower. And perhaps this afternoon, I could help you with Adrian. I have kids, I can do the diaper thing."

Fallon is eager for the help with Adrian. I spend the afternoon helping her out and looking after her, like I promised Stavros I would. She's a beautiful woman, as stubborn as my brother, and she's gentle with Adrian. She lets me change the little man's diaper and then she feeds him.

"You don't mind, do you?"

"No. You're a mother. You feed your child whenever you must. Yiayia even fed Galanos."

"That's disturbing."

I shrug and respond, "In my family, you get used to disturbing."

"I guess you do," Fallon says, wincing as Adrian chomps down on her sensitive breasts. I glance away from her chest as she adjusts her nipple in his little mouth. Fallon swears and adjusts her wet breasts again and I excuse myself, giving her the space to manage it. I know she wants more company, but... I can't. In a few months, I'll be a father all over again and I'll have to rip my child from Tisha's breast and take him or her safely back to Greece. I haven't exactly got a bulletproof plan. Around noon, my phone rings and I think it's Stavros, but it's Zoe.

"Papa, they are sending me on the plane to London and taxi to Oxford," my daughter says. Her voice brings me grief that I would normally numb with liquor.

It hurts not to numb myself anymore. I have to face all my feelings, even the darkest ones, like my fears that I failed Zoe as much as I failed Carlotta and Antonio.

She sounds so *grown up*. Fuck. How have I missed so much?

"Do you need money?" I ask her. I want her to know that at least I'll always provide for her. Zoe giggles and her laugh makes me feel alive. I love my daughter.

"No, papa. I need to know if my bedroom has a TV."

She's like a little Carlotta already.

"No TV. I'm enrolling you in a Montessori School," I tell her. "Where you'll be studying so you can be very smart like Carlotta and go to Oxford."

Zoe makes a disgusted sound.

"No, papa! I want a pony. I don't want to go to boring school, I want to ride horses and run around with the trees and only study Italian."

"We'll discuss when you get here," I say, "But get here safely."

"Ciao, papa."

I wince. Maybe I shouldn't have sent her to safety in *Italy*. But she'll be here tomorrow. While I work on enrolling her in school, I can spend more time with Zoe. Fallon brings me lunch and then I call Antonio, who doesn't answer. He's better at taking care of himself than any of my other children. And probably in class, I realize. In the evening, I go for another 10 km run and have dinner with Fallon. 8 p.m. rolls around and Carlotta's not home yet. I'm agitated.

"I need a drink," I grunt.

Fallon holds a sleeping Adrian against her chest and presses her finger to her lips before whispering, "You can't. You quit."

"Why? So I could care for a daughter who isn't here."

"She has helpers, Lou. She probably wants a little independence."

"Independence got her here," I mutter bitterly.

By 8:30 p.m., I hear a car in the driveway. Carlotta's assistant helps her out of the backseat and he's laughing. They're both laughing. Carlotta's voice rings across the parking lot. And then two other people get out from the other door. It's Tisha... pregnant. And she's with a man. A boy.

FORTY
DOWN TO THE TEETH

Tisha steps into the house gingerly, and the oaf has his hand on her back. He's the man I saw her with earlier. Her boyfriend. I freeze when I see the group of them walk into the house. I feel suddenly stupid and uncomfortable.

"Tisha!" I blurt out, and my voice sounds strange and strangled. Tisha turns to Carlotta, who clings to her attendant, Marco, dutifully and says, "Your dad's here. I thought you said he was out for tonight."

"Sorry," Carlotta says absentmindedly, giggling and leaning more against Marco, "I must have forgotten."

I try to play a good host and greet Tisha's boyfriend in a booming voice, "Welcome. Um... who are you, young man?"

I stick my hand out to shake the young man's hand. He looks obviously British, all the way down to the teeth. I hate him.

"Mason, sir," he says in an agonizingly posh accent.

I shake his hand and then squeeze it. Mason yelps like a stuck dog and pulls his hand away.

"Sorry," I say, grinning, "firm handshake."

"I can tell," Mason whines, his hand bent like a hurt paw.

"Nice to see you again, Uncle Lou," Tisha says casually. She grabs Mason's hand, interlocking her fingers with his as he winces. My cheeks burn. They follow Carlotta and her attendant toward the living room. Fuck. I've made a fool of myself. Again. Getting into a pissing contest with a child and squeezing his hand like that because of her. Tisha is back to calling me Uncle Lou again. I lost my chance with her. Forever.

I think of nursing my wounds in a bottle of vodka, but I pester Fallon and Adrian instead. Fallon calls Stavros on the phone, unhappy to hear that Papa and Yiayia have set sail again, and this time, they may be off the grid for good. Somehow, I doubt that. Our grandmother has a way of turning up.

Fallon falls asleep eventually while my daughter and her friends engage in some mixture of studying and laughing. Marco loves Carlotta, of course. I see the way he looks at her and satisfy my fatherly rage by telling myself I *could* break every bone in his hand if I wanted to. But so far, he hasn't moved his hands too far down her back and he doesn't flirt with her when he knows I'm looking. But he flirts... and my daughter flirts back.

At least I know this one's responsible.

I move funds around in the family accounts before bed and message Galanos. I have to stop thinking about that ape Tisha brought into my home. They're all Carlotta's friends. And I'm... her father. An old man. I ought to act like one.

Galanos doesn't message back right away. He ought to join us in London soon, and I suspect he knows exactly where Yiayia is. If Stavros can't find her, Galanos is our next best option. Stavros and Gal don't get along. No one gets along with Gal, but at least he *fears* me. Galanos doesn't respond before I fall asleep. I get up early for a run and when I walk into the kitchen, the fridge door is open with someone bent over.

"Fallon?" I whisper.

Tisha gasps and sits up straight, dropping a carton of French fries. She tries to bend over to pick them up, but she struggles.

"Don't worry. I'll clean it up," I offer, hating that it's her out here. Hating that I'm staring at what she's wearing. She's gained weight since I last saw her, but she's perfectly filled out and her breasts are enormous. The giant orbs move against each other as she resigns herself to accepting my existence.

I'm hard. Bursting.

She shuts the fridge door and I turn on the kitchen light, hoping to shame myself out of the erection I'm sporting.

"You're up early," she mumbles, ignorant to my plight.

"Heading out for a run," I grunt, moving past her to open the fridge and grab some chilled water. She watches me with a funny look in her eye. Hesitation?

"Oh. Yeah. Carlotta said it was okay if we all slept over," she says.

I nodded, my jaw clenching. She's *sleeping with him* in my house.

"Sorry to spring this on you," Tisha babbles, "But... Mason knows I'm pregnant. He doesn't care because I'm giving up the baby. So. That's it."

"Right. I'd better head out for my run," I say, hoping I can force myself to be responsible. If I touch her, I won't control myself. I know what I'll do to her and... I'll have no qualms about it. She's carrying my child. She's mine.

"Wait. Loukas..."

She touches my forearm, and our eyes meet. What it felt like to kiss her comes flooding back to me. My tongue gets dry and her fingers squeeze, digging into my arm hair and closing around me. I'll lose myself in her. Again. And then I'll ruin everything.

"What is it?" I say, trying my best to sound gruff. It's over between us. She has a new boyfriend.

She asks with frustration, "Why did you come to London?"

I give her a version of the truth, "Carlotta wanted to return to school."

I wanted this. I wanted to see her again. My daughter comes first, but I'd move to the end of the Earth just to glimpse Tisha in the distance. Having her this close is excruciating.

"Oh."

"Your boyfriend will wonder where you've gone," I warn her.

Don't get too close. Don't lose yourself, Loukas. Tisha ignites an insane part of me. A part of me that's reckless enough to touch her. I don't care if she has a boyfriend. She's carrying my children, holding a part of me inside her. Tisha West belongs to me... and this other man makes me angry. I don't want him to have her.

"I haven't slept with him," Tisha says, "In case you cared."

I nod and raise my eyebrows.

"I don't know how he can stand it," I tell her, "Not sleeping with you has always been... my greatest struggle."

Tisha drags me close to her and kisses me. Hard. I push her away.

"No," I say, "We can't. We can't do this again. I can't go through this."

She grabs me against her chest and kisses me again. She kisses with that furious urgent inexperience, her tongue sliding out of my mouth and over my lips before she juts her tongue into my mouth. I can't stop myself. I kiss her back. Tisha needs to remember that she belongs to me. Every part of her...

But then I stop myself again and let her go. She falls gently against the counter with a soft gasp. And then she begs.

"Please," Tisha says, "Don't go. I... Mason's... Mason and I only went on *two* dates. He's thirsty."

"Thirsty? Tisha. Please. Don't justify unfaithfulness. We can't."

"Why not?" she says, "I'm having your baby."

"No," I answer gruffly, "I won't hurt you again. I can't."

She says, "I *love* you, Loukas. I am *in love* with you."

"Stop it," I hiss, "I'm leaving for my run."

Tisha leaps onto me and kisses me again. Fuck. She's strong. And I can't exactly toss her off. *She's pregnant.* With my baby. I put her on the counter and kiss her. She spreads her legs around me and then flicks the light in the kitchen off. We're together again. Screw going on a run. I'd rather go for a ride.

"Pull your dress up," I whisper, "Hurry."

"I want you, Loukas," she whispers.

Her breath is hot and tempting. I imagine how wet she is and I'm rock hard.

"Are you wet for me, little woman?"

"Yes."

I kiss her, pushing my tongue down her throat. Her thighs wrap around me and my stiffness bursts against my trousers. I need her. Now. I press my lips to her neck and grab some of her between my teeth. Tisha moans.

"Did you fuck him?" I ask her gruffly.

"No," she whispers, "I couldn't. I can't..."

I grab her cheeks and kiss her lips.

"I missed you," I confess, "I missed you every day."

She slides her panties off and I place my fingers between her lower lips. She's soaked. My Tisha... I close my eyes, leaning in to kiss her again as I slide my fingers between her thighs. Tisha moans as I pull away from her and when I open my eyes, I notice the lights are on. And then I hear that man's voice.

"What the fuck!?"

His hand snaps away from Tisha's soaked inner thighs as I whip around. My daughter stands in the kitchen in her bra and a thong, half-naked and holding onto Mason's hand.

"Were you cheating on me!?" Mason yells at Tisha. I don't pull away from her. I push myself against her protectively as Tisha wraps her arms around me. She's still wet. I could still slide into her. My logical brain (thankfully) overrides the urges that still pulse through me as I hold her.

Protect her, Loukas. Protect her.

Mason screams, "Were you cheating on me?!"

"You were the one cheating!" Tisha shoots back, "Why are you holding Carlotta's hand?!"

She wraps her thighs around me, but she has a wild terror in her eye. This is it. This is the moment Carlotta finds out about us.

"Tisha? Cheating with who!?" Carlotta asks, side-stepping the fact that she'd clearly just hooked up with Tisha's boyfriend. Unfortunately, I am not in a position to critique my daughter's behavior. My dick nestles right against Tisha's crotch, still straining for freedom from my trousers.

"Your *dad*," Mason yells, "Your dad's *fucking your best friend* on the kitchen counter."

Carlotta lets out an anguished shriek and then screams, "You bitch! You slutty bitch!"

Carlotta, not caring at all that she's blindly fumbles on the counter for a lockbox behind the toast. Fuck. She knows about Stavros' guns. Tisha hops away from me and pushes Mason.

"You *liar*. You said you would not fuck Carlotta!"

"She's really fit," Mason drawls, "I'm sorry I lied but... it was easier to use you to get to her."

Carlotta has a gun now and I'm searching for mine, but Carlotta reaches hers first and points it in the general direction of Tisha. But really, she could hit any of us. And kill us. Thanks, Stavros. This idiot's paranoia will kill us all one day.

"Everyone shut the fuck up!" Carlotta yells.

Tisha shrieks and races behind me. Mason immediately wets himself. The smell is as immediately pungent as the action itself. Fuck... This is who Tisha dates when she's not with me? I feel less threatened instantly.

"Carlotta," I say calmly, "Put the weapon down. Stavros doesn't leave the guns loaded."

"Do you want to find out?" she hisses.

She doesn't need to scare me. She just needs to scare the other two. Carlotta's hands shake and she breaks down. Crying.

"How could you!?" she yells, "You fucked my dad!"

"You fucked every boyfriend I ever had," Tisha yells back, "Do you know how hard it's been to be your friend? You're skinny, white, blue-eyed and *rich*. You only liked me because I was your loser best friend."

"That's not true," Carlotta snarls, "We were best friends because

I always listened to your stupid boy problems. And anyway, if you weren't a loser, you wouldn't have fucked my father," Carlotta sneers.

She's still crying. Heartbroken.

"You fucked Mason! So we're even," Tisha says, "And you hooked up with Ashton. And Devon. And Dylan."

"How many people has my daughter hooked up with?!" I snarl.

"Shut up, Papa!" Carlotta yells. She returns her attention to Tisha, waving the gun at me instead. I hold still, praying that neither of us calls the other's bluff.

"No," Carlotta says, "We're not even, Tisha. I want the truth. All of it."

"We can tell you the truth when you put the gun down," I say calmly.

"SHUT UP!" Carlotta shrieks, "Shut up you *liar!* You fucking *pervert.*"

"Hold on," Mason mutters, "Does that mean... is that baby... his baby?"

Why do idiots always choose the worst imaginable times to wise up? Carlotta's sobbing continues and her finger hovers over the trigger. She's not mentally well. She'll kill all of us. She'll hurt Tisha. My heart throbs as I struggle to control the situation. My daughter's sobbing intensifies. Tisha's calm, like she trusts me to get her out of this.

Little woman, I hope you have your faith in the right man...

"He's right, isn't he?" Carlotta shrieks.

Think, Loukas. How can you all get out of this *alive?*

FORTY-ONE
AN APOLOGY

"Yes. He's right," I say, "Tisha's pregnant."

"I hate you, Papa," she says, "But I hate Tisha more..."

Mason screams as Carlotta pulls the trigger. He lunges dramatically between Carlotta and Tisha. The gun isn't loaded, so Mason's effort to take a bullet for Tisha fails. He lands on his face and groans like he's been shot. I grab my daughter and rip the gun away from her, throwing it across the room. Tisha, still thinking Mason's shot because he's moaning like a stuck pig, kneels beside him screaming his name. He starts taking off his shirt. I'm unclear why.

Carlotta thrashes in my arms, screaming about how much she loathes me.

I know she does. She *must*.

"Carlotta, stop."

She elbows me and gets away. I catch her again and Carlotta strikes me. Then she stumbles back. She can't see what to hold on to and she falls over. I catch her before she hits the ground and she lands in my arms. Tisha cradles Mason's head and then helps him to his feet.

Mason's fuming.

"Don't call me!" he yells as he chews her out and storms off. Tisha lets out an anguished sob and then says, "Carlotta, I'm sorry."

Carlotta pushes me off her and sneers at her, "*Slut.* I knew you were poor, but I didn't know you were desperate enough to *shag* my father for money."

"Stop it, Carlotta," Tisha says, "You're lashing out."

"When did this start? How long have you two been fucking behind my back!"

Carlotta's red and doesn't know where to focus her eyes. But they're wild. And hurt. This betrayal cuts deeper than any other. She's been more honest with me than before, and I've lied. I fucked her best friend and lied about it. For months. I don't have a choice anymore. I need to tell my daughter the truth because she deserves it.

I answer calmly, "It started a year ago," I say, "And... I love her."

"Don't say you love her," She yells, "Are you crazy? She's *my age.*"

She's distressed. But she's not wrong. Most people would agree that Tisha is far too young for me. But I'm Carlotta's father, damn it. I can't have her parenting me.

"I don't need a damn lecture from you. You're my daughter," I grumble.

"You need a lecture," Carlotta sneers, "You need to stop being a pervert. And Tisha, you can go home now. Don't bother sitting with me in class. I need to talk to my father alone and I am not interested in a slutty liar."

"Carlotta, wait... We can talk about this," Tisha begs, her voice cracking, "I didn't mean to."

Her voice sounds so hurt. I expected this would hurt Carlotta, but I selfishly never considered that coming clean could hurt Tisha too. She cries again, "Please, Carlotta. I'm sorry."

"You're not," Carlotta sneers, "Did you enjoy laughing at me behind my back as I complained that my father never cared about me? Did you sleep with him while gossiping about stupid I was?"

"We never talked about you," Tisha blurts out.

Carlotta's cheeks turn purple.

"Silence," She hisses, "You disgust me."

"I love him," Tisha cries, "Please... I didn't mean to fall in love with him. But I did. Let me make it up to you. We can still be friends."

"No," Carlotta says, "We can't. I'm sorry I slept with Mason, but this is worse. He's my dad. He's the only person who has ever loved me. You didn't have to steal him."

Carlotta walks away slowly. Tisha lets her go and then changes her mind, and tries to follow her. I grab her arm and stop her. Tisha's eyes are filled with tears.

"That was horrible," she whispers.

"I know," I say, "But... we're both alive."

"That's not a consolation," Tisha says angrily, "She's right. I know how much you mean to Carlotta. She loves you, Uncle Lou. She's always hated sharing you. You're her precious Papa."

I snort and mutter something about her treating her "precious papa" like garbage. Tisha approaches me and presses her hand to my cheek.

"I've been selfish," she whispers, "I wanted a guy so badly, I didn't care about hurting my best friend."

"Don't say that."

"I can't come between you and Carlotta," Tisha says, "Trust me. If my dad was still here..."

She chokes up and then finds the strength to continue, "If my dad were still here, I wouldn't want anything to come between us."

"We have a child together," I say, "She knows. We can't stop her knowing. For our child... we can make it work."

"Uncle Lou, I'm trying to end things," Tisha says, her voice warbling, "I don't want to but I can't hurt Carlotta. She's my *best friend*."

"She hooked up with your boyfriend," I point out, "Carlotta needs to learn that you aren't just her best friend. You're a person. A woman."

Tisha shrugs and explains it away, "She knew I didn't really like Mason."

"I want you," I say, and it feels good to say. It feels good that this isn't a secret. The look on Tisha's face tells me she disagrees with my philosophy on the matter.

Tisha sticks her nose in the air, putting on a look of "responsibility". I'd like to *responsibly* hoist her up onto the counters and finish what I started. She shrugs and says, "It doesn't matter. We have to do the right thing."

I squeeze her forearm and pull her against me.

"You aren't going anywhere, little woman," I murmur, "I'm not letting you go. Carlotta will have to accept us."

"I should go home," Tisha whispers, "Please... Let go of me, Loukas."

"No," I whisper back, kissing her neck, "You're coming to my bedroom tonight. Because you're *mine*. And now that everyone knows, I intend to have you."

She kisses me back. I've won. For now. I drag Tisha back to my room and strip her clothes off. When she's in her underwear, I kiss my way down her stomach until my lips land above her mound. I peel her panties away from her supple brown flesh and lick her outer lips until she moans. Tisha moans louder than I've heard her before, and I eat her with abandon. Every inch of her spreads itself for the taking. My tongue slides along her slit, easing between her lower lips and then pressing inside her to press her to a climax.

I pull away from her, and she lets out a little groan.

"What is it?"

"The baby," she moans, "I can... *feel* it."

I pull away from her and touch her stomach. Tisha gasps and then jerks away from my hand. I crouch on the bed over her and follow her gaze. She stares at my crotch. Excitement? Reluctance?

"We shouldn't," she says, "Not tonight."

"We're through the worst of it," I murmur, "Let me have you."

I press my crotch against her. Tisha gasps and moves her hips against me. I have her pinned to my bed and my cock rests right against her bare pussy, ready to slide between her lithe brown legs. Tisha shakes her head, but keeps her arms wrapped around me firmly.

"I'm *very* close to taking you," I whisper, "Let me..."

"Okay," she whimpers as my tongue traces my initials on her neck, "Just a little."

This woman drives me mad. How can I get *a little* inside her? I grab her hands and pin them over her head before I ease my dick from its cotton prison and rest it against her soft, engorged mound. I rub her lips and then find her entrance. Tisha gasps as I slide an inch inside her.

"I can't stop myself," I grunt as I squeeze her hands over her head.

"Don't," she says, "don't stop..."

I thrust the rest of my length between her legs and Tisha cries out. I make love to her recklessly, each thrust driving the headboard against the wall. Tisha's legs spread around me and her body responds to each merciless movement from my dick. As she climaxes, she struggles to break free from my grasp, but I hold her there... *Mine. She's mine...*

When I finally climax, she tries to crawl away, but I pull Tisha against me. Her body slides back against mine, relenting to my grasp. We're both covered in sweat. I hold her engorged nipple between my fingers and roll it around as I pull her close to me. My cock rises to attention again. Her sweaty back presses against my chest and I love it. I love how she smells. I love the smell of *woman* filling my room.

"I owe you an apology."

"For what?" she whispers.

I reach between her ass cheeks and move my thumb against her backdoor. Tisha gasps, but then nestles her ass backward.

"That's not a *normal* apology."

"I hurt you," I murmur gruffly, "But this time, it won't have to hurt. I can make love to your ass."

She squirms against me and slides back so her backdoor pushes against my thumb.

"Tonight," she whispers, "Do it tonight."

She's perfect.

FORTY-TWO
WINGS, 15 WHITE ROSES, A PISTOL, A COWBOY HAT

Taking her ass pleases me. She squeals and moans as I slide inside her, but she accepts me well and begs me to finish in her tight backdoor. Once we've made love in every position imaginable, we fall asleep together. We don't need to hide. Tisha proves more restless than I expect because of her pregnancy. She kicks in her sleep, bites my forearm like a rabid bulldog, and then lies *across* me with her butt sticking up in the air.

We're both abruptly awaken from this strange sleeping position by Fallon bursting into my bedroom and then *shrieking*. Adrian, hearing his mother's upset, immediately bursts into tears. Tisha squeaks and scrambles off me, hiding behind the pillow like it's not too late.

"Loukas are you crazy? What the hell are you doing? Do you know what time it is? Do you know what's going on in your own damn house?"

"Does Stavros whip you for all this damned nagging?" I snarl, mostly because I've just woken up and I'm frustrated at Fallon literally catching me with my pants down. I grab the pillow from Tisha and press it over my crotch.

"Watch your mouth or I'll throw this baby at you."

"You can't lob your child like a volleyball."

"Watch me," Fallon says, "Now get your ass out of bed. Carlotta's gone. Marco's helping her move everything out of this house."

"What?!"

"They're in the car. If you hurry, you might catch them. I tried to stop her but... she's a girl in love."

I launch out of bed in only my boxers and the car speeds down the driveway, away from the manor.

"CARLOTTA. CARLOTTA WHERE ARE YOU GOING?!"

I sound crazy. I *feel* crazy. I don't want my daughter to leave. She's not ready. Anyone could take advantage of her condition. I can't let her out of my sight again. Not after she lost hers. Tisha catches up with me, a blanket around her.

"Where is she going?"

"I don't know," I say, "I'll call her."

She doesn't answer. She doesn't answer Tisha's call either. Fallon walks outside with a blanket pulled over Adrian's head. And a letter for me. Once she hands it over, she takes Adrian back in from the damp and cold. My hands tremble as I open the paper. Tisha steps closer to me, worry written on her face. She's limping slightly from our adventures the night before...

The handwriting isn't my daughter's. She's had her attendant write it for her. But the signature is hers. It's scratchy and wobbly, but this is my daughter's work.

Dear Papa,

Enjoy your life with Tisha. I will not be a burden to you any longer. Do not contact me. I do not need your help to finish Oxford. Marco and I will take care of my personal affairs together. Tell Tisha that she can have you. I am not your daughter anymore.

— Carlotta

· · ·

I am not your daughter anymore. Bullshit. She's *mine.* She was mine the moment I laid eyes on her. When her mother died, I knew I couldn't afford to be a failure anymore. I stopped cocaine. I stopped my addiction to hot models and hotter yachts. I dedicated my life to this child. Carlotta and I may have a tense relationship, but she will never stop being my child. Fatherhood isn't a job... it's who I am. A father.

My beautiful baby girl. I would do anything to protect her. I would do anything to keep her safe. I've killed before and I would kill again if it meant keeping her safe. I'll kill Yiayia the next time I see her, just for stealing Carlotta's mother from her. Carlotta doesn't understand how deep my love runs for her. No one could ever steal a father's love for his children.

If Stavros is smart, he'll squirrel my grandmother to safety and warn her I know the truth. Tisha snatches the letter from my hand and reads it.

"This is horrible," Tisha whispers.

She's taking every word seriously with that youthful emotional timbre to her voice.

"It's nonsense," I snarl, "Melodramatic. Carlotta will return. If she doesn't come back by tomorrow, I'll retrieve her myself. She's my daughter and I'm not letting any more of my children out of my sight."

"What does that mean?" Tisha mutters.

Yes. I've decided about her. With Stavros after Yiayia and our secret exposed, I am in no mood to hesitate. I have Tisha West where I want her and I won't let her go again.

"It means, Tisha West... We're getting married. And we're doing it today."

"Um... don't I get a say?" she protests, pulling away from me. I grab her wrist and pull the nineteen-year-old close to me again.

"No," I snarl, "We've had enough games. Do you love me?"

"Yes."

"I love you. And we're having a child. I know I purchased your pregnancy, but the deal will be off. As my wife, you'll have whatever your heart desires. Oxford University. Money."

"*Wife*?! Loukas, we can't just... get married!"

"Why not?"

"Because... what about my dream wedding?"

"Damn it, Tisha... I'm not letting you get away again."

Her eyes soften like a doe's. My grasp on her tightens. Tisha works my fingers apart and interlocks them with mine. My shoulders relax.

"Right," she whispers, "And you don't care about a dream wedding because you've had like eight weddings already because you're *ancient*."

"Careful, little woman."

I grab her waist and kiss her. Hard. Tisha lets me dip her and clings to my neck. When I rest her on her feet again, she shakes her head.

"This is crazy."

"Yes," I tell her, "I'm a crazy Greek man in love with a young woman... and I want to marry you, Tisha West. Now."

"Can I update my Insta at least?"

"With *what*?"

"I don't post a guy unless I get a ring."

"I haven't given you a ring..." I mutter, barely understanding what she means.

"You will. And you're my boo for life soon, so I can post you now."

"Tisha... please, hurry it up."

She stands in front of me and pouts, taking a picture of us. She stares at it grinning.

"Ugh, it's so good. Your eyes are sexy as hell. And you're serving hot older guy looks. Mysterious."

She posts it and then her feed pops up.

"Is that my brother Gal?" I snarl, snatching the phone. Tisha grabs it.

"Loukas, you uncouth beast, give that back."

"Are you hiding something?"

"If I can't watch your sex tapes, you can't go through my phone," she says.

"Does your phone have *sex videos* on it?"

"No," she says, "But... still."

I don't listen to what she says next because I see Galanos' post. He's on a boat and he isn't in Albania at all. He's lying to Stavros. He's on Yiayia and Papa's yacht, and from the looks of the mountains in the background, they're close to England. I need to call Stavros. *Now.*

"Lou, are you listening to me!?"

I shake my head and hand the phone to her.

"Sorry. No."

"I *said*," Tisha repeats, "My phone has nudes. Which you can't see."

"Nude photographs? For who?"

"I sent them to you."

"No. You didn't."

"Yes. I did."

"I don't know how this stupid phone works," I grumble and hand it to her. Tisha rolls her eyes.

"And anyway," I tell her, "I don't need pictures of your ass. I believe I know it well enough."

She pushes me, and I chuckle, shoving my hands in my pockets. I glance over at her. She's beautiful.

"Get in the car," I tell her, "We're eloping, little woman."

"Okay. But we need all the crucial elements of my dream wedding."

"Okay," I say, "What does Tisha West need for her dream wedding?"

"A bucket of KFC wings, fifteen white roses, a pistol, and a cowboy hat."

The best part is, she's serious. I'd been waiting my entire life for a woman like Tisha.

FORTY-THREE
CUNNING

t takes a day of scouring the city and spending time with Tisha before we're ready. She's serious about her wish list.

Tracking down the cowboy hat is the hardest, but I set it on Tisha's head as she gleefully picks through her bucket of chicken for the "best bits". She doesn't care that her face is all greasy. I don't either. She's gorgeous. And her cravings barely add any weight to her frame, which I worry about. She needs cushion for the baby she's carrying.

I try not to cluck around her like a nervous hen. But it's difficult. She's carefree and I'm burdened... by my forties.

"We should go find Carlotta, shouldn't we?" she says, chewing vigorously on some chicken skin and then licking her fingers.

"We aren't married yet," I point out to her.

"You were serious about that?" Tisha says, just pleased to have her cowboy hat and chicken.

But I was very serious. No matter what I do, Carlotta runs. It's time to let my daughter know that if she can do whatever she wants, I'll do the same. And I'll still be there for her. Because she's my child. And a father doesn't let any of his children go —

including the child in Tisha's stomach. She's bigger than I remember her and definitely showing, but I'm smart enough not to tell her that.

"Yes, I'm serious."

"That's old-fashioned, Uncle Lou."

"I'm old-fashioned," I grumble, "And you'd better get used to it. I'm *keeping you.*"

"You make me sound like something the cat dragged in."

She chomps her chicken bone open and starts sucking out the marrow. Oh, Tisha.

"That's not it at all. I love you, Tisha West."

I stop her from walking so she knows I'm serious.

"The worst is over. Carlotta knows... but she'll have to learn to live with it. You are carrying my child. You're... the love of my life."

Tisha nods and finishes her chicken bone. I call an officiant. You learn to keep these people on speed dial wherever you go in my line of work. This man knew Ofek, and he remembered well what happened the last time Ofek crossed paths with a Pagonis. He agrees to meet us at a small Greek Orthodox church downtown. Tisha finishes her chicken and I clutch the white roses as I hurry over with her. When we burst into the small church, Tisha gets quiet. We sit in a pew toward the front as we wait for my contact. Tisha puts her now washed hands on mine.

"I am stuffed," she whispers.

"Hm," I murmur, "Good. It's good for the baby."

"You can feel it, you know," she says, "If you want."

"It's hardly larger than an apple," I mutter. Tisha takes my hand and presses it to her stomach as she whispers, "Ours."

How could I have ever considered leaving her? I take my fingers and interlace them with hers. Tisha rests her head on my shoulders.

"Does that mean in an hour, I'll be a mob wife?"

I snort and mutter, "You'll be a *studious* wife. I'll have you finishing Oxford. And perhaps... we can buy a house together."

Tisha straightens her back and then gets serious. She sighs and begins dutifully, "Loukas... as your future wife, I have an important announcement to make."

"Oh?"

"I... have no money. I can't afford a house. I can't even afford rent. I only dated Mason because he offered to pay next month."

"Can't afford rent? How are you living?"

"I'm getting evicted."

"Tisha!"

"What? I was having fun in Greece. I didn't have time for a stupid job."

"Don't expect to work in the family business," I mutter, noting Tisha's previous enthusiasm for all things mafia. The last thing I want is her involvement in family drama or worse. Tisha pokes her elbow into my side and giggles.

"I'd be great at the family business. No snitching. Ride or die. Shooting people... so *awesome.*"

"Shooting people does *not* inspire awe. It's serious."

"Whatever, Loukas. I won't shoot just anyone. Only people who get between me and my man."

"I'm your *man* now, am I?"

"Yup. But when you get my *late* engagement ring and then my *late* wedding band, you'll be my real man."

"I have an engagement ring," I murmur. I keep it in my pocket. A gift from my mother before she left us. When Carlotta turned eighteen, I tried to give it to her, but the ring didn't fit and she said it was old-fashioned, anyway. I take the gold ring out and slide it onto Tisha's walnut fingers. The ring fits. It has a single stone in the center, a pink diamond.

"Did you get this for me?"

"It's a family heirloom."

Tisha slips it on her finger and stares gleefully. One problem solved. She just loves me. She doesn't care about the glitz and the glamor. She only cares about Loukas. It's... different. But I love that about her. I love everything about her.

The officiant arrives, and he mumbles an apology. I hand him the cash, which is all the Greek bastard cares about, and then he performs the ceremony. I've had my fair share of weddings. I've done the big Greek family wedding with the insane drinking and the uncles and the aunts. But nothing compares to this. What I share with Tisha, I share with no one else. She says "I do" with a glowing smile on her face and I say the same.

When I kiss her, I don't want to let her go. I plan on *never* letting her go. I grab her hips and kiss her until the officiant clears his throat.

"It's official," Tisha says gleefully, "I'm a mob wife."

The officiant clears his throat and shouts to the back of the church, "Excuse me, but I'm conducting a service. If you could please wait—

And then there's a gunshot. Loud and cracking. The officiant hurtles over the altar and blood spurts from him. Tisha screams. I hold on to her forcefully. I need to get my bearings and get Tisha to safety.

"Run," I hiss, but I don't know where she'll go. Tisha lets go of me and I shove her toward the back of the church where I'm sure there's an exit. I turn toward the entrance and reach for my gun. *Fuck.* It's Papa. Three henchmen. And then Yiayia enters the church, holding her cane. Tisha's scurried off, but they know she's here. And they have the advantage over me. Galanos walks in behind them, his hands in his pockets.

"Hello, brother!" Galanos says, chipper as ever, then he turns to Yiayia, "I told you it would work."

"Excellent, Gal," she says, her voice wheezing like she's out of breath from walking in here, "Go find the girl."

"Gal," I snarl, "If you hurt her..."

Gal walks up to me and pats my shoulder. He leans in and whispers three words that send a chill down my spine. Then Galanos disappears into the back and I hear two gun shots. I wince. But I don't have a choice. I have to keep Papa and Yiayia busy.

"What are you doing here? You didn't just come here to assassinate me and Tisha."

"I learned to accept *one* black grand child. You couldn't expect me to sit back and accept *two*."

"That's it, then? Blood purity?"

"Yes."

"Liar," I snarl, "You killed Carlotta's mother. You killed every woman I loved."

Yiayia rolls her eyes and spits, "You are *so* melodramatic. Women are not for Pagonis men to love, especially not the gutter trash you and your brothers drag up from the ghettos of North America. Why can't you be more like Galanos?"

"Galanos. The man who just killed a nineteen-year-old girl?"

Papa sticks his gun back into the holster and pats his mother's shoulder.

"Mama. We've taught him a lesson. The next one is dead and there's a football game on. He's learned."

"Weak little shit," I snarl at my father, "Go watch your football game. There are three other men. I can't harm Yiayia as long as they're here."

She smirks as I say the word 'harm'. Unlike Stavros, I won't hesitate. I've taken no vow against killing. I suffer no guilt if I know I've done the right thing.

"You hurt Carlotta," I murmur, "So you should kill me if you don't want to die yourself."

"I don't need you dead," Yiayia says calmly, "I needed to abort your child. What I *need* from Loukas Pagonis, is understanding. You cross me again with another bitch or another fight and I will kill your daughter. Carlotta's in the hands of someone who works for me. And you have a choice... go to your dying woman in the back of this church, or go to Carlotta."

"No, Yiayia. I won't do that," I say calmly.

The doors to the church thrust open and Galanos fires. Three shots in quick succession. Stavros bursts in a few minutes after and finishes the job. Yiayia's henchmen are dead. My father has already dropped his gun and surrendered, which we all could have expected. Yiayia turns around slowly, confident that none of us will shoot her. And she's right. But she doesn't account for one important factor. Tisha, wielding a *thankfully* unloaded Kalashnikov, slams it on Yiayia's head.

"Take that!" Tisha screams as she lands her forceful blow.

Yiayia falls without making a sound. Galanos' three words burn in my ears. He could have been lying when he said those three words. But I trusted my younger brother, not having much of a choice, and for the first time, Galanos didn't let me down. *Stavros sent me.*

Very cunning, Stavros.

FORTY-FOUR
CARLOTTA & MARCO

Galanos yelps and crouches at her feet.

"You fucking idiot!" he squeals at Tisha, "Did you kill my grandmother!?"

"I didn't hit her that hard!" Tisha protests. I rush over to my wife and rip the gun out of her hands. There's blood on it. I squeeze Tisha close. If Yiayia's dead, we'll have problems. But if Tisha didn't knock her to the ground, I don't know what I would have done.

Stavros crouches next to Yiayia, but I'm distracted by Tisha. I hold her and kiss her.

"I'm fine, Lou!" she says, pushing me off, "And I didn't kill that racist old woman... but maybe I should have."

"That's not funny," I mutter. But Yiayia's words about Carlotta are still at the front and center of my mind. One of her people has Carlotta. That stupid attendant. He wasn't interested in her. He was taking advantage of her. Stavros announces, "She's alive. But unconscious. We need medical help for her."

Galanos already has his phone out, and he's speaking to a doctor. He has better English than any of us (except Tisha). Tisha now realizes how serious it is that she knocked an old woman unconscious.

Stavros now worries about the man my father shot, and he yells at Papa to get his ass out of the car and drag the body to the back of the church. One remaining henchman, more loyal to Papa than my grandmother, helps him move the body. Tisha stares at the gruesome scene. The officiant who married us is dead and all we have is a certificate in my pocket proving that she's mine.

Facing death turns Tisha's concern to the old woman she's just walloped over the head.

She whispers to me, "If she dies... do I go to jail?"

Stavros snorts and mutters, "If she dies... the bloody woman is immortal. I ought to finish her now."

Galanos pushes him, "That's your grandmother. Finish her and you'll contend with me."

It must be nice to be the favorite. I put my arm around Tisha and kiss her shoulder, "She'll be fine. Trust me."

I don't know if Yiayia will survive. I'm hoping she doesn't. That will spare me the guilt of having to murder my grandmother to avenge my daughter. Maybe that's what Tisha wanted to do in her own misguided way. But she's in over her head. This isn't her scene. I take her away from Yiayia's unconscious body for fresh air. She claims that she's fine — just hungry.

The doctor comes. He's accustomed to working with us when we're in England, but always recommends we leave his country as soon as possible. I don't think he likes the Greeks. It takes Dr. Cotton twenty minutes to arrive at this small church in Oxford, not too long all things considered. We adjust Yiayia's position on the floor. Galanos props up her head with a pillow from the altar, and we wait. She's still breathing when he examines her, but he mostly makes inaudible noises in English that not even Tisha can decipher. His prognosis is vague. Dr. Cotton believes her injury to be serious, which any of us might have guessed.

"Take her to the hospital," Dr. Cotton recommends, "There's a discreet private hospital that can assist you and keep your family business private. And Pagonis boys? I never want to see your fucking faces again."

Papa stops listening to the football game on the radio long enough to help us get her to a private room in a countryside hospital. Then he leaves to bury the man he killed. The hospital workers figure out we're mafia quickly. It's probably Stavros, dressed like the living dead as usual. He should have had a normal goth phase like the rest of us, but he's all about crisp lines, knuckle jewelry and scaring the shit out of people. There's only one person who isn't scared of him and she comes loudly stomping into the office with her newborn, demanding access to her husband.

Fallon arrives at the hospital with Adrian and drags Stavros into another room so they can argue about whether it's safe for her to take part in family drama with a newborn on her teat. Once Yiayia's settled, I have a more important task. Tracking down my daughter. But there's a detour. Tisha's talking to a nurse, about to lead her into another room.

"Tisha, I'm leaving."

"Wait! Lou. She wants to help me see what I'm having."

"Isn't it early for that?"

"Technology has come a long way since the last time you had a kid."

I had Zoe not as long ago as Tisha thinks. Thankfully, my daughter has tutors and horseback riding instructors to look after her all day, so she hopefully won't notice that we're gone. Zoe doesn't know about Tisha. I don't think she'll care. If she does, I think Tisha will win her over. She's won over Gal, clearly. He hovers nearby, glancing up at her and then turning his attention back to his phone.

"Fine. Let's see."

I follow her into the other room. The nurse puts Tisha on a bed and she lifts her shirt eagerly. Her stomach barely protrudes forward when the nurse slathers mysterious gel on her tummy. I hold Tisha's hand. Her fingers interlace with mine and emotion catches in my throat.

"No," I tell the nurse, "Stop."

"Unc—Loukas," Tisha says, "What's wrong?"

Panic surges through me. It happens every time I'm in this situation, but this time it's worse. This is Tisha. I've messed up a lot in my life and if I screw up this chance to do things right, I'll never forgive myself.

"I can't do it again. I'll mess up. Another kid..."

"Relax, Loukas," Tisha says, "You're being weird. Ignore him. He's emotional because I'm his *fourth* wife."

Now it's my turn to be embarrassed. The nurse gives me a disapproving look and then beams at Tisha. The little woman has quite the skill at charming everyone around her. The nurse continues with her implements and then says, "I'm surprised you're not bigger."

"Um... thanks?" Tisha squeaks, trying to look over her stomach.

"What do you mean, nurse? Is the baby healthy."

"There are two babies. Boys."

"Boys?!" Tisha says, sounding distressed.

"By the looks of it, yes."

"Boys," I whisper, running my fingers over Tisha's hand. The nurse hurries off to more important work after helping Tisha get the gel off. She sits on the edge o the bed and leans over.

"Tisha? You don't seem happy."

"What am I going to do with a *boy*?"

"Two boys," I remind her, "And I didn't take you for a sexist."

"I'm *not* sexist!" Tisha snaps, "It's just... I never thought I'd have boys. Or twins."

Twins. The reality hits her. Tisha jumps out of bed and says, "Well! Before I freak out, we should go."

"Are you going to tell anyone?"

"Yes," Tisha says, and she hurries past me and sits next to Galanos. My brother has a new tattoo healing on his hand. As Tisha whispers her news, Gal smiles and then taps something out on his phone. Maybe I could leave them both here and solve this on my own. I try to hurry off. Especially with Tisha and Gal whispering to each other in hushed voices. But Galanos notices me and follows me with Tisha in tow.

"What do you want?" I snap at them.

"We want to help find Carlotta," Tisha says, "to take my mind off the fact that I'm having twins."

Gal puts his arm around her shoulder, and my throat constricts. Why is he touching her like that? Holding her... I try to fight off the jealousy, but find that it barely works. Gal must notice me turning seventy-five shades of purple because he removes his hand and sticks them into his pockets.

"Tisha and I have an idea about where she might be. And Tisha says I need to be less of a prick. So I'm helping."

"Did you tell him we were married?" I snap at Tisha.

"Lou, stop acting so jealous. It's embarrassing," Tisha says.

Gal grins and elbows her, "You didn't tell me. Were you hoping we could start something up?"

Tisha smacks him with one of her roses, sending white petals spraying everywhere.

"Liar," she snaps at Gal, "I told him, Loukas."

"She did," Gal admits, "Congratulations. I will hereby give up all attempts to sleep with Tisha West."

"It's Tisha Pagonis now," she announces proudly.

"Carlotta," I say gruffly, "Now."

My daughter is still my priority. Yiayia's lucky I didn't finish the job Tisha started. I hasten toward the exit. I vainly hoped that Yiayia would awaken and I could shake the information about Carlotta out of her. That won't work. Not now, anyway. Tisha and Gal hurry behind me. My brother's blond hair is slicked back, and he wears a floral shirt halfway open with a pendant dangling there. I think about the necklace I found around Geo's neck and how I put his body into the ground. Bastard. That's what he gets for touching my family.

And Carlotta... I have to save her from the same fate. Yiayia messed with the wrong women when she touched Carlotta and Tisha. I glance over my shoulder and Fallon waves at me as she takes her biracial baby into the room with Yiayia still unconscious. She would have never brought Adrian around Yiayia if my grandmother were awake. I wonder if the baby's presence will lurch her out of her slumber.

The doctors are running their little tests. I'm less worried about Yiayia surviving than Tisha going to prison for her reckless act. Either way, it's my job to protect her now. If only Galanos weren't here. My annoying younger brother is too much of a flirt. And Tisha's my wife now. My protective instincts are in overdrive. I was never fatherly toward her. The type of love I had was always... this.

"I got suspicious when I heard Marco speaking Greek," Tisha says, "I didn't think he could work for your family."

Galanos explains Yiayia's ties in London and our trade routes in England. I didn't know he was so well-versed in the family business. Stavros has been trying to get him to take life more... seriously.

"He's a hired hand. They wouldn't have gone far. He's waiting for instructions," Galanos says, barely comforting Tisha. I reach for her hand and grasp it. But she's still worried. And pregnant. I don't want to put her in danger. But I feel that after getting shot at, Tisha's even more excitable than ever about her new 'mob wife' status. I might have to ban her from the television so she doesn't dive into too much danger.

I wish Gal could do better than his useless platitudes. Every moment we waste, Carlotta could disappear forever. We search Oxford's campus and waste valuable time turning up nothing. Carlotta still won't answer her phone or any of the other "direct messages" Galanos and Tisha try to send her. Galanos turns red with frustration as some message pops up on his phone.

"Is it her?"

"No," Gal says bitterly, "it's your *son*. Don't you keep track of your children?"

"Watch your mouth, Galanos."

"Antonio dropped her off at the airport. She's returning to Greece."

I haven't seen Antonio in days and I didn't think to call my son. I feel foolish.

"Blind!?"

"She has that idiot with her. Her *attendant*."

"He's taking her to one of Yiayia's spots, then. We need to go back to Thessaloniki."

"I have *a class on Monday*," Tisha complains, "I can't come."

Galanos rolls his eyes and picks his phone up after punching in a number.

"What are you doing?" Tisha says.

"Calling Latrice," Gal says, "She can take your notes for you."

"Who the hell is Latrice?" I murmur.

"She's my cousin," Tisha says, "She does the influencer thing, so she knows Gal. And she lives in London."

"How does she *know* my brother?"

"I introduced them," Tisha mutters and she sounds like it was a mistake. I can't imagine what Galanos has done to the poor girl. He speaks in rapid English and appears to arrange something for Tisha.

"Go to Greece," he says, "I'll stay here in case Carlotta changes her mind. And I'll babysit Zoe."

Galanos taking responsibility? I suppose he's twenty now. I was a mess at his age. Maybe my little brother deserves a chance.

"Can I trust you with Zoe?"

"I heard about what you did to Geo," Gal says, "I'm not stupid enough to mess with your kids. Believe me."

"We can sort this out soon," I say, "I'll get to Carlotta and fly back."

"I'll stay here anyway," Galanos continues, "For Yiayia. No one else cares, but she's still our grandmother."

"You'll put up with Papa?"

Papa sees Galanos as a threat to his perpetual golden boy status. He loathes his youngest. Galanos runs his hands through his hair and shrugs, "I have other reasons for wanting to stay in London."

"Thanks, Gal," Tisha says, hugging him. My heart still flips as she touches him. *She's my wife*, I remind myself. That won't change. I won't allow it to. Tisha and I hurry back to the house where we say goodbye to Zoe, who barely looks up from her horse-themed video game. I hate flying, but there's no faster way to get to Carlotta. Tisha and I board in Heathrow for the Greek coast. First-class seats are the best we can do on such short notice. Tisha curls up and pulls a blanket over herself as she leans on my shoulder.

"Twin boys," she whispers, "can you handle that, Loukas?"

"You're young," I tell her, "We can have as many children as you'd like."

"I should be in class," she says, "But... I owe it to Carlotta. She ran away because of us. Because we were selfish."

"No," I tell her, "not selfish. Those boys you're carrying are my children too."

"I betrayed her."

"Yes," I murmur, "We did..."

I kiss her hand and hold Tisha close.

"But I'd burn the entire world just to hold you," I whisper as I kiss the top of her head, "I hope we're blessed with many years together, little woman."

"I love you, Uncle Lou."

"I love you too."

I've always loved her. And I'll never stop.

Tisha rests her head on my lap and falls asleep until we land in Thessaloniki. If we're lucky, she'll only miss one day of class. If we're *very* lucky, she won't miss any of her classes. At the airport, they all recognize me. And stare. We return to the villa. Cassia and Sandros are there, tanning by the pool. Stavros had Sandros working in Egypt with Cassia, selling weapons to a group of young rebels. They're back — I suppose. Carlotta didn't come here, but Sandros knows one of her friends from town and rises from his tanning bed to help us track her down.

When Sandros takes Tisha inside to track down the friend's phone number, Cassia lifts her head.

"You fucked her?" she asks.

"Cassia, it's none of your business."

"Fallon tells me everything," Cassia brags, "But Tisha? Really. I didn't see you going for a girl Carlotta's age. Does she know you're old?"

I throw a pool noodle at Cassia, who laughs maniacally. My sister and I are, thankfully, on good terms now. Sandros makes a splendid match for her. He takes all her madness and passion, and he knows exactly what to do with it. Tisha walks back onto the pool deck, distressed.

"Loukas, we have a problem," Tisha says, "We found Carlotta and Marco."

"That sounds like good news," I grumble.

"The police have her," Tisha blurts out.

FORTY-FIVE
PRISON

"**P**OLICE?!" my voice booms.

"She broke into the Adamos estate and killed three brothers and their friends with Marco. He wasn't working for Yiayia. He's a double-agent working for Carlotta."

Working for Carlotta? Where the hell did she get the money? My heart sinks. It's me. I give her money whenever she asks and I never think to verify what on earth she does with any of it. But I recognize the names. Carlotta refused to tell me, but I'm a father — I have my ways of finding out.

My stomach lurches. The Adamos estate. The men Matilda hired to hurt her.

"I don't understand," I growl, "Yiayia hired that man to *kidnap* her."

"Looks like Carlotta was two steps ahead," Tisha says, "The cops have had her for half a day. She won't talk. They've apparently beat her attendant up pretty badly."

"She's blind!" I roar, "They can't have her in *prison*."

"The case is airtight," Sandros says, materializing nervously behind Tisha, "They can send her to prison now."

I told her not to do this. I told her to let me handle this. If Carlotta let me kill them, no idiot Thessaloniki cop would have hauled me to prison. But she's a woman and with her family scattered across Europe, they're holding her and doing God knows what to my daughter in their custody. I feel the veins bulging around my neck and my blood pumping furiously like an animal. I need to act. I need to *hurt* whoever put her in jail. But to successfully do that, I need to think. I need to get calm.

"Tisha, you need to stay here. Sandros, we need two AR-15s and three of the men from the village. Two black jeeps and tear gas."

"Loukas?!" Cassia snaps, sitting upright, "Shouldn't you try *talking to them* first."

"What the hell do I need to say? They will give me my daughter, or they'll suffer."

Tisha clutches her belly.

"Loukas," she says softly, "Cass is right. What about the kids? Not just ours, but... Zoe? Antonio?"

"They have Carlotta..."

"Don't you get it, Loukas?" Tisha snaps, "Carlotta's a big girl. You've done your best and you don't need to keep feeling guilty. You do *everything* for Carlotta and she doesn't appreciate you. She wants you to love her, but she wants her independence too. You don't always have to jump in and save her!"

"I can't let your best friend *die*."

"She won't die!" Tisha protests, "It's Carlotta. She's always fine. You raised her well enough to always survive. She can handle mafia life. She doesn't need you to save her."

My heart thuds in my chest.

"You want what every woman wants," I snarl, "You want me to choose. You or my daughter?"

"No!" Tisha yells, "You've made it clear that Carlotta will always come before me. But what about our sons? Are they going to sit here abandoned in some mansion because you're running off to save a girl who has made it clear she can save herself? I'm not a little girl and neither is Carlotta."

Cassia takes her sunglasses off and clearly listens keenly, but Tisha doesn't care who wins this argument.

"Carlotta will always be my little girl," I snap.

I don't want to be angry with her. I want to hold her.

"I was someone's little girl too. When you *kissed me*."

"You were... seventeen."

(Cassia gasps, but I ignore it.)

"Exactly. Carlotta's older than that. Let her handle things. Just once. Trust that she has a plan."

"What would you have me do?"

"Don't talk to the cops," Tisha says, "Let me talk to them. Trust me, Carlotta and I have gotten out of a few scrapes with the Thessaloniki police."

"I'll take a pistol. Just in case."

Sandros nods. Cassia puts her sunglasses back on and flips over so she can tan her back. I take a pistol and let Tisha drive the Jeep. She parks outside of the police station and hurries inside. Fifteen minutes takes an eternity to pass. But then she emerges. Carlotta and Tisha together. Tisha leads Carlotta into the backseat and shuts the door. Carlotta still doesn't say a word until we're back at the villa. Her attendant is noticeably absent. Tisha leads her to a chair in the living room and gives Carlotta a cigarette. She's done with her patch. Tisha drags me out of the living room and into the kitchen where Carlotta can't hear us.

"Aren't you going to say a word to her?" Tisha hisses.

"You didn't say anything either."

"You're her father!"

"You're her best friend..."

"We need to go talk to her," Tisha says, "Together. She's mad because... I told them they could keep her attendant in custody."

"You did?"

"I *negotiated*, okay? I'm new to this whole mafia thing. I didn't know which family to threaten, and I *definitely* didn't have any fingers to cut off."

"I'm disturbed about what you think my profession entails," I murmur.

Tisha snaps her fingers aggressively in front of my face.

"If we talk to her, I can get back to class by Monday. Come on."

Tisha drags me to the living room where Carlotta smokes her *second* cigarette. I glower at her, which she can't see. Tisha stands away from the cloud of secondhand smoke.

I say my daughter's name, knowing that she wants nothing to do with me, "Carlotta."

"Papa? I don't want to hear your voice unless you explain why you fucked my friend."

Carlotta's testy, and I deserve every bit. I betrayed her. I took advantage of a young Tisha West and then... I *married* her.

"I don't want to talk to you about that. I want to know what possessed you to shoot four young men," I grumble, pretending to have the higher ground.

The worst part about Carlotta is how her recklessness reminds me of myself. I wish she were like her mother. Soft. Innocent. But my daughter is all Pagonis: hell-fire and lightning bolts.

"They hurt me. I told you I could handle it," Carlotta sneers.

"You almost went to *prison!*" I yell. I want my daughter to understand the gravity of what she's done. They might have let her walk out of the station, but there will be a bribe. They'll want *money*. That's how this city works, like any other. The Adamos family will at least want us to pay for the funerals.

Murder is still a problem without prison.

"I don't care," Carlotta says coldly, "I worked hard to plan this. I fooled Yiayia. And I fooled you."

The second part brings her pleasure I didn't expect. There's no remorse. She got her revenge on Matilda and she got her revenge on the men who harmed her. She doesn't care who she had to hurt along the way. The beautiful blue-eyed girl I raised is ruthless.

My tongue hangs heavy in my mouth. I would die for Carlotta. I would do *anything* for her. Why didn't she let me do this?

"Is that what you want?" I mutter, "To humiliate me?"

"I want you to let me live my life, papa!"

"What about Tisha?"

"What about her?"

"You stole her from me," Carlotta sneers.

"He didn't!" Tisha says, "Carlotta, you're still my best friend."

"You're a snake."

"I saved your ass," Tisha yells, "And it's not my fault your dad is ridiculously hot!"

"Hot? That's disgusting!"

"It's not disgusting. He's hot, and he has a big dick."

"TISHA!" Carlotta and I scream.

Tisha clasps her hand over her mouth. She *definitely* didn't mean to blurt that out. Hearing the panic in her gasp, Carlotta laughs. And then I laugh. I break up the laughter by saying, "I'm sorry, Carlotta. I didn't mean to fall for Tisha. And I don't want to steal your friend."

"We need a custody agreement then. Fridays are for the girls."

"Fridays? What about when we have twins?"

"Twins!?" Carlotta shrieks.

"Surprise..." Tisha mutters, glaring at me.

"I am still taking custody of your Fridays. Papa will have to change the diapers."

"So you can accept this?" Tisha asks disbelieving.

"As long as I never have to *see* it. I can accept it."

Tisha wraps her arms around Carlotta, who hugs her (and nearly burns her hair with her cigarette). I sit across from the girls.

"Is this a good time to tell you we're married now?"

Carlotta screams and starts walloping Tisha with a pillow. But they're happy. And they're friends again. We're not quite finished with family business, but we're close to the end. Sandros can help me get Yiayia's boy out of jail and then we'll go back to England in time for Tisha's class on Monday. My phone rings as I walk out of the room, my wife and daughter in a friendly embrace.

"Hello?"

"Loukas," Stavros says, gasping, "It's about Yiayia. We need you back in England. Now."

FORTY-SIX
ENGLAND

Tisha stands over the bed, crying. I hold her hands.

"It's not your fault," I tell her.

"I *hit her* over the head!"

"Shh," I whisper, "Stavros has arranged it all. You won't get in trouble."

"I'm not worried about getting in trouble, Loukas," Tisha snaps, "She's... a person."

"Yiayia?" I ask, clarifying whether we're talking about the same grandmother who killed my exes and led to my daughter's blindness.

"Yes," Tisha says, frustration in her tone, "She's a person. And now, she's in a coma because I got caught up in the lifestyle."

I seriously don't know what Tisha means half the time. But she's so... cute. Especially now, with her reddened nose and mulberry cheeks. She sniffles and wipes her nose on her sleeve. I fight the fatherly urge to lecture her. She's not a little girl. Tisha is my wife.

"I'm sorry, Yiayia," Tisha whispers, "I didn't mean to put you in a coma forever."

"She's safer there," I mutter under my breath. Tisha hears me but pretends she didn't. I won't kill a defenseless old woman and for the first time in her life, Yiayia's truly defenseless. No wit. No minions. Except Papa, who holds his mother's limp hand and sobs, occasionally blowing his nose into a handkerchief or cursing under his breath at an online poker loss. He didn't react to the news of my marriage, but I expect little from Papa. I raised my siblings more than he ever did.

After giving us time alone with her, Stavros and Fallon enter again. Fallon takes Tisha into her arms in a warm hug. I missed when they became friends, but if Fallon approves of Tisha, that must mean something good. Stavros sighs.

"Galanos is heart broken. He hasn't moved in hours. You should talk to him."

"You did the best you could," I tell Stavros, "She's alive, isn't she? What more do we need."

Papa clears his throat and speaks for the first time in several minutes.

"You should all leave. I'll look after her. Mama... precious mama..."

He kisses her hand and breaks down in sobs again. The color drains from Tisha's face. Fallon sits next to Papa, who instantly puts his hand on her thigh. *Way* too high up. Fallon smacks him and his hand drops dutifully to his side. Fallon puts her arms around Papa's shoulders and tries to help him through his grief. Stavros leads the rest of us out of the room.

"We got here as soon as we could," I explain to him, "And I have Carlotta back in class."

"Good," Stavros says, "But we have trouble. The Adamos family..."

I pinch my brows together and massage my temples. Stavros' cheeks turn red as he fights back his temper.

"Your *children*, Loukas. Do you think you could control them for one second? Or is the problem that you can't control yourself?" he sneers.

Tisha steps between us and puffs up her chest. She barely comes up to Stavros' neck.

"Hey!" Tisha says, "Don't talk to *my husband* like that. I don't care if you're ten feet tall and *really* muscular, but I won't let you talk to Lou like that. He's a wonderful dad, and if Carlotta messed up, he'll help work it out. Just because he's old doesn't mean he doesn't have feelings."

Only someone her age could think I'm *that* old. I try not to let her see that it gets to me. Tisha, for her untamed tongue, loves me. That's all that matters. Finally, having her. But pissing off Stavros might take things a little too far. Even for her.

Stavros starts, "Look here you little..."

And then he trails off and grins. His grin turns to laughter.

"Loukas... how the hell did you find this one?"

Tisha seems ready to hide behind me again once she realizes that her impulses might have poked at Stavros' sensitive spots. But my brother, for all his faults, has a relatively good nature.

"I didn't find her," I muttered, "She found me. Brooding in some corner of Thessaloniki."

Stavros snorts and says, "Yes. Well, Tisha. I won't disrespect *your husband*. I'm glad we both agree he's nearly *elderly*."

Tisha's mouth drops open a bit and then she scowls and tries to think of something quick to say, "Loukas isn't *that* old. That's not what I meant. But he's a wonderful dad."

"Yes. He'd better be, hadn't he?" Stavros says, eyeing Tisha's slowly protruding belly, "Before you become a father to newborns at your advanced age, we will need to handle the Adamos family and unfortunately, we will need to petition Galanos for help."

Galanos sits at the end of the hall in the hospital on a bench, holding his phone in his hands. For once it isn't illuminated. He looks depressed — a condition I normally associate with Stavros and not my blond younger brother. Stavros mutters something about Fallon and Adrian before hurrying off to Yiayia's bedside. Tisha follows him. I suppose I don't want her providing Galanos with a shoulder to lean on. I'm the older brother. It's my job. I approach the bench and sigh as I sit next to Gal. My muscles are stiff. I need a good run to work everything out. Galanos's eyes are wet with tears.

"I don't care about anything anymore," he whispers.

"Oh? Five million followers not enough attention for you."

Galanos shoves the phone into his pocket.

"Yiayia was like a mother to me. She taught me that even if I could never live up to my older brothers that it didn't matter. I was a Pagonis... not just a shit head little kid."

"You *are* a shit head little kid."

Galanos bites his lower lip.

"She was protecting me," he whispers, "I see that now. In her own fucked up way, she encouraged me to be tough because she didn't want me to end up like Papa. The spoiled and coddled youngest."

"Trust me, Gal. You're spoiled."

"What if I want to grow up?"

I laugh and pat my brother's back. He sits up straight, like I've made him self-conscious. He's not such a *little brother* anymore. He's twenty, and he looks every bit like Stavros at that age. But blond. The hair is different, but his eyes are blue, like ours. He's a Pagonis man through and through. He loves women the way all of us do.

"You don't need to grow up," I growl, "We handle the family business and you... shop. And brag."

"Real men don't do any of those things," Gal snaps, "I don't want to be a fucking joke. Yiayia... she might not be here forever. It's time for me to stop hiding beneath my grandmother's skirts. It's time for me to choose what kind of man I'm going to be."

"Have you been talking to Fallon?" I ask suspiciously. My brother's wife enjoys flexing her past as a psychiatric nurse with her experiments on my fucked up Greek family.

Galanos shrugs.

"It doesn't matter," he says, "If I want a beautiful woman... one who stays with me forever... I need to be a man."

"It's your lucky day," I say to my brother calmly, "The Adamos family. We need your help with them."

Gal winces and shakes his head before protesting, "I can't."

"Yes, you can. Carlotta's in trouble. Prove yourself to this family by taking some responsibility."

Galanos opens one eye and mutters, "You are *far* too good at guilt trips."

"You can help."

"I dumped Thalia," Galanos explains, "For good."

"Oh?"

"For Carlotta, I'll try my best to help."

"And for Yiayia," I say, "Despite her cruel ways... there's a part of her that wants us to fight back against her. She wants us to be ruthless."

Galanos' voice gets low and sharp, "I am already, ruthless, Loukas. Trust me. And I am ready to stop playing silly games and join the family business."

"Swear it in blood?" I murmur.

I don't need to say another word. Galanos slips a pocketknife from his pocket and cuts his palm and then mine. The bonds of brotherhood are impossible to break. Even for Yiayia.

Galanos slips out to discuss business with Stavros and I return to the hospital room where Papa, Tisha and Fallon sit next to each other. Papa has his flask tipped to his lips, Tisha holding his shoulder on one side and Fallon on the other.

"What is this?" I grumble.

"He needs *help*," Fallon protests, "He's mourning."

"Not you too... Since when did you women get so soft on Yiayia? Have you forgotten whenever the old bat awakens she'll have not one but *three* black grandchildren. And she's racist!"

Fallon and Tisha exchange glances. Papa glares daggers at me. Fallon mutters something to Tisha, who drags me out of the room, frowning.

"Loukas, your father's heart is breaking."

"*Now* you want to get involved in my family drama?"

"I'm a Pagonis now," Tisha says proudly, "I'll never rat. I'll never snitch. I'll stay loyal. And that means getting through this *without* sending your Papa on a violent revenge quest. I did this to this mom. It's called playing it cool, Uncle Lou."

"I'm your husband," I mutter, "There's no need to call me Uncle Lou all the time."

Tisha grins and wraps her arms around me. I can't resist her. I take her in my arms and hold her close.

"I enjoy calling you Uncle Lou," she whispers, "It reminds me of being a seventeen-year-old girl, hopelessly in love with a guy who I never thought would look my way. And now... I'm having *twins.*"

"So you've come around on the matter of boys?"

"If they're anything like the Pagonis boys I know... bring it on, baby."

I kiss her. My beautiful, nearly twenty, Tisha Pagonis.

THE END
Get text message updates on new books: https://slkt.io/gxzM

Order the third book in the series, the story of Galanos and Latrice. If you enjoy romance books with plus-sized female leads, friends-to-lovers plot lines and most importantly dark BWWM mafia romance, you will love the story.

https://bit.ly/4seduction

ABOUT JAMILA JASPER

The hotter and darker the romance, the better.

That's the Jamila Jasper promise.

If you enjoy sizzling multicultural romance stories that dare to *go there* you'll enjoy any Jamila Jasper title you pick up.

Open-minded readers who appreciate **shamelessly sexy romance novels** featuring black women of all shapes and sizes paired with smokin' hot white men are welcome.

Sign up for her e-mail list here to receive one of these FREE hot stories, exclusive offers and an update of Jamila's publication schedule:
bit.ly/jamilajasperromance

Get text message updates on new books:
https://slkt.io/gxzM

EXTREMELY IMPORTANT LINKS

ALL BOOKS BY JAMILA JASPER

https://linktr.ee/JamilaJasper

SIGN UP FOR EMAIL UPDATES

Bit.ly/jamilajasperromance

SOCIAL MEDIA LINKS

https://www.jamilajasperromance.com/

GET MERCH

https://www.redbubble.com/people/jamilajasper/shop

GET FREEBIE (VIA TEXT)

https://slkt.io/qMk8

READ SERIAL (NEW CHAPTERS WEEKLY)

www.patreon.com/jamilajasper

JAMILA JASPER

Diverse Romance For Black Women

MORE JAMILA JASPER ROMANCE

Pick your poison...

Delicious interracial romance novels for all tastes. Long novels, short stories, audiobooks and more.

Hit the link to experience my full catalog.

FULL CATALOG BY JAMILA JASPER:

https://linktr.ee/JamilaJasper

DARK MAFIA ROMANCE PREVIEW #1

Sample these chapters from my best-selling Amalfi Coast Brotherhood Italian mafia romance series while you wait for my upcoming romance series.

If you enjoy dark & twisted mafia romance stories, you can binge the entire completed series on your eReader.

Enjoy the free chapters.

Click here to sign up for text messages about my new release:
bit.ly/textjamila

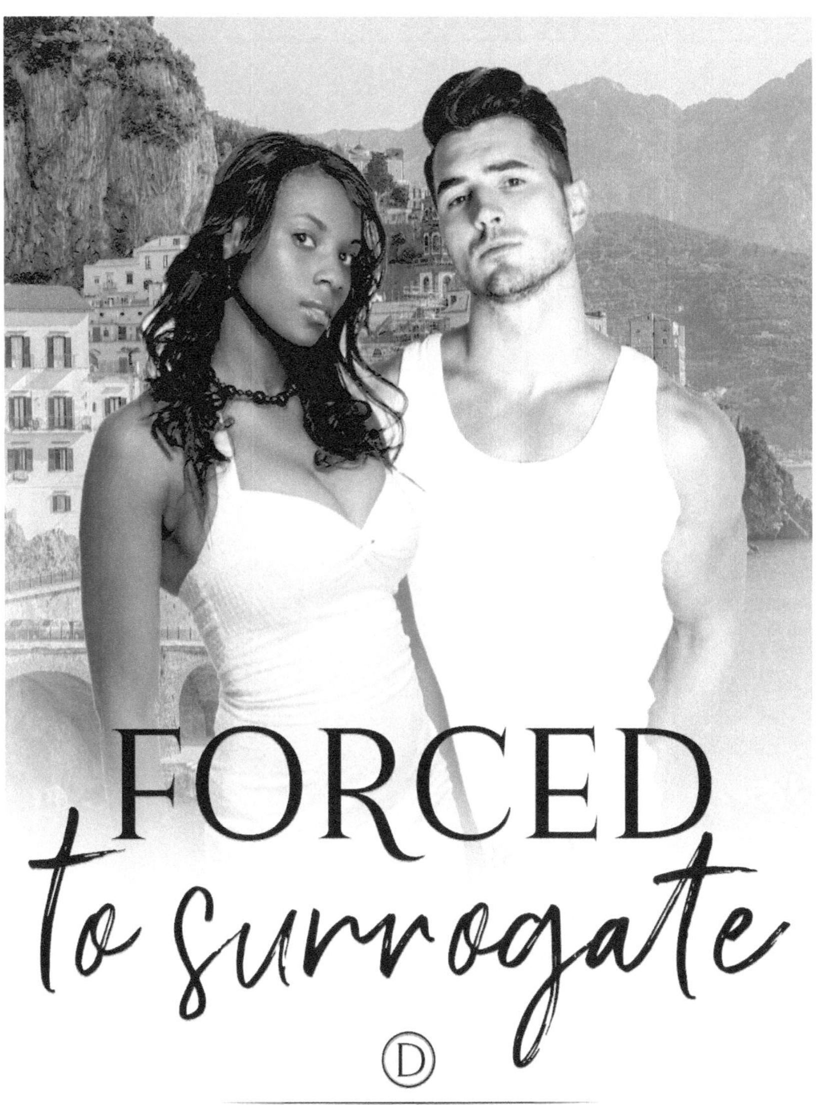

FORCED
to surrogate

BWWM DARK MAFIA ROMANCE

the amalfi coast mafia brotherhood #1

JAMILA JASPER

DESCRIPTION

The last thing Jodi remembered was a shot of tequila.
Next thing she knows,
Italian sociopath Van Doukas has her chained in his basement...
And he's claiming she agreed to become the mother of his child.

There's a detailed contract and everything... with her signature.
Jodi will do whatever it takes to get away from him...
But she doesn't count on the 6'7" Italian Stallion being skilled with
his tongue and excellent in bed.

SERIES TITLES

Forced To Surrogate
Forced To Marry
Forced To Submit

CONTENT AWARENESS

dark bwwm mafia romance

This is a mafia romance story with dark themes including potentially triggering content, frank discussions and language surrounding bedroom scenes and race. All characters in this story are 18+. Sensitive readers, be cautioned about some of the material in this dark but extremely hot romance novel. The character in this story is ***forced by circumstance*** into her situation.

Enjoy the steamy romance story...

ONE
PRODUCE A PURE ITALIAN HEIR
VAN DOUKAS

There aren't enough cigarettes in the world for meetings with my father. The boss. Tonight, I meet with him to discuss something 'very important'. He calls everything 'very important', but tonight, I know exactly what he wants from me.

He wants me to kill again, this time for my foolish sister, who can't seem to keep herself out of trouble. Everyone in the family heard about what happened to Ana by now. That idiot Jew was foolish enough to put his hands on her with witnesses and expect nothing to happen? That's not how the Doukas family works, which he'll soon learn.

You mess with the Doukas family, we retaliate. If the Jew had any wits about him, he would disappear from the Amalfi Coast and head for the mountains or Sicily, or somewhere we don't have ears. He could go to Albania like Matteo. Maybe then we wouldn't find him. But fuck, I don't want to carry out another hit. Why can't that lazy fuck Enzo do it? Or better yet, Eddie. I carried out my first hit when I was two years younger than him. We spoil the new generation and wonder why our family falls apart.

None of this would be my responsibility if Matteo would get over himself and come down off his fucking mountain.

I stop my motorcycle and approach my father's front door. The all white old European style mansion sits on an excessive and opulent lot on the coast, right above the cliffs with a long path to the beach, a 'fuck you' to the tax collectors and the government who want to stop us from doing business.

Most of my siblings still live here, but I prefer keeping myself far away from papa and his... associates.

I can hear the party from the entrance. Seriously? On a fucking Tuesday afternoon? I assumed he called this meeting because he was working for once. He's intertwined in a different business based on the noise filtering outside. Please, Lord, let me not walk in on my father having sex with a model... *again*.

I open the front door to our old family home without knocking and immediately regret it when a completely naked foreign woman runs giggling toward the door, too high and drunk to feel self-conscious, exposing her completely nude body to a stranger. At least I didn't find her twisted in bed with papa, although this isn't much better.

"Oh! Good afternoon, sir!" she teases me in crude Italian, spinning around to show off her assets. *Whore. Foreigner. Her tricks possess little interest to me.* My brothers Lorenzo and Matteo would sway more easily.

"Where's my father?"

She giggles and spins around again. Fucking hell, I wish the ground would swallow me up. My father's prostitutes do not interest me.

"Your papa?" she says, standing to face me with her legs slightly apart, daring me to ogle more of her body. I have no interest in whores and I want her to answer my fucking question.

Before I can answer, another one of my father's toys saunters into the foyer, naked. This one is young—she looks eighteen just about—far too young for my father. I grimace and keep my gaze firmly fixed away from the nude females. Just because the men in my family are bastards doesn't mean I have to follow suit.

If we don't conduct ourselves with respect, how can we expect the respect of the Amalfi Coast?

"Yes. My father. Sal," I grunt, failing to hide the irritation in my voice.

The woman ignores my irritated tone with her response.

"Oh, he's in the back with Boyka. I can take you there after we take you to bed upstairs."

How much is he paying these women? We're still struggling to get Jalousie off the ground and he spends all his money on Slavic hookers.

"Not interested. I have a meeting with him."

"Are you sure?"

I don't dignify them with a response. I walk past the girls, keeping my eyes away from their bodies. Where the hell is my father? I pass the long hallway with the family portraits and follow the loud music and the louder giggling from near the pool. The familiar sound of pool jets betrays papa's location.

He's in the fucking hot tub again, I know it. He spends all fucking day in the hot tub, dishing out orders and expecting work to happen without him lifting a fucking finger. It's a fucking miracle anything gets done around here.

My father chuckles loudly, and I brace myself before approaching him. He's the boss and you don't question the boss, even if he's your father and even if he cares more about partying and women than our family — than our future.

When I enter the back patio, the pungent smell of tobacco and marijuana surrounds me. Judging by the bottles of vodka on the ground, the piles of cigarette butts and the other piles of detritus, they've been at this fucking party since last night.

Fuck. I put the cigarette tucked behind my ear into my mouth and approach my father's outdoor speakers, unplugging them and stopping the little dance party happening around his hot tub. Three women, each wearing next to nothing with their tits out belly dance for him while he chuckles loudly, his fat stomach causing waves in the hot tub. When the music stops, they stop too and look up at me indignantly.

They don't have to ask who I am. The ones who don't know Van Doukas can tell that I'm related to Sal. I have my father's eyes, but thankfully, I don't have his overweight body or his bald head. The girls make booing sounds at me, but I brush them off.

"I'm here for our meeting," I say sternly to papa.

He chuckles and nods. "Yes. The meeting. I almost forgot."

Almost? He doesn't look like he's fucking prepared for a meeting.

Papa dismisses the girls, except for one — Boyka. She slides into the hot tub next to him, twirling his thick plumes of chest hair around her fingers and sliding his freshly cut cigar between his lips. Nauseating. Papa coughs after a puff and taps the cigar over the edge of the hot tub.

"You're early."

"I'm twenty minutes late."

"Oh?"

"Papa, you said it was important. Shouldn't we conduct this business alone?"

None of the girls are dumb enough to rat on Salvatore Doukas, but unlike my father, I don't see the sense in taking risks.

Boyka's hand moves down my father's chest and I don't want to imagine what sorry shriveled part of him she touches next. I just want my orders so I can get the fuck out of this bachelor pad.

"I'm getting old, Van," he says. "I'm getting old."

He didn't call me down here to bitch about his old age. I furiously puff on my cigarette, waiting for him to get to the fucking point. Papa grunts as Boyka touches something... sensitive. Cristo...

Watching my father grunt through a hand job might be the only thing worse than watching him stick it to a woman.

"Do you mind postponing your fucking hand job until later?"

Boyka's hand rises guiltily from the water and I choke down bile.

She really was touching the old fuck. I shouldn't swear at him or set him off. Papa might seem old, but he can have me killed. Any of my brothers would do it if he gave the command. Tread carefully, Van.

"Maybe I should leave," Boyka says, giving me a flirty glance as she plays with her tiny pink nipples.

"Yes," I snap. "Please get the fuck out of here."

Papa scowls. "Be respectful, Van. Boyka is a very dear—"

"I said please."

Papa smirks. "Boyka, return in thirty minutes. If we're not done..."

"We'll be done," I interrupt, glowering at my father. I don't have all afternoon for his games when I have the club to attend to.

Boyka reluctantly leaves.

"Are the women in this house allergic to fucking clothes?"

"None of them are allergic to fucking anything."

I'm not doing this with the old man today.

"Why did you call me here?"

I start another cigarette. I keep swearing I won't touch another, then I spend five minutes around papa and change my mind.

He leans back in the hot tub, displacing several pints of water over the edge.

"I'm tired, Van," he groans, leaning back and rubbing his forehead.

"From working?"

My father doesn't pick up on the sarcasm. He hardly leaves his fucking hot tub anymore, and he hasn't done anything even remotely resembling working at either of the nightclubs, restaurants, apartment complexes or construction sites around town.

If it wasn't for me and Enzo, he wouldn't have the fucking time to boink Boyka or whatever the fuck he does with all these young Slavic women.

I still have to tread carefully around him. He's still my father, my boss, and I must obey him.

"Yes," he says, coughing. "From working. I need someone to take my place and lead the family soon. I want to retire, Van. You and I both know I need a break."

He spends every fucking day on vacation while his sons and nephews run his businesses. Vacation? We're the ones who need a fucking vacation.

"Perhaps you should contact Matteo about that."

My older brother spent his entire life preparing to be the boss. It's not my fault he fucked off, leaving his worthless children with us, I might add. I'm already halfway through my fucking cigarette and he hasn't closed in on the point.

Papa scoffs. "Matteo hasn't left Albania in four years. He left his children, his business, his fucking money, and he's not coming back. Give up on him."

"You're the one who trained him for the role. Send Enzo after him. Better yet, send his fucking son."

I don't want to go into the mountains to bring my jackass older brother back and I don't want to have this conversation with my father.

"Why don't you go to Albania?"

"Every time I'm in the same room as Matteo, he tries to kill me," I remind papa. I love Matteo, but he isn't exactly easy to get along with.

I'm surprised a woman tolerated him long enough to allow him to give her Eddie.

"Fair. But I need a replacement, Van. I don't want to be the boss anymore. I can't take the stress much longer."

Stress? What stress? Does my father seriously think sitting in his fucking hot tub banging whores counts as a job?

"Have you considered the role?" He asks before I can spew something disrespectful in my father's direction.

"Why would I want to be the boss of this fucking family? It's filled with degenerates, fuck-ups, people who need more violence to be kept in line. I kill enough as it is. You don't want me to be the boss and nobody in this fucking family wants me as the boss."

"People respect you, Van."

"People fear me. There's a difference."

Papa nods. "Exactly. Personally, I think you would make a good boss."

"I disagree."

But I don't completely. Yes, the job would be horrific and I'd have even more blood on my hands than I do now by the end. I could bring honor back to our family, clean the streets of our scum, stop the Jews from fucking with our shit... but I can't. Not with Matteo gone. Even in the fucking Albanian countryside, he would find out what I did and Matteo would kill me.

"No," Papa replies calmly. "You don't. But I agree with your assessment that you're not quite ready."

"I never said that. I said I didn't want the job."

Nobody smart wants my father's job. He spent twenty years walking around with a target on his back before he built up enough trust, enough loyalty, enough captains in the streets of Italy to ensure his safety. I don't want to lose my freedom.

"You didn't have to say anything. I know my son."

"Hm."

Arguing with my father is entirely senseless.

"You need an heir, Van."

"What?"

"I will give you the leadership of this family without the ritual, without the sacrifice and without the financial investment required. All I want is an heir."

"Why don't I go up to fucking Albania, then? Because I can't produce a child out of thin air."

Papa chuckles. "Don't you have women? If you want a woman... I filled this house with them. I have very young ones too. Eighteen. Nineteen. They make good mothers."

"I am not interested in fucking teenagers."

"Then find a whore like that old Greek Pagonis fuck. I don't care how you get the heir. You can prove how serious you are by giving me a child. I'll be generous. I'll give you a year."

"I don't want this role," I snap. "So the likelihood I'll produce an heir is slim."

Papa laughs, which only infuriates me further. There's nothing funny about bringing a child into the world.

"You can't lie to me, Van. You were always the most ambitious child. Maybe it's because you were smack in the middle and we didn't pay any attention to you. Who fucking knows?"

My father spent little time raising any of us, except for Enzo, and look how that fucking turned out.

"Thank you for the psychoanalysis."

Every time I visit my father, my desire for alcohol increases exponentially, along with my cravings for nicotine. He brings the worst out of everyone, especially me.

"No problem," he says, again ignoring my sarcasm.

"What happens if I don't produce an heir? Eh? You still need someone to take your place."

"I make this offer to Lorenzo if you don't produce what I want."

"What?" I would have at least expected him to mention one of our cousins, one of the very obedient captains from the northern coast, or even fucking Eddie, Matteo's 18-year-old son, would be better than my irresponsible fuck of a brother. That old fuck really knows me well because he just said the only thing that could get me to reconsider his stupid fucking offer.

"You heard me."

"Lorenzo would ruin this family. For fun."

"I know. And it would become your responsibility to save it. You would have to act as the boss to save Lorenzo from himself. You might as well earn the position."

Fuck this old man...

"I don't want a family life, papa. I don't want the fucking wife or the fucking family. I want this life. It's what I'm good at. Business. Killing. More killing. That's who you taught me to be."

I'm not a man who can picture himself kicking around a football with my children or taking them to the beach. I'm not built for seducing women for more than a night and dealing with the danger of introducing them to my life or worse, hiding it the way papa did with our mother.

He can pretend it's not his fault what happened to her, but we all know the truth. No woman deserves our life. I can't afford to react. He loves when he can draw a reaction out of me.

Papa continues, as if my reaction is irrelevant. "Part of this life means having a family. I can't expect my other children to carry on my bloodline."

"Matteo has a son. You have a fucking bloodline. Why don't you make him the fucking boss?"

"Eddie? Eddie will not survive long the way he lives."

"That's a way to talk about your grandson, eh?"

"Have another cigarette, Van."

I'm already on my fucking third. But I'm not in a position to turn down his offer, considering the shit he wants me to deal with right now. An heir? I thought he wanted me to kill someone. Producing an heir in a year... It's just fucking impossible. I stick the cigarette in my mouth and light it.

"You can't let the family fall apart. We aren't the only people who would suffer. What would happen to our people, good Italian people, when the only people around they can get money from are the fucking Jews, who hate our guts?" He says.

I can't let his guilt trip work on me.

"I want an heir."

"Hm."

"Consider what you would sacrifice by turning down my offer, Van. It's not just about the family. It's power. You act like you're a fucking saint, but you are my son. You enjoy power. You're just too much of a stuck up cunt to let yourself enjoy it."

"Thanks papa."

"You're welcome. Now, onto the matter of the Jew."

Fuck. I hoped my father would only piss me off one way today, but if we're discussing the matter of the Jew, I won't leave here tonight without an assignment. Someone else could easily do this job, but he wants me to kill. Because I'm good at it.

"I suppose none of my other brothers have the free time to do this?"

"I don't care. I need you to do it. The cunt offended this family."

"Perhaps we waste too much time retaliating for every offense. Ana told you to drop it."

I'm taking a risk just questioning his order, but he's pissed me off so much that I stopped caring.

"Decision making isn't women's work. It's our work. The man signed his own death warrant. I want it done soon. Call me when you finish the job."

"Hm."

"If you don't like the way I run this family, Van, you know what to do. I want to retire. Make an old man happy."

Drugs and whores are the only things that make my father happy.

"An heir," I scoff. "You want me to have a fucking bastard child to continue your bloodline? A bastard won't have any loyalty to his family. Children have a mother and a father, a mother they spend all their time with. If I fuck some poor woman, you won't have an heir. You'll have a problem on your hands."

"Then get creative. If you need to get the baby and kill the mother, do what you must."

What's happening to this family? When did we lose our way and talking about murdering women for our own ends? Papa... This life changed him. It was slow, but it changed him completely. Too bad there's no getting out.

"Thank you for the advice."

"You're welcome. Now get Boyka back in here and get the fuck out. I need relief."

"Good evening, papa."

I drop my cigarette on the ground without bothering to step on it. Maybe my father's right — it's time for him to retire. But how the fuck will I get an heir? I need help.

There's one person I can call on for assistance in these matters. I don't like involving the Greeks in Italian business, but... they're our cousins. She answers after a few rings and it sounds like she's at a nightclub. She has an inordinate amount of time for parties...

"Ciao?"

I can barely hear her over the sound of the music.

"Miss Pagonis. It's Van."

She giggles. "Duh. What's happening? You finally have work for me?"

"How soon can you come back to Italy?"

Click here to learn more about where to buy the book:
https://www.jamilajasperromance.com/blog/forced-to-surrogate

MAFIA PLAYMATE
PREVIEW #2

BOSTON IRISH MAFIA ROMANCE SERIES

Mafia Playmate

Mafia Property

Mafia Surrogate

Mafia Possession

Mafia Stalker

Click here for the complete collection:

www.jamilajasperromance.com/catalog

CONTENT AWARENESS

Read this passage if you require content warnings for sensitive material. I do not give detailed content warnings that will spoil the plot, but be aware of this note.

This is a mafia romance story with dark themes including potentially triggering content of **all** varieties, violence, frank discussions and language surrounding bedroom scenes and race.
All characters in this story are 18+
Sensitive readers, be cautioned about some of the detailed romantic material in this dark but ***extremely hot romance novel.***

DESCRIPTION

A large pink box arrives on Aiden's doorstep with a woman inside.
His mail-order bride arrives in her birthday suit and tied up in knots
with a pretty pink silk ribbon.

Aiden never requested a dark-skinned beauty...
His family would never approve of such an impure connection.

Who is this woman? What does she want?
A note in the box reveals the truth...
**The woman in the box - *Valentina* - is a gift from an anonymous
sender who wants something dark and twisted in return.**

CHAPTER
ONE
AIDEN

*You have one job in the Murray family. You grow up, you get your marks,
you listen to Pa, you marry a nice Irish girl, preferably a blond or a
redhead with lighter features.*
You do what Padraig Murray asks.
*You pray everyday and you keep your rosary wrapped in your pocket. You
stay loyal. You keep our bloodline strong.*

Pa demands a meeting with me now that I'm back in the
city. He claims it's important, but it can't be that important
if he wants to meet me during the Red Sox game. It feels
good to be home. There's something special about Boston, but
maybe that's just it – paradise is wherever our family is.

After Pa, I'll go home and see Roscoe, my Rottweiler. Then get my
shit together and call my younger brother Darragh to check in on his
training and find out if Rian's around. Over the weekend, I'll head to
Leominster to visit Callum and then Sunday after church, stop by to
see Ma and Odhran. I brought a gift home with me for Tegan, Rian's

daughter, and I can't wait to see my niece's face light up when I give it to her.

If there's one thing I don't miss about being home, it's a never ending list of shit to do.

I meet my father at our usual casual meeting spot, Mulligan's, a place where we aren't afraid to celebrate Irish pride. A place where you can catch the Red Sox game and no one can catch your conversation. *It's as much home as anywhere else.*

I spot my father hunched over the bar from the street, his face illuminated by a warm orange bulb as he watches the pre-game announcer talk. I prefer football to baseball, but Pa bets on all their games, so he likes to keep his eye on the Red Sox each season.

When Pa calls, you answer, and he's desperate to know about the affair with the Italians – what the fuck happened, have I found the renegade cousins who pissed off the Italians, and whether I've killed them yet. *I haven't.*

It's all bad news and my ass is on the line if I don't find a way to sort out all the shit that happened in Long Island. At least we're guaranteed peace with the vicious Italians. *Those greaseballs aren't any better than the blacks. 'Trust 'em as far as you can throw them', Pa told me. But for now, we have peace and that's what matters. At least to me.*

I enter Mulligan's and the conversations fall to a hush. *Aiden Murray's back.* I clear my throat and the conversations continue. But there are more phones pulled out than before and two guys sitting in the back leave. I don't hate the reputation I have. Most of the bar fights I earned this cutthroat reputation in were Darragh's fault, but that doesn't change what people say about me.

Darragh, my younger brother, can still throw his weight around in the ring, but he got his practice here, in this fucking place. Our last fight here was over a girl. Darragh kicked some Puerto Rican's ass and a few of our boys jumped him outside... I don't know what happened to the guy after.

My father slides a twenty-dollar bill across the bar to the

bartender, Finnegan O'Malley, a one-eared ex-hitman, who in turn fills up two glass pints of amber Sam Adams. Pa's already several drinks ahead of me. *Great. The news can't be that bad then.*

I pull out a bar stool next to my father, who barely acknowledges me, although he must've caught me entering the bar through the reflection on the glass behind the bartender. He shoves one of the pints across the bar towards me. He knows I prefer Guinness, but I don't mind starting with this. I can see my dad's reflection in the glass. He looks older than I remember. He's pushing 70, so I shouldn't be surprised by the large streaks of gray through his slick hair which was once blond, but changed color throughout his life, settling on a dark chocolate brown, like Rian's.

I glance at the television to check the score, but the game hasn't even started yet. I can smell the alcohol coming off of him already.

"You can have a Guinness after you drink this," he says. "I heard you did good work with the Italians."

He sounds raspy, but calm. My tension dissipates. This is just a normal, father-son meeting. Nothing to worry about.

"I didn't find Eoin or Robert. Haven't heard fuck since they all screwed with Vicari," I say as I take a sip of my beer.

"Maybe the Italians killed them," he says. "They're a violent, vicious group of people."

"Yeah."

Like we're ones to talk. Pa's done with his Sam Adams already and waits patiently for me to catch up, as if I could catch up to a man who's been drinking for an hour. At forty, it's not so easy for me to keep up with long nights of drinking. I don't know how he does it.

He waits for me to have a few more sips, his eyes glued to the television. Chris Sale throws the first pitch. It doesn't go so well. My father glances down at his glass and sighs. "It's going to be a long night."

"That bad this season?" I grunt, glancing up at the Detroit batter sliding into second.

I've been too busy to keep up with baseball. My father grunts. Yeah, it has been that bad.

"Any other news?" I ask him, finishing off the Sam Adams. Dad grunts and snaps his fingers for the bartender, Finnegan. The buff, tattooed bartender hustles over as dad orders two Guinnesses without opening his mouth. Bad news if he's drinking Guinness.

"Cops got Rian last week. They're charging him with manslaughter."

Manslaughter?

"What did he do?"

"What the fuck do you think he did?" Dad responds calmly. "He killed somebody, they caught him. That boy's not careful enough and I have to pay to get his ass out of trouble. Maybe some prison time would do him good."

"That's what you said the first three times," I grunt. Sale throws a good pitch and my father's face visibly brightens.

"If it weren't for Tegan, I'd let him spend a few extra years behind bars," Dad confesses. "Your mother won't let me do that to his daughter."

"What's going to happen to her?"

"I don't know," my father says. "No one has seen the kid in a week."

"What?" I growl, sipping at my beer and hoping this is my father's idea of a joke since he sounds dangerously unconcerned.

"What do you mean no one's seen her? Is she with her ma?"

My father shrugs.

Rian's notoriously bad taste in women landed him with a child he should have never brought into the world. She's a sweet girl, but doomed by a mobster father and a whore mother.

Her ma doesn't live in Boston anymore. She wants nothing to do with Rian.

"Where does he say she is?"

"Last time he saw her was the night he got arrested," Pa says before taking a sip of his beer.

"What about the cops? Did they give her to his lawyer or something?"

I don't have a single paternal instinct in my body, but my mind courses with worry over Tegan, despite my father's calmness.

"She'll turn up," he says, pouring more alcohol down his throat.

Fuck, Rian. My brother must be an even worse parent than our father. His daughter's missing and he's behind bars and there's no one else to look for her except...

"I can find out where she is. Once I get Roscoe and take care of–

"It would serve him right if something happened to her," my father says coldly. "Her mother isn't Irish. He keeps fucking up. I'm tired of cleaning up his messes. Now *drink*. This is not why I asked you here."

I bristle at his comment, but it's just Padraig Murray. This is who he's always been and my brother should have had the good sense to keep his dick in his pants. I made it to forty without fathering bastards all over Boston. Rian should have been more careful. I drink a few more sips, but I can't let this go. *Who else will worry about the fucking kid if not me?*

"How the hell did Rian let this happen? Can I talk to him?"

"Best that none of us talk to him. The cops listen to everything. I can get messages into the prison and messages out, but I don't want you talking to him."

"Fine," I grunt, finishing off my first round of Guinness and ordering us another. I try to pay, but my father stops me and then finally answers my other question.

"Your idiot brother trusted a woman," he says. "He wants a mother for that little girl so badly, that he's willing to do anything. He's willing to kill for a woman who doesn't deserve him."

"I didn't know he had a woman," I grumble.

"*Had* is correct," Pa says. "She's dead."

I wish I could tell you a chill ran through me, or I had some other human response to my father's announcement. I don't need a university degree to understand what he's implying. Rian had a woman, she got him locked up, so my father had her killed.

"Will that affect his case?"

"No," Pa says. "It was very clean."

"Who?"

"None of your business, Aiden. You worry about your shit, I'll worry about your brother."

I want to feel sorry for Rian, but he deserves it for crossing our father. This is what happens when he pisses off Padraig Murray. More problems for all of us.

"How much time is he facing?"

"Three years since he's been in jail before. I tried to get that stupid motherfucker to get his life together, but your brother just wants to be a fuck up."

"Who's the lawyer?"

"Someone from Nigel & Bancroft."

At least he isn't cheaping out like he did for Rian's first case. I don't want to push my father's buttons, and despite his outward calm, he must be furious at Rian for drawing more attention to us, but Rian has his uses.

"It's Rian," I remind him. "Crazy fucking Rian. We need him out soon. There are some jobs only Rian has the balls to handle."

Padraig snorts. "He takes after my father. Too proud and too violent for his own good."

We created the monster Rian Murray is. He's our responsibility.

"He needs another woman."

"He needs a woman who isn't a fucking spic," my father spits. "At least the child looks white."

"What about this previous woman? What'd she look like?"

"It doesn't matter," he grunts. "She's dead. Now drink. We have more important things to talk about than your idiot brother and his shitty taste in women."

I drink because Pa commands it. I do everything he commands

and have since I was a child. I have the burns and scars to remind me of what happens when you disobey my father. At first, I hated him for what he did to me, but to keep an organization like ours together, you need to inspire fear.

You have to be cruel to survive – that's just how the world works. I can't let Tegan go. The second I see Darragh, I'll ask about her and track her down.

I drink so I don't lose my temper. He doesn't give a fuck about Tegan. No one does. Maybe he's wrong and one of my sisters took her in. But who would do that? Evie's saddled with her drunkard husband and two unruly kids of her own – Katie and Patrick. Kiara's off at university and Maeve's sixteen, too young to have any involvement.

"I need to tell you something important," my father says somberly, as if there could be something more important than my missing niece right now. I'm burning with desire to leave, but if I get up without my father's dismissal, he'll hurt me. Or someone I care about. Not like there are many of those people yet. It's foolish to get close to people in this life.

"Then tell me."

If he notices my tightening tone, my father doesn't acknowledge it.

"There's a plot against my life. I don't know who. I don't know why but... there's someone out there trying to kill me," my father says, the faded tattoos on his knuckles even more wrinkled than I last remember. He's getting older, but aside from his physical appearance, he shows no signs of slowing down. If anything, he's desperate to prove himself more. If he wasn't ordering more killings than necessary, maybe Rian wouldn't be locked up.

I don't want to dismiss his concerns as paranoid, but he's the leader of our family. There's always a plot against his life. It comes with the territory. My father doesn't have to worry because he has us. *Family.*

"Fuck that," I grunt. "No one would be stupid enough to try to kill you. April 2013, four days after the bombing. An entire decade ago. That's the last time anyone tried."

I was thirty back then, old enough to be the one who ended that war before it started. Back then, we only killed when necessary. I got five tattoos that year, one for each kill. Each a painful release, each representing a necessary act to keep my family safe.

My father smirks and keeps drinking. He shrugs. "That's what I thought. But I'm serious. This time is different. This time the bastards might just get me. I'm getting old, Aiden. Most guys in our line of work don't make it this far."

"What happened?" I grunt, urging my increasingly drunken father to get to the point. His cheeks blaze tomato red with alcohol and his blue eyes swim with tears, again brought on by drinking rather than any emotion. He grunts and knocks his biggest gold ring against the bar's surface contemplatively.

If anyone tried to kill him, surely Darragh would have mentioned it. He's responsible for keeping our father alive.

"I feel it in my bones," Pa replies. "Someone wants to destroy our family."

"Yes," I grumble. "Our cousins. But they're gone and if they were anywhere near this city, we would have heard about it."

"I don't know. Something big is coming for us. I feel it."

"We can make decisions based on feelings now?"

"Cut the shit, kid. You know my instincts are good because you're like me. You can smell shit before it hits the toilet bowl."

"I'm home. If anyone tries to kill you, they'll have to get through me, Darragh, and Callum."

My father smirks. "My boys. I'm proud of all of you. Except Rian. He's a piece of shit."

Ah, Padraig. Honest as fuck, especially when he's drunk.

He might not be proud of Rian, but he still loves my brother enough to spring for decent lawyers and to make sure Tegan goes to the best day school in Boston. Once she's old enough, she'll go to Milton or Dana Hall, or another nice private school where she can meet someone to untarnish her sullied blood, that is as long as I can find her. If Rian's behind bars, she could be anywhere. Hopefully not with her mom's people.

She belongs with us, even if Rian made mistakes. She looks like us and that's good enough to cover up his shameful behavior. I don't know what Rian was thinking with that Puerto Rican chick. Tegan's mother was low class.

Let's hope my brother's behavior doesn't come back to haunt all of us. Let's hope his daughter is safe, sound asleep somewhere and protected.

"Thanks, Pa," I mutter, uncomfortable with even this much emotional closeness between us. I love my father, but trusting him too much is dangerous. Rian found out the hard way that it isn't worth it to defy our family beliefs, and it definitely isn't fucking worth it to screw around with the wrong women.

"And Aiden? I need you to hurry the fuck up and find a wife. I'm getting old and I want to retire, but I need a family man to lead this family. You're the oldest. Why the fuck can't you keep a woman? Do I have to send you back to Galway?"

He wants a real answer.

"Not interested in chasing after girls, dad. All they want to do is take your money and ask where the fuck you're going. I've had enough."

"That old dog won't take care of you when you get old."

"Neither will some Boston snob who could take my ass to the cleaners in a divorce."

He laughs, which is the best reaction I can hope for. He quickly moves along to talking about the game and his plans for the business, and then asks me questions about Long Island. They're a mess out there, but doing better under John Vicari's leadership. We're developing a few buildings together and are prepared to make a lot of money in the real estate game. John does cleaner business than his father. Too bad the old man died of a heart attack... that's the word anyway.

"I need you to find a nice girl," my father reminds me once he's almost blackout drunk. He can barely keep his head up. *Great.* I'm not dragging his ass outta here tonight. If he wants to get so wasted he can't sit up straight, I'll leave him for Finnegan.

"We have this conversation every time we talk."

"This time, I'm serious. I want to retire. I don't want you bringing home no spics either like the Duffy boys."

"Fuck's sake, Pa. You can't talk like that around here anymore."

"I can say whatever the fuck I want. I want Irish children. Irish fucking children and I need you to have a wife so I can retire."

"Retire any old fucking day you want," I growl. "It'll be good for you to stop worrying about who I fuck or marry or the fate of the fucking family."

"The fate of the family matters," he says, taking another sip of his newest glass of beer before rubbing condensation off the sides with his napkin.

"I'm too old to have kids," I growl. "I'm too old to get tied down. You and mom were lucky you even found each other."

That's bullshit and we both know it. They stay together because they're Catholic, because back in the eighties, my dad killed someone for her father and won my mother like a prize. He also put a baby in her quickly and then kept her pregnant. There's nothing romantic about their love story or marriage in the Murray family.

"If you can't find a girl, I'll find one."

"The last girl you found me was a crazy fucking redhead who wanted to bring Roscoe Jr. into the bedroom. No thanks."

My father shrugs. "She was white. Do you know how hard it is to find a white girl around here who hasn't been fucking ruined by some fucking Puerto Rican or black guy?"

"What do you want from me, Pa?"

I know what I want. I want an end to this conversation, and I want my father to give me a fucking break about women and dating. All the Irish and Catholic women in Boston know to stay away from us, and the ones who don't learn their lesson pretty fucking quickly.

"Find a nice white girl with big tits and blond hair and get her pregnant so I know you're fucking serious about family. That's what I want."

"Give me time."

He continues, getting to what I suspect was the original point he wanted to make before the liquor got to him. "And get your ass to the site in Back Bay tomorrow bright and early."

"Why?"

This is the first I'm hearing about something wrong at the Back Bay construction site. I know something's wrong because my father doesn't do anything bright and early unless there's a problem to solve.

"You'll find out tomorrow. You just got back. Go home. Pet the dog. Your mom's tired of walking that big fuck. He nearly knocked her over near Harvard Square."

"How is mom?"

"Pissed off."

"Why?"

"Eh. Upset about another woman. It's nothing."

It's nothing. Dad just got his second mistress pregnant and even if we all know about it, we're all supposed to pretend it's no big deal that our elderly father knocked up a Irish teenager who he supposedly hired to clean the construction company office.

I hate how he treats our mother. What's the point of having a family or a woman if you hurt her? There's no getting through to him, but I have to try for my mother's sake.

"You treat her better, pa. Seriously. She needs you."

He grunts. "Get your ass home kid and get a white girl pregnant."

"Thanks, dad."

"If you can't find one, I'll find a good Irish girl who needs a green card and bring her over to you!"

My father is the last person I want picking my romantic partners. I mutter something to him about cutting back on liquor, then I pat my father on the back and leave the bar. This is the closest we've felt in years, but there's still a wall between us and there always will be. I felt closer to him when I was younger, when it was easier for me to justify the life I led. I know I'm a screw up, I know I don't belong anywhere near a woman or a family or any of the fucking things my father wants from me.

He knows it's wrong to bring a kid into this life, but he did it anyway. He knows that we're villains, but he doesn't care. Fuck, I don't care either, I suppose. I'd just rather not ruin a perfectly good woman.

I drive out of the city listening to rock classics on the radio. Just as I turn down my street – I live at the end of a cul-de-sac – I notice the large box on my front step. There are only five large houses at the end of this cul-de-sac, all of us with wide open well-maintained lawns around traditional New England colonial houses.

The box on my front step is fucking enormous – and I don't remember ordering anything for delivery. My hand moves swiftly to the pistol under my seat. I feel no fear as I reach for the gun and slip a mag out of my pocket. I feel ready.

Leaving the city for any amount of time always carries a risk, especially since I didn't exactly leave the place with a house sitter. The last time my teen brother Odhran house-sat, he trashed the place and had a threesome in my bed. I hop out of my black GMC Sierra with the gun under my coat and approach the box slowly, glancing furtively over my shoulder for anyone who might have eyes on me.

The box has holes in it. It's large. Pink. Wrapped in a bow. I reach for the bottom of the box and try to lift it. *Fuck.* It's heavy. I drop the box and I swear I hear a sound coming from inside it. *Is that possible?* I try to peek through the holes but it's too fucking dark and something's telling me opening this box will be a shitshow. It has to weigh about a hundred pounds. Maybe more. I'm no weakling, but it still takes a measure of back strength to lift a box that fucking heavy.

I open my front door and greet Roscoe Jr., my rottweiler, as he bounds towards the door to greet me. His coat looks shiny, the nub of his docked tail wags back and forth. Pa's choice, not mine. He runs up to the box and sniffs at it a bit.

There's definitely something in there and it gets his attention because Roscoe utters a low bark.

"Roscoe, go lie down."

Once he heads off to his bed, I throw my doors open wider and eye the giant box to decide how to carry the fuckin' thing. I would call Rian if his stupid ass wasn't in jail. I could call Callum, but he's still hung up on some fucking girl and won't answer my calls because I won't sugarcoat my opinion of him. Then there's Darragh... He's probably twice as drunk as Padraig. Not a good option either.

I'll have to carry the box myself. I stretch a little and then grab the edges of the box and grunt as I carry it a few feet inside my doorway. I set the box down more gently. *Is there something alive in there?* If it were an animal, I suspect Roscoe would be barking from his spot in the house, but he's laying down as I commanded, gazing at me curiously and wagging his tail.

He's probably wondering why I'm not taking him for a walk since I'm back. *At least he didn't bite the sitter this time.* I close my front doors and then search for an opening on the giant pink box. Finding none, I start with the ribbon and peel it away. The box comes up to my waist. It's *enormous.*

If it didn't weigh a hundred fucking pounds, I would assume it's a novelty gift or something extra special from one of my brothers. Which of my piece of shit brothers would get me a welcome home gift? It's not like either of them are here with a six pack of Guinness right now...

I peel the top of the box open and there's another box inside it, also pink. I open the second box and stumble backwards as I expose the contents. I don't mean to act like a fucking idiot, but I nearly fall over, because this is the last thing I expected to find on my doorstep. I just got back to Boston... How long has that box been out there?

Holy fuck, why isn't she screaming?

I gain control of myself and approach the box again, heart pounding because my second assumption is that the human female in the box might be dead and that's the reason she hasn't made a sound. The sick thought twists my stomach into an unyielding knot.

I slowly approach the box again, ignoring my heavy breathing, focusing instead on taking in as much information as possible about the situation. I move the flaps of the box open and stare at the woman's face.. Suddenly, her eyes snap open before swiveling around and looking me directly in the eye..

Holy fuck, this woman is alive.

"What the fuck is this?" I grunt to myself. Not to myself. I'm not alone. I dry swallow and run my fingers through my hair. She's black. Someone tied up a black woman in a pink ribbon, wrapped her up like a gift and put her in a box on my doorstep. This has to be a sick joke.

I'm almost too scared to reach into the box and touch her, but I have to touch her to get her out of the fucking box. Whoever this woman is, she ran into the wrong fucking people and ended up in the wrong living room.

I have tattoos and vows of loyalty to prove how I feel about people like her. "Don't worry. I'll get you out of there."

I don't know why I'm bothering with comfort. I reach into the box and grab her at the base of her spine before hoisting her out of the box and gently setting her on the ground. My stomach lurches. This is some sick, twisted shit. Whoever did this to her stripped this woman naked, bared every inch of her dark skin, the color of Arabica coffee, and wrapped her in a pink ribbon, contorting her limbs and running the ribbon over her bare breasts, between her thighs and in loops around her body so she's wrapped up like a chocolate present.

My body has an unconscious, primal reaction. I could unwrap her like the present she's been wrapped up to be, but I need answers quickly.

She has a gag in her mouth, a round white ball that keeps her lips spread open and hooks at the back. Her eyes roam around the room in terror as I reach into my pocket for my knife. I've killed people with this knife and now I'm using it to save someone.

Her skin prickles with goosebumps as I touch her. I apologize, but I need to brace myself against her to get her free. I press the serrated edge to the ribbon and make the first cut.

I cut her legs free. She groans as her legs fall in a curled heap. She cries out and tries to jerk them again, but however long she's been in that position was far too long for her to have full control of her legs and hips.

"Don't move," I remind her. I touch her skin again and my stomach lurches. Fuck, her skin is so dark. I look pale as fuck touching her and even putting my hands on her drives guilt through me. She's black. She's the wrong kind of person. I run my tongue piercing over my lower lip as I focus on all the parts of the ribbon I have to cut free.

When I have her limbs mostly free, she rolls onto her side, groaning in pain as her arms and legs curl in an awkward and splayed mess next to her. Even her wrists bend at an unnatural angle. I know she's alive, but the woman still looks dead.

I swallow slowly. What the absolute fuck is this?

"I'll take the gag out, but you can't spit or bite or do anything of that nature. Do you understand?"

She stares at me, but she can't say anything. I approach her mouth slowly and reach around her to find the clasp of her ball gag. I unhook it and take it out of her mouth. She groans again and winces in visible pain as she attempts to close her jaw. She slowly moves her hand to her face and rubs her cheek, groaning.

I crouch next to her, staring at her in awe, knowing that I shouldn't but am completely incapable of taking my eyes off the naked woman in front of me. If her nudity makes her uncomfortable, that hasn't sunk in yet. My cock stiffens inappropriately in my pants and I clasp my hands in front of my dick, refusing to take my eyes off her.

Her breasts are small, but they protrude forward in tiny, dark orbs with nipples that are even darker than her extremely dark skin. Holy fuck, I didn't know nipples came that dark. My eyes widen inappropriately and I pray she doesn't notice my leering. Who sent this woman to me and what exactly did they send her for?

Christ, Aiden. Get a grip. You're staring at her crotch now and it's obvious.

She's waxed completely and my gaze snaps to the bare, dark brown lips. I wonder what this strange woman conceals between those lower lips and what color her flesh is between those thin, toned legs. I clear my throat.

"Who are you?"

"Read the card with the gift," she manages to say, with a raspy voice and an accent I can't place.

"I asked you a question."

"Read the card with the gift," she repeats.

I raise an eyebrow and walk towards the box. There's a large card at the bottom, about 8 x 10 inches, printed on thick paper. I pull it out of the box and read the note, muttering it out loud to myself. *What the fuck is this?*

Dear Mr. Murray,

We hope you enjoy your object. Your task is simple. Use the object wisely. Have unprotected sex with the object and film a 4K quality video.

Compress the video file and send it to the email address below.

The object may be initially unwilling but both of you will face strong motivation to comply. The object understands that documentation of her existence belongs to us and if she fails to comply enthusiastically, we will destroy her identity.

If we do not receive the video within one week of today's date, you will both lose what's most important to you.

Tegan Murray counts on you to succeed. We have possession of the girl and you would be wise to listen to our orders if you or your family want to see her safe.

Do not call Padraig Murray. Do not call anyone else, or you will both suffer.

It takes less than a second to fire a bullet.

You must comply. When you're finished with said object, it is yours to keep.

Sincerely,

Your Benefactors

OA

"What is this sick shit?" I growl, throwing the card back into the box, causing the woman still kneeling on the ground to flinch. My heart thuds.

These people have Tegan and this woman might know where she is and who they are. I won't be a part of this sick fucking game.

Click here to order Mafia Playmate:
https://bit.ly/bostonirishmafia1

PATREON

13 SEASONS OF SERIAL CHAPTERS

NEW preview chapters published WEEKLY on my Patreon.

Read all 6 seasons of *Unfuckable* (Ben & Libby's story)...

UNFUCKABLE

For a small monthly fee, you get exclusive access to over 375 chapters of my first completed bwwm dark and spicy serial romance, as well as the spin-off serial...

DESPICABLE

The second serial, despicable has 300 chapters available for all Patreon subscribers to access instantly and... we officially have a **third completed spin-off bwwm romance series.**

And yes you get access to all of this at the $5/month tier with more benefits at more pricey tiers.

The third serial is about Clover + Thomas. Thomas has a shocking connection to a character in the second serial and Clover is an all-new African American female lead.

POWERLESS

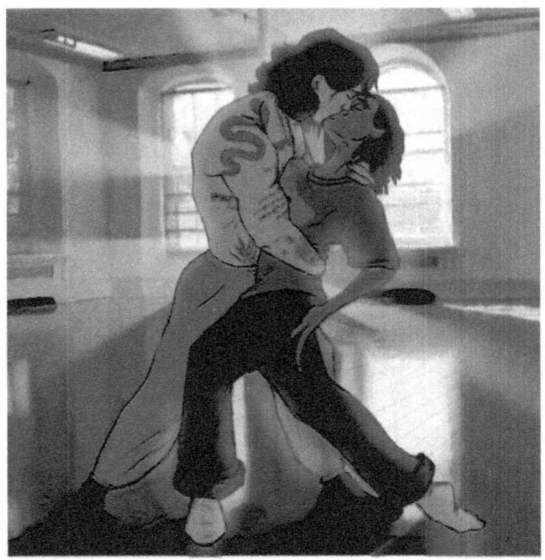

This series has three *very long* "seasons" of chapters, the length of five full-length novels all-together.

You will probably have over three months of binge-reading before catching up to current content, making this one of the most 'bang for your buck' author Patreon subscriptions out there.

Don't take my word for it.
Check the post history:
www.patreon.com/jamilajasper

PATREON HAS MORE THAN THE ONGOING SERIAL...

INSTANT ACCESS

- NEW merchandise tiers with **t-shirts, totes, mugs,** stickers and MORE!
- **FREE paperback** with all new tiers
- **FREE short story audiobooks** and audiobook samples when they're ready

- #FirstDraftLeaks of Prologues and first chapters **weeks** before I hit publish
- Behind the scenes notes
- Polls and story contribution
- Comments & LIVELY community discussion with likeminded interracial romance readers.

**LEARN MORE ABOUT SUPPORTING A
DIVERSE ROMANCE AUTHOR**

www.patreon.com/jamilajasper

THANK YOU KINDLY

Thank you to all my readers, new and old for your support with this new year.

I look forward to making 2023 an INCREDIBLE year for interracial romance novels. I want to thank you all for joining along on the journey.

www.patreon.com/jamilajasper

Thank you to my most supportive readers — my Patreon subscribers!:

Queen Ke

Jamie C

KimW

Warrior_pprincess

SavageSam

Roslyn H.

Katrina

LMSYT

Lainey R.

Naomi

GrumpyMillenial

Jay

Asia A.
Angela D.
Danyelle C.
WakeupMakeup Slay
Jocelyn F.
Nikki O.
Cdublu
Carla
Jonathan
Kelly
Jessica
Jasmine
DARSHELL
Dawn
Tiabuena3
Leigh
Yvonne
Ashlee
Crystal
Marshybabyyy
Shout
Quaniquequia
TK
Kayla
Shronda C.
Ma-Eyongerie
Kayla
Chantell
Kheiara
ophelia
Vickie
Cass
Kamil
Kaela

Love

Miryam

Charlene

Summer

Lola

Eryn

DD Davis

Symone

Deborah

Beatrice

Valescha

Khadija

makhalaab

Kaya

Glitter Garden

SavageSam

sybil arroyo

Ncsportsfan79

Jessica G.

Danielle

Yola

Joslin

Alexciz

Stacia

Ayanna

Asia

Hailey

Kaya

Nikki

Naomi O.

Jessica J

Chakiya

Noelle

kourtnee

Martha

Nikki Valentina

xjkpop

Valeria

BlkBae

SweetS

Msteeq

Rhonda

Darrah

Killa

Shavon

Misty

India

Kassandra

Imani

Nala

Chantell

Benvinda

Roger

Lexi B

Zapphire

Vbrooks

Tasha G

Kiera

Valencia

Stacy

YANITZA

Texansgurl76

Emma

Tinette

Jenny

Mariah

Nale

Tanisha

Trenita

Shelle

dulcemaria413

Shanice

Letarsha

Tania

Neeka

Julia

Linda

Lisa

Jiannie

Jillian

Tameka

Asia

Scarlette

Olwyn

R W

Fayefaefee

Brianna

Tiffany

Katie

Diamond

Kera

Tia

Love Reading

Dominique

Sheria

Jennifer

Georgette

Monique

Wendolyn

King Turtle22

Jessica

Nic M.

JustChill

DJC

Atira

TheeLastHokage

Yvonne

Chrissy

Janelle

Rian

LaRonda

LaRonda

Deanna

dlawson382

Jasmine

Haley

Belinda

Sercee

Yvonne

Jadelock

Farah

Tamiya

Quin

J.Payton

Geek Girl

Ashley

Rubi

Pilar

Sandra

Jurnee

Anni

Shannet

Joneesa

GlitzyHydra

Amanda

Barbara

Brianna

Jamica

Lyons

MARY ANN

Marketia

SarahD

LoverofHawaiiHearts

ceblue

Yolanda

MonaGirl Lewis

Dianna

Mary

amna

Nysha

fayola

Ty

Abria

Shyra

Andi-Mariee

Jamila

Naee's World

KEISHA

Jennett

Fredericka

Candece

Chante

Pholuv

Lydia A

Sabrina

JM

Jackie

Mo

Natrilly83

Ashaunte

Tolu

Margaret

Wendolyn

Lori

Dionne

ZLB

Kristina

Nicol

ELBERT

A. Harris

Jesi

Brenda

Desiree

Angela

Frances

LaShan

Only1ToniD

Debbie T.

Tiffanie

April L

shawnte

Kay

Lisema

Yvonne F

Natasha

Colleen

Julia

Amy

Jacklyn

Shyan R

Kiana B

Pearl

Javonda

Sheron

Maxine
Dash
Alicia
margaret
Love2Read
Juliette
Monica
Sandhya
MaryC
Trinity
Brittany
June
Ashleigh
Nene
Nene
Deborah
Nikki M
Dee
TyKira
Kimmey
Laytoya
Shel W
Arlene
Judith
Mary
Shanida
Rachel
Damzel
Ahnjala
Kenya
momo
BJ
Akeshia
Melissa

Tiffany

sherbear

Nini J

Curtresa

REGGIE A.

Ashley

Mia

Tink138110

Phia

Sharon

Charlotte

Assiatu C

Regina

Romanda

Catherine

Gaynor

BF

Perpetua

Tasha G

Henri Ann

sara

skkent

Rosalyn

Danielle

Deborah J

Kirsten

ANA

Taylor R.

Charlene

Louanna

Michelle

Tamika

Lauren

RoHyde

Natasha

Shekynah

Cassie

AnnaBooms

Keitheena

Nick R

Gennifer M

Rayna

Anton

Jaleda

Kimvodkna

JaTonn

Jazmine

Anoushka

Raynischa

Audrey

Valeria

Courtney

Donna

Patrisha

Jenetha

LaKisha J.

Ayana

Taylor

Christy

Monica

FreyaJo

GRACE

Kisha

Christine

Alexandra

Amber

Natasha

Stephanie

LaKisha
kristylove7
Cynthea
DENICE
Latoya
monifacd .
Doneishia
Mariah
Gerry
Yolanda T
Yolanda P
Susan D
Phyllis H
Alisa K
Daveena K
Desiree S
Kimberly B
Robin B
Gary S
Stephanie MG
Georgette A
Kathy
Marty
JanetDaniels
Megan
Shelle
Delores
Janet
Lydia
Phyllis
Freda
Charlott R

<u>Join the Patreon Community.</u>